UP, INTO THE SINGING MOUNTAIN

Richard Llewellyn calls himself 'an expatriate Welshman who now lives in the world and will stay there'. When he was sixteen he went to Italy to learn hotel management, but took up painting and sculpture and learnt eight languages in Venice instead. At nineteen he enlisted in the Regular Army. In the 1930s he lived in this country, working in the film industry and beginning to write, first of all for the theatre. Since the war he has lived mainly in North and South America.

His novels include: *How Green Was My Valley, None but the Lonely Heart, A Few Flowers for Shiner, Mr Hamish Gleave* and *Chez Pavan.*

Up, Into the Singing Mountain

RICHARD LLEWELLYN

NEW ENGLISH LIBRARY
TIMES MIRROR

For Nona with love

All of the characters in this book are fictitious, and any resemblance to actual persons, living or dead, is purely coincidental.

First published in the USA in 1960
First published in Great Britain by Michael Joseph in 1963
© Richard Llewellyn, 1960

*

FIRST NEL PAPERBACK EDITION MAY 1976

*

NEL Books are published by
New English Library Limited from Barnard's Inn, Holborn, London, E.C.1.
Made and printed in Great Britain by Hunt Barnard Printing Ltd., Aylesbury, Bucks.

02917 4

1

If you will tie a little blue cloth about such everyday things as socks and shirts and some handkerchiefs and a suit, then I suppose a bit of the dust from where you have been and even a smell of the soap you have used will go in there as well, and while I was shaping the knot I looked up as if a hand had been put steady on my shoulder, and I was seeing where they had been with me, and trying to think what else I might have done, or perhaps should have said at those times to put me in a better place, with more to show for my years and less, much less, to be sorry for.

Then to wait, looking at the candles, listening to this little house creaking tales of its time even before I was born, and reminding me of good seasons we both had known, and some that were bad, and in sudden loudness bringing into the room all those so far away, and them too, long gone.

Strange that a word or a look at the proper moment will change the whole cage we live in, and the places of all those perched. If I had looked a small second longer at Bronwen those years ago, or if I had opened my mouth to say what I wanted, I am sure I would never have been standing hopeless when I came home at last, with nothing to come home to, and having to go from there empty, O, empty again. Nobody ever knew I had been in love with her since that Saturday afternoon when she came up the hill to see my mother for the first time. Some will say it is silly to think that a child can fall in love with a young woman, but they are the kind to tell you how to wear your hat. Wife to my eldest brother she was, and a widow with two boys when he died in the colliery, so if I thought of her in love and with every wish to kiss, I saw my brother beside her, and that was enough. If those times were now, I swear I would have her off somewhere else to live where nobody knew us, and marry in joy. But then the faith was still in us, and it was not enough only to want our own way. There were others to think about, and beyond them the Law had to be kept. Often I have wondered when did we stop using our heads like that. Mind, everybody thought the same. If we had tried to marry we would have been in serious trouble, though I am not sure what kind and I have never bothered to find out. We were afraid of the notion of doing or even of saying anything that might spoil the quietness of the life between us. Bron could have married a dozen men, quick. There were plenty of splendid girls I could have asked. But there is no must about marrying. There is one woman, and one man, and nobody else. Bron felt the same as I did, and if she lived lonely, so did I, though in that distance I will swear there was more of love than in all the twining arms.

The two little boys were strength for us both, and I worked for the family, and under this roof we lived all those years, though Bron had my mother's room in front, and I stayed where I had always been.

Yet one word could have joined us. We could have gone off to be married and we would have left this little house to go to one better, more fit for those of substance.

But I left it only to go away.

Nothing more dense ever stood at a street corner on a winter's evening, with a bag in one hand and the timbers of the wall bed weighing the other shoulder, those years ago, trying to make up my mind if to go this way to Town, or the other way to the mountain. If I had gone to the mountain, I would have landed in the other valley and made a business with Rhys Jones, Carpenter, because he had asked me, and I might have become a millionaire with him, and having a house like his in London, and motor cars, and my name in the paper every other day for good advice to the young, or giving somebody in need a shilling or two, or opening a Chapel Social, or anyway, busy and long retired, with plenty in the bank and a thumb to the nose for everybody.

But I only heard the colliery engine whistle a high little tune that reminded me of being far away, so off, one foot before the other, I went. Perhaps if I had walked to the station I might have seen the last train in a U of lights going round the curve, and laughed at myself, and turned back home to Bron.

Luck, it was, that Thomas, Carrier, came along in the wagon, and stopping under the lamp, and I can see his red

6

face and blowing breath even now.

'Are you finished, or starting, or only looking?' he was shouting. 'Or are you tired for a bit of help?'

Luck, I meant.

Because if I had said, then, that I was off home, I suppose he would have run me up the hill to the door. But I had a bag in one hand, and the timbers of the wall bed on my shoulder, and my best suit on.

'No,' I said. 'I wanted to catch the last train to Town.'

'Climb up, Huw, my little one,' he said. 'I am going to claim Geraint Lewis' crates from the yard. Come you. It will be company.'

In that way I went, and no chance to change my mind or speak to anybody.

Luck, because Thomas, Carrier, was never one to talk even when he had the horse and trap, and he was more careful with the wagon and two pair. But he told me, while the wind blew to perish, that Geraint Lewis was home after years away in South America, and he had kept them up all night at the Three Bells with tales of adventures better than a lantern lecture, everybody said.

'Well, you would never believe what he was telling them in there,' he said. 'Our Mr Gruffydd, Pastor, remember? Well him, there he is down there, working for somebody, and never near the chapel, not even a verse or a hymn. Everybody was struck dumb, there. You could rack your brains why he would be in such a place, isn't it?'

Luck.

Mr Gruffydd's watch was in my pocket that moment, never stopped since he gave it to me, and every word spoken that last time was in my mind. But I said nothing, and at the station I helped with Geraint Lewis' three crates and a tin trunk, and I looked well at the labels for names and the port. Up I went that night, and walking in the early morning through the Liverpool docks, full of ships and flags wonderful to taste a strangeness, and I had a good drop of tea with some builders round a fire, and they said the ship Geraint had come back on was over a little bridge in the other basin, and one of them came with me, so kind he was.

Luck, no doubt, because the agent said she was ready to sail and a ticket to Port Madryn was twenty-two pounds, all found, and a cabin to myself. Whether to say yes and go, or no, and edge down the gangway, bag and timbers, and look a fool in front of a couple of sailors.

So I paid, and signed papers, and he took me to a cabin, and off, because somebody was shouting. I had time to fit the wall bed timbers round the cot, and open my bag, and make the cabin look like home, and the floor began to shiver and the whistle was blowing, so out I went. I lost the way up and down ladders in smells of tar and linseed oil and cooking, and when I went out in the sunlight, the agent waved his hat to me from below on the dock, and a rope splashed in the water, and there was a yard of it between the ship's side and the quay.

One day, a cabinet-maker in a good way of business, and the next, only a few hours after, somebody on a ship, off somewhere and knowing nothing.

Well, well.

I will always see that water bright between me and the land, with bits of straw and paper in it, and a tin with its lid in a lift like the agent's hat, wagging side to side on the ripples. So much on earth I have found since is like that bright little space, keeping everything away by the reach of an arm only a little longer than your own, or the tone of a word, or the want of a look, but enough, and even though everything you love is there in front of you, it is denied, why, God knows, and off it goes from you, and nothing to be done.

But if I felt thrown-in-a-pit then, it was joyous songs to the beauty to be endured about three weeks and all the Atlantic Ocean later when I saw Port Madryn. A few old sheds and huts, and some baulks and planks for a dock, and nothing but low hills of pampas bush, and rain in hanging clouds, and the shine of mud by the mile.

A welcome for kings indeed, and knowing nobody. But it was like warming your hands to see a railway, even if it was only one line, with carriages and trucks and an engine under a corrugated iron roof. They told me on the ship I was coming to a rough old place, so a train at any rate was a comfort.

Mari Ann Gwythir sat in the corner out of the rain heating a little kettle over a couple of sticks. Tall and thin she was, in the clothes of years before, and her grey hair combed tidy and curled with lamb's fat glittering with rain-drops, and her face wrinkled like a soft russet in a beautiful smile of strong teeth, and eyes shy to be looking, and grey as the rain, lifting the crinoline with one hand and holding towards me

8

a gourd the size of a pear with the top cut off, and a few inches of silver pipe in it, and I saw the hand brown and hard as a root.

'Welcome to the Colony of Camwy,' she said, in the Old Language. 'May your visit be happy for every moment and all trouble only a dream.'

She told me that the gourd was called a maté, and the pipe a bombilla, and the green liquid came from the crushed leaves of yerba, a plant from the north. Bitter, no doubt, that first time, but a reviver good as tea, and I had a couple of sucks, and handed the maté to her, ready for more.

'Thank you,' I said.

'Would you like another?' she asked me, shy, she was, and over sixty, but like a girl in Sunday school.

'If it can be spared,' I said.

'You should never say Thank You,' she said. 'Have your fill, and when you are tight full, then say Thank You. Because here, when we say Thank You, we mean Enough. No more.'

'Well,' I said. 'I would have thought that rude.'

'Have your manners, and go without,' she said. 'It is lovely to talk to somebody from home. I am going, now just. But I will never believe it. I am in shivers to be there before the snowdrops have gone. And to see the primroses and crocus. I will put my face to them for hours.'

But sorrow was in me, because I knew that her dream was late, and the snowdrops were long past, and the primrose and crocus would be gone. She wondered if it would be a great change to go back to the Old Land that she had left thirty-five years before with her mother and father among the other pioneers, and she pointed up the Bay of Nymphs to the narrow beach and the cliffs where the sailing ship *Mimosa* had landed them. That year was before I was born, but white hair and wrinkled or not, I felt that she was much younger than I had ever been.

In the time we waited for the ship to unload and take on cargo she told me about the first years and the droughts that burnt the harvests and dried the river, and with her I tasted the weeds they boiled to keep alive, that to this day they call Welshman's Cabbage.

With charcoal she drew the River Camwy from the Atlantic all the way across the desert to the mountains of the Andes, and the railway going from Port Madryn inland to the City of Lewis. But it looked very short, and she said they had spent all the money on that piece, and they were still about six hundred miles from where John Evans had built the City of the Mill in the Enchanted Valley.

'All the land here is taken, and the earth without water is useless,' she said. 'Some of the young men followed the Indio hunters across the pampas and claimed good land over there in the Andes. Plenty of water and timber, and pasture over the ears, they say. I have never been. There was always too much work here. But they are having a hard life because there is nobody to buy the crops, and not enough wagons to bring it here to the coast.'

'Will it be best for me to go to the Andes, or stay in the city?' I asked her. 'I will settle where there is work.'

'Work there is wherever you turn,' she said. 'The flood of two years ago and the one this year again ruined everything. Nobody has got a door to fit or a window to shut, even the few with a house left standing. If I was a man I would have gone to the Andes long ago. Only the strong will bide there.'

'Not much use for me if there is nothing to be sold,' I said.

'Work, and you will be paid to the penny if it is twenty years from now,' she said, and then, it was, that I saw her age. 'You have come as a foreigner. You will learn or not. Nobody will teach you if you are not to be taught. Only be thankful, and have trust.'

The sailors came to call her, and she took her bonnet dry from a bag to put it on, and indeed, making a bow of the ribbons, she looked a white-haired sixteen, with eyes gentle, and quiet in the hands, and a washtub fresh of aired clothes about her, and she dipped a knee, and I raised my hat.

'You shall have the kettle if you want,' she said. 'Will I leave the maté box with you? I was going to give it to the peons.'

'They have got their own, Mistress Gwythir,' Jones, Price Special, said, from the other end of the roof. 'If we are here for hours, a maté or two will warm the cockles, aye.'

So she gave me the kettle and a tin box full of yerba, and off she went through the mud, holding the wide skirt far enough up to show men's boots, and perhaps it was men's white pants, too. It was blowing cold enough.

'One of the richest in the Colony,' Jones, Price Special, told me. 'Her father cured the cattle and sheep. She is the same with people. She has got her own medicines. Where babies are coming, she is there first. But never married. A

10

few tried, mind you. From the way you were looking, I thought you were hanging your hat, too.'

'She was kind to me, and I thought her lovely, indeed,' I said. 'Has it got something to do with you?'

'No offence, Mr Morgan, joking, I was,' he said, and going back. 'Bryn Jones, I am. Shipping manager for the Co-op. Farmers' Co-operative. If you are in want of something, only tell me. Nobody will have it cheaper. Always a price, special. Whatever I can do, it is done, worldwide.'

'Thank you,' I said. 'The first I want is to find a lodging. After that, a chest of tools fit for a cabinet-maker's shop.'

'Youngest sister of her just gone for lodgings,' he said. 'A widow. Two children living with another sister to help with the farm. Good house, brick built, sheets to the beds, best table in the Colony. The widow Morwen Glyn, and say I sent you. A list of tools, and I will have them by the next mail.'

Well, you would have to be drunk to believe the ride in that train, and if I have ridden many a time since, I never laughed as much as on the first, to be getting off, all of us, and running about to gather little dried branches for the engine, or help to push the train up hills, and running to jump on before it went too fast, and then off, to push again before it stopped. Jones, Price Special, told me there was no coal in the country, and timber was on the other side, in the Andes, up to six weeks of hard travel for horse and mule trains, and no hope of selling cargoes of fuel for a good price because people had the pampas bush all round and they could gather it free.

I was booked to the City of Lewis, and when the train stopped, I thought we had to push again. But the guard said we were there, and all change, if you please. Outside the station was smaller than our village, a couple of streets criss-cross and a house or two beyond, and a run of shops, but with more wagons and traps waiting in the front than I had ever seen in my life before, and horses that would make you stop, even in the rain, to look.

The house of the Widow Glyn was part of the few brick shops, with a door between two windows on the ground floor and a roof of corrugated iron painted red. A couple of taps with the knuckles, and she came herself, in black, with a white shawl on her shoulders and an apron starched to be heard a mile away, and eyes so black, and shining, and direct, that you might feel a blush coming to think she knew a little more about you than she ought, even though in her was some of the same shyness I had felt in Mari Ann Gwythir. Now, of course, I know what it was, but at that time, I was in a new country, among people speaking the same language but of a hundred years before, with the manners of that time, and a wonder to me, as if the clock had slipped, and I had come from sleep. They were quieter, gentler, kinder than I had known, and I had to be silent, and listen, and try to make up my mind if they were really what they seemed, or only in pretence.

It takes a long, long time to lose the poison of towns.

Up went her hands when she saw the kettle and the tin maté box, knowing them for her sister's, but when I told her where I had them, I thought she would faint, and the next moment I was sure she would eat me. Nothing was too good for one straight from the Old Land, and out came the best china and silver, and the big teapot, and off went the children to find new bread and cakes, as though there were not enough in the kitchen. But I soon found out she was right, because in a few minutes the house was full of people come to shake my hand and ask me who, and when, and where, and so warm to bring tears, and if I had any doubt about work, I had none when tea-time was over because everybody wanted a cabinet-maker, and I had enough offers to keep my sleeves rolled for a couple of years.

Next was to find a shop, but it was hopeless. They were building again up and down the river after the flood had swept the farms to the sea, and there were no workmen to be had. But wood needs a good roof and sound walls and a dry floor. Other carpenters I have seen working in a sty. But I like tools in a proper place, and dry timber, so a shop it had to be. The Widow Glyn knew I could have plenty of help to build my own place farther up the valley. But if I was going to stay as a lodger, it was a long ride there and back, and time in the saddle was better to be spent with the plane and chisel.

'Well, look you, Huw,' she said, one night over the candles. 'I will make a bargain. I will build the shop as you want it, with my own peons from my own pocket, outside here. But you stay, is it? It is years since there was a man in the house. If I was younger, people would talk. But my lovely days are gone. I am too old for their tongues. Rupert went too soon, see, and the clock was driving me silly, tick-tock. If I build, will you stay?'

'I have got money enough, Mistress Glyn,' I said. 'I can build.'

'Not on my property,' she said. 'If I build, you will stay and pay rent. But it will be my property, not yours. Will I build, then?'

I should have said no, but at the time it would have been silly. I had the best lodgings in the city, with cooking nearest to my mother's, and a big room and a feather mattress in the wall bed, and a good chair by the fire at night, and shelves of books, so there would have been something wrong with me if I had wanted more, besides a shop in the middle of the main street, and nothing to do except go outside to it.

But I began to be sorry about six weeks or a couple of months later when Mr Gruffydd came to see me. The shop was built and I had been working, and he stood in the door, with the sun strong behind him, and in rough clothes he seemed to come twisted from my memory, and darker, smaller, as though I had always been wrong.

'Well, Huw,' he said. 'Last time, you were wearing Davy's trews.'

'No, Mr Gruffydd,' I said. 'Owen's.'

'Well, of course,' he said. 'Ivor, Ianto, David, Gwilym, Owen, you. And how are they all?'

But if he was careless in the way he said it, the hunger was sore with him and dry in his throat, and he had missed out the names of the girls.

'Well,' I said, careless, too. 'Ivor, you remember, died in the colliery just before Dada. Ianto is in New Zealand with a coal importer, and two children in the last letter. Gwilym is married, five children, and superintending a mine in Canada. Davy is in the United States, two children, with Owen, not married yet, in Detroit, and doing the work of engineers. Thousands they are earning.'

'Good,' he said. 'Clever in the head, both.'

'Bronwen is still in the Valley and married again by now, I suppose,' I said. 'Ceridwen is a district nurse and living with Mrs Tom Harries. Her husband was killed by the Boers. Olwen went to Oxford with a scholarship and became a Bachelor of Arts. She is in a college as a mistress.'

'A Bachelor of Arts, Oxford?' he was whispering, in frowns of wonder. 'Pity your good father could not have lived to hear it. Pity, indeed.'

'It was the little bit he and my brothers left in the box that helped her to go,' I said. 'And we haven't heard a word from her since, either.'

'Well,' he said. 'There are ways of living a life, Huw. Letters depend on a lot of things. And your good mother?'

'Gone from us,' I said. 'And thankful.'

'Thankful,' he said.

'Yes,' I said. 'To be off, with my father. She sat for hours after he went, and every moment getting smaller. She only lived for Olwen. When she was ready, I could have carried her. A little box of feathers.'

'I think of her with love,' he said. 'She fed me when I was thin. And stitched and darned for me, too.'

'Good,' I said. 'Angharad is back from South Africa, again. No family. Iestyn is dead. She is the owner of everything.'

Vyrnwy Beris was hitting his anvil a little chime before the overarm thump of the sledges, and putting one in, silver, between each thump, and then bouncing a chime to tell that the iron must go into the forge again.

'I came in as soon as I could,' Mr Gruffydd said, in a stronger voice. 'I have got a good house, but not much furniture. I can make an offer for at least three months of your best work. Everything there is yours. Come and go when you please. If I had known, I would have gone to Port Madryn to meet you. But it seems you are busy.'

'I am looking for helpers,' I said. 'There are very few not in work.'

'Too much to do and too few to do it,' he said. 'Plenty of money and no idea how to use it. If I leave you now to buy my stores, will we have something to eat?'

'Certainly,' I said. 'You could come in the house with me.'

'No,' he said, looking up the street. 'I will wait for you on this corner when midday puts hands together.'

He had gone only a moment, and from her back door the Widow Glyn came over the stones pushed by El Pampero blowing from the west, and holding down her apron at her knees and trying to help the pins in her cap.

'Let me tell you something now,' she said, breathless, not with the run but from what she had to say. 'I am sorry, but we are not on terms with Mr Gruffydd. Nobody in the Colony. We begged and begged him to give us a service when he came first. But never. And why? Well, we found out he

14

had trouble with a woman where he was before. And he was sent from there. See how he lives with the Indios out in the camp? Shame is full in him. But sure he must never put a step in my house. Tell him from me, will you?'

I looked at her longer than a moment.

'About Mr Gruffydd, everything there is to be known, I know,' I said. 'That woman is my sister. She was married. Now she is a widow. He was pastor to us for years. It was thought to be wrong for him to visit for a cup of tea when her useless husband was in South Africa. There was no sending from there, either. Mr Gruffydd sent himself. For the same reason he is outside, here. To have a breath of air from mouths of muck. Go back in the house and look to yourself.'

'You will dare to say that to me on my property?' she said, in a high voice, and trying to go higher. 'I will say everything to be said on this piece of land, please to remember, Mr Morgan.'

'It will take me two minutes to pack and be off,' I said.

'We have got an agreement, now, wait,' she said, holding out a hand to settle fur. 'No use to lose the temper.'

'Our agreement is for rent by the week for my lodgings, and this shop, and storage in the yard,' I said. 'There is nothing on the paper about wasting time with old chat. I will be in the house for tea. I am out at midday. I am saying this on property I am paying rent for, and no more to be said, if you please.'

If she wanted to say something back or not, she had no time because El Pampero bent the lilacs almost to the ground, and took her skirt up in front, showing two stockings of white wool tied in bows above the knee with narrow red ribbons, and very good, too, but she made a noise like a goose on the nest and pulled the skirt down, and ran bent double from there, and El Pampero chased her to the door, and while she had to press the handle, she was almost like an umbrella blown inside out.

'I know the colour of your garters, and your hams are beautiful, indeed, never mind your lovely years have gone,' I shouted to her. 'Will I do a little bit of chatting, now then?'

The door slammed to drop plaster, but I never heard a word after that.

He was on the corner when I went out, and I turned him past the front windows, certain that the Widow Glyn was having a look through the lace, and of course she was.

'They are the same here as they are at home,' I said. 'Peep and chat. Another country and an ocean between, but no difference.'

'It is nothing to me,' he said. 'When I found I could trim a bit of land, and build a house, and rear a flock of sheep, and make something where nothing was before, I had peace. Chapel, religion, preaching, evangelising, no never again.'

Work with the saw and plane will do wonders for the shoulders, and I had worked hard in the years, so that he was not much taller or broader than I was. He had shaved his beard and his hair was short, greyer than I remembered, still plenty, but there was nothing of the lion that once had been. Before, perhaps because I was a boy, he had seemed a big man, and tall, with something inside him that might have been burning until you almost thought you could feel the flame reaching you. Perhaps he knew what I was thinking, because he smiled, and nodded across at the space behind Dalar Roberts' stables.

'I suppose you have been to many an asado by now, Huw?' he said. 'Did you bring a knife?'

'Yes,' I said. 'And wearing it in the back of my trews good as any gaucho. I like eating in the open air. A healthy custom.'

'From the old conquistadors,' he said. 'A piece of meat from the grill, and a crust, and a mouthful of wine, and the poorest man is a Caesar in the purple. I asked for an asado in the hide today. The heat of the coals goes through the leather and cooks without searing. For me, it is the only way to eat steak. Cut, and see.'

He was talking of little things, and other things, and of nothing at all. But I knew well what he wanted to talk about, so I waited. The asado, which is a Spanish word for roast, was in a pit at the end of the yard, a ring of burning logs, and on iron stakes, whole sheep and half a beef, and on an iron mesh, sausages and smaller fry. About a dozen men sat out of the smoke, and Kankel swung the beef to cook on the other side.

'A little different from your good mother's table, Huw, but it fills, and it has an advantage,' Mr Gruffydd said. 'There is no washing up after. Wipe your mouth and your knife, and go, thankful.'

That asado is in my mind even now, not because the steak was the best I had ever put teeth into, but because from that

16

moment I was ready to follow the wagon track across the desert to the Andes.

'It will be better later,' Mr Gruffydd said. 'Autumn is best for travelling, because now the dust blows straight in your face all the way across, and the sun is in your eyes all day. Some like to travel at night. But not with cattle. A lot of foxes and too many pumas in places. A man can lose his profit soon enough.'

Funny it was to hear Mr Gruffydd talking about pumas and cattle and profit. Another sort of language from a different man, and something in the voice not of him I remembered.

'I am out of my chair, Huw,' he said, as if he had seen in my eyes. 'If I have lost, very well, but I have gained more. I am only sorry I never wrote to tell you to come here. There is plenty of room for good workmen, especially now, after the flood. I know many who lost farms in their families from the pioneers. Everything, stick and stone. No better than peons. Common labourers.'

'But they had help, surely,' I said.

'For the poor, there might be a wish in piety, with a few potatoes and a hambone, and perhaps the loan of a shovel,' he said. 'Anyway, it has been something like the other life to see you. Tell me, now then. How is Angharad?'

In the way it came from him, he might have scrawled the name in blood across the sky, even though he was looking at the mule teams coming from the stables. So I looked at them, too, and told him everything I could think of in minutes and minutes of remembering, and more colour came in the weather of his face, and his eyes smiled as well as his mouth, and he even seemed taller.

'Will the old address find her?' he asked me.

'Certainly,' I said. 'Everything there is hers. She will sell the colliery and the iron works, and she will probably sell the foundry and the strip mill, and everything together in South Africa. She has got docks there, and ships. Think of her out in the scullery a little time ago, and now with everything in the world, and called Madam. That old tomboy with the red hair, look.'

'Not red,' Mr Gruffydd said, looking as if I had used bad language. 'Titian, it was, not red. Is it darker, now?'

'Well,' I said, and wondering how to say it not to take the light, and sure to sit down to a letter the moment I got back, with underlining for Titian, so that she would use her brains.

'Of course, she is older,' he said. 'There must have been a change. But I would know her again, sure, wouldn't I?'

'Good gracious, and she would know you,' I said. 'She is older, well, naturally. Us, too.'

'Yes,' he said, and sad. 'I think of the years flung, like old slippers. But she mustn't sell any of that property, Huw. If there is one lesson I have learnt, it is never to sell one inch of the land, or one brick over it. He who owns the land owns all. She must be warned.'

'I am not sure she has much interest in property,' I said.

'I didn't, until I had none myself, and nothing to work with, and nowhere to go,' he said. 'You were lucky. You had a trade in your fingers. Mine was in my heart and mouth. Fortunately I met a family on the ship. When you come to stay, you will see them. But choose your time, Huw. Ride every day. Saddle sores are funny in the mouths of comedians. Under your trews, they are less than a blessing. Mind what I say, now.'

Well, thank God I did, because like that I met Lal.

2

Every afternoon when the doors of the City were closed, and
the streets were silent for the hours of siesta, I went to the
stable and took Merri from Kankel, and walked her down
the back lane not to make a noise, and mounted under the
poplars on the road to the river.

Those shadows of deep green light and the smell of rich
pasture are with me now, on the way past the farm of Ieuan
Williams, and the gate of Daniel Jones, and the fields of Idris
Ebrill and Gil Walters, and Matthew Dowlais and Idwal
Rowlands, and Alun Jenkins, and Elisha Thomas, and Evan
Tudor and Asaph Hughes, down to the willows, and the pool
where Merri liked to sip her nose. Sometimes I fished, little
beauties that hot from the grill tasted like a cream from
heaven, or else I went the other way to the harbour for
lobster, crab and shrimp that the Widow Glyn would cook in
a soup to make you shut your eyes and think you had put a
spoon in paradise by mistake.

But oftener I went to a patch of land on a low hill and
bare of anything except the pampas bush, and while Merri
grazed along the river, I was on my knees picking up beads
made from all sorts of stones and in every colour, until I had
a hatful and pockets, too, for the inlays of a screen I was
making spare-time at the shop.

Like that I saw Lal.

I must have picked up pounds of beads, and I had four
leaves of the screen covered by the afternoon in late spring,
with all the flowers out, and a blue sky, yes, blue, the very
breath of Patagonia, and the green walls of the poplars all
the way along the river, and the white hills beyond, and she
galloped from the trees, side-saddle, wide-brimmed panama
curling above her eyes in the strong breath of El Pampero,
and a red coat and a skirt of white corduroy, and black boots
polished to see yourself, and lace about her throat, and black

19

and silver harness on a black stallion with four white socks clipping across the short grass and pulling up on his hinds at a touch, and standing, still, a dozen yards away from me.

A thick plait with a red bow lay over her shoulder, and she swung it behind, staring across the pasture, and all that moved were the willows behind her, and the light in her eyes from the sun.

Somebody had been hammering all the time I was there, and over the brush I could see a peon setting fence posts in the meadow about two hundred yards away. She saw him, too, and drew a carbine from the saddle holster, and aimed and shot while I turned my head, and I saw his hat fly, and he fell, but he was up, and scooping the hat as he went, taking the horse's mane and vaulting, no saddle, and off, split.

She turned to slide the carbine in the holster, and there I was, standing with my mouth open. For a moment I was sure I would have the next, looking at her eyes that always reminded me of the light from a bed of deep red wallflowers, and even with some of that scent, but they altered and she frowned surprise at my hat nearly full of beads.

'Whoever you are, think shame to yourself,' she said, in the contralto that comes from trained lungs. 'How long have you been robbing cemeteries?'

I could have dropped.'

'Cemeteries?' I said. 'Is this one, then?'

'Those little things you are picking up were put about the necks of Tehuelche women with love,' she said. 'What would you say if a Tehuelche opened a grave of your family?'

'Every one I will put back,' I said. 'Thank you for telling me.'

'You speak like a foreigner,' she said.

'You of the North kept more to yourselves,' I said. 'The language has got more cut to the blade.'

'So you are from the South,' she said. 'From Tierra del Fuego?'

'No,' I said. 'South Wales, girl.'

'O,' she said. 'No wonder.'

'No wonder what?' I said. 'We had a few more Romans and Normans and Saxons down with us. Let me hear you speak English.'

'My father took us from school because we were taught it,' she said, and smiling, O, a smile. 'My grandfather would

20

never allow one word in the house. But he could swear in it. So can we. If I catch you near a grave on this land again, you shall judge my command, too.'

'How was I to know it was a cemetery?' I asked her, and looking at the scrub and pebbles.

'Did you think it was a natural mine of little beads you had found, then?' she asked me. 'Everything done, only missing a bit of string? If you had gone farther to the river, you would have seen the bones and skulls. The flood took the earth away. So you found beads.'

'Yes,' I said. 'I might have found a man with a bullet in him, too.'

'I could have killed him ten times over if I had wanted,' she said, as if it were no matter. 'Once a fence is up and they have put it on the map, it is hard to prove who the land belongs to. This land belongs to Maes Corwen. Those who cannot learn will be taught. My compliments, Mr South, and remember, the Tehuelche are good friends of ours and we are good friends to them. What you are stealing could put you before The Twelve.'

With no move that I could see, the stallion was up on his hinds in a turn and off, four white socks in a thumpitathum-pitathump, and the plait and his tail were straight out, as if El Pampero held them for me to see how long they were.

Old Tibbald at the bookshop told me about The Twelve on the way back when I was in the kitchen for a cup of tea. English, he was, and tall with a bit of weight below the chest and not much breath. Blue in the eye, and cold until he smiled, and a good man in and out, and a scholar in Greek and Latin, and in his own language splendid to listen to, and I often did. Messrs Shakespeare and Milton and Pope I thought I knew well, but he taught me how little, and he presented Mr Chaucer to me among a crowd of pilgrims, and before that shining one I have been barefoot ever since.

'Twelve men chosen from among the electorate,' he said. 'Not in itself judge and jury, but they inquire into what is substance and what is not. Where they find guilt, they recommend trial in the Argentinian courts. An old Welsh custom, excellent of its kind, and in perfect accord with the constitutional law of this country. Saves time, trouble and local feeling. Are you in any danger?'

'Not that I know,' I said.

I will always remember that cup of tea he gave me, not

only for the pattern of black and red and gold in the china but because of the blue look that came a long way, and went farther.

'Delighted to hear it,' he said, and no more.

'The door will be bolted every night after this,' the Widow Glyn told me the moment I put a foot in the house. 'There are bandits and old murderers shooting and killing here. A poor man has been found dead from a knife in the throat, and now just, one of the Orozco peons came in with bullet holes all over him and shouting because old bandits robbed everything he had. The police are after them.'

'Well, well,' I said, remembering one shot from a carbine. 'He was lucky to come from there. Where was all this?'

'Up the river,' she said. 'This side of Maes Corwen. I wouldn't be one of those girls riding in and out, not for ten seasons' harvest. They think it is the pistoleros from North America.'

'I thought this was a land with never a crime, or a blow, or even a rough word,' I said. 'You told me, for one.'

'It is true,' she said. 'Only now we have had this Walty, or what he is called. All over the Territory, he is, killing Indios and stealing their horses and cattle.'

'They should catch him, quick,' I said.

'Go to the desert, and give advice,' she said. 'Ride for days and see nobody. Where will you look? If I was alone in the house, I would be off to sleep with Marged Prosser to be safe. Husband and three grown sons she has got.'

'Pity,' I said, to change the tune. 'Maes Corwen, is it a farm?'

'Yes,' she said, and no more.

'And how many girls riding in and out?' I asked her, pretending not.

'Three,' she said, and struck a match for the candle. 'One father, and three daughters, and him widowed, yes, and here is me, and two children on the farm, and peons in the camp, and nobody else, and good night.'

Protest meetings were all over the place next morning, and crowds in all the shops and coming in the house for a cup of tea and more talk, and I had to shut the door to get some work done. But when I looked out to hear the Reverend Mr Armon Tudor making a good prayer from the back step, who should be standing with a bag full of shopping, and looking as if butter would melt and quick, only the girl of the day before, in a long blue dress and a hat with white flowers.

'Save the wicked from their handiwork,' Mr Tudor was praying, eyes shut, and hands about the Book. 'Sinners we are all. But murder, the placing of a bullet, the point of a knife, these are crimes we must banish from our dear land. Peace on earth, it is also a commandment. Pray for them, for their salvation, for the victims. Pray for the light. Amen.'

The crowd Amened, and Harries, Sawmill, went forward, smoothing the white beard and moustache to speak.

'Most reverend and respected Pastor, and friends,' he said. 'There is no doubt we should have a fund for rewards, because if men are going to find these murderers, they will carry their lives easy. I will start with twenty pesos for the capture of the one who killed that poor boy yesterday, and twenty more for that one up the river. Shooting and killing have never been in my lifetime in the Colony. This is the first. I will pay to make it the last.'

Everybody nodded, and moved, and a crowd went to put money in the hat, and my lady took out her purse and went through them all to put with the rest, and saw me, because I happened to be adding a couple of pesos at the same time.

'Somebody is going to have a lot of money for catching those criminals,' I said. 'Shooting for a miss is a crime, too, so I am told.'

'Robbing a cemetery is a crime against the living and the dead,' she told me, as if we had never spoken before. 'Every bead not put back is a curse. Remember that.'

She turned from me and went on the steps, and spoke to the Reverend Mr Tudor, and he looked out at the crowd, and his eyes were almost the size of his mouth.

'A moment of your attention, if you please,' she called, and the voice alone would have brought silence. 'It is said that a peon was almost shot to death along the river yesterday. The only peon I know was the one putting fence stakes in Macs Corwen land. He got one bullet. From me. I took the hat from his head to remind him, and all others, that Maes Corwen land belongs to us, and nobody else. Thank you.'

She looked once where I was standing, as at paint on the wall, and went down, and off, and everybody was looking at everybody else, and most of them were saying Quite Right, Too, and I went in and shut the door.

I found out soon enough that Lal was eldest daughter of

Vrann Corwen, with a place along the river you could put a whole county in and never find again. Vrann's grandfather had been one of the pioneers and like all of them, a slave to the plough, and his son after him, saving every grain, leaf and hair, and giving nothing except sweat, so that when they died, they left behind leagues they had cleared as settlers, and other leagues they had bought over the years from neighbours, and Vrann came into a little empire, and Lal, Doli and Solva ruled as three princesses, and worked the land, cattle and sheep as good and perhaps even better than if they had been born as men.

Shamed though I am to say it, from the moment I saw Lal I forgot everybody else, even Bron. Not altogether, indeed, but when I thought of her, it was only to hope that she was happy with Matt and having peace in her life that she had missed before. In that way, short, we throw off the dreams of years. It surprises me now, remembering the hopes and sighs, and all the rumblings. Sure it is that if I had opened my mouth that time, or looked only a small second longer, I would never have left the house, though thinking back now, I am almost glad that I did.

Every hour of the days after I met her I was trying to have a reason to go up to Maes Corwen. It was a long way and I had a lot of work, so there was no excuse for losing a whole day and night.

She came to me instead.

The moment I heard her voice, I knew, and turned in a spin and tipped the gluepot over my apron, and treading in a pool, and trying to apologise and pull my feet free, and she leaned on the door to laugh. Well, I had to get out of my shoes, and walk sockfoot to shake her hand and she was laughing, deep, free, beautiful, and I laughed too, and we stood there like a good pair.

'A cousin of ours is getting married,' she said, while she wiped her eyes. 'We thought we would ask could you make a small copy of my great-grandmother's coffer for a wedding chest for her. But you will have to come to the house. My father says it shall not be moved in case to bring bad luck.'

'I will be there tomorrow,' I said quick. 'And I have put the beads back, every one, please to know. There are the spaces, see, empty.'

'Sad pity to spoil pretty work like that,' she said, looking at the screen. 'May I buy it?'

24

I would have given it to her, and the shop, too.

'Well, yes, I suppose,' I said. 'Instead of the beads, I will inlay with patterns of wood. This, or the chest, first?'

She gave me a look from the side, not black but brown in fire of red, a marvel.

'The wedding is on the day after the harvest, so sharp is the word,' she said. 'At what time will you be there tomorrow?'

'If it is five hours ride, at about nine o'clock,' I said. 'But I am not sure of the way.'

'I will meet you where the road leaves the river,' she said. 'Good-bye, now, Mr South.'

The pale blue hat and the big red rose at the side had just gone round the corner, and I was scraping the glue back in the pot, and at the door was the Widow Glyn.

'Well, well,' she said. 'Visitors.'

'It would never surprise me,' I said.

'Money with the order,' she said. 'Advice from one knowing plenty. Vrann has got a finger and thumb like winter's ice with a peso. He owed poor Rupert hundreds, but I could never get back not one. Nothing signed, see.'

'A moment with a pen, and a stamp, after, will settle everything,' I said.

'He is without a word in eye or hand,' she said. 'Too far up the valley to go to school. Trouble over that again. Three daughters by his wife, gone, poor girl, before her time, and his fault, no doubt. But he had wives among the Indios, and twenty or more children, known, all out in the Territory. If he gives them his name, they will have shares equal with the girls. Twenty-something shares instead of three, and equal shares for the wives, what will be left of Maes Corwen?'

'When it is my business I will think about it,' I said.

She put a forefinger under her right eye, and pressed down to open it wide.

'Watch out,' she said. 'If a man married one of them, she would bring him nothing except a little bit of a strip not enough to keep a cow, and Indio thieves by the dozen for relations.'

'If it was my family I would be worried,' I said. 'What is for dinner?'

'Broth of celery, roast beef, Yorkshire pudding, new potatoes and sprouts,' she said. 'Apple pie and cream to follow. Is there something missing, then?'

'A good cup of coffee, after,' I said. 'You have put the habit strong in me.'

'There are more I could put,' she said, from the door. 'Come quick when I call, not to let the plates go cold.'

'I must have time to wash,' I said. 'Shall I come to the table smelling of glue, then?'

'Come as you like, and no words from me,' she said, out of the door and the cool draughts bringing back her voice soft. 'Is something to be said against a man working hard and earning good profit? Not in my house. Never.'

If I had thought for a moment I might have found something clotty in the cream, but the way of those who never use their heads is blown by the spice of flattery leading always by the nose, and when the time came and I was made to think, it was too late.

If the banks of the Camwy are not among the few calm dreams of the world, I will wait in the sounding of harps for better. Clear water runs sometimes over sand and pebbles from the harbour, with many a pool under willows, and always blue in the shade of poplars, or shining through the rushes, sometimes in the shallows breaking into fingers with little islands between, and everywhere alive with duck and heron, and birds prettier than a wish. Along a deep stretch that always made me think of a rod and fly, the track turned off, and Lal waited below a mound thick with flowers, where she told me the river had pushed Aaron Humphries' garden during the flood.

'You must have ridden well,' she said. 'I thought you from the South were better on a bicycle.'

'Practice and progress,' I said. 'We had good roads, not tracks. In any case, I have got my knees now, but you can raise money I will never be in a horse show. I will wait for a motor car, instead.'

'Mo-to car?' she asked me, as if she had just seen a bogey. 'Mo-to? What is that, then?'

'Mo-tor,' I said. 'A machine coming from engineers. My brothers have been working these years to make them so that somebody knowing nothing can drive one.'

'I can see you from the South will have a big advantage,' she said. 'But I will be there before you, side-saddle.'

'At twenty miles an hour, side-saddle will be something to see,' I said. 'The wheel will always be the master of a pair of reins.'

'Never,' she said, flat. 'Could you throw a lasso from this moto?'

'Pasture is for animals, and roads for others knowing better,' I said. 'When there are more of us from the South here, there will be roads.'

'Room to swing a cat is an estate for those coming from the warren,' she said. 'I want room at least to swing the boleadoras.'

'Swinging the lead I know,' I said. 'It came direct from the North.'

'You copied too well, and made a habit,' she said, and lifted the front of the saddle, and held up leather thongs sewn to three stones, one the size of a fist, the second of a billiard ball, and the smallest half of that again. 'These are the boleadoras, Mr Morgan. A gift from the Tehuelche to the pioneers. Do you like roast ostrich?'

'I thought an ostrich had only feathers for Sunday hats, and sometimes for a bit of dusting,' I said.

'The South has still plenty to learn,' she said. 'Did you see them over there?'

She held the smallest stone, and swung the other two above her head in a sound that held warning of a cracked skull, and the stallion went at stretch gallop towards the pampas. The birds of brownish grey with long necks, all running off on legs too thin to be seen reminded me of my zoo book and looking at the pictures by the fire at night, bringing me home again, and making me feel that this was only something to live through before to wake up. But the mare taught me again, and off she went, and nothing I could do to hold her. Lal and the stallion were shadows beneath a dark circle that flew in a loop out of the dust, and turned, spinning direct as if put there about the neck of the tallest ostrich, and wrapping tight, dragging him flat. She was off the horse, and putting a foot among the feathers and holding the head to unwind the thongs before I reached her, and a peon came from somewhere behind me, and slipped head-down off his horse, running to take the long neck and give it a good twist. But she left him there, and mounted again easy as I sit myself in a chair.

'At least, you have seen a cast of the boleadoras,' she said. 'When will you start lessons?'

'Cabinet-makers have plenty to learn in their own trade,' I said. 'Horses and cattle are beyond me. But I would like to own a few and a bit of land.'

'And look after them in a moto, is it?' she said, with a smile the sun might have risen in. 'Where will you buy?'

'I will earn the money first,' I said.

'When you are ready, tell me,' she said. 'I know the land and I know cattle and sheep.'

'I will have enough to start when you buy the screen,' I said. 'Now you have got time to think.'

'If you buy a farm, you will have a house,' she said. 'Then you will have to stay here, is it?'

Riding across Maes Corwen pasture then, it was, that I first knew I was willing to live there. Until then I had always thought of myself as a visitor, kindly welcomed and giving everything a trial, but sensing myself a little left out of the ordinary run, and the land itself seeming to offer hospitality but always with little frost coming in some moments to warn that any stay comes to an end soon enough.

But cantering into hot sunshine towards the red roof among trees, for some reason, perhaps because of her beside me, I felt myself held and willed to be part of the meadows and the pampas beyond, of the cattle moving in a sparkle down by the river, of the hills white above the poplars, of the little pinkish clouds like babies' fists in the sky, and of the pioneers, and all they had cleansed by their sweat and hallowed with their bones, and left for others, even me, to enjoy.

Perhaps the feeling got into my knees, or my hands, but Merri was off, leading the stallion, and going faster than I wanted towards the garden in front of the house, and Lal calling behind, but no matter, I had all I could do to clutch the front of the saddle and stay up there, and it was no surprise to me, when the front door was so close I could see the buds on the hollyhocks, that Merri sat down and slid to stop herself, and I went over her neck and into the pink hydrangea.

'Well, fancy, now,' Doli said, with her head round the door. 'I thought I had seen a few in my time, indeed.'

'He is a beauty from the Rhondda,' Lal said, in the saddle looking down at me with an elbow on her knee, and a hand under her chin. 'Mistress Doli Corwen, allow me to introduce Mr Huw Morgan, if you insist. A wonderful rider, too. In a moto.'

'Come in, boy,' Doli said. 'Did you hurt?'

'If you have got a good cup of tea with you, it will cure

everything,' I said. 'I believe you have got a kinder heart than your sister.'

'Turn to the youngest,' Lal said. 'Kindness and Solva are like sponge cake and red-currant jelly. A match, indeed.'

'There is soft you are, girl,' Solva said, and she spoke quieter than I ever heard anybody, yet each word was plainer than if she had shouted. 'Somebody will have to mend the old butter churn, again, see. I am stuck in middle, yes, and no hope to make another kilo. How do you do, Mr Morgan, excuse my hand all wet.'

'Mr Morgan knows how to mend it,' Lal said. 'A special piece of Christmas cake with his tea, if he can.'

'I will give an estimate,' I said.

'And you shall have an estimate for your dinner,' Doli said. 'One peso for you, and ten centavos for the horse. Hay is coming scarce. Stay to tea, the estimate will be more.'

'I have got plenty in the saddlebag, thank you,' I said. 'There is grass by the river. First the chest, for measures, and afterwards the churn for repairs. Charges by the hour, tools and wood extra.'

'No charge for the bump,' Doli said.

'Two blooms off the hydrangea and leaves in shovelfuls,' Solva said, whispering. 'Brought in casks from the Old Land, and a fortune in freight, my grandfather said.'

'More than twenty years of looking after,' Lal said. 'How much is that?'

'Every moment is costing,' I said. 'My injuries might stop work for a week or more. There is a doctor, and a good advocate in the city, one to patch the damage, and the other to assess, and justice after.'

'The doctor is in Bahía Blanca, and the advocate is in our family,' Lal said. 'The only justice was smoking a pipe in that chair behind you, yesterday.'

'A reduction in case the three of you are on the jury,' I said. 'For my dinner I will mend the churn, and for my tea and Christmas cake, I will sing to you.'

'Mend the old churn,' Solva said. 'Singing we have heard, thank you.'

She took me through a long room, dark to keep out the flies, and down a passage to the dairy, with stone troughs all round the walls to hold the milk, and butter tubs on the floor, and pails and yokes, and a big wooden churn tipped off the axle. But there were no tools or wood and the store

29

was locked, and I went off round the house to see what I could find.

A big place it was, to be sure, stacked with many a good rick, and ducks and geese about the pond, and poultry of all kinds in the yard and splendid roosters like living jewels picking about the manure heap. At that time I suppose they must have had a thousand or more eggs a day, though they were not worth collecting once they had enough stored for the winter, because everybody in the Valley had hens and nobody wanted more, and in those days there was no market. The barns were filled to the roofs with hay and grain, and beyond the fence, miles and miles of corn grew all the way to the hills. But it was grown only because it would grow. Wheat and barley could be sold, yes, but rail and shipping dues took the profit, so most of the farmers let the cattle eat and thrive. Under the apple trees I was to the ankles in a rot of fallen fruit, and the plums were deeper still. Apricots, damsons, nectarines and peaches lay like colours in a carpet, though thinking back now, there were square acres of garden there, to say nothing of the groves of cherry trees thirty feet high and more, and currants growing wild that would take prizes for size or taste, and a stretch of berries of every kind never to be bettered anywhere. Through the window I could see that the toolshed was kept like a parlour, with every tool racked and every horseshoe on its spike by sizes. The ploughs and farrows were oiled and the handles were scraped clean and smooth, and the harness had been soaped and the metal greased, and the floors were swept, and a sprinkling of carbolic lay on the air. I found a good log out on the woodpile but no loose tools, and Doli said her father had the keys and he would be home from working on the dam, if I wanted to wait, at the end of the week.

'Him, work on the dam?' I said. 'Why, with all this?'

'To have water here, boy,' Doli said. 'Everybody has got to take his turn to dig or carry, no?'

'No farm without water,' Lal said. 'No water without a dam and canals. Him, and his father, and his grandfather worked years with the river. So have we. And everybody else.'

'Plenty of peons, surely,' I said.

She turned and went from me.

'Some there are,' she said, careless. 'For real work, there is nobody to trust except ourselves.'

An hour with a sharp axe and a knife, and I had the churn working, and Solva turning the wheel, and in lyric soprano singing the ballads of an older time brought with the pioneers, gay tunes and sad ones, and poetry strange to me, and I could have stayed struck, only listening to her. But I had to measure the coffer, in wood of teak that I had seen only a few times in my life, the last a couple of days before. But I said nothing. Mr Tibbald had a pile of empty Havana cigar boxes in his shop that would do for a cedar lining, so for the making there was no more to think about. But the girls were not so sure. They wanted something good and they were willing to cut down the oldest apple, or walnut, and they were even talking of putting a blade in a great briar that had been growing for donkey's years.

'Cut them all down if you think it will serve,' I said. 'But remember you will have to wait a long time for your coffer. That wood will have to season. She will have had a family by the time it is ready.'

'Not if I know Jenkin,' Doli said. 'He will have to season a bit, too. If then.'

'She didn't want him anyway,' Solva said, in the little voice. 'Billo, it was, she wanted. If Vrann tries that with me, I will use a scythe on him.'

'Wait until somebody says something,' Doli said, and looked at Lal, but no look for me. 'Jenkin has got a farm flat on the river, and twelve leagues. She will live a good life.'

'I wish her everything, and a kiss from God,' Solva said. 'But I would go with the first Indio rather than be told who to marry.'

'Is everybody told who to marry here, then?' I asked them, and Lal was cutting the bread thin, and Doli was putting teaspoons in the saucers, and Solva was waiting for the kettle to boil with the teapot in her hand, and they all stopped and looked at me.

'Not told, exactly,' Lal said, in doubt. 'But even with animals, the blood must be considered. I agree with that. Some of our girls have gone off with Latins and Slavs and who. You should see how they live.'

'Not all,' Doli said. 'Beth Prichard has got a beautiful family, and so has Meriel Gwynn. The others are well used to idleness, and a lot of dirt and sousing in wine, so no trouble.'

'I haven't seen any of our women living like that,' I said.

'Wait you,' Doli said. 'You will see a few of the men, too. A wash they will have by accident once a year if they fall in the sheep dip, and colds in their old noses, after.'

'They could sneeze their last, and I would call the kites to pick them clean,' Solva said. 'Indios can be forgiven their habits. But ours, no.'

'Better combine property,' Lal said, spreading butter to fill the pores of the bread. 'Too much hard work goes in wine-shops, and profit to nobody except foreigners.'

'The Tehuelche they will clean out,' Doli said. 'Us, too. If we let them.'

'You can say nothing about Beretroff, anyhow,' Solva said, away from us and into the teapot. 'Slavo, yes, but always polite, and a lovely moustache.'

'You have not got a word in common,' Lal said, up, from the bread and butter, and her eyes big in the shadow. 'No use to think like that, girl. Marry somebody you can talk to, at least. Have your children decently at school, and a house with a chair to sit down in.'

'I will marry who and when I like,' Solva said, in the little voice, over the boil of water. 'Nobody shall tell me. Do girls in Wales have to ask, Mr Morgan?'

'If they are over the age of consent, no, I don't think so,' I said.

'Consent to what?' Doli asked me.

'Don't be dull, girl,' Lal said, busy with the knife in cur-rant bread. 'To consent, you must say yes. To what, then?'

'Well, in that event, the age would be eight or nine, here,' Doli said. 'But they only live together.'

'Marrying, I said,' Solva told her, putting down the pot and leaning across the table, not in a temper, but eyes wide. 'Nobody shall say one word. There will be no Jenkin for me. No interbreeds, and no crossbreeds. Healthy children, I will have, even in the dirt and drunkenness. But where I am, there will be neither.'

She ran from there, and the door slammed.

Doli poured milk for the tea, and Lal put the plate of currant bread in its exact place.

'Sugar, Mr Morgan?' Doli said.

'Two spoons, please,' I said.

'She shall never go to the city by herself again,' Lal said. 'We will lose her, Doli.'

'Tell her not, and she will,' Doli said. 'The jams are in

these dishes, Mr Morgan. Scones under that cover, muffins under this. Smallcakes by there, and sausage rolls near your plate. Help yourself, and eat plenty, please, for the long way to go back. Keep room for the cakes. They are at the window to cool.'

'Between the Widow Glyn and you, they will be rolling me on rails from the shop,' I said. 'Is it healthy to eat so much?'

'No,' Doli said. 'Only nice.'

'Too fat by ten kilos,' Lal said, eating plain bread and butter, and watching Doli with a muffin dripping greengage jam. 'Nothing so ugly as fat.'

'Saddle-racks there are many,' I said. 'A girl with some upholstery is comforting to the eye. Nothing more comforting than Doli have I seen since I came here.'

'Well, my beloved soul, listen to the estimates, here,' Doli said, with her mouth full. 'For nothing you shall eat and drink busting for ever. Come soon and often, boy.'

'Mind the hydrangea,' Lal said. 'What will you charge for the coffer, Mr Morgan?'

'I will see what the wood costs, first,' I said. 'But I will have to write home for copies of the lock and hinges.'

'Go to the Co-operative in the city,' Lal said. 'Mr Rhos Phillips. Ask for what you want, and put it on our account.'

'Put the wood on the account, too,' Doli said. 'Then we will see what an old swindler you are. You are eating in a peck with you, boy, and still cakes to come.'

'Enough I have had for three weeks solid,' I said. 'Show me a cake and I will be sick over the table.'

'That cloth is fresh from the wash and an hour with the iron,' Doli said. 'Take him from here.'

Solva came back with the bolt of brocade for lining the coffer, heavy, with a feel of satin, threaded gold, and sewn in colours with flowers and Chinese junks, that Doli said their grandmother had been given by the captain of a ship wrecked on the coast. Carefully they wrapped it in a length of muslin, and put it in the saddlebag, and on the way home I was thinking how strange it would be if the ship that had been lost was the wreck I had found with the teak panelling.

And about Lal I was thinking, too.

3

3

A couple of days' work down at the harbour, along the strand of shells and sand turning in to the river, and a hard time I had, stripping teak from the cabin and scraping off the barnacles. But my best find was underwater, and it took almost a week longer to pull loose a lovely bit of rosewood from a place that must have been for the master's wife perhaps, almost unmarked by damp because of the list of the deck and the strong timbering round it. I had my eye on all that was left, and every foot of it came in useful for many a good suite. Indeed, how people can let a hulk rot on the shore is beyond me, because common sense should tell them that only the best timber goes into a ship.

James Smalcote and Voldemar Zhdanov came alongside during the first morning to give me a hand with the lifting. They were both big men, and bearded, with hair to the collar, and wearing leather trews and jackets well-sewn and fitted, and Indio slippers. They could have been brothers, but James was from London, and Volde was a Russian.

They worked a home-made boat with squared ends, and oars like telegraph poles, but it floated, and the day's catch of shrimp and lobster they sold round the farms for the week's expenses. Voldemar spoke good English, and James told me he had been to a university and got into trouble about politics, and escaped, but he never talked about it. James said they had met in the south somewhere, both from a ship, without a centavo between them and getting work together, or starving and caring nothing, because to starve half and half is to share half a meal, and saving enough to come north into better land and more chance of work. In some part they helped a Tehuelche family, and one of the girls wanted to follow them and the father made a gift of her, so then there were three, and she made everything easier. She brought her own troop of horses and guanaco skins for a tent and sleeping rugs, and in buying and selling she got the Indio price, and more of everything, and if they wanted extra and had no money, she helped herself. One shop they went into, James said, she had a knife for each of them, and a kettle, and even the blade of a plough, all taken bare-faced and pushed under her skirt. But they always sent back and paid when they had the money, and in that way they had a name for being honest, besides good workmen and savers.

Only lately they found the Valley of the Camwy, and they had a few sheep and a couple of head of cattle, and a hut they had built farther up the river, with enough of a garden to keep them in vegetables, and a little corn over for the poultry. That year they were hoping to get credit and rent a piece of land.

'If we had some of these places along here, we'd have money in the bank inside a year,' James said. 'You speak Welsh, don't you?'

'Poorly, according to some,' I said. 'Would it help you?'

'As much as Michaye speaking Tehuelche,' he said. 'There's a girl up the river. Near the salt flats. I go down every night where she lives. She waves when she sees me, but she always runs. Not a word of English. Her father's a proper bean-pole. About seven foot high, he is. If I don't do it right, I can see me getting me neck broke. Could you help me?'

'To go courting?' I said. 'Troubles I have got, thank you.'

'When I knock on the door, I mean,' James said, and in his voice were the hours of his dreams. 'I want to talk to her old pot-and-pan and set things right. Get spliced. I tell you, I start thinking of a wife like that, and a house, you know, like, and a garden, and sort of get down to it, and make a bit of brass. Alys Caerog Evans her name is. She's fifteen. I got it from the bloke in the Post Office. I want to drop her a line. Would you write it for me?'

'Come to my shop, and we will have an epic,' I said. 'But respectable. Mr Eynon Caerog Evans is an Elder of the Chapel.'

'Know him, do you?' James said, in hopes.

'I have only seen him there,' I said. 'Do you want to know the best way? Never mind scribble, and love to her. If she waves now, she will kiss later, and no trouble. Him, not her, you should think about.'

'Tell me,' he said. 'I'd rake the cinders out of hell for her.'

'That one has got a voice,' I said, hearing Voldemar la-

laing down on the beach mending a net. 'Bring him to Chapel, and let him stretch an octave with a hymn or two.'

'Volde's got no time for religion,' James said. 'Nor me.'

'For the girl, not religion,' I said. 'If he can sing as good as he can la-la, and if you open your mouth with his, they will think you are ready for the blessing, both. After, you will shake hands with everybody at the door, and Eynon Caerog Evans will be one. If you are invited to an asado after that, will it be a help or a hindrance?'

'Brains,' James said. 'Now I know why I teamed with Volde.'

With them I had a midday lobster grilled on hot sand, and Volde made a tomato sauce I will never forget, and I shared my steak with them, and they took the other loaf and half a cheese, and I made Volde fill up his water-bag with the rest of the wine, and you would have thought I had given them a coach and pair. Michaye ran down from the high grass when we were having a wink or two in the shade. Farther up the coast she had been looking for them, and she came laughing and scolding, tall for a girl, in a leather skirt and a pink blouse with an Indio sash of many colours, and Volde lifted her to sit in the ark, and they went out on the sunny green water, with the food and the kettle and the maté, and I suppose three people happier you would never find.

But looking at Michaye and the light in two braids of ink silk, and the smile without teeth of a settled spirit, I thought of Vrann Corwen, and Indio wives, and many children, and I came to understand much more than I had, and perhaps even a little more than I wanted.

Porfirio Hernandez I met the last evening, driving his flock up to Port Madryn, and resting them in the grass along the shore. He and his Indio herdsmen helped me to lift the timber up the track to the Widow Glyn's wagon, and then it was that I found out what a fool a man is without a word of another's language. Porfirio and the herdsmen spoke only Castellano, so we had to pull faces and use our hands. Of course we got everything done, but it took longer than it should, and from that moment I made up my mind to speak the language of the country.

But there I ran into squalls from the Widow Glyn, because it was her I asked first about a teacher.

'To learn what?' she said, as if she was deaf. 'Why should

you weigh your mind with something you will never use? Who would you talk to?'

'The others,' I said, surprised at her. 'Beyond us, and a few who speak English, I am helpless.'

'But with those you will have your money,' she said. 'Who else has got a peso? Which one of them could give you an order in Castellano? Paying with what? All the Tehuelche and the Basques and the Italians who deal with us, speak Welsh. Let it be good enough for you.'

No more was said then, but I had a talk with Mr Rhos Phillips at the Co-operative Stores when I gave him the order for the lock and hinges.

It took only a moment to see in him a preacher, but put to business instead, and quiet, but strong. Small, he was, and black hair brushed back flat, and a clipped beard and moustache, and pince-nez on a ribbon to point.

'Do me the kindness to look out of that door, Mr Morgan,' he said. 'If you can see a tree, it was planted by the Welsh. If there is grass, the Welsh put it there. If there is a flower, Welsh women brought the seeds in their bosoms. If there is water, the Welsh dug and ditched and dammed it. These streets were planned and stamped out by the Welsh. These houses and the farmhouses outside are Welsh. The shops are Welsh. The railway was built by the Welsh. The sewers were dug by the Welsh. The Bank is Welsh. This Co-operative is Welsh, staffed by the Welsh, and the books and accounts are in our language. There is only one cemetery. Go there, and see. It is Welsh.'

'But there is a lot of Spanish,' I said. 'Why is everybody against it?'

'They are hoping to keep it Welsh, especially the old pioneer families,' he said. 'Remember, this is called the City of Lewis, in the Welsh language, not Castellano.'

'And is that why they always call it a colony?' I asked him.

'Of ideals, and hopes, yes, and it was that, once,' he said. 'A place they wanted where they could speak their own language and worship in their own way. Strong people, too, and willing to suffer. Not like us today. There was nothing then to comfort. Some improvement we had in style when families came from Wisconsin a few years ago, and a couple from California and Brazil. But not enough. No influence from the outside. In truth, you could call us a forgotten people.'

'Patagonia I always thought of in the same way as Brobdingnag, not existing,' I said. 'Darwin and Swift made about the same impression.'

'The Tehuelche's big feet gave Patagonia its name, so you have got a good parallel,' Mr Phillips said. 'But they are dying from the land the same as us, and the same reason. No brains. No ability in business. No professions. Not enough lawyers or doctors or accountants or engineers. No real education. Most of them go to Buenos Aires and live off the profits from here. You have seen all the Italians? Good they are, too. Spaniards and Basques in plenty, and everybody from the Arabian Nights is peddling safety pins one minute, and before you can turn, they have got a wineshop. But they have all come to a land ready cleaned and waiting. No trouble to them. And Buenos Aires is sending soldiers and politicos like the flood, a little at first, coming stronger, and after that over the roof. The language is losing, and religion will follow. And the strength that kept the old ones going went out on the flood to the Atlantic. No man has any faith in a god who robs him of everything.'

'A picture for Jeremiah,' I said.

'Better than to play Job,' Mr Phillips said. 'A dream has put to sea. Nothing to take its place.'

'But they have all got their properties,' I said. 'A good harvest to come, plenty to eat and drink, and the Co-op to buy everything from. No doubt about it, the conditions are much better here than in Wales. I am staying, for one.'

'Of course, I was talking about the vision of other days,' he said, and his face said nothing. 'The facts of today, and the material outlook are different matters. These locks and hinges will be here in two or three months, Mr Morgan.'

'Too long,' I said. 'The wedding is after the harvest.'

'Ships take their time,' he said. 'A search through stocklists robs the clock. Eight weeks, for a miracle.'

'It will happen here,' I said. 'That chest will be ready, or I will have three girls hitting sparks out of me. May I have my account, please?'

'You have got credit, Mr Morgan,' he said, and passing a hand over inches of letters all spread anyhow on the table. 'It is easier to deal with accounts once a month or quarterly. With these thieves about the place, we prefer not to have cash on the premises.'

'Then there is more in my pocket for a little longer,' I said.

'I have never heard of anybody not wanting cash before.'

'It is a co-operative,' Mr Phillips said, and very patient. 'If you have got extra money you would like to invest, please to remember us. We can always accommodate. Eight per cent per annum, compound. Better than the bank, and a help to the community.'

Straightaway I went down to Vyrnwy Beris, and found him in a smell of burning hoof at the back of the smithy, beating a sheet of iron red from the fire and using a sledge in each hand, swinging them overhead easy as I use a tack hammer. Shorter than me, he was, but thick in the shoulder, with arms the size of any other man's legs, and so strong that he could hold two Shire stallions pulling against him, and the day came when I thanked God for it.

He looked at the hinges and lock, and went out in the light to look at the clasps.

'This work I always wanted to do,' he said. 'Wasting my time with a lot of old shoes. A man could be proud of giving a bit of something good for a lifetime, see. I will heat metal ready tonight, and pour tomorrow. Flatten and polish, a day at least. Parry Jones will make that lock and a key. Come Saturday, or I will bring it, sure.'

Good as his word, Saturday morning, in he came, and put down those I had given him to copy, and the others he had made of hammered steel, bright and solid and special screws to fit.

'You know something about it,' I said.

'When you get work like this, come running,' he said, black, and stuck in his grime and sweat. 'Pleasure I had, see, and hoping for more.'

'I will pay you twice what you were going to ask,' I said.

'Double, and still you will pay nothing,' he said, out, in the street. 'Money is for work. Pleasure is for pleasure, and good-bye, now.'

Well, I got the teak for nothing, and Mr Tibbald gave me the cigar boxes for nothing, and the lining was for nothing, and the lock, hinges and clasps were for nothing, so for nothing I gave the chest to the girls when they came in for the Saturday shopping.

To see their faces was to be light and lifted in a cloud, and I had a couple of kisses from Doli, and a few from Solva, but somehow it never came the turn of Lal, because with the noise they were making with OO's and O's, a lot of people came in to see what they could, and the place was shouting full.

But I got a look and that was thanks enough, because I will swear it left a little place on the back of my brains, and I can feel it even now, and see her, too, in brown velvet, and a wide brown velvet hat and yellow roses, O, and beautiful.

We had an asado at the back of Evans, Up, called that from living up the valley, because his brother living at the other end was called Evans, Down. The eldest brother was called Evans, Sideways, because he was too fat to go face-first through a door, and the youngest, with a twist in the fork of something wrong with his gottings that never let him sit square to a saddle, him they called Evans, All Shapes.

The girls had to go home early because their father was coming home from the dam, and they took the chest wrapped in blankets like a child not to get a bump, and off blowing kisses they went in the trap with red wheels, and two creams, and Solva with the whip, and I suppose I went back treading on froth of gold to the shop.

There was plenty to be done, and only me to do it, never mind that I offered free apprenticeship to any of our boys ready to work. Every pair of hands was needed on the land, or at the dam, and there was no skill to be had, so I was up to my neck from just after dawn, making bedroom suites, and china cupboards, and dressers, and all sorts of furniture for houses emptied by the water.

Late it was on Saturday afternoon, and I heard the door open and a man stood in the dark.

'Rhinberry Winn, I am,' he said, as if he had a bad cold. 'Harries, Sawmill, is shut, and so is Morris, Carpenter. I was wondering.'

'What?' I asked him, at thin shadow.

'If you could make a coffin,' he said. 'I would be very obliged. The burial must be tonight or early in the morning. The sun is too hot, see.'

'Cabinet-maker I am,' I said. 'Never have I made a coffin and no intention. Good work, and good wood put down a shaft for no good reason.'

'No, not for no good reason,' he said, coming in the light, and I saw the face too pale, and about him a look of the trampled. 'My wife has gone from me.'

He leaned on a chair, and his clothes were too big, and

40

weight pulled down his head.

'If you will let me pay for the wood, and lend me the tools, I will shape it myself,' he said. 'I was in hopes she would have something better. The best I only had from her. She shall go with the best, too.'

I put an arm about his shoulders, and he turned quick to me, and leaned the dusty head, and cried as if I was the only solid in his life.

'Sweet of my heart, she was,' he said. 'Always beautiful to me. I have got plenty of money to pay, Mr Morgan. I will give it all, only for my little one to have the best.'

'Go out by there, and make a maté,' I said. 'Ready late this evening. No need to wait. I will bring it.'

Cutting firewood and filling a kettle are small things that help to pull the salt, and while he was out there, I went down to Vyrnwy Beris and found him washed but not dressed, reading a paper in the kitchen. Sorry he was to hear about Mrs Winn, remembering her at school, and picnics on the river. Into the smithy he went straight, to make handles of coiled iron, and polish brass to stamp with her name and the date. The Widow Glyn cut up a couple of her mother's silk dresses to make quilting with cotton wool, and by the time she had finished on the sewing machine, I was ready with the shell, and with brass-head nails, and the handles Vyrnwy brought in, well, the Widow Glyn said if I would promise to make her one like that, she was ready to get in herself, and go comfortable.

We went in Vyrnwy's trap out along the river to Maes Hafod, white by the moon in standing wheat, and pitch below the trees, and we heard the woman singing soft when we turned in the gate.

Vyrnwy was down and carrying, so I stayed in the trap and turned the horses, and Rhinberry ran from the house, and came to the side, trying to push money.

'Take it,' he said. 'I looked only once, but I know what she would say. She will go from here lovely, indeed. Good work, and good wood, and a good, good girl, yes, I will swear.'

Vyrnwy got up beside me, and we had a nod.

'I am a cabinet-maker, and nobody shall pay me for work not mine, Rhinberry,' I said. 'So good night, now, and God rest a hand soft on the house.'

'One day there will be something I can do,' he said, looking up at me. 'Remember me till then. Rhinberry Winn. I will remember you, and I will bless with every breath.'

Back home, the Widow Glyn had cooked a big supper and a lot of people were there, so I had to go up and change, and Vyrnwy, too. We were all at the big table in the front room, and the plates were coming full and going empty, and the wine was going round, and I was thinking of bed, but the Reverend Mr Armon Tudor came to sit next to me, and ready to talk.

'I hear you know Mr Gruffydd from before,' he said. 'We have always been sorry not to make his acquaintance. If you should see him, will you tell him I would consider it a pleasure to welcome him at the house? Besides that, a duty. After all, no crime was committed.'

'Two things I have got to say,' I said. 'First, Mr Gruffydd's business is nothing to do with me. Secondly, I will not carry messages. Everybody knows when he comes here. Or you could send a letter.'

'Well, not that I meant to offend you,' he said, in a stare. 'If you are a friend of his, you have duties.'

'One is to mind my own business,' I said.

'Ah, Mr Morgan, a lot of us say that to escape our share of good work,' he said, hands together, and in a good preacher's voice. 'This man has been with us for years, coming and going with never a word or sign. But his training and vocation taught him differently. Where are we complimented? Where is he? That is to say not a word of his doctorate, and the truth imposed in him, and perhaps in you, in the name of the Founder, who calls every one of us to testify. The chapel is open for every sinner.'

'Amen,' the company said.

'I know nothing, and I have no interest,' I said. 'The only reason I go to chapel is to hear a good hymn. If there were no voices, there would be no me.'

'That is an utterance near to sacrilege, Mr Morgan,' Jared Perkin said, and looking round the table. 'For worship, and no other reason you should go. To find your soul, and the grace to give thanks for life, and health, and the blessings of abundance.'

'I will do that with a hymn, and a word,' I said. 'I am not a chapel man. The voice of a choir is prayer enough.'

'But not enough to save you in the Hour,' Silas Ieuan Pendar said. 'A coffin you made for the unbaptised and un-

42

consecrated. Another matter for the Judgement. I am not sure if I should be at the same table.'

'Move to another,' I said. 'Any coffin I made held the love of a good man. Be happy if I will make one for you.'

'Well, indeed, you are a new kind with us, Mr Morgan,' Evans, Sideways, said, and his fingertips just touching across the waistcoat. 'It is wrong to speak in such a manner to one who requires your respect, and you increase the wrong by speaking in front of us.'

'Then keep your ears from what I am saying,' I said. 'I spoke for him, not for any of you.'

'Wait, now,' Mr Tudor said, standing, and holding up a finger. 'There was no intention to cause argument. I believe when Mr Morgan has lived with us a little longer, he will find that we are different from his present thoughts of us. Perhaps you take sustenance from the Bible, Mr Morgan?'

'Sometimes,' I said.

'Then I extend an invitation to join us at the class,' he said. 'Monday, Wednesday and Friday, seven o'clock and Sunday school at three.'

'I have too much work for the moment, but thank you, and perhaps there will be time later,' I said. 'But generally I enjoy the English Bible.'

The Reverend Mr Tudor pulled down his coat, and settled his collar over the black patch.

'Thank you for our generous and excellent supper, Mistress Glyn,' he said. 'Nobody, I am sure, will ever leave this house except comfortable in body and in spirit. Disappointments, of course, we all have at times. But we must be patient, and judge not. Good night, Mr Morgan. We shall probably meet again.

Everybody went to the door except Vyrnwy, but only the Widow Glyn came back, and fell in the big chair I had made for her, and rested her head, with her hands on the arms, looking at me as though I had crawled from somewhere.

'Everything that came from your mouth was a mistake, and wrong, and no hope to change it,' she said, from hilltops away in the far desolation. 'I was thinking to put you comfortable with us. Are you senseless, or did you know that every man at that table has got his million or two in the bank? Every one of them can put work in your way, money down, cash. Anything you want you could have only for the asking. And you speak like that to Mr Tudor? And Silas

43

Ieuan? And Jared? Never mind brains, where is sense in your behaviour?'

'If you ask questions you will get answers, as they did,' I said. 'Mr Tudor speaks with those millions well in his eye. I heard him in his chapel.'

'Right, you,' Vyrnwy said. 'You know yourself everything is coming very changed here, Morwen, not like it was. If I ever go to chapel, I am there to sing a hymn or two. And if I go to Sunday school, the reason is a good cup of tea and talk to a few after, no doubt about it.'

'You are not in fears the roof will throw flame over you?' she asked him, whispering, and back with her head, and opening her eyes to see devils dancing on his shoulders. 'If I will die this minute, I never thought to hear you talk in such a way. Brought up with me, same class and same teacher and same lessons as me, every minute for the years, and now you are saying something different to me because Huw talks with the wickedness in him, and the sloth of wine bibbers and smoking. If your mother could hear, she would have fits of the spin in the tomb again with her, poor old woman, not cold.'

'A good one to talk, you are,' Vyrnwy said, and laughing. 'When did Rupert go to chapel, then, hot or cold? A red letter, six foot high, every time. And before you were married, you only went to be chased through the trees on the way back.'

'There is lies, lies I am hearing,' the Widow Glyn said, looking round the room to see where monsters were kicking in their stalls. 'In my own house, you will dare? A girl is different. Boys, too, Vyrnwy Beris. If I had to go in the trees sometimes to find my horse, is it right to blame me now? You make me jump when you say that. What will Huw think of me? Who can point a finger? Not you, for one, never, now then for you.'

'I am off home,' Vyrnwy said, and put his pipe in his pocket. 'You are come very serious all of a sudden, Morwen. But I remember Rupert very well, too, and carrying him home here drunk many a time, round the back not to be seen. And when were you in chapel, those days? Will we have a little stroll, Huw?'

Stars alone lit the front of the shops pale, and there was fire above the engine shed beyond the station. Dogs barked from a distance, a little noise making the silence stretch into something that had a sound of its own, that I have never heard anywhere else, and that always reminded me of the voice of the twin of loneliness.

'There has been too much of hammers in my mind before, but what you were saying there tonight I think I can agree with,' he said. 'I'm sure a lot of us are going to chapel to do some singing after the week, and see each other and have a good talk. Do a bit of business, too, if nobody is listening. Even without a preacher, there are always Deacons or Elders. But the other side of it, I have got to think. It is very hard sometimes, indeed. What shall it profit a man to gain the whole world and lose his own soul? Often I think of that while I am fitting a shoe. For money I do it. Work, it is. But I would like to do other things. And where is the chance? With what prayer?'

Sometimes you can think, and sometimes the mind seems to float in an oil of its own, bringing words, and the look on faces, and the walk of somebody, or music never heard, though how it comes or where it is kept I could never tell. That night, in the quiet street I was thinking of home, and chapel as a boy, and our family sitting in a linc, and my mother passing a sweet to Angharad, and from her to Ceridwen, and from her to Owen, and from him to me, and another coming down for the next, until everybody had one for the sermon, and the look on my mother's face if we made a noise taking off the paper, or sucked too loud, or cracked with the teeth. None of us needed a hymn-book or psalter, and we could follow the lessons under our breath from most of the Bible, and go on with the verses where the reader left off, and a sixpence from my father for the one who could go on the longest. It was always close between Ivor and Davy and Ceridwen and they generally got a sixpence each or split one between them, and we got pennies for trying, but none of us were any good after the Book of John to the end of the Bible, and Ivor was the one who said that in those books a lot of smallcoal was mixed, and in the push and pull of Peter and Paul, poor Christ got lost and never to be found again. That was why we read only the books of the Old Testament, and Matthew, Mark, Luke and John and nothing more in the New, because Revelations was full of dragons and smoke and smiting, and my father said that we all had a bit of that to come, and no use to read about it and have goose-flesh all over and go upstairs frightened, but better to read from the old ones singing in or out of pain, or from a Voice easy to tell from all the others, and have a bit of hope, and take peace to bed.

Five hours at least we had every Sunday in chapel, with morning service, Sunday school and service in the evening, and during the week, there were Bible classes, and readings and lectures, never mind choir practice and sessions of hymns. Chapel, in truth, was the goodness of our lives, and looking back now, I wonder what would we have done without it. An influence it was, no doubt, in bringing together everybody, family by family, so that the missing could be asked after, and the travellers followed wherever they might be, and prayed for by name and place, so that everybody knew where they were and what they were doing. Nobody could come looking like a tramp, so best clothes and clean linen and polished boots it had to be, and there again was a double discipline, because a decent appearance brings good manners, or if not, a clip in the ear to cross your eyes would be the least to expect, and the strap when you were home, and bed, then, and bread and water for supper. But a great deal had to depend on the pastor, and in my years he was Mr Gruffydd, and he used to say that a chapel is open to be full and if he wanted one empty, he could lock the door. A lot of good he did the morning he found Zoar Brethin and his family missing, and kept the chapel waiting to go down there, and found some of them out of bed and round the fire, and Zoar still in, and went up there and took the bed in pieces under him, and threw the bedclothes from the window, and Zoar followed him out in his little shirt and went at him with fists, but Mr Gruffydd tripped him into a tub of freezing water and pulled him out, and gave them all five minutes to dress. Back to chapel then, and everybody turning to see what, and who, and Zoar was in such a temper, he sang the hymns too loud, and everybody hished him to go softer, but the more they hished the louder him and his family, and then everybody had to shout not to hear them, and Mr Gruffydd said it was the best bit of singing he had ever heard, and we would have advantage with more of it. From that morning on, Zoar was leader of hymns, and never missed a moment after, and family, too, so proud he was, and the only one to be more surprised than him must have been the old Devil himself.

Certain it is, that without men like Mr Gruffydd nothing

moved because there was nothing there to make it. In our chapel, we knew well enough after he had gone. Nobody tried to stop this one from going off to find a choir more to his liking, or that one from going somewhere else. A few came to be out of the house while the Sunday dinner was cooked, or because it was close to go without trouble, and others stayed home to read the papers. And the few came to be many, and soon there were none, and no chapel. Blame, then, but too late.

I had just as much of the blame as anybody else, and I saw it very clearly strolling back to the house. A lot like me knew what was right to do. It had been with us from babies, but coming to be grown up, we had left it, though it would be hard to say why except that our fathers were not there to keep us on the road, and harder to find what good had taken its place. The old ones had known a Faith, but it was surely not in us, and the signs were plain enough to see. There were still men like my father, but they were the old, not the young, or of my age, and not the growing children, either, and in a moment I was back in this very room, and hearing Bron telling me to mind my own business, and she would look after her sons in her way and no interference from anybody.

'But Bron,' I said, and so surprised.

'But, but,' she said. 'They have got more to do today than put their noses in the Bible. Studies they have got for two hours every night from school. Lucky to be in bed by ten, and up again at six. They are going thin, the pair of them, with old books, here.'

'They must study or be mending roads,' I said. 'Scholars you were given, and think yourself blessed in heaven. You would have plenty to complain about with a couple thick in the top. Study comes easy to them, thank God. But a few verses from the Book will bring rest to the spirit and spice to their wits.'

'Spice your own,' she said. 'No more will be pushed into those two while I am here. Besides, who are you to talk? Are you their father?'

She had never spoken to me before like that, or looking like that, either, and I turned to her, eye to eye, as I had not done for the years I had been in the house. Of course, we are all fools down here, and sometimes I think I must be the biggest fool of the lot, and cruel beyond words, for then, and only then, I saw that Bron was going old with her, and showing the lines of tiredness to thread her beauty, and in her back was a shape that had never been there.

Beauty, yes, nobody more beautiful than Bron, then or now or for ever, and sweet, too, as a woman is sweet, and gently patient, with smiles inside a smile, and laughing instead of tempering, and in a temper, funny.

But she looked at me then, old in the face, and cold, nothing in the eyes, and a sound like a knife on the window-pane in her voice.

'Well, Bron,' I said. 'Who am I? Brother to him that was their father, and no more.'

'Yes, no more,' she said, and she laughed, if scratching like that is a laugh. 'A lodger you have been for years, and now you think you are come to be something more, is it? Well, let me tell you once for all. No advice about my sons. No words to them, and no looks, never mind what they do. I will do all the correcting and every bit of encouraging. I want them out of this valley and to pass their examinations, and have a position and a good salary and to be free of us, with old washing hanging up in the kitchen, and a lot of old stuff out in the back and no room to grow a flower. I want them to have a house all clean, and tidy rooms, not this old den. Furniture you make for other people, but nothing for us. Not one respectable piece of wood in the place.'

There was no need to be told that the washing was my overalls, and other things, that always missed washday because of late hours from work, or that my timber and stores filled the back yard and had for years, and not a single thought about it in my mind. Furniture I knew I could have made, but I was set on putting as much in the bank as I could to buy Bron a house of her own. What else was in my mind at that time, God only knows, but sometimes we must have a kick to wake up.

'If it is furniture, you want, I can make it,' I said. 'The washing I can have done by Mrs Jenkins, and the back yard I will clear tomorrow, and Madoc, Trellis, will plant a garden for you. Perhaps that will let you feel a little more respectable, is it?'

'Respectable?' she said. 'Since how many years has anybody in this valley, or any other, though me respectable?'

No need to tell me I was a brother-in-law living in the house and nobody else except two boys. Never, I will swear, for all the years, had I thought about it since a time, long ago, when she had gone up and locked her door. From that moment there was no more to be said. Fool, yes, and fools exist, but it takes time to find out.

So I looked at her, and she looked at me, empty, cold, with the smile that was part of the laugh, though never of her.

It came in my mind, then, that Matt Humphries was always at the house for supper, or Sunday dinner, or a cup of tea, always with a joke for her, and help for me, or taking the boys somewhere, or being quiet and comfortable in a chair with a book. He had always wanted to marry her, and I had thought she was unwilling, if, but only if, I had ever thought at all.

So I looked at her, and she looked at me.

'Do you want me from the house, Bron?' I asked her.

'A bit late for that,' she said, same voice, same look.

'I can go, and I will be no trouble to you,' I said.

'You own the house,' she said. 'If anybody goes, it must be the boys and me.'

'It went in your name years ago,' I said. 'And everything in it.'

'Except you,' she said.

From the way she said it, there was nothing for me to say, and only one thing to do, and I looked at her, and the words were in my mouth, and I saw her face change, and her eyes were Bron's and if she had spoken, I knew I would hear her voice that I loved, but then I knew she would say she was sorry for being short, and I would say something, and everything would go on as it had.

Until the next time.

No.

Without a word I went from there, and ran across the hill to Matt's shop and found him working the lathe in the back.

'Listen, Matt, you have known me too long to waste time,' I said. 'Are you still wanting to marry Bron?'

'O, Huw,' he said, and such a look came in his face, and so sudden, that I felt struck to the floor. 'Nothing, not a whisper have I said these years. But if Bron would marry, I would walk as a prince among men. My oath is on it.'

'Why not tell her,' I said.

'I did, time after time,' he said. 'But always she said no, you had to be looked after. She had her boys. And what would people say, and how could she live knowing you were in lodgings, or well, anyway, no. So I said, right you. I will wait. Nobody else for me.'

I looked down at the head of him who had carried love so gently, and I thought of myself, and selfishness.

A shake of the shoulders I gave him, and ran out, and back to the house, and up the stairs from the yard not to go through the kitchen, and along the passage to the room we called the Scholars' Retreat, that I had made with shelves for the books, and desks for the boys. They were both writing by the lamp, and I put a finger over my mouth.

'Not a syllable, now,' I whispered, and pointed down, through the kitchen ceiling. 'Do you want to earn a sovereign each? When you hear me go downstairs, be quick to go in my room. The wall bed timbers you will find roped, and my bag. Take them out by the back window over the roof. Meet me on the corner, is it?'

It took very little time to unpeg the wall bed, and pack my bag, and dress. No thought was in my mind where to go, but the look on Matt's face was enough, even if I would have braved a legion of the damned rather than hear that sound in Bron's voice again, and I heard the boards shake upstairs only a little when the boys went flying on tiptoe to earn their sovereigns.

'Are you leaving us, Uncle Huw?' Gareth asked me, under the lamp when he came burdened. 'Does Mama know?'

They could have been my boys, because from babies I had known them, and Gareth's voice and eyes were his mother's, and a heart can be broken with a thought, too.

'Now, listen,' I said, and rough, for business. 'Say nothing, or you will be in splendid trouble for leaving your books without permission, and your sovereigns will go in the box. I am off for work. Not a murmur to your mama, and nothing to anybody else, and we will all be the wiser. Good night, now, and behave yourselves, remember.'

So, off they went, and off I went.

And there I was, under the Southern Cross. Under it I mean, to stretch my neck back to look at it, and not a proper cross I was sorry to find, because one star is smaller, and none of them very big, but the Southern Cross that some think is only a sailor's tale, there it was over my head, and

50

me under it in the City of Lewis, in Patagonia, all the way down in South America.

And only for a look not looked long enough, and something to say never said.

4

The Widow Glyn and many another, I am sure, thought that I started going to Moriah Chapel because of the talk that night, but in fact I went to see if Lal was there, although if I had used my brains nobody would have had to tell me that the family went to the chapel at Gaiman, farther up the valley and much nearer Maes Corwen.

Moriah, taken from Genesis, in the Hebrew language meaning Provided by Jehovah, was the first building the pioneers made in brick, but how long, or how many of them it took, or what they went through to put it up, only Jehovah knows. Then, everything had to come by sea, and there were few ships. No timber was to be had because none grew, nor was there cement, or slates for roofing, or glass for windows, or nails, or any little luxuries, putty or paint or varnish, and for tools, one saw-blade, kept like a jewel of price, and a couple of hammers and axes, and their knives. A stretch of high ground they cleared near the river to give them water, and they slapped the clay into shape by hand, and fired the pampas bush to bake the bricks for the floor and walls, and roofed it with rushes and plastered mud.

Provided by Jehovah, yes, as strong as hands and sinew could make it, and held with the sweat of work and the music of many a good verse psalmed or sung.

A little place it was, built from the memory of another at home, perhaps, and from the outside telling that the architect had many a time looked helpless at his helpers, and in some places gave way to love of their willingness, or to the clay that never came to be the shape he had in his mind. But Faith saw it and Faith built it, and when the last slop of mud was level on the roof, all the trumpets up above must have sounded, or if not, the trumpeters were idle and not fit to keep royal music.

Windows were in and paint and varnish were on when I

got there, but it was still plain inside, and even in the door I got the scent full in the nose of hard living, and I began to know the secret, then, of that shyness in the women and the gentleness in the men, and the strange shine in their eyes, which was self-denial and triumph in a shriving of confidence that nothing could win against the spirit that had gone into them with the blood of their fathers, and the milk of their mothers.

Listening to the hymns full-sung and in the Old Language sharp with the accent of the scholar, I knew that Moriah could teach a lot more than one from another world had presumed to think, and far from going there only to see a girl and follow a tune, there might be profit in going to see myself. Strange enjoyment it is, but I was calling myself names, and from the side of my eye a handkerchief moved up and down, and James Smalcote and Voldemar Zhdanov were on a bench at the side, still in their leathers, but clipped and combed and shaved to glisten.

Volde in certain surety had a voice, the deep Russian hymner, and all of us were not slow to follow, and after a few lines of the first verse, all the bassos went out of their places to be near him and sing together, and with that vibrant thunder to help, we had something to sing to, and sing we did. No surprise it was to anybody that after the service they were all over him, and there was no need for me to say a word, and when I did, James was talking to Alys Caerog Evans and her father and Mr Armon Tudor, and in a corner Volde was humming a tune for a group of them to catch with tenor and baritone, and the girls were coming in after.

James nearly squashed my hand and he could hardly say a word, he was so full of spit and thanks with him, and Alys smiled in a way I know well, so I knew that not a moment was being wasted, and that for once I had done something right.

An asado we had at Gethin Probert's, and going to it over the fields and crossing the Camwy by the stones, seeing the valley wide and far through pale blue haze, and the river in a flash of hot sun, and everywhere to the chin in ripening wheat. A couple of threshing machines just off the ship at Port Madryn came up the rise and along the verge in a chiff and chuff, new, and bright red with brass in a sparkle. The drivers were the proudest men I have ever seen, riding in high seats with their hats to the side and chewing a toothpick, and if they smiled at the cheers, never sparing a look from the way, like corduroyed Dioscuri on scarlet stallions, flinging black manes over seas of wheat green as their sisters' eyes.

'They should never have brought them on a Sabbath, but at least, now we shall have some work done better than before,' Mr Armon Tudor said. 'Too long we have threshed with horses and the flail. This year we will be done in a quarter of the time and far more profit to everybody.'

'I should have thought the Co-operative would buy enough for all the valley, and hire them out,' I said. 'They would pay for themselves time and again.'

'I dare say,' he said, and quiet, as though he listened to other things. 'The wheat on this farm had a gold medal in the Chicago Exhibition, and more have been won in Paris. The world showed its best in both places, but we came away with the prizes. And who took notice? Nobody. What happened after? Nothing. We have got few machines of our own, no ships, and the railway is owned by bigger thieves than those going loose in the Territory this moment. If we had machines and a railway and ships that were ours, and prices to fit, we would flourish. As it is, the ends touch, but never tie.'

'And I thought the railway was ours, and a blessing,' I said.

'Of the same shape as the plagues of Pharaoh,' he said. 'We put up the money, and they brought the scum of the world to build it. The moment they were here, they ran. Rag and tag. If you can see tramps and drifters today, them they are. Not content, more came shipped until they had enough. It cost many times its proper price, and the freight charge is twenty times what it is worth. We are not businessmen, Mr Morgan. Give us some land and a roof, and plenty on the table and enough on our backs, and a little in the bank for old age, and a pipe and a paper, and let somebody else worry. I think Mr Gruffydd would have a word to say, too.'

While I watched him, small, and the wrong shape in the long Sunday frock and wide hat, and taking out his knife to be whetted, I could have laughed to think that my eyes were not being opened, but pushed apart. I began to understand that on the surface all might be slow and taking time from the progress of seasons, but beneath, and almost unnoticed like the little shake in his voice, a move was there to bring feet from the mud and come further out of the last Century and enter the one we were in. But a mention of Mr Gruffydd got no change from me.

'The same at home,' I said. 'A few talking about Home Rule, and Self Government, and progress, whatever that is, and the rest with their faces to football or the fire, and having a strike when they feel like it. A funny lot, we are.'

'No, Mr Morgan,' he said. 'Not funny. A tragic lot, we are, and you will never see more of the essence of tragedy than in that little place we have come from. A temple it was. A tomb it is, and a memory it will be. If I go on, I will spoil what you have to eat. Till tomorrow.'

The Widow Glyn brought table linen and salt, and her son Rupert and Phair, her daughter, carried cushions, he sixteen and she fourteen, and both taller than their mother, with some of her looks, though fairer from their father, but the same eyes, black, direct, and seeming to know more, though of what I could not have told anybody.

Eating a cut of beef, a rib of lamb, or a pick of sausage and other meats from the grill, with a half loaf to cut it on, out in the air of the garden, with the wine bottle going round, and talking all the time, will pass a couple of hours prettier than any way I know except two, and one of those is work. By the time we had finished, the bones hung white on the spits, only crumbs were on the ground, and the demi-johns were empty, and everybody looked for shade to stretch out and let the goodness take its time. The Widow Glyn had gone in the house with the women, and the children were off with others, and about sixty men were on the grass under the shrubs and poplars and in the orchard, most of them sleeping the moment they were flat, and I was looking at blue through the leaves and wondering how it was I had never known peace before, and screams came from the other side of the house, and boys thrashed a way through the tamarisk and shouting that Indios were stealing the horses.

The very grass seemed to sprout men, no hats or coats but running, on every face the same look, and not one to be in front of, and I went with them, round to the corral at the back. Far out in the wheat we saw them, and those behind swinging lassos to keep the horses in a troop, and dust like clouded diamonds shining about them.

But not a single horse left behind.

Some of the men started to run across to Blethyn Morgan's place with the nearest stables three miles or more away, and younger men followed the tracks of the thieves, to be lifted when the others caught up with them, and the rest went towards the city to find horses, and to rouse the settlers, and call the Frontier Police.

But the Widow Glyn stood fast in my way, and there was no moving her.

'You will come now to the City, and quiet to the house,' she said. 'You can do nothing out there with them. They will track for weeks if they have got to, and you have never spent a night in the open, never mind a day in the saddle. What use will you be? A fever the first thing, or fall and break bones or have a sprain. If you take a step, I will hang on your coat, and the girls will help me. Now, for you.'

Like a little boy I had to go back, because there was sense in what she said, but I made up my mind that never again would anybody tell me I was useless. Sleep out, and ride a horse all day were two items to practise, and on the walk back among all the women and children, I swore it.

Tom, Tot, the smallest man in the city and among the oldest, was the only one to be seen standing in the middle of the crossroads with a gun longer than himself, and telling everybody to go home quiet, and be good, and wait till their fathers came back.

'If the Indios find that little man for a policeman, they will tread on him in mistake,' I said.

'I hope so, and they will put a foot in the wrong place,' the Widow Glyn said. 'He was Sergeant of Fusiliers, and medals from India and Africa. With that gun I have seen him shoot eggs thrown in the air, never missing, and hit a clay pipe from a man's mouth the length of the field. Why do you think he was left there?'

'Old, I thought him,' I said, ready to apologise.

'Go you, and tell him,' she said, and laughing. 'How many Indio women he has got in the camp nobody knows, or how many children. Two real wives buried here, and Mrs Tom is turning twenty, and a baby six months. Go, you, but be quick to run. A shocking temper he has got, over in a moment, but then too late.'

'Do Indios often steal horses?' I asked her, to go on another foot. 'If it is usual, how can the men work, and chasing all the time?'

56

'It is something in these last years,' she said, and pointing to the children to go from the room. 'Perhaps the flood took their horses, or else somebody is giving them money or drink to steal them. Horses are costing a lot today, especially ours. Pedigree they are, trained special, and not to be bought for anything. Not a single man will be in this valley till they are found, I can tell you. Then there will be a few Indios less.'

'But you were one who told me the Tehuelche were always our best friends,' I said.

'Pish, good gracious, them today were no more Tehuelche than you,' she said. 'You could tell that from the way they were riding. A lot of use you would have been. The very worst of the half-breeds, they were, and perhaps a few bad whites. Or it might be this one running loose in the Territory. I am worried to my soul for the children's Auntie. She will have to come in to us. Out there alone, she is, and nobody for miles.'

But though a couple of messages were sent, there was no answer, and when Mrs Roper Hughes came in the day after for her shopping as usual, she was not through the door and she called the Widow Glyn an old ewe for thinking silly. A big woman she was, tall, and brown plaits round and round her head, and fists like hams in brine with her. One look at her mouth, like a mare's with a tight bit, and her eyes lit like the edge of a ploughshare, and there was no more to say, but plenty to think. But she walked round the shop very slow, and touching chairs and tables, and standing to watch till I was coming restless.

'Will you drive out to the farm for me Mr Morgan?' she asked me, in a voice nothing like her size. 'Please to look at the house and tell me what you could make, and for how much to be comfortable. Everything I had went to the river, and I have never had the heart to look at a stick since. But this chair of Morwen's would be lovely in the evening, indeed. A dresser like that, and a set of blue china, and I would feel like home, and having peace at last, see.'

No man can hear that tone in a woman's voice and say no. A house she wanted, and pictures on the walls, and things in order, and a teapot ready. Every woman cried out in her, so clumsy she was, but longing for little things made her dainty again, and nothing daintier than the way she passed a hand over the gloss of the table, and rubbed it with her coat to polish out the mark.

Later in the week I went in the Widow Glyn's trap, because Merri had still not come back, and neither had most of the men. Every other day messengers rode in and gave the news, but there was nothing except that our trackers were well behind them, and we could expect to hear they were knocking the sin out of them at any time, and soon.

Mrs Roper Hughes had a place far from the river, but with the canal running along one side, so there was plenty of water, and the land showed it. We went through half a mile of kitchen garden with cabbage and lettuce and root vegetables that might have been grown for giants so huge they all were, and into a flower garden long overgrown to take every breath with wildness and colour, and along a path in an orchard, and there was the house, of plastered mud, and two little windows to get your head through, and a roof of corrugated iron. She came from the ditch walking like a man and carrying a full bucket in each hand and no trouble, and her face with the pulled-down mouth was turned to me, ready to shout, but her smile came as if it was not often in use, but brought out slow, not to tear the wrap.

Inside were two rooms, both with a mud floor sprinkled with water to keep down the dust, and a fireplace in the first with a kettle and some saucepans on hooks, and a box against one wall and a couple of nailed-together stools, and next door was a bed piled with sheepskins, and a box beside with a candle, and a curtain to hide clothes.

'This I built with peons after the flood,' she said. 'A lovely house I had with my husband, all bricks, and eight sash windows down, and five up, and all the floors waxed wood, and my mother's silver and china, and good furniture in every room. I sat out there on a raft that night, and I heard it all fall in the water. When I came back there was nothing. Nothing, I was glad, then, poor Roper had gone.'

I listened to the space in her voice where the pain should have been, but there was nothing because it had all sunk into her, and I understood her mouth and eyes.

'Well, now, let me have your opinion,' I said, as if no tale could make me sorry. 'First, you will have to lay a level floor or everything will rock. Tiles for both rooms, and plaster for the walls. Think of a Pembroke table to rest against that wall, folded, opening for four to six places, and chairs to match, and a chair like Morwen's for the fireplace, and a miniature dresser against that wall. Under the window, a tea table, round, and two oval-back chairs padded blue. Bedroom, I will make a round head and shorter foot for the bed, the whole raised on a three-inch step off the floor, and a chest of drawers with a looking-glass and a pull-out slide, and a double wardrobe, all in the same wood. Before those are in, I will send Morris, Carpenter, out here to do something to the doors and windows, and then there are curtains to choose and stitch, isn't it?'

I heard the fall of her knees on the floor, and she was heaving sighs that hurt only to listen to.

'Nobody has wanted to do something for me,' she said. 'Nobody has helped. Let me finish, thank you, and go from here.'

Back to the trap I went, and through the orchard, and the garden, and thinking of her life, lived lonely, and I was glad to be going to the City.

The Widow Glyn liked the plan for the rooms, and the little models I made of the furniture, and sent them off with the boy. Back he came with a trap full of flowers, and boxes of fruit, and sacks of vegetables for her, and a message for me to say that Mrs Roper Hughes was dreaming for the day to see the first piece in the house, and please to make it the chair, with compliments.

Well, that style of chair had been popular and I had made several, so the parts were only wanting the putting together, and the Widow Glyn made a back-and-seat cushion in thin red leather, stuffed with duck feathers, but when it was all ready she wanted to keep it herself and send her sister another, so I had to promise one for the other side of the fire-place before she would let it go.

Past three o'clock one morning, it was, when the men came back with the horse thieves, and we heard the quiet knocking on doors first, and from the window we saw them, with torches and lanterns, and the main body going past towards the prison at the barracks, and the air strong with the smell of dust and horses. Mathias Rowlands told us that eight Indios had been hurt by the boleadoras, and two shot, and two got away, and the rest were prisoners. The troop passed by the house and all the Indios were trussed with their hands behind, and tied to their horses facing the tails, and I was sorry for the way their chins were down on their chests, as if their heads might break off, and under the leather binding their arms looked dried of blood.

Next morning there was excitement enough, because somebody had cut the prisoners loose, and they had gone over the barracks wall. The police had a roasting worse than any asado from everybody, but worst from the girls going round and round the barracks in sulkies or on horse, and calling as they passed, so that you could hear it down where we were. But roast or not, the prisoners were never seen again, and nobody knew a name or a face.

'Not one was Indio,' Billo Harries said in the shop. 'They all had good boots and Sheffield knives. But they were in a scatter and we had to chase them one by one, and when we had them all together we came back too quick for questions. We should have put them in Mog, Moke's corral. Now they will try again. But next time, more careful.'

Every day that week the men were out in small troops beating the scrub and all the uncleared ground, and along the river in places where nobody had been for years, but though they ran many a fox and started any number of ostrich and guanaco, and caught wild horses nobody knew were there, nobody saw a single Indio except those with a right to be where they were, and everybody went home.

But once was enough, and up the valley everybody started wearing a revolver strapped over their trews, and carrying a carbine, and a longer knife, even when they came into the city.

'A disgrace down here,' Idris Beynon, the Bank, said in his bubbly old voice, and buttoning his jacket and unbuttoning it. 'In the Andes, or the desert, yes, in case of a puma, or some trouble. But here, where is the use in carrying one? Extra weight it is, and no good to anybody, and looking rough, indeed. The valley has never been a place for violence. There are police, and paid. Keep the law, and the law will keep you.'

'But not our horses,' Asaph Hughes said. 'If we had left it to the law, none of us would have a horse today. For one, I am carrying my six bullets in, and forty-four more in my belt. Let me see anybody touch a horse or anything else of mine, and we will see which law shall be kept.'

'You will go before The Twelve,' Idris Beynon said.

'Evidence, first,' Asaph Hughes said, and laughing. 'Under a few shovelfuls, who will tell?'

'I speak for those with respect for a soul, and another's life, and knowledge of good and evil,' Idris Beynon said, and his pale blue eyes were shinier, and angry, but quiet. 'We are not a lot of braggarts and hypocrites. There is no place among us for the pistolero. Those who live by the sword shall perish by the sword, remember.'

'And those who live to steal shall perish in the stealing,' Asaph Hughes said. 'I have worked too hard to let somebody take one chew of grass without my permission. And having ears, hear ye not?'

Two sides there were from that moment, the elders not so many in number, but strong because of more property and more money, and expecting the Colony to follow their advice. But the younger men and others not so well off were impatient, and there came a Sunday when Mr Armon Tudor was preaching on the Sixth Commandment, and first one, and another, and then a crowd of men all got up and went out, and their families with them. Volde and James were two of the few to stay because they had not understood a word of the Welsh. But they agreed with those outside.

'This past couple of months we've been losing cattle,' James said. 'Eight head means a lot to us, you know. Besides that, the sheep are going. Come down, and I'll show you the fleeces the dogs dug up. That's animals slaughtered on the spot. Who is it? Michaye's put the word round, but none of her people know. Don't these blokes ever count their cattle and sheep? Are we the only ones?'

To Gethin Probert I went, and the narrowness came to his eyes, and the hollows in his cheeks were full of anxiousness.

'Well, Huw, upon my Sam, if I think of it, the only count is when we brand the cattle, or dip and shear the flock,' he said. 'Harvest is with us now, and no time for the next month. But no doubt we shall find a difference.'

The whisper went round, and everybody was quiet instead of all the happy noise of people talking together as it usually was after Chapel, and many went away instead of going on to the asado at Will Martin's, and Volde and James were given most of the meat and bread to take home in the little boat.

'I will go out to my sister's tomorrow, and from there to the farm and my places in the camp,' the Widow Glyn said. 'I will have a count of my stock, and see if I have lost. Tegwyn, Toldo, will cook for you and clean the house, and I will send my sister to see if everything is nice. And if not, speak up. She will be paid well.'

Tegwyn, Toldo, was called that because her husband had

died only a month before the flood took her house and all the horses and cattle and sheep and poultry. She and her two children were saved, and Indios helped her to build a toldo of logs with the tops leaning together and skins over like a big tent, and there she lived, digging the land by herself, and coming in to do washing or look after somebody's house to earn enough for food, and seed for the plots. Nobody gave her anything or tried to help her because they knew better, and one woman with old clothes to spare went in the river with a foot behind her, and after that people let her alone, and only gave her work. A good girl and reddish fair she was, in her twenties and nothing to look at, and never a word for anybody except the Indios, and she spoke Tehuelche as one of the family from being brought up in the Territory.

Three days she was in the house before I had a word from her and then by chance, because I saw her face when she was looking at the little models I had made for Mrs Roper Hughes.

'Something like these you are wanting, is it?' I asked her.

'For the children,' she said, as if she had shame, quick, and folding her hands in her apron and looking through the door. 'I will pay my work for them, if you please. They have seen nothing good, and they will grow without knowing anything, and a disgrace to their dada.'

'Have them,' I said. 'If you can bring me some guanaco and fox skins for a bed cover, I will give you a good price or make you the value in furniture.'

'Right, you,' she said. 'In the Spring I will build a house. There will be room to put things tidy, and my children will walk clean. A table and chairs I would like, and a cupboard for the dishes. But I will pay for these little ones, first.'

'A present to the children,' I said. 'They have done their work, so there is no price.'

'I will pay,' she said, and going dark in the face, and eyes blue out of the shadow as if lights were behind them, clear, like an animal. 'No man will give me. Nobody shall give me. I will work, and the work will pay.'

'Very well,' I said. 'Your children are too young to say yes or no for themselves. If they were here, they would say yes. But the models are not for sale, and no more shouting, if you please.'

At midday I went to Damaglou's on the hill for dinner and to talk to the customers in from the other end of the valley, or from the Andes, or somewhere between. Idwyn Thomas was there, and he came over to give me Mr Gruffydd's compliments, and to say he would be in soon, and could he have a couple of comfortable armchairs ready to take back with him, and if I had newspapers or news from home, he would be grateful.

'I will have a parcel ready for you in minutes,' I said. 'Was he looking well?'

'Always the same, him,' Idwyn said. 'We crossed trails out on the Camwy at Indio Crossing. There I will leave the parcel when I go back. The finest sheep I have ever seen, he had with him. In a couple of years he will have a place of his own. When will you have a piece of land, Mr Morgan?'

'When I have got the money,' I said.

'Find a piece, put in your papers and pay the taxes, and wait to pay for the title,' he said. 'If you will wait too long, every inch will have its owner. Basquos are coming everywhere, each month more. Good boys, they are. They will soon be more than us. We will all be speaking Basquo.'

'Our fault,' I said.

'Of them at home,' he said. 'Not enough here, and not enough coming out. I have got cattle and a garden here in the valley, and a couple of leagues for sheep in the Territory, and a place for cattle and a stretch of timber up in the Andes. Only three weeks in the year I am having at home, and my wife crying every time I go from the door. But I tell her there are years in plenty to sit with her. Eight children I have got, so if they are to have a fair chance when I go, I have got to have enough for eight good parts, no?'

'They are lucky to have such a father,' I said.

'I had a good one,' he said. 'I will hope to be half of his kind, and I will do well. But we are forsaken by those at home, Mr Morgan. Land of My Fathers, yes. For my children, the land of their grandfathers, and no thanks to anybody.'

Looking over the little city, with the board walls and half-scoured smells of Damaglou's behind me, and across the valley spreading gold among the willows along the river and between the lines or poplars about the farms, and the bare white hills behind, I could even feel that forsakenness in the sag of mud roofs on some of the houses and the faded red flake of corrugated iron over the others. Two dusty streets of brick-fronts down, and two across, and a few mud huts

63

outside, and the stone houses of the railwaymen, and a house for a girls' school with a bare space in front, and lines of washing, and horses tethered to walls in sprinkles of hay or green splashes of grass, and all the traps and wagons with the shafts up and leathers coiled, and groups of men in the shade drinking maté, and not a move anywhere. A sabre glittering between the legs of a sentry outside the barracks held a severe note, even though I knew the heels of his boots were worn to the nails, and his tunic was more patches than uniform. Ruffles of dust out on the road were traps bringing in the afternoon shoppers, and the engine-shed pipe blew steam, but the sound of flies coming too close to the ear was louder. A couple of Indios squatted in wrinkled cones of leather with a black shock on top, and putting out a hand to look between finger and thumb, and eating, and putting their hands in to search again, taking no notice of the dust when I passed, that was everywhere thick, and never off the boots, and shoulders and hat, and always in steady promise of mud for the winter.

A railway halt, it was, and no more than a place to live for those keeping a shop, or working for the line, and where the shiftless could drink their wages of months in a couple of nights.

But in truth no city because no spirit, and no capital because no country, and not a village, either, because no conscience. Moriah Chapel, monument of the pioneers, was far outside, and nothing of them was inside except the values they had created by clearing the pampas. But the first men and women had cleansed land and spirit together with the plough and prayer, and growth had come with a hymn.

That afternoon, in the city they never saw, where so few were left to sing, and fewer still to pray, the other valley I remembered well, that was dying of the same dross, and this, of the Camwy, came much closer in my mind.

Inside the shop was always hotter than outside, but I never closed my eyes after the midday meal, and I began to saw long timbers, and soon I was wet down the back, and a trip to the well and a bucket of water did good. In the outhouse I went to wipe, but the piece of old stuff was gone, and a folded towel in its place, with a bowl and ewer and a tablet of soap on a stool. By the time I had finished thinking if they were for me, or for a visitor, I was dry, and back I went to the shop.

But the little models were gone from the bench, and where they had been was a tea tray, with toasts of ham and cheese, and cream cake, and a treat to see. With the Widow Glyn, tea had always been at the table in the house, and at least forty minutes out of the day. Tea in the shop was in between work, and a better taste with more done, and I said so to Tegwyn when she came for the tray.

'An empty house is no good to eat in,' she said. 'Work helps for a comfort. I will always go outside. The water and the towel is put for you. Tomorrow I will turn out the cupboards in your room. Moth is in there. The models I have taken for the children. You are right. They would say yes. I will tell you their thank you tomorrow.'

She went away side-saddle on an Indio pony, and I saw the box under her arm, and her eyes made me feel as if more light had come to the evening.

In the next couple of hours I made a doll's house, and painted it, and I thought of the one I had made for Olwen, and wondered where she was, and from her to Bron, and Ceridwen, and the night went in writing to them, and to Dai Bando and Cyfartha, and Thomas, Carrier, and Ellis the Post, with messages for everybody I knew through the valleys. Many others I could have written to, but they seemed too far, and most of them too busy. There was nothing much to say because nothing was happening, though when I wrote to Amyas Wilkin, a great one for putting in the paper who was married, and who was dead, and how everybody was dressed and what was provided for supper, and told him about the Indios stealing the horses, he wrote back and said not to pull his leg, and the only Indios I would ever see were still in a book, and if I had nothing better, then save my time, and his, too. So many I have found like Amyas, to say that if it happens to them, very well, but if it happens to you, no. Most of that denial is envy because they have got only streets and lamp-posts to look at, and nothing better to do than go in a pub and be drunk. But if it is a small feeling of no odds, it can still be strong enough to come like bad breath from their letters, so Amyas never got another word from me, and he was happy, and I am sure I was happier.

But it was a tussle to write, because letters have got to be about something, and every day was the same with us, and Sunday could be told from weekdays by shut shops, and a couple in best clothes for chapel, or out for a visit. Galardier, the barber, kept open, but he was a Frenchman, and a pagan and he would tell you to your face. Damaglou's kitchen, and Beretroff's and the other wineshops were never closed, and neither was Trodd's, Split. Two doors down from the shop, it was, a place so small that it was known as the Split in the Wallpaper, full with a dozen, but generally with forty or more, where a lot of business was done on Sunday mornings, and a certain place to find everybody unwilling to go to chapel, either because they were Lutherans or Hussites or Methodists or Anglicans or Adventists or Reformists or Wesleyans or Presbyterians or Roman Catholics, or any other label to stay off their knees. Many a one had a good excuse, I suppose, though the best I heard was Lal's when I went to Gaiman one Sunday, and found her with a class of children under the trees, and Doli and Solva farther over with others.

'The chapel is too hot for the little ones, and too ugly for me,' she said. 'The sound is better from the outside, and the preacher is twenty minutes too long coming to the Amen. Will you go in?'

'I will sit by here and listen to you,' I said. 'What are we learning today?'

'Nothing,' she said. 'I am telling them how they were dressed in the days of Jesus, and what they were eating, and where they had their money, and who was ruling and why. If they can only see and hear now, they can learn when they are older. And you will have to sit straight, or go off to lie down, because if they see you with your hat over your eyes, I will have no attention.'

'Then I will look at your hat,' I said. 'And I will give attention to everything else beneath.'

Surprising even now the pink in her face, and the quick turn to go, with long black skirts breathing through the grass, and lifting the veil higher before she sat, and trouble to take the marker from the place, and having to bite at each fingertip to take off her glove, and a good slap for it when it was off, and another for the marker, and a fly that got in her veil was rolled up in it to practise his buzz, and all the time everybody sat still because the riding crop shone from the back of her chair and its use was known.

It was easy to see the people she spoke of, and hear them, because they were like those to be seen every day about the valley, and bringing water from the well, and cutting wood, and skeining wool by the fire at night, and doing a bit of weaving between milking the cows, and herding sheep, and living in the same mud-plaster house and pulling the plough through the fields, and growing something in the garden with a little wall to keep out the goats and chickens. It was no surprise when she read from the Bible to hear Jesus talking to his men as Vyrnwy might to his helpers when they took the patience from him, or Mog, Moke, when he was trying to teach how to tame a mule, with the same quietness, and sense, but a sureness that if anybody wanted trouble, there was plenty and to spare.

Listening to the children's voices joining in the last hymn, and El Pampero floating the sound among the boughs and leaves and over the river to the red shine of wheat ripe for the scythe, I thought of home, and the family, and of being a boy again, and remembering so little of what I had been taught, and yet it must have gone into me because I still had it.

'I wonder how long this will last,' I said, on the way down to the asado at Daniel Jones'. 'Many a one today cares nothing about it, and how many live it?'

'We will add to them, then,' she said. 'It is like manners at table, or learning sums. Where shall we be, without? Plenty of them say they don't believe. My father for one. Never near the chapel since he was from the reach of my grandfather's belt. But he will be the first to want a good, full service when he goes. Most of the people are good, here, and why, except the chapel taught them.'

'What was it they learnt, and where does it show?' I asked her. 'How many are like the money-changers? And all in the front seat, there, singing to push a hole in the roof.'

'As long as they take the trouble to be there,' Lal said. 'Without it we might all be sorrier. If they had enough put into them to deal fair, we can be thankful.'

'A long way from being fair to being sorry for harm done to others,' I said. 'There might just as well have been no Jesus and no Calvary. Who is sorry?'

'I have never been sorry for Jesus after He was in the tomb and out without a word to His mother,' she said. 'Tramping up the old hill there, poor girl and two angels telling her He was risen. Why couldn't they go to the house to tell her?'

'Well, Lal, there is a fine thing to say,' I said. 'Angels,

67

they were, girl. Why should they go to the house?'

'To save her climbing all that way, and the worry, of course,' she said, and songs in the air for me because I had used her name and no notice from her. 'Sitting on their bottoms, there, and letting her come breathless? I would have had a word or two to say. Doli would have every feather from their backs.'

'They were put there to tell whoever was coming,' I said. 'They had orders, and they obeyed.'

'If they were angels, they would know who was coming,' she said. 'And who would be the first but His mother? Yes, and poor Mary. Who said a word of comfort to either of them?'

'They had enough to say for themselves, especially if they were like a few at Maes Corwen,' I said. 'Why were there no women apostles.'

'The easiest to answer,' she said. 'Too much to do in the house. Only the men have got time to traipse, and tope, and chatter.'

'Teachers they were, girl,' I said. 'Like the teachers we have got now, but a new message. We have got collars and ties and bowlers, and it has come old and not believable, like a tale from Box, Quiff. Good while he is telling it, and after forgotten.'

'Nobody forgets except when they want to,' she said. 'A pity, but there is not enough in the Bible. For people not able to read, and certain to see the end of the world the next minute, yes. I am nobody, but for me something is missed. Too many tales about what will happen if I do this or that, like putting dogs in the gaps to keep the sheep inside.'

'Sensible,' I said. 'They are needed.'

'A good shepherd will close the gaps, first,' she said. 'It is very easy to pretend to know more. But night after night for years we read only the Bible when my mother was with us. Always we had questions, and always she said to believe. I suppose we still do, in a way. Now you know why there are no women apostles. Too many questions.'

'They might all have been answered very tidy in that day, but missed from the writing,' I said. 'Have you got a knife to lend me? When I put mine in my trews this morning, my waistcoat was too tight with me.'

'I will cut for you, like a little boy,' she said. 'Well done, medium or crude?'

'Underdone,' I said. 'And bread with a good black crust. Sliced sweet tomatoes and a heart of lettuce and a sprinkle of chives. Oil and a drip of lemon for dressing.'

'Leave room for strawberries and cream,' she said. 'We picked baskets of them early this morning in case you were here.'

'Sabbatas, three of you,' I said. 'Wonder to me the Book is not smoke in your hands.'

'Not in mine, Mr South,' she said. 'I was doing the washing all day yesterday. Doli was all the week up at the dam, and Solva came back last night with the cattle.'

'You were alone every day and night of the week?' I said. 'Nobody with you to take care?'

'Only the Remington, and a Lee-Enfield, and a Mauser, and two Colts and a Smith and Wesson,' she said. 'Go, you, and sit soft on that sheepskin over by there, and I will bring to eat, is it?'

She went to the fire and I watched her among the crowd, easy to see from the black velvet hat she wore high on her lovely head and tipped down in front, with the brim up at the sides and to a peak, with little pink and blue flowers filling the middle, and talking to Doli while she sliced with the sure strokes of a butcher, and Solva coming up, in grey, with white flowers round a little straw, and all of them laughing and Doli trying to pick sausage off the grill and getting her fingers grilled and stamping her foot when she dropped one.

Three less like sisters I never saw. Lal, dark, and slight at distance, but close to, bigger than you would think, and strong enough to drive a team of mules. Doli, not fat but wide enough, and fair especially under a red hat in the sun, and eyes blue as the river. Solva small, not thin, and far from weak, and straw-stalk fair, and eyes granite grey that could be harder than her voice was soft, or with a smile bright as running water. But all three had the same mouth, full, with a shine, to make you feel you must turn your eyes or go closer to kiss and taste. Many a one would, but it was known that if they were not as strong as men, there was still enough to give respect, even if a look was not warning to send chills through the scalp of a hedgehog.

Plenty of families were there that I had never seen, and my hand was soft from shaking. But the difference between them and most of the people down toward the city made me remark while we were eating.

'They were the first of the pioneers, down there,' Doli said. 'Masons and carpenters and workmen. They took the land at the harbour and along the top of the river. They had to look after themselves more as a family. Not even matches to light the fire. The others came in later with more money, and tools and their own furniture. They cleared this land and farther up. There were miles between my grandfather and his neighbours. We were more on our own, I suppose. A lot went away because they could never make a year's wages. That was how we got our extra land. My father always buys what is offered. I will, too.'

'We will be lucky to see any of it,' Solva said, as though a butterfly had spoken. 'But how they will divide the house between more than thirty of us, even the lawyers will have trouble. Eighty-eight keys to the piano, so we will have three-and-a-half keys each, I suppose. Have you played on three-and-a-half keys, Mr Morgan?'

'Two keys I have got to my name,' I said. 'One to the tool chest and the other to the shop. Blow down them, and you have got doh and soh.'

'Fah you would have to blow to see any key of ours,' Doli said.

Lal had said nothing, and the pieces of beef she cut went into her mouth with the little cube of bread at the same rate, no hurry, and calm in the face, which made her so beautiful I was pretending to look for the wine to take my eyes away.

'All we have got to do is marry well for ourselves,' Solva said. 'If my husband has got a couple of hectares I will soon make it four, and six after, and then leagues. A good house, then, and what more to ask?'

'Why is the subject brought up?' Lal asked, in quiet that was worse than a shout. 'Is it interesting for somebody?'

'I suppose,' Doli said, mouth full, and a sprinkle of salt for the next bite. 'I would have interest to know who will come to me for a marriage.'

'Your turn will be soon enough,' Lal said. 'So let the time arrive. The salt if you please, and if you are not too stuffed to turn your head, that piece of crust by there. And here is Nelya Peninnah paying us a visit, so eat well.'

It was not in her voice or eyes, I will swear, and yet the alarm hung, and when I stood to give the visitor good day, I saw. Big she was, and her belt pulled tight made her bigger above and below, and her eyes were almost too big for the sockets, a blue, palish and wet at the lashes, and looking over her nose a little to the side in a smile of the nostrils that said I am better than all of you, and I can do what I like, and I have, and will, and a look under the eyelids at me that was like a bucket of hot water.

'From B.A. on Friday we came, and drove over in the new coach yesterday, and such a journey, dear God,' she said, coming closer. 'We had a month there, and after M.M. has bought cattle and sheep here, and wool above the dam, we shall be home for two years at least.'

'So you will have your seventeenth winter with us, is it?' Doli said. 'Practice to knit anyway. If there is a sheep with wool good enough, yes?'

'Knitting, my heaven above, home I said,' Nelya Peninnah told the grass at my feet. 'Wales, of course. I will be in a finishing school for young ladies, and in between I am going to Paris and Berlin and Madrid and Rome, and everywhere. First class we are going to London.'

'Ask Mr Morgan to give you the address of his sister in Oxford,' Solva said, in the little voice much littler. 'And I hope she will finish you before it will be one of us.'

'Tck, well Solva, and Sunday it is, too,' Doli said, and putting more in her mouth, and speaking over the lumps. 'I am ashamed to be sitting here and listening. What were you saying to her, girl, rude old thing you are?'

'Give our compliments to your father,' Lal said, with politeness in a veil before her eyes. 'We are sorry not to have seen him, but welcome is waiting if he finds time to call at Maes Corwen.'

'Tell him to bring twelve thousand pesos to clear his account two years old,' Solva said. 'Then I can settle the books, and he can be off to London, and finish you and him together.'

'Ho, but you should have sent your bill to B.A.,' Nelya Peninnah said. 'I will tell him, and you shall have it, cash, first thing. Do you think it is something to us? Always you have been nasty to me, Solva Corwen, only because you are jealous, nothing else. Everybody knows why.'

'Go from here before I will flatten your udders,' Solva said, in a voice so small you would have to take a pin. 'Nobody is jealous of a cow in heat.'

'Only because I could be Señora Beretroff any time I want,' Nelya Peninnah said, with her nose further up, and her eyes further sideways, and wetter, and laughing. 'And no Indios in my family, either, please to notice.'

'Pity,' Doli said, mouth empty, and watching. 'You have practised often enough to be anybody's señora, and with generous help of Indios as well, family or not, no doubt. Go back to your wagon and drop off for everybody else, you slut.'

'Sticks and stones will break my bones,' Nelya Peninnah said, and a skipping rope and the playground were in her voice. 'You are jealous, all of you. But M.M. told me, if you had our money, you would have room to talk. Now, for you.'

Off she went, with her bottom this way, slow, and that way, slow, and pulling the long white skirt, and waving a little handkerchief for air.

'You would do well never to say anything,' Lal said, soft, a blessing. 'Nothing is there to be hurt. The hide of a wild pig is rotten silk by comparison. Have you questions, Mr South?'

'Yes,' I said. 'Who is she, who is M.M., and why does everybody say B.A. instead of Buenos Aires?'

'She is Nelya Peninnah Morse,' Lal said. 'M.M. is her father, Matithiah Morse. Matti Mumpo, he is called, and you will know why when you see him. B.A. is shorter, like a nickname. It is always impressive to speak familiarly of the Capital, isn't it? Have you been there?'

'For three days,' I said. 'No wonder everybody wants to go.'

'I will be there the moment I have got my share,' Doli said. 'I will spend every centavo before to come back. If.'

'Save more, and go home, girl,' Lal said.

'If I will have more than my share, I will be paralysed to move anywhere,' Doli said. 'I wonder if Mr Vrann Corwen has been doing more talking? That one was very fast with her mouth about Indios.'

The grey dress passed beside me, and Solva was up and running towards the garden, crying in a splash of sobs, but Lal put a hand on Doli's shoe to stop her following.

'Leave her,' she said. 'She will feel better, and think a little less of Mr Beretroff, I hope. The bell will go in two minutes and nobody ready. Will you come to school again, Mr South?'

72

'For a moment, yes, Miss Corwen,' I said. 'I am going to have a cup of tea with Tegwyn, Toldo.'

'A valiant one,' Doli said, getting up. 'How are you so privileged?'

'Volde Zhdanov and James Smalcote are helping her to make a little boat to cross the river and save time,' I said. 'I will have a hand in it, too.'

'When will my screen be ready?' Lal asked, wiping the knife on a handful of leaves. 'You said you would buy land the moment you were paid.'

'I will start the moment you call me Huw, Miss Corwen,' I said.

'Call her Lal, boy,' Doli said, and picking up the sheepskin for a good shake. 'She has called you Huw behind your back long enough.'

'Doli,' Lal said, and knives under the hat. 'Enough, is it?'

'Nothing good to say about the Widow Glyn, either,' Doli said, very careful in folding the sheepskin. 'When you are from there, she will breathe.'

'Doli,' Lal said. 'Another word, and I will never be responsible.'

'For that old widow, too, if she makes a move,' Doli said, over her shoulder. 'Quiet your face, girl. Only telling him what he knows, I am.'

'Nothing to do with you,' Lal said, back to me. 'Hisht, and stop your lies now. You are bringing disgrace.'

'Disgrace, go on, girl,' Doli said, and lifting her skirts to run. 'If the disgrace is called Huw Morgan, I will love him like a brother-in-law, is it? Have you got brothers, a disgrace like you, Huw?'

'One not married,' I said. 'But he is in North America.'

'Tell him I am in love with him,' Doli said. 'I have been looking at Lal, so I know how it is, and what to do.'

'Doli,' Lal shouted, and ran. 'I will have you in the trough.'

'If they call you Huw, I can too, yes?' Solva said, behind me, and putting a hand round, and taking the handkerchief from my pocket. 'I am sorry I ran away, and no apology.'

'It is nothing, girl,' I said, watching a pair running behind the roses. 'For use it is. Make a good blow.'

She did, too, and settled her belt, and pushed the handkerchief in at the side.

'It will be washed, and I will give it to you when you

come next,' she said. 'Will you do something kind for me? Tell my sisters I have gone home. Too much fire is in my head to see a word this afternoon. And I am the same as Doli. I would love you for a brother. Good-bye, now, Huw.'

5

Only a woman has sweeter scent than wheat in the time of harvest, and that year I was brought to know it without hope to forget.

Many a summer I had gone to my uncle's farm over the mountain to help with the threshing, but that was only three fields, and his neighbour's two, and a few others farther on, which to me was a world, and when the bags were stacked, I was always proud to think that a bit of my work had helped to fill a railway truck to the top and no room to spare.

But when I had shut the shop that morning and taken Merri down the river to Idris Ebrill's farm we passed a train of six-team mule wagons, the first I had ever seen, each holding three truck loads, and Eiluned, his wife, told me there would be another train out that night before the threshers moved next door to Watkin Williams'.

'Two trains of wagons have gone over to Chile, and three to Buenos Aires, and a ship is coming for cargo to Europe,' Idris said. 'This year will be good for some, anyway. But most of us are without a buyer or a bid. Sometimes I wonder is it worth putting in the seed in case the sacks will rot before to find a market. And of course, the buyer knows it, too, so we take off our hats to his shadow if it only moves near us. Farmers are fools. We have got to scrape for every centavo. Beggars in gold, we are.'

But no shadows were in the fields except beneath the engines, and the wheat travelling up the feeders, and under the straw sheds where the older women cooked and washed up, and everybody went to eat a sandwich and have a drink, because of course, the young women were all in the field and doing as much as any man. Threshing is a hard job in hot sun, but many hands made nothing of it, and work that might have taken one family a month was over in a day or two, because all the farmers locked their houses and brought

75

women, children and peons to the first farm, and finished
there, and went on to the next, sleeping in the camp until all
the valley was threshed and loaded or housed. If I was in the
way or not, nobody told me, but I did what I could and
many a time I saved a few hours with a repair, and in any
event, the shop was too hot, so I poulticed my conscience
with work of another sort. For one thing, I found how easy
it was to sleep out. Before I had always though of pneu-
monia or something in the lungs, and my mother worrying
about wool next to the skin and the draught in howls
through the house from open windows. But to see children
going to bed in the stable and no noise was a lesson, indeed.
A few branches on the ground, and sheepskins over, and a
small frame of twigs and straw over the head to shelter from
dew, and sleep, then, as an archangel.

Wake, as if you never closed your eyes, with a moon still
shining, and the black shapes of women moving across the
fires like witches, and men squatting to put a match to twigs,
and the maté tins rattling at the bucket by the well, and
dogs barking at somebody going too near the house, and if
you were not out of bed before the smell of frying bacon
came to raise the juice in your mouth, you would dribble
while you were putting on your socks and boots, although a
dip for the head and shoulders in a ditch would knock any
taste out of you in a crimp of ice, but in the line and passing
the fires, with a loaf of fresh bread too hot to hold, you
would be tasting plenty and swallowing pints by the time it
was your turn to take the rashers off the fork, or slice your
piece of steak. All the eggs and bacon you want, and fresh
bread, butter and jam, and a jug of tea or coffee, and the
worst of hard work will be out of the way before you know
it.

Small repairs on wagons I did in the mornings, and everybody thankful, and a bit of stacking later, and some bagging
and tying, and the noon asado was always ready before I
was. The one I liked best was of sucking-pigs in a pit and
covered with cinders, and lifted out on the iron net or the
meat would have come from the bones, and crisp, with
potatoes in the skin packed about them, and with cold apple
sauce, and a glass of wine freezing from the river, sure it is
that emperors have never had better. Then to lie in the grass
of the orchard and watch the parrots chasing through the
tips of the poplars, and fall asleep betting which will win,

and waking to hear the engine and the whistle blowing, and all the men putting boots on to start again, with the hottest hours gone and ten more to go. Sixteen hours was a short day in those weeks, and the only time off was for food, or a maté and a smoke, and a couple of hours on Sundays for a service. Up before the sun, and to bed before ten, asleep before the eyes were shut, waking to the moon, or to the stars almost as bright, and coming to wonder why streets one after the other, and houses stuck together, and rooms to be crossed in a couple of paces had always before seemed right and proper. It might have been then, in waking to blue morning, that I knew I must go soon to the Andes.

That weekend Box, Quiff, the saddler, had to go in for repairs, and I went with him to see if the shop was still there, but everything was quiet, locked, and Mrs Trodd, Split in the Wallpaper, came to tell me that Tegwyn, Toldo, was in every morning to clean, and the Widow Glyn was still in the camp, and please to do the pleasure of coming in for a drink.

The Split in the Wallpaper was a narrow place with a narrow bar, no more than a wide plank down one side, and just room for Trodd, Split, or his wife to push behind and serve. Both were thin, looking as though they had been left for years in the dust to wear away and have a polish, and the shiny bones of their cheeks, and her hair that once had been red and now was pale sand, and hanging in a droop past her ears, and him with a long moustache the same colour, made them look like two from a piece instead of man and wife.

'Welcome to you, Mr Morgan, welcome indeed,' Trodd, Split, said. 'We have been struck not to see you, no, never, not once near the door, yes.'

'The only time I am thirsty is for tea,' I said.

'Me and the Mrs were going to have a good cup now just,' Trodd, Split, said. 'Will Mr Box join us?'

'No, indeed to damn,' Box, Quiff, said, and the long yellow fall of the hair over his right eye, that wetted over a finger with a comb to curl gave him his title, was mixed with the long yellow brush of his moustache, and he looked like a wild pony trying to see through hay. 'A flask or a bottle of something, yes, or a good couple of quarts of beer, yes. But I will go to hell if I came in by here for tea, aye. Beretroff is only a spit and a half from the door, and I can have what I want.'

'Not there, not today or tomorrow, spit farther, too,' Mrs

Trodd screeched from the kitchen. 'Matti Mumpo have closed him down. Account owing and not time to pay, so out he went, and the clothes on his back, poor boy.'

'Poor boy,' Trodd, Split, said, and nodding the wink of one weak blue eye at Box, Quiff. 'Miss Nelya Peninnah had both her feet, and something else in there.'

'Don't, now, Willie,' Mrs Trodd, Split, screeched again from the kitchen. 'I can hear every word, mind you. Nothing to do with us, so save it, now then, disgrace she is.'

'Doubling our trade, see, till somebody else opens, and nothing to do with us,' Trodd, Split, said, both eyes shut. 'If Beretroff had sense, he would have her to the Justice, and marry. A good one, he is. But slow, damn, to bleed your nose, yes.'

'Marry it?' Box, Quiff, said. 'You never heard of Perino, Two Wells, and his brothers? Working for M.M., they were, and fresh from Italy, not a word of the language, six of them, and her not thirteen, and no strength to pull their trews on, any of them.'

'Box, Quiff,' Mrs Trodd, Split, screeched from the kitchen, and hitting something on a tin tray. 'Be so good to remember who is present here, and not one word more, now then.'

Trodd, Split, winked one eye looking one way, and one the other.

'Those three Basquos on her poor father's place there, at the Bend,' he said. 'Poor father? As bad, and worse. But the old Basquos had no pull to take the skin from an onion between them.'

Mrs Trodd, Split, came in with the tea, and looking very severe at the bread and butter, and sharp with the spoon to ladle sugar, and filling the cups as if she was drowning something.

'Useless to talk, and a disgrace to us, I have always been saying,' she said, to the quiet. 'One born like that, and nobody can lift their eyes, in case to treat us all in the same way. My father would have put a horsewhip to her.'

Box, Quiff, drank three fingers of whisky in the same way I was drinking tea, and a nod to fill again.

'She would be just as bad,' he said, no joking this time. 'A madness, it is. Even a little girl, no man could stand near her. And don't forget, a man can be put in prison. You have got to think well.'

'And whose fault?' Mrs Trodd screeched, again, and the

78

iron roof threw it down. 'Does a child find out for itself? Nobody in the house to look after her. Always in the shop, and full of people, and out in the yard with the men, or everywhere in the camp. Well?'

'No mother, yes, and Indios to nurse, yes,' Box, Quiff, said. 'But she has caused more than her share of worry. Old M.M. has got money. He has got his trouble, too.'

'I am not sorry for him or the girl,' Mrs Trodd said, and tipping up the cup to look at the leaves. 'Rude to Mr Armon Tudor she was, and saying she had no intentions of kneeling in Chapel, and she would sit, like the gentry. Who did she have that from, I would like to know?'

'That friend of hers, Mr Gruffydd, out in the Territory, perhaps,' Trodd, Split, said. 'He has got the best of M.M.'s flock on interest while they are away, somebody was saying, here.'

'Perhaps it was not Mr Gruffydd,' I said. 'It sounds like everybody but him.'

Mrs Trodd gave me a look, straight, and through.

'An excuse can be found for everything if you are expecting favours,' she said. 'A big favour he has got from M.M. Who would put that idea in her head?'

'Nobody here would say such a thing,' Trodd, Split, said. 'Outside, she had it. Here, she has got to speak to somebody before they will speak to her, if then. We are disgusted beyond words.'

'You have got a little den where everybody comes to tipple and gossip,' I said. 'If the girl was here you would say nothing to fear from her father. If Mr Gruffydd was here you would keep your mouths shut. If I come here again, it will be with a bucket to swill out.'

Too long it took me to put money on the counter, and they had time to look in their minds, and at each other.

'Speak for yourself and your conduct two doors down,' Mrs Trodd, Split, screeched, and the bluish eyes coming in a polish dry as the cheek-bones, and the sand mat hanging down beyond the red lobes, and her top teeth coming loose. 'Do you think you have been lodging there all this time and nobody knowing? Swill yourself out, and think disgrace to take advantage. Older than you she is, and two children, and a widow, and not safe. You will be married, and fit to come in here before you will put a foot across the doorstep again. Go, you.'

She swept the money off with the flat of her hand, and I left it there, and went out in the quiet street.

The same words, and the same sort of misery to speak them had always been, through the years, about Bronwen and me, but if I was used to it, and hardened, it could still bring the white before my eyes and the red behind to blind. No doubt I should have gone then and there to pack everything, and go somewhere else. But that might have been to satisfy the gossips and make a gift of more room to talk. To stay, to give them nothing, to take no notice seemed better.

Box, Quiff, came behind the shop, and stood in the door.

'I told the pair of them what I thought for spoiling my drink, Sunday, too,' he said. 'Always after somebody, they are. Wait you, the Widow Glyn will moult when she hears. They have never been friends, see, ever since Rupert was going in there to soak, and them greasing in every other minute to ask her for what he owed. Take advice, and let it go with the river.'

If I had taken my own advice I would have been better served. But the rage of the moment did the talking, or perhaps I was decided by thought of the comfort I would lose, and the silliness of packing everything and nowhere to go, only because of chat from the worthless.

Back we went to the camp, and it was like coming home to be with them all, and join the choir round the red logs and drink hot chocolate and rum, and to bed again in the sheepskins, and breathing flat on the back, up into the dark middle of the Southern Cross.

But the fruit of that day was not long coming to a fine ripeness, and I think I knew when I saw Doli trotting through the camp towards the thresher I was on, and waving to me to come down.

She turned to a quiet place among the weeds on the canal, and let her horse graze, and came to meet me, all in black among the golden stalks, and if there were no smiles, there was something of mischief in her eyes, and even in the way she put the crop under her arm and pinned up the veil, I could see that she was in stitches to have a laugh, but too important to show it, so I made straight my face, and went close.

'Huw, we are friends, and it is the business of all of us, and no offence,' she said, all sounding like one word. 'What is this we are hearing about the Widow Glyn going to marry you?'

Well, I started to laugh.

'Me, marry who?' I said. 'Good God, I am the furthest.'

'Everybody has been told you are going to marry,' she said. 'Solva heard it in Gaiman the other day, and she told me, but we didn't tell Lal. She heard yesterday from Jones, Price Special, at the Co-op.'

'He shall have a special bit of price from me, too,' I said. 'There is nothing but the air about it. The Widow Glyn has been kind to me, and fair in business. There is no woman better, and no more to say. If there is talk because I am lodging there, that is no business of mine. Tell Lal from me.'

'Why not come home with me now, and tell her yourself?' she said.

'Why should I make a journey to take notice of gossip?' I said. 'Let them do the travelling. When the work is finished here, then I will come. When are you going to thresh?'

'Among the last,' she said. 'And the wedding is only a day or two after.'

'Only let me know when,' I said. 'Come and have to eat.'

'Plenty at home, thank you,' she said. 'Besides, we are not very friendly with these down here. I might open my mouth if they talked too much.'

She went up in the saddle in a way you would never believe for a big girl, and I went back, and from that moment I saw the difference in everybody. Either they turned when I was near, or they were looking somewhere else, or they were taking too much interest in what they were saying to notice I was by. It can be comical to see grown-ups behaving in such a way, but they do.

'We have no liking for the Corwens or any of that lot up by there,' Aaron Jenkin told me, while we fed the belt. 'Keeping all the water for themselves, they are, and not letting a drop come down here.'

'The river is running deep enough,' I said.

'The flow is away from us,' he said. 'Canals we have built at the top to spread through all the valley, and dams to hold the water to run down here. We are always working up there, but Corwen and the others will wait till we have gone, and fill up, or open, or cut troughs, and then we have nothing. So if you are friends with the Corwens, or any of them up there, be careful down here. And double careful because where you are lodging is a private house.'

Somebody having little rubber bands put round him would feel as I did then, easy to snap, but a nuisance and not worth the energy. Never mind how much she said to me about her lonely life and her weeds, or the hints that fell with weight to smash the tiles, the Widow Glyn's care for herself and all her scruples of behaviour brought her dearer to my mind, even without memory of her kindness, than if anybody had said anything, and I could even find myself becoming angry, though whether for the way she was talked about, or from injury to my sense of delicacy or justice, who knows, and at those times there is no desire to ask even if you could have an answer. On top of that, I was being told who should be my friends, and who not, and what might happen if, or if not.

There is nothing like a push to do something you have wanted to do to make you do the opposite. Children we always are, but we give ourselves other excuses, and when a peon came from Vrann Corwen to ask if I would go to an asado, and Michaye galloped in at the same time to say she was sent by Tegwyn, Toldo, because the boat had a leak, off I went to Tegwyn, though nothing I wanted more than to see Lal at Maes Corwen or anywhere else.

Michaye crossed the river and trotted down the other bank towards the harbour by a way I had never been, that went wide to the hills, and open, no trees, and not a house or a bit of plough, and I knew, then, how all the land on the first day must have looked to the pioneers.

Dry, it was, dusty in the winds, and covered with pampas brush, and no green except along the river, and nothing moving, not even a bird, and in that quiet, no hope, and nothing for the spirit, less for the heart, and for the next meal, nowhere to look.

Only to see it, and think of them, I shivered, and Merri went into a gallop and I was thankful to catch up with Michaye.

By that time, I had a few words of Castellano, as the Spanish is called, from talking to people in the shop and listening to others, and trying to read Don Quixote with a dictionary, though what I had from Mr Cervantes was very little to do with the language spoken in the street. But it all came as grist, and when I tripped on a word, Michaye gave it as one giving sweets to a child, and that way I learnt more. But she gave me a shock when she told me that Volde and

James were going to the Andes, and she was with Tegwyn, Toldo, until she went home.

'But you are married,' I said.

'Never,' she said, and looked at me with black eyes, not like the Widow Glyn's, but full of smiles and yet empty, like a cat's, and she hit the pony, and went in front and stayed there all the way.

Nothing was wrong with the boat, except that Volde and James had used thin nails, and some of the battens had started. Merri went to graze, and I worked with a stone and a handful of moss to caulk the gaps, and when she was floating and not a drop coming in, I went up to the clearing.

The toldo was far enough away from danger or overflow from the river, and about twelve feet high, shaped like cards leaning together, and covered with skins, one end shut with logs, and a vent at the top for the smoke. A few acres of kitchen garden had water from little channels cut from the river bank, and Tegwyn came from hoeing a bed of new plants, and her dress was wet from the heat and close to her, and hair hanging, and hands and bare feet black with mud, and caring nothing.

'Besides to thank you for the boat, I have got compliments from Mr Gruffydd,' she said. 'He came in the shop this morning on the way to Port Madryn. If I saw you, he said to say he would be back on Wednesday, and please could he have the chairs, and thank you for the papers. Michaye was doing nothing, and I had work, so I sent her to be useful.'

'Thank you,' I said. 'No word from the Widow Glyn?'

'Still in the camp, so Gomer Davies thought this morning,' she said, and serious. 'She has had loss to put grey in her hair, he said, and so has he, and he was in to see the Justice. Some of the men have left the threshing to go out there. Thousands of sheep will be lost, he said. And no tracks anywhere. Will you have a cup of tea, Mr Morgan?'

'Or a maté,' I said, not to be a trouble.

'Tea I always drink in the afternoon,' she said. 'For the sake of the children as well. They have got too much of the camp round them day after day. One decent habit will help, anyhow.'

'Is maté a bad habit, then?' I asked her.

'No, indeed,' she said. 'I like maté with milk and honey. They always have it in winter against the cold, and my husband used to put a spoonful of rum. But I want them to know something better. I will have it when I have my house.'

'Where will you build it?' I asked her.

'On the land I have got in the Territory,' she said. 'With the rest of the vegetables this year, I will buy my roof at the Co-op. The posts and doors are there waiting, bought year before last, and my husband had plenty of bricks and cement, and a lot of other things. I will have glass windows, and a beautiful iron stove. From a ship, it was, with brass rails. We shall live nicer, and I can work the sheep as well.'

The voice without any feeling, and the steady way she put the teapot on the stones, and took bread from a cloth to cut slices, and never looked from what she was doing, for minutes on end, I will say now, gave me a very small opinion of myself. To be alone out there and looking after two children was enough, but she was riding to the City to work for hours every day, and coming back to tend the garden and clear the water channels, and milk the cow, and make butter, and wash, and wipe, and everything pin-clean for every minute of the day everlasting. Then, in the light of her hair, I knew how the pioneers had been, and what sort of people they were, and beside them what a smallness I and my kind had become.

'If Michaye is going back to her family, you could keep her for help,' I said, to say something. 'I was surprised she would leave James and Volde.'

'No use to me,' she said, filling the pot from a tin. 'And no use to them, if they are going to do something for themselves. James Smalcote could never bring Alys Caerog Evans to partner anything with her about the place, could he?'

'She is a woman, too,' I said.

'She will do well in the camp, or in one of these,' she said, and a nod at the toldo. 'What, in a house? Could she scrub a floor? Or polish a window? Could she use an iron, or cook something for a family? Beef, or a soup or rice she would get, and fried dough, and maté. Six babies in five years, and every one of them with Indio habits. He would always be away from home, and what, when he came back? A baby from every man who clapped hands outside the door. No, Mr Morgan.'

'You are hard in your judgement,' I said. 'She has a little use, surely.'

'Go down and look at where they were living,' she said, as if that was all the answer had to be. 'Both my brothers went

84

off with Indio girls. I know what I say. Both of them died in the camp. The shares of the farm my father gave to them were sold for bottles. Their children are white Indios. Where are they? What are their names? Sugar in your tea, Mr Morgan?'

'Two, please,' I said. 'I will be at the house tonight and working, so there is no need for you to come for a couple of days. I can make breakfast.'

'I will be there tomorrow morning, and every day,' she said. 'Paid I am, and work I will. Cheese with your bread and butter, Mr Morgan?'

'Thank you,' I said. 'How long will it take me to be in the City?'

'Down the river till where they are building the bridge,' she said. 'Over the water, and straight, twenty minutes.'

Her children came running while I was saddling Merri, he with a bamboo rod and line, and she carrying a tin with little fishes. They looked like her, the boy about five and the girl three, white-fair from the sun, brown in the face and legs, and the same pale straight eye, distrusting, and when I wanted to pick them up, they were off.

'Tame they will be in a house,' she said, putting on a pot of milk. 'Till the morning.'

I went down to the new bridge and watched them putting in the uprights, and crossed to meet Gilead Gwain, the carpenter in charge, not old, but looking it, with a long brown beard, and hair to his shoulders, and a wide hat, and a corduroy suit, and bare feet in cloth slippers.

'The other bridge went away in the flood,' he said. 'Lessons I had from that. This one is stronger. It will go down from age, and nothing else.'

'Those supports are very thick,' I said. 'They will put a wide face to the water. The river will have something to push.'

'Two-thirds in the ground they are, and a lot of hard work,' he said. 'If you will stick to cabinet-making, I will be glad to employ my time with carpentering, and we will both earn enough to buy bread, and let us put our face wide to that, and push, one and one, is it?'

Off at a canter, and back to the shop, and I had been there long enough to put out the tools, and in came Beretroff, and bending his head very civil in the door, and looking at me like a little boy trying to think of words, and a child himself, except for his height, and a big middle, and black hair combed in a parting, and the black moustache. A clean man he was, always in clothes that had been under the iron.

'Señor Morgan, I speak little Castellano,' he said.

'I speak less,' I said.

'I desire work,' he said. 'When you are satisfied, then pay me. I can sleep here, and I must have one plate a day to eat.'

'Do you know something of wood?' I asked him.

'My family,' he said. 'We make very fine work in Europe. I want to be a carpenter in fine work. No more wineshops.'

I put the plane on the table, and showed him the other sizes in the chest. Off came his coat, and up with his sleeves, and into it he went. You have only got to see a man pick up a tool, never mind use it, and you will know.

The moment Beretroff tapped the blade, I saw at least one man I had been looking for, and when the plane started to shave, I turned my back and went out to make a fire, only to let him know I had seen all I wanted.

Vyrnwy Beris came in later, and looked, and looked again.

'Well, Beretroff,' he said. 'What are you doing here?'

'Working,' I said. 'And doing well, so far. Have you an interest?'

He looked at the yard, and I followed him out, down to the heavy timber, and he stopped.

'Because this boy had dealings with that spread-legs girl of his, old Matti Mumpo said he would have him out of the country, or ruin any business he was ever in,' Vyrnwy said, and looking thin at me. 'One to watch close, let me tell you. There is a lot he can do for, or against.'

'Beretroff will stay till I find him no use,' I said. 'Shall I turn him to the street because somebody has got a peso or two?'

'Not only that,' Vyrnwy said, and kicking a splinter. 'M.M. can put a lot of people against you. You might not be able to get stores or timber.'

'To hell with him,' I said. 'What else?'

'I came to ask you to an asado tonight,' he said, and laughing. 'Bring Beretroff if you want. I was never in his shop, but I have got nothing against him for selling a drop of wine. There is one thing we have found out, for sure.'

'About what?' I asked him.

'Mr Matithiah Morse,' Vyrnwy said. 'Elder he is, and big in the chapel. A great one to handle the plate for collection, and dutiful in the act of prayer. And promoter of wine-shops?'

'Is something bad about them?' I asked him. 'A business is a business, wood or wine. Trodd, Split, for one,'

'But the Split is only for us, not Indios,' Vyrnwy said. 'We can get drunk, yes, but not all the time. Drunkards never work, and so no pay. The wives go to get credit to have food. With credit in food, and more in wine, and nothing to pay with, then either an order from the Justice to sell up for debt, or offer the farm, or the land, or the flock, or the cattle. At what price?'

I looked into his eyes, and he looked down at his boots.

'Are there many like Mr Morse?' I asked.

'Enough,' he said. 'Basquos and Turkos and Arabos have done just as good. Ten years ago, all the Indio chieftains came to me to shoe their horses. How many today? They have drunk their horses, and their land and titles. You know Kankel? His grandfather on his mother's side owned more land than you could ride across in a couple of weeks. Everything here was his. Kankel has got a place to sleep in the stable. Matti Mumpo and company, prayer and hymns to order, barrels of wine a speciality.'

'How many of our people?' I asked him.

'Matti Mumpo is the only one I know, but not one of the pioneers,' he said. 'One of the late ones in, he was, about twenty years ago, and capital to help, so he never had to work. He only bought in. Then a shop, and wagons and teams, and interest in sheep, and dealing in wool, and cereals, and cattle. Who is surprised to see millions come to him? Especially with that Eias, Snuff, to help. If they own one half of the valley between them, it will be no surprise.'

'Do I know Elias, Snuff?' I asked him.

'I hope not,' he said. 'In Buenos Aires he is, doing the selling. They say he will marry Nelya Peninnah, and we pray he will.'

'Only one Elias I have ever known,' I said. 'He stole my father's turkeys.'

'Elias, Snuff, would steal your father,' he said. 'Eight o'clock at the back, and bring Beretroff.'

Most people were out in the camp, and the city was quiet except for El Pampero and his dust, and a few in to buy stores, so there were only about twenty of us at the asado, and nine of those women, under the eye of Mistress Kathi

Jones from the school and having theirs in the house with Vyrnwy's sister, Alwen, because their dresses were starched against the heat and she was worried they would have marks from the forge.

We were sitting on the anvils and everywhere, and each one with a chicken from the spit, plump, and tender to save a chew, and in walked Eynon Caerog Evans, filling the door, and looking about and shading his eyes under the lamps till he saw me, and over he came.

'Where is Smalcote and that Russian?' he said to me, rough, as if he had been shouting.

'Gone to the Andes, so I heard,' I said.

'From Tegwyn, Toldo,' he said. 'She told me. I am looking for them. My daughter has gone. Horses she has taken, and a lot of her clothes. But she will regret to her dying day. No daughter of mine shall marry a foreigner.'

'Foreigner?' I said. 'Smalcote is English.'

'Foreigner to me,' he said. 'Can she talk to him?'

'He is a good boy, and hard-working, and she will go many a month of Sundays to find better,' I said. 'What do you want of me?'

'You are friends,' he said. 'Where are they?'

'If I knew, you would be the last to have a word,' I said. The whip came up in his hand, and I stood ready.

'Right, you,' he said, and quiet. 'You have made yourself a name since you have been here I can expect nothing else. Never speak to me or come near my place again.'

'Be sure,' I said.

He went to the middle of the forge, and told Vyrnwy that he had posted a reward for information. Some of the men went with him, and Vyrnwy came over to me and slicing flat strips off a drumstick with a knife like a razor.

'You are making wonderful friends,' he said. 'More like this, and you will have a colony on your own.'

'And in peace,' I said.

'He is in a temper because somebody took the girl and no word to him,' he said. 'Everybody will agree. If he is against you, they will all be, too. He is one of the old families, and honest, and nobody with a word against. You have come now just, and one of your friends is Mr Gruffydd, and others you have got at the top of the valley, and you would rather read the English Bible than the Welsh, and you are a single man in and out of a widow's house as if you owned both, and you have got somebody working for you who is marked for destruction. Worse than that, you made a coffin for a non-believer to put in unconsecrated ground.'

'I would like to meet a few more non-believers,' I said.

'Rhinberry is worse,' he said. 'They even say he is a Mormon, mind you.'

'Mormons believe in God,' I said.

'So do Mohammedans,' he said. 'But there is only one real one, and that is in Chapel. Now you know your offences.'

'A broadsheet,' I said. 'And what, to my credit?'

'Only that you are hard-working, and saving more than any other single man in the city,' he said. 'And you have got a good place to work, and lucky, and so is the Widow Glyn, because you might have been a drunkard like Rupert, or not steady with the rent, or an idler. Reading the English Bible is for the lettered, and the Reverend Mr Armon Tudor is respected because he can read it all the way through without once looking in a dictionary. And nobody could have told you about Rhinberry, and if they had, there was still a coffin to be made, and nobody to make it, and you refused money. And Mrs Winn is very peaceful where he put her up in the rocks with a little spring to give water for flowers, and a lot of them are thinking of going up there, because their bones will be safe from the flood, see, and ready to stand up, every bit in the right place, when the Promise is fulfilled.'

'Now strike a balance,' I said.

'Tell everybody to push a thumb,' he said. 'Split a chicken with me. Still hungry I am, and a pity to waste.'

Alwen came to ask if I would speak to Mistress Kathi Jones, and over we went to the school, and a little room with the china sets behind glass in a cupboard, and a family of white dogs, one behind the other on both sides of the mantelpiece looking towards the clock, and a bit of fringe everywhere.

'I hear your sister is a Bachelor of Arts, Mr Morgan,' she said. 'I was wondering if you have time to give lessons in English. There are very few here and the children need it.'

'In that field there is many a rabbit hole,' I said. 'I would soon be to my neck.'

'I will put you down for as many times as you can come,' she said. 'If the Colony is going to trade, it must have English. It is the duty of all of us. The matter of fees can be spoken about later.'

'I learnt it from books, and for nothing, Mistress,' I said. 'If I pass it to somebody, it shall be for nothing, or for Castellano in return.'

'If you would like books, come to the house and have what you please,' she said. 'The newspapers are old but readable, if you mind how you turn the page. Castellano you shall have. I am told you know Lal and Doli and Solva Corwen. Pupils of mine, they were. When they come in next, bring them to tea, and we will talk more.'

Those little rubber bands I could feel again, but it was kindness in her and nothing to annoy, I suppose, but the sand was in my teeth to think that people would push me to do something that I wanted to do, instead of letting me do it without the push, in my own way.

Beretroff went before I did, because he had been given a bed in the loft by Vyrnwy in case of looks from the Widow Glyn about sleeping in the shop without her permission. That, anyway, made me feel glad because it seemed that whatever I did was likely to be a hoof in the wrong place.

Round the back I went to put out the lamp in the shop, and I was passing the timber racks, and my arm was touched, and James Smalcote was standing there, and behind him, Alys Caerog Evans. Neither of them needed telling to be quiet, and they came in the shop and I shut the door.

'We had to come in to get married,' he whispered. 'She won't go without the papers. But the Justice is closed and he's going up the valley for the threshing, first thing. We can't go anywhere. Everybody's after us. Would you be a real pal and give us a shakedown here?'

'Her father is very angry with her,' I said. 'You, too.'

'We know all about it,' James said, and very tired. 'We can't go on the roads. Can't go through the farms. Can't go anywhere. Then Volde thought of you. He's watching the horses over the river.'

'You could make sad enemies for me,' I said to Alys. 'Are you sure you want to be married? Why not speak with your father first?'

'I have spoken with him every day for my life,' she said. 'No difference. James is the first I have loved. I will only marry him, and nobody else. Off to the Andes, then, and have a piece of land and a house, and settle.'

Little, she was, and a blue eye, clear, and even without the laugh always ready for it, and a voice that seemed never to touch the sides of her throat. But she was like a block, there.

'Right, you,' I said. 'Come behind me, and not a sound.'

Out I went and across the street towards the barracks and the house of the Justice. Dark it was, and they crossed running, one at a time. I waited till they were in shadow, and went round the house to the light in the back room, and the Justice had his sleeves rolled up, and a big sheet of paper across the table, and painting another notice to be stuck on the wall outside the office, that El Pampero always peeled off before anybody could read it, and for that, Justice, Dab and Blow, they called him.

One of sympathy I had always found him, and a friend of Mr Cervantes, and of mine as well, and he was patient, as ever, to put shape in my splutter of Castellano, but he twisted his moustache and said he was much afflicted, but the office was shut and they should have come before five o'clock, so I called them from the door, and in they came. He started explaining to James, and I took Alys to the corner.

'Use a bit of glimmer, girl,' I said. 'Put your arms around his neck, and pool tears, and wet his old shirt with him. If you want to get married, get married, and no old nonsense from anybody.'

Well, I will give that girl plenty of due, but the words were not from me before she was howling to wake them in the back streets of New Jerusalem, there, and running to the Justice and hands about his neck, and him, poor man, staring, and James wondering if I had said something to her, and looking at me very old-fashioned, and then Mrs Justice, Dab and Blow, came in. Spanish she was, and a lovely dancer after an asado, with long black hair and a red shawl, but different when she saw Alys leaning, and Mr Justice with an arm about her. But in a moment, Alys had told her, very quiet and her cheeks shining with tears and her eyes blue and soft, and the Castellano sounding lovely between the two, and then Mrs Justice said something to him, and he started to argue. The more he was saying, the more and louder she said, and then he shrugged, and went to put on his coat, and she took the candle, and Alys by the hand, and went out, and the Justice took James and myself through the passage to his office, full of chests and crates and rolls of paper and folios. A couple of servants put a cloth and more candles on the bare table, and Mrs Justice brought in Alys, with a lace shawl over her head and a bunch of flowers from the garden tied in a ribbon, and the Justice came back with a couple of bottles and put them under his chair.

All the columns in the book were filled, and for minutes the room was alive with the noble sound of the quill joining two into one to suffer and cherish unto death. Signatures were put, and stamped with wooden blocks, and Alys kissed James, and they were crying, and everybody shaking hands and kissing, and the cork came from the bottle and Alys was telling everybody how happy she was, because James had no more of the language than I, and somebody tapped on the window, and nearly came through.

The Widow Glyn was looking at me, first, and making signs to the Justice.

The maids ran to open the door, and I went quick in the back room with James and Alys.

'We can go anywhere we like, now,' James said, and holding the folded paper like a sword. 'Nobody can't say a word, can they? You know where to come, don't you? If there's ever anything we can do for you, it's done.'

A kiss I got from Alys, and I watched them go out, arms about, and nothing in the sky so bright as their eyes for each other. The thought was in me, then, that she could have been Lal, and I might have had an arm about her, and going off to Damaglou's for the double room in front.

But the look on the Widow's face was not one to forget.

'It is not in my mind what they will say about you after this,' she said, tired, and draped with dust. 'Eynon has got men all along the valley looking for them. And I have got a headful for myself, indeed. Sheep and cattle are missing and a lot of horses. I am sick to think what it will be when the count is full. And two dead tonight.'

'Home, you, and sleep,' I said. 'Plenty of time in the morning. I will light the bath for you.'

Out I went, a good excuse to say no more, and the fire was going well by the time the horses were at the house, and the peons calling good night to her, and the front door closing and the bolts tight in. The water was almost at the boil when I went for a stroll over to Damaglou's, but it was shut and no lights. Everywhere else was shut, too, and no light in Vyrnwy's front, and no sound anywhere but a breeze scraping up dust in little coils, and my boots treading slow to be back at the house late, and the Widow Glyn asleep, not to have more talk about Mr and Mrs Smalcote or anything else.

Round the back I made sure the tub had been used, and I banked the fire down, and went in and locked the door and put on my slippers in the dark kitchen, and upstairs quiet on each stair, to my room. The candle was alight by the wall bed, and the window curtains were drawn, and I opened the wardrobe to hang my jacket and waistcoat.

But I turned from the looking-glass quick enough to see a head on my pillow, and I went over there, and raised the candle.

The Widow Glyn pulled aside the clothes, and smiling, beautiful to dream about, and hair in three plaits, and looking not a day older than her daughter.

A man can do plenty full dressed in the light, and give him a pulpit and he will go on for hours about purity and goodness and one thing and another. Some there are who say that a man should commune with himself and be strong to deny, though a fine time it is with a candle, and braces flapping, and a bit late for lectures when a woman smiles at you white from a bed one moment, and the next, pinching out the candle finger and thumb.

'A wedding is for others,' she said, in whispers. 'But ours only for us, yes?'

Well.

No use to argue, indeed.

6

To be in love with two women is held by some to be non-sense, and perhaps they are right. But strange it is to think of one fondly, to protect, and yet to have the mind on another, with a hunger that hurts in the heart.

Of course, there is a lot to be said about keeping Commandments, and treading in the narrow path, and behaving yourself. But when the woman is the Widow Glyn, it is a good man to say Go From Here, although I have listened to a few who said they could, but I am sure they were never given the chance. Many an hour while I was working I knew I was in the wrong and thinking I ought to go, quick, and live in accord with the teaching, for what good it would have done.

But one look at the Widow Glyn, and I was water.

Perhaps that is the punishment, never to be able to say No in temptation, or to have easiness in the conscience, or to think clearly for the future, or have any surety for the present. Before, to anybody coming in the shop, I could be free with them, knowing I was paying my way and no harm anywhere. But after, I felt that everybody had been right to gossip as they had, and if it was small comfort, there was none in thinking that I should marry the Widow Glyn.

Lal was always with me. But the Widow was nearer.

There was nothing against her in marriage, either. She owned properties from her father and mother and from Rupert, and she had an account at the Bank and money invested in the Co-operative, and rentals, as she would tell me at any moment of the day, never mind that she lived in the fashion of her mother. Comfort she had, and whatever she wanted the Co-operative could get for her, though beyond a good table and whole clothes and a solid house and the best horse and trap in the City there was not much she could want, except somebody to share it with her.

She surprised me.

As my landlady, she was exactly as she had been before, not a word or a look different, downstairs in front of the Indio helpers at any rate. But she was prettier to do little things for me that had not been done when I was only a lodger. My clothes were not better brushed or my boots more polished, or my laundry whiter or my shop or my room swept cleaner. It was the air about them that looked different, as if another kind of mind had been at work, and a gentler touch had ironed and starched and brushed and scrubbed and polished. There was no longer a look about things that they had been done because it was usual. Everything went softer to its place, and going in the house I began to feel more settled, or quieter though I suppose others noticed nothing at all, and they would have thought me turned in the head, or perhaps purblind with the evil that was in me.

But if what we were doing was evil, it showed nothing in the Widow Glyn. She seemed to change better by the hour, and all about her was younger, and she spoke with more tone to her voice. The black dresses and the shawl went first, and in colours she looked run from twenty years, and her braids shone under lacier caps that kept off the dust, and framed her face and showed the white neck and made her eyes blacker, quicker to smile, and never coming near me, but speaking a couple of yards off, and turning away, and looking back, and laughing, and brisk to be at work on something in another part of the house, or sharp with the Indio girls to do this over, or get that done.

For sure I knew why Adam had wanted to wear an apron of fig leaves. Something, it was, nothing much but just enough to hide his appetite, and his weakness, even from himself. Perhaps it is why a lot of us hate nakedness. If we had gone to Mr Justice, Dab and Blow, for a few scratches on paper and a couple of stamps and rigmarole with the garlic of his breath, we could have come home to do what we liked, and two fingers to all the world. But without him, shaved or not, and garlic or not, and his page of scribble, it was wrong, and guilty we had to feel.

Never had I known how it was to be naked to the world, no matter what I tried to think, and unable to meet anybody in the eye, though that was no punishment for what I was having, and I expect Adam felt the same, so I came to understand the story of the Garden a great deal better, and the Apple and the Serpent became friends of mine. About the matter of Bronwen I knew more, too, and it was plain that if the door had not been locked that time, and locked in my mind ever since, we might never have been able to live in that house for all those years and letting everybody think what they pleased.

Eyes alone, without the tongues, might have poisoned us.

But the only time I tried to talk to the Widow Glyn about it, she made a tff! with her lips, and spoke about what we would have for supper.

Those days, in any case, I was stacked with orders, and any time extra I worked with Beretroff, though there was no need for me to do much, except to rough the designs and choose the wood to be used, and leave him. The Widow Glyn looked hard, bright and black at him the first time, but except to say that from wine to wood was change for the better, nothing more was said because she knew I had need of a helper. Only a couple of days later, Donato Urrisbiscaya came in and Beretroff left his bench and brought him to me with a bow that always meant he had something important to say. Donato was tall and broad as a Tehuelche, but thin from not much to eat, and honest in his look, with a grey Basquo eye like an owl, and a sudden little laugh that would have you doubled without knowing why. Beretroff said he had just come to the country, and looking for work as a wheelwright and coachmaker. The idea had been in my mind for long enough, so I gave him the run of the yard to build me the champion trap of the valley, and if he made a success, we would go in business together.

By the time he understood my Castellano, he had his coat off, and the only times I saw him after that was in clouds of shavings at the end of the yard, or sitting by the fire for a maté with Beretroff.

Jones, Price Special, came in with tools and odds from the ship just docked, and gave the news from outside while I looked at the invoice. A talking newspaper, he was, and knowing more about everybody than the people themselves.

'What is heard about the Cassidy lot is bad, too,' he said. 'They have taken an Indio chieftain in the Territory, and wouldn't give him back without money, but it was hidden, and the poor wife had no idea where, so they sent him back on his horse, dead, aye, and his tribe are after them.'

'Who is this Cassidy?' I asked him.

'A pistolero from North America, they say he is, but nobody here has seen him,' he said. 'The chieftain was one of the richest of the Manzaneros. They are from the Apple Tree country. Apple is manzana in Castellano. Listen, if they kill one white, they can kill two, see. There are enough of them to kill us all. One of my uncles was murdered by them. Cut in bits alive, him and four other boys. Once the killing starts, who will stop it?'

'The police,' Beretroff said.

'Police?' Jones, Price Special, said, and putting up his hands to the ceiling. 'Where will they go? Fit to wink at the girls and bloat bellies with wine? Going down to the river to fill their casks, and drowning, then, a couple at a time. Two under yesterday, again, and no hope. We shall need more than police if there is trouble. There will be a meeting about it at Maes Corwen before the thresh. Mistress Doli asked me to say will you be there, Mr Morgan?'

Whether from the way he said it I imagined something else was in his mind, or if it was only in mind, but I thought he was ready to hear me say no.

'Yes,' I said. 'Did you tell Mistress Lal I was going to marry Mistress Glyn?'

'Well,' he said, and the red coming in his face. 'Well, indeed, Mr Morgan. I only happened to mention I had heard.'

'Who from?' I asked him.

'Well,' he said, and looking about. 'I forget for the moment. Everybody is saying so, here.'

'When there is talk of marrying, I will be the one to do it,' I said. 'Put your nose in my affairs again, and you shall have more than a price special. Free it will be, and good-bye now.'

But if I had the weight of a few worries extra for Merri to carry, they were gone the moment I got to Maes Corwen because Solva came running from the house and laughing beautiful, and saying she had heard that Beretroff was working for me, and she was sure I had given him the place because of her, and well, it would have taken crowbars to put a word in, so I shut up and sat to a tableful that would have served multitudes and baskets over. Only by listening I found that Lal had been out in the camp with all the peons to look for missing sheep and cattle, and Doli had taken her place at the dam with the men.

'You girls work very hard,' I said.

'We did much more when we thought it was ours,' Solva

said. 'Mama worked in the house and out in the camp all her life. By her we were trained. But if Indios are going to have it, what good to trouble?'

'Are you sure?' I asked her.

She looked round at me from the stove, and her eyes were frozen, and a little smile to make them glitter.

'Would it make any difference?' she asked, sweet to wrinkle the mouth. 'Perhaps you had better talk to my father, first. Then you would know. None of us do. But of course, Lal has no interest. Not like Doli and me. She cares nothing.'

'In what matter?' I asked her, knowing very well.

'Look,' she said, and no patience. 'You are old enough. The Widow Glyn has been running to Tibbald for hats. Six, mind you, in only one week. For years she has gone about in Rupert's old cap. And bolts of cloth from the Co-op, in colours, and china, and carpets, and towels. Why? Since the ground was dug, she had used what she had left in the house, and going everywhere in black. Singing, she was, for anybody to hear, in the Co-op back room, there, and choosing a double bed. A doubler? Everybody knows she has never slept on anything only a couch of her mother's since Rupert was taken from the house, and the bed burnt for health. Now, Huw, tell me. Why do you think she could change so much?'

'Nothing to say, even if I had been paid, nothing.'

'On top of that, you stayed from the asado you were invited to by my father, and no word why,' she said, going out of the kitchen. 'Ask yourself what Lal was thinking.'

She was in the larder for a few minutes, and I was trying to give myself the words and have my voice in a level to say them.

But I could feel the Apple stuck tight.

'Of course, we might not have the right to ask anything,' she called through the door, careless as throwing a coat over a chair. 'Nothing has been said, except joking. Nothing for business, no? So we have got the wrong bull's tail here. No hope from the start, everybody.'

'If I knew where Lal was, I would go, now,' I said. 'Her, I will talk to, nobody else.'

'She is twenty leagues out in the camp, and where, after that, you would have to ride to find out,' she said, coming in with a basket of peaches. 'There is nobody here to take you, pity, too. But she is bound to be here this week, and Doli with her. I am putting everything ready for the cooks. They will be here with the threshers three days from now.'

'Price Special said the thresh would start tomorrow,' I said.

'It should,' she said. 'But my father and the neighbours have had big losses in sheep and cattle, and they are out to know why, thresh after. So stay. Plenty of room.'

'If I am here a couple of days doing nothing when there is plenty in the shop, there is no excuse,' I said. 'Besides that, even if I slept ten miles down the river, people would swear you and me had been practising to marry. I will be back in three days, and no suspicions, except a few I bring with me.'

She laughed with the hair falling in her eyes, and O, I could hear Lal.

'Bring that old Beretroff, too,' she said. 'Only for me. Tell him you saw me, and I asked kindly after him.'

'Do the same for me with Lal,' I said.

'Another language, and nobody to speak it, only you,' she said. 'Be here for the thresh. I will tell her.'

Off I went, and in some ways thankful, because there was time to practise what I was going to say. Perhaps because I was more at home by then, I turned off across the pasture instead of following the river, and went direct towards the city, wondering at the crops of vegetables, and the fields of uncut corn for feed, and I came to a gate I knew well, and only to give Merri a drink I went down, through the garden in glory of autumn roses, and towards a little house I hardly knew.

'Come in, Mr Morgan, and seven times seven welcome,' Mrs Roper Hughes called from the doorway. 'Look what a couple of willing ones and a few days' work will do, yes?'

The roof was painted red, and the walls had been whitewashed, and two big windows were in, and the door was pale blue. In the kitchen were dark blue tiles, and the fireplace had been built with pointed stones, and the little dresser was against the wall and filled with blue and white china and some silver pieces, and the other furniture was all in place and waxed to make you blink, and everything floated in the shine of the floor.

'Morwen did a bit of bullying, see,' she said, opening the door to the bedroom, and the same shine, but the suite looked very good, with the new linen and a coverlet worked in colours, and a white goatskin rug. 'She came with the furniture, and the trap full to the top. Goodness gracious me,

girl, I said, have you sailed from your wits, here? No, she
said. But a sister of mine used to smack me for being naughty
or untidy, and I am in shame to see her living like an old
Indio. Sheets, she has brought me, and tablecloths, and
china, and everything new, look. And the price is terrible,
indeed. But could I be angry, and having it about me? And
I could give you a good kiss for your furniture, but Morwen
said nothing about the price.'

'She paid me,' I said.

'Good, she is,' she said, and eyes full. 'In disgust with her
life till now, but underneath, always good. Of course, she
shall have it back, every centavo. But I am glad, because
Mari Ann will be home soon, and think what she will say.
A cup of tea, now, and open a pot of special damson-and-
rum, and bread from the oven, is it?'

'Thank you,' I said. 'I want to be in the city before dark.
Have you heard anything about Mistress Glyn and me?'

Her eyes were half shut, smiling, and looking out in the
sun.

'Yes,' she said. 'And glad, too. Not from her, though. She
needs somebody. She had a terrible time with that other one.
Half-brother of my husband, he was. Same mother. An old
mule of a woman. Drowned in the flood, she was, and
nobody sorry. She lived with Dilys, the sister between me
and Mari Ann, where Morwen's children are now. A teacher
she was, so they are having good lessons. Are you sure no
tea, Mr Morgan?'

'Thank you,' I said. 'Any message for Mistress Glyn?'

So suddenly, a little of the same look was in her eye as
there had been in Solva's, a freeze and a smile together, and
a new sureness, and a picking of the cuffs and belt.

'To thank her for paying, and love,' she said. 'Good afternoon, Mr Morgan.'

What I was thinking on the way back, I will never be sure,
but it was a boiling of everything, and every way I turned I
could see I was wrong, at any rate in the eyes of others, and
by the time I gave Merri to Kankel and watched her nuzzling
at the clover, I had made up my mind to leave the house, but
keep on the shop and yard.

But of course, the Widow Glyn had gone to see her
children, and Tegwyn had no notion when she would be
back, and Mr Matithiah Morse had called to see me, no

100

message, and after an argument with him, Beretroff had gone.

'Gone where?' I said.

'He only raised his hat, nothing else,' she said. 'He put things tidy, and took his box, and went. The Basquo might know.'

Donato looked very sad, and from all I understood, he said that after loud voices and disturbance, Beretroff had come out and said good-bye.

The shop was left clean by a workman, and the emptier for that, and I knew what strength I had lost. All the other matters of the day were small beside it, but they had their effect, and they helped to build a rage against Mr Morse like a plant in a twist with ugly leaves. Tegwyn said she would soon find out where Beretroff had gone, and I told her to tell him to come back. No smile was in her, and no pity, and I sensed she thought I deserved what I had.

But there was no news after a couple of days, and the Widow Glyn was still away, and I was up at sunrise to finish before going to Maes Corwen, and the door was pushed wide, no knock or word, and a stout man in black put a square-crowned bowler hat on the counter, and a walking-stick beside it, and took out a handkerchief to wipe all round his face, and laughing quietly to himself as though he enjoyed the wipe and laugh together.

'An early bird, one like me, and worms in the beak before anybody else, yes, Mr Morgan?' he said, and giving the dew-laps a good pat all round to be sure. 'I was at the hotel for the night, and I thought I would pay a call. And Mistress Glyn not at home, shame, yes. Be sure to say how sorry I was. Busy we both are, so no time to lose. Matithiah Morse, I am, and I would like to know if it is your intention to have that Slavo back to work here?'

'If Beretroff will come, he will be welcome,' I said. 'Is it your business?'

'Yours, too,' he said, and laughing to himself, and wagging his head, and folding the handkerchief neat. 'Let me speak to you, first, as an employer. Supposing you set a man in business, and gave him your trust, and told him not to supply certain goods to certain others. Supposing you found him supplying contrary, and the supplies being misused. What, then?'

'Have it in the open with him,' I said.

'And if you proved that he had done what you had told

him not?' Matti Mumpo asked, and laughing between breaths. 'If you brought a dozen witnesses, and him not a word to say, would you tell him to go?'

'Perhaps,' I said.

'Perhaps,' he said, and laughing more. 'Not only in business, but everywhere there is an example to be shown forth, always, yes? Would you tell him to go, and if you found him in a business where he could do more harm, you would see he was sent from there?'

'I would have to hear the facts,' I said.

'Would I have your permission to hear the facts for myself, and have him out?' he asked me, and leaning, laughing across the counter. 'Some of us make up our minds very quick. Once made, and the words said, no more, yes?'

'Yes,' I said. 'But he is not a dishonest man.'

'He was used dishonestly, then,' he said, and laughing so much he had to wipe all over again. 'Will you guarantee he will keep from it if he was allowed?'

'He will do no harm here,' I said.

'No harm, but more business for himself and others than he will do for you,' Matti Mumpo said, and breathing harder to laugh more. 'A consignment of wine yesterday, look, coming to me, bought by him on the road before it got here.'

'He learnt something,' I said.

'Bought with whose money?' he asked me, and almost crying in the handkerchief. 'Where will the wine go? To make a few drunk? For what? Listen well. Beretroff never works in this valley again if I can help it.'

'He is a good workman,' I said. 'If he was making his money in wine, why would he be a carpenter?'

'To be near his friends across the street,' Matti Mumpo said, in fits, there. 'Wait you, if he is let, he will have a bigger place than ever. But I have warned him. Never again in this valley.'

'That is for you to say,' I said. 'His place here is ready for him.'

Matti Mumpo blew his nose, still laughing, and set the handkerchief in creases, and put it in his hat, and the hat on his head, and took his stick and went to the door, and turned, and looked at me through a laugh, to the side, and morning sun was pale along the lashes, and from the eyes I knew Nelya Peninnah's father.

'Good day, Mr Morgan,' he said, and breaths in between,

and a flourish, like a bouquet of hands. 'The last time I will say it where I am standing, is it?'

Donato had not come when Kankel brought Merri, but going past the Co-op, Jones, Price Special, was tying his horse, and I went over.

'You know something about wine,' I said. 'What is the reason for Matti Mumpo wanting to push out Beretroff? He works well for me.'

'Wait now,' he said, holding up his hand. 'It is more than my existence to offer one word about old M.M. He has got money in by here, and a word to say in everything. The wineshop he let to Beretroff because the land is his, and the wine was shipments from Mendoza, up there in the North. Instead to have a dirty old place for drinking, it was clean, and fair prices. If Beretroff had stuck to selling by the glass or bottle, very well. But he was selling barrels, and nobody knows where they went. Looking after Number One, he was, like a lot of us, and caught.'

'But why shouldn't he sell barrels?' I asked him. 'Everybody here has got a barrel in the house.'

'Except the Indios,' he said. 'And anybody too poor. They are the ones who drink, and go in debt, and sell everything. And who will get the blame? Him who sold the wine? They never blame the one drunk. So there were a few words, and Beretroff crossed the road to you. And listen. If you want to walk tidy, be from in front of Matti Mumpo. Compared with him, old Satan is in his infancy. Good-bye now.'

Very few were on the road out, and I cut an hour off the ride by the short way, but even so, the news was at Maes Corwen before me.

'Tea parties you are having with Matti Mumpo, is it?' Doli said to me, when I was putting Merri in the corral. 'Wait you, there will be more leaves than tea, and not long, either.'

'Where did you hear?' I said, and very surprised. 'Only this morning I saw him.'

'He has been talking for longer than that,' she said. 'Say nothing in the house to Solva. Where do you think Mr B. is now?'

'Not at the shop,' I said.

'He is with Miss Nelya Peninnah,' Doli said. 'They have gone up the coast.'

103

'You are better than Price Special,' I said.

'From him we had it yesterday,' she said. 'Nobody will be here till midday, so come you and eat in peace. Lal is putting the machines in place, and Solva is out with the other girls seeing to the asado. I am cutting bacon for the morning, so you can help me.'

About twenty girls were in there, all busy with dough, or pastry, or chopping something or stoning fruit, and more were in the dairy, and others coming in every minute. None of them were known to me, so I had pleasure to hear all their names and give them good day.

Beautiful, many of them were, too, and whether black-haired or red, or fair, or somewhere in between, or whatever colour in the eyes, or tall or short or fat or thin, not one could have come from anywhere but Wales, and certain it was that unless a man was hooked, first cast, a fine time he would have trying to make up his mind between them. Everybody had something to do, and each one could do another's work, so hands were never still, or if they were, somebody soon put something in them, especially old Mistress Eirene Vaughan, in a lace cap and sleeves rolled and round spectacles from her grandfather that she said were better than a dozen pairs of eyes, with special glass to see idleness.

An appetite I got from a marvellous smell of fruit pies from the oven, and soups coming to boil, and herbs being crushed, and celery chopped for roasting the poultry, and my eggs and bacon came with extra relish, and listening to voices soft in harmony of songs that had the age lovely in them, and yet were always young.

But about me was thought of Lal, and after I had sliced bacon enough to cure me of pigs for ever, I went out to the fields and I saw her on the high seat of the thresher, and over I went.

'Well, stranger,' she said, and the same smile. 'We have been hearing tales about you. Are you with us till the finish?'

'If I am allowed,' I said. 'I am told the tales displeased you.'

'Does it matter?' she said. 'There is work, and the days go just the same, pleased or not. If you will give them a hand with the roof of the shed, it will save time. I must go to the stables. Till later.'

So off I went to help with the shed for the serving tables,

and that was the last I saw of her for three solid days. Working, of course, she was, and so was everybody else, and if she was avoiding me it was well done because there was no effort. Her father was away during that time and so were the owners of most of the farms near by, but on the fourth day, in they came, and tireder or longer faces never were.

Vrann Corwen led on the finest horse I have ever seen. About forty men were with him, all of them whiskered and ragged and burnt black, each with a rifle, and a revolver on the belt, and with packs as if they had been out for weeks. A rough lot they looked, every one of them over six foot, and very different in manner from the farmers in the valley, more assured, sharper to speak, readier to joke. All the threshers stopped work and ran to take their horses, and over to the asado pit, then, and talking while they had to eat, and I saw Idwyn Thomas, the only one I knew, serious.

'Some of the boys went on to warn them in the Andes,' he said. 'We will finish the thresh, and go out again. Thousands of sheep and cattle are missing. If they are lost, it will be a worse year than the flood for a lot of us.'

'Is Mr Gruffydd among the losers?' I asked him.

'He is farther out, and to the south,' he said. 'The worry is whether the robbers are Indios, or some of the half-breeds out there. The sins of the fathers is more than only a few words in the Bible, see.'

Vrann Corwen was much taller than I had thought, and eyes like Doli's and a voice like Solva's, very quiet, but it went a long way, and when he climbed on a wain, everybody stood close and silent.

'We are going to finish all the farms in half the time,' he said. 'One more day to settle business, and we shall go out towards the Andes. We will be back when you see us. Work well, and finish soon.'

The change between any thresh in the valley and that one of Maes Corwen could be told in a word.

Silence.

Nobody stopped to talk, or have a smoke, and the women brought food to the men, and boys and girls ran with the maté and a kettle, or pots of tea, and the engines pumped and the steam hissed all day and white in the night, and some of the men and women went to sleep, and others worked on, but everybody was working before dawn, and as Vrann had said, we finished in less than half the time, and moved to the next place within the hour.

The only times I had seen the girls was when they came in with the loaded wains, or if they brought food or drink to the machine, and Vrann worked where he could, and one more tireless would have to be a machine. But when we finished, he came round to where I was, and put out his hand.

'At last, a moment to speak,' he said, with something of Doli's smile, too, so I knew that Lal was most of her mother. 'The girls have often spoken well of you, and indeed, you have done well here. Will you be coming with us to the Territory?'

'One with a shop in the city is not much good out there,' I said. 'If I was better on a horse, yes.'

'Wise,' he said. 'We will talk more at the wedding.'

Solva came while we were saddling in the corral.

'Will Beretroff come back to you?' she asked me.

'If he wants,' I said.

'They say he was sent from you by old M.M.,' she said. 'Did you allow it?'

'I allowed nothing,' I said. 'His place is still open.'

'He is with Nelya Peninnah,' she said.

'Mouths are saying so,' I said.

'I would put an axe in her,' she said, quiet, even with a little smile. 'He is too good to be a toy for that one. And she is not good enough to be even a rainditch for him. He is a fat old fool, but he could be made better. She is a pit without end, amen.'

'Strange she can push a sensible man like him to do what she wants,' I said. 'One with brains, he is.'

'Other things, too,' she said, and turning her horse. 'You could be one to find out. I saw the looks she was giving you.'

'Why not give him a look of your own?' I asked her.

'With a ring on my finger, and bells on my toes,' she said. 'He will come to no harm. And perhaps I will find somebody better. Especially if we have our property. Nobody will want any of us without, will they?'

Well, I was thinking about that, and Lal came from the stable in the trap with red wheels, and an empty place beside her, so I gave Merri to Islwyn Hughes, and stood in the way till she stopped.

'Any price for the seat beside you,' I said.

'A little chair to sit down in to put my slippers on,' she

said. 'Ours are all too high. I am giddy for a week, bending down.'

'Have you got a shape you would like?' I asked her.

'Anything that will come from your shop that is sit-down-able,' she said. 'The chairs you made for Mrs Roper Hughes are the talk of the Colony.'

'If that is all there is to talk about,' I said. 'Doli was saying there was plenty about something else.'

'The Widow Glyn and you,' Lal said and turned the mare into Plenydd John's gate. 'What will stop people talking? Only the right word in the right place.'

'Which word, and what place?' I asked her.

'Yes, in Chapel,' she said. 'Morwen is happy to tell everybody she has found a man she can admire. You. There is a funny word, too.'

'To admire?' I asked her. 'Why, funny?'

'Wrong word, wrong place,' she said, and put the whip in the holder, and slipped the reins out of the brass rings and gave them to a peon. 'We know her language. Admire says everything, about her, and about Mr South.'

'And Mr South is allowed to say nothing,' I said.

'Anything he wants, but everything has been said, and nothing more to say,' she said, and got down, watching the peon undoing the harness. 'Sorry I am, too.'

'No need for that,' I said, sitting up there, ice, I was.

'Need,' she said, and looking over to the threshers starting, and the steam rising. 'If there is one, there cannot be another. Good-bye, now.'

'Lal,' I called after her. 'Why?'

But she waved her gloves and walked on, and I was still sitting there in the empty trap, shafts up, passenger to nowhere and dry in the mouth. Why I was not down and running after her would be a good question, but the Serpent is not part of Adam and Eve for nothing.

The strongest rope is not tighter to bind than that slippery one, and well I knew it.

No argument and nothing to be said.

7

Standing here now, and thinking then, I suppose the Garden was stripped by Mr Gruffydd when he came in for the winter stores, but nobody would have taken him for an Angel, and if he had a Flaming Sword, it must have been in his smile. Breath was out of me to see the change, so young he was, and laughing, and walking as if with wings at the ankles between the timber racks to the shop.

'Loss is not putting a long face or a short step in you, then,' I said.

'No loss,' he said. 'A splendid season we have had. You will see when I bring the selling flock in. These others let the sheep go. Not a foot of fence for a couple of hundred leagues. For how long do they work out in the camp? A month a year to shear and dip or mark the increase? You have got to be there ten months out of twelve, at least, and men riding the fences every day. With good weather, and plenty of feed, no loss. Thieves attack the unguarded.'

'Mr Matithiah Morse is fortunate in his associates,' I said.

'Matti Mumpo is a businessman,' he said, going quiet, and I could almost hear the wings fold. 'Best sheep in the Territory, and buying the prize rams every year. He will soon have the prize flock, too.'

'And a daughter,' I said.

'Poor girl,' Mr Gruffydd said, and looking through the window at Donato, busy with the spokeshave. 'Everybody is given a nature, Huw. Not one of us is asked if we want it. We must do what we can. Nelya Penninah has been spoilt, for one thing. But she is only sixteen, turned. There is time, still.'

'She is with Beretroff,' I said. 'A good workman. Why he should want to leave the bench for her, God knows.'

'Be careful she will not put her claws in you,' he said, looking straight at me. 'I came to tell you I have had news from home. Everything is well, there. Did Angharad write to you?'

'She is staying with Olwen,' I said.

'She will be here for the first flowers,' he said, and his voice changed, and his face was almost as I had known him. 'I have got you to thank for more blessing of hope than I have had in my life. Perhaps Olwen will come with her. But I have been in despair to think where will they stay. Not at this cattle pen of an hotel, here. There are no good lodgings. How could they be put in a wagon? Where, then?'

Well, I suppose the right words to make the right question will be like the pattern cut in metal to be a key, and places are in our brains for the question to fit, because the answer comes from the mouth quick as if we had never thought for a moment, even if, after, we wonder where and how we could have had any notion.

'I will build a house and a shop of my own,' I said. 'Business is doubling every month. A man wanting to marry has got to have a house, to begin with.'

He was looking at me in a way I knew well, that told me he wanted to say what he would rather not.

'If it is capital or credit, I can help,' he said.

'All I will need of both I have got,' I said. 'Wait you. I will start looking for the land outside, where there is room, and water for a garden. I am comfortable enough, yes, and busy enough, too, but I am tired to be here.'

'I am glad, Huw, glad from my heart,' he said, and turning about, speaking with his back to me. 'Leave this place. Go from the reach of their eyes, at least. From their tongues you will never travel far enough.'

'You have heard a little, too, then,' I said.

'To spare,' he said. 'I will help with everything. At the stables, we are. We have all got a wagon. More comfortable, and not so crowded as Damaglou's. Have an asado with us tonight.'

'Right,' I said. 'I will tell the Widow.'

We had gone on, those days, with nothing said, and everything done. Strange it is, that if you are doing something you know to be wrong, all can go on as before as if nothing is given plain speech. Open your mouth, and you will hardly believe it is you speaking, and you would much rather stop your ears than listen. But you know it is true, and the truth, then, belongs to a monster.

When I came back that night she was waiting for me in the kitchen, starched cap, black shawl, white apron and wool slippers, and not in the chair I had made for her, but in the worn crate nailed to be a seat, with the dog's basket under, and a bit of carpet on top for the cat.

'Have you got time before you go up?' she asked me, when I was through the door.

'Yes,' I said.

'Late, you are,' she said, and no turn. 'The supper is cleared these hours.'

'I had plenty, thank you,' I said.

'Is it right what they are saying, you are looking for another place?' she asked me, with salt and vinegar, and knitting fast, still without a look.

'Clever with their mouths, they are, but not so clever as that,' I told her, because I had said not one word to anybody except Mr Gruffydd, and besides, I was thinking of the wall of planks between the shop and the washplace, where anybody could listen if they wanted. 'You have heard only what is in your head.'

'Hob-nob with that one, and out all hours, yes, but for me, giving my time and all in my house, and making everything the best and nothing too much trouble, only insults,' she said, still knitting. 'If you are going to make a habit of talking with the worst of the camp, perhaps it is time to think again.'

'Perhaps,' I said.

'Too good to you, I have been,' she said. 'Everybody is saying I am a fool to myself and no thanks to come. Your conduct is a disgrace beyond words. No shame, no thanks, nothing. And I am alone in the world, nobody except myself and my poor children. Thank God to have a roof.'

'I am paying for my share of it,' I said.

'You have never paid for what they are saying about me,' she said, and pushing in another needle. 'If you can have what you want, satisfied you are. If you were a man you would have said something before. You wanted only a bargain, Huw Morgan, and you found it.'

'What I found was in my room, that I pay for, laundry and sundries extra,' I said. 'If I was not a man, you would have a complaint.'

'Not complaining I am, only saying,' she said, and putting the knitting down. 'What shall I tell everybody? You know how they look. You know very well what they say. You, only you can do something.'

'Yes,' I said, 'You are right. No doubt about it.'

'O, well, now then, I knew you would think so, at last,' she said, and threw the knitting in the basket, and sat up, hands folded, looking at the fire. 'I have thought long about it, see. We will have to put everything to paper, first. A property agreement we will have, and I will get an advocate to do it in B.A. Nothing of mine will pass to you, in case you do go before, like poor Rupert. Half what you make will come to me, and on that we will live. For your share, you have got the run of the house, and the shop and everything free. And a good marriage, and comfortable for life. Moderate in drink, clean habits and a hard worker. Nobody could ask for more.'

'Of what?' I asked her.

'Well, of a man,' she said, surprised she was, looking up at me.

'You are counting points like cattle in a show,' I said. 'So many for the head, so many for the neck, so many for the barrel.'

'Points are not counted like that,' she said. 'Say only what you know, and less confusion.'

'I know I will make no agreement,' I said. 'No confusion, there.'

'Wait, then, wait,' she said, and held up a hand. 'Now, listen, Huw. We will live contented if we have both got what we want. Tell me where you are not willing and I will come the halfway with you. Will I say fairer?'

'I will pay for everything I have had, and the cost of the shop,' I said. 'Nothing from you I want.'

'Nothing?' she said, high in the voice and seeing somebody instead of me. 'But a bit of mine you must have to exchange what I am having from you, isn't it?'

'I am having nothing from you, and you are having nothing from me,' I said.

'Oh, well,' she said, and sat back. 'Right you are. I will do the paying in the house, and we both keep what we have got, yes? That way you can save and later we will talk about sharing. Nothing to mix, and no papers, and no old advocate to pay. Very sensible, yes. Yes. Good. Well, I will be going in the big room, back, tonight. You will be in your own room, is it? Until.'

'Until what?' I asked her, fool, like wanting to know the colour of black.

'Well, until the marriage,' she said, and getting up, and stretching, and taking off her cap, and letting the hair fall. 'Notice in the paper tomorrow by mail to B.A., and visit to the Chapel, later, and tea for everybody in the City, and an asado after Chapel, Sunday, to announce, yes?'

'No,' I said, and looking for the words to follow.

'Listen, now,' she said. 'Be sensible, Huw. No use to look sour because I am having a different room. We must save everything, is it?'

'Nothing to save,' I said.

'Blame yourself,' she said. 'Shame it is, to you, not me. No use to behave like an Indio.'

'They have been better behaved,' I said. 'Who would know they were in the house? And no shame anywhere, except with us.'

'Will you blame me, now, because I have said I will be in the big room, back, till the marriage?' she asked me, in whispers and picking up the knitting basket and holding it close. 'That night we were single, both. And those two going off, papers signed, everything. If there is shame, take it to yourself, Huw Morgan. There was no need for you to be forward ever since, and well you know it.'

'True,' I said. 'But where was I forward, except in my own room? Mine, remember, I am paying for, and nothing owing.'

'Two days are owing this moment,' she said, and a slap for the basket. 'You are not getting out of paying for it, either, remember.'

'Two weeks you shall have, and two weeks' notice I will be moving,' I said, and took the money from my pocket. 'Except to clean, please to ask permission to enter.'

'Never will I ask, and there will be no permission when its anything of mine,' she said, and looking past me almost with a smile, and in an ordinary voice. 'And you shall never have the chance to say the words, either. Sleep in the shop if you want, tonight. Never come in my house after. Clear out your business from my premises and go not later than twelve tomorrow. Lock and stock, or I will have the police on you.'

'Good-bye,' I said, and went.

In that way, a couple of minutes soon told, I left the Widow. Perhaps if I had known how she would use the knife, after, I might have listened to good sense, and spoken softer, or to say it plain, with more cunning. But I was angry, and

112

at fault, and she was in the right, from her side, and I saw it
very well. She had to look after herself, and she was in a way
to have success, except that I had never thought of myself as
a workhorse for somebody else, and nobody would catalogue
me for a partner, and neither would I be part of the furniture to be used when she wanted.

'You are well advised,' Mr Gruffydd said, before he went
back. 'Property and money, and flocks and herds, very well.
Soft words, yes, sometimes. But if you married, you would
hear them only when a banner was waved by the man in the
moon. What is the use of that for a wife? Leave it, now.'

Trouble I had next morning to find a wagon to take everything away. Rather than sleep in the house I went across to
the stable and had a bale of green hay from Kankel, but I
missed the sheets, and a good cup of tea, and I was scratchy
to wake and thinking it over I was blaming myself, especially
to find not a wagon in the yard, and everybody out in the
camp.

Donato helped me to pack, and then it was that I saw how
far I had come and what a big business I had made. The
stock of many kinds of timber was fifty times more than I
had ever dreamed of owning, and the tool chests were full of
the world's best. Outside in the back lane we put it all, with
the help of Indios sitting about, but it was coming to noon
when three carts bumped in the ruts, and a man called me
through the dust.

'Rhinberry Winn, I am,' he said. 'Good morning, then,
and peace everywhere. I heard you were in want of a wheel
or two, yes? Bullocks I have got, if it is the same. Slow, they
are, but we will have you anywhere you say, no cost.'

That was another thing I had forgotten. Well, not forgotten. But too much to do to think.

Where I was going.

'It is no trouble,' Rhinberry said. 'A barn I have got, full
made of timber, and empty. Take that for the time, and look
for better, yes?'

So off we went to Maes Hafod, and my shop came alive
in the barn. A good big place it was, of solid oak from ships,
and a roof of wooden tiles from the Andes, cool in summer,
and warm in winter. The shop went in one end, and Donato
was in the other, and nobody has ever had better. Beds we
made, and Rhinberry brought mattresses from the house,
and sheets, and from Indios on the farm we had coloured

blankets, and carpets, and covers for chairs. In a couple of days, I was better off even than with the Widow, and wondering why I had never stirred myself before. Rhinberry had at least a dozen Indio girls about the house for cooking, and laundry and cleaning, and some to spin wool and others to weave, and a lot of men curing fleeces and making rugs of fox and guanaco skins, very soft, and a luxury to have on the bed.

But custom fell off because nobody knew where I was for a little while, and by the time they did, the word was through the valley that I was cutting to pattern, and lodged in the house of an Unbeliever, and finding my level.

Doli told me, lovely fat old lump of a girl she was, when she came over just before the wedding.

'You will make no excuses,' she said, and very severe, inside the shadow of the barn, and light shining in her hair loose under the wide straw. 'We will have you to the wedding if we will come with lassos to drag you.'

'I will be there,' I said. 'Is Lal still cross with me?'

'Your business to find out,' she said.

'There has been a lot to do here,' I said. 'It takes time to put everything in order.'

'A word takes no time, only to say, and off, then,' she said. 'Did you think it might be wanted?'

'It seems silly to leave work only to say something,' I said. 'There is always time to talk.'

'Nothing so important as work, Mr Morgan says,' Doli said, looking up in reverence. 'Good God, boy, work there will be in plenty when you are dead. Half a day to ride, and wish good morning, and have a cup of tea, and to eat, and speak for yourself. Back then, and do a day's work in half the time, and know somebody is better for it. Are you ashamed because you are living here in sulphurs with an old unbeliever?'

'Ashamed only because I have not been here all the time,' I said. 'Tell Lal. Where is she?'

'At the dam and working for two with the new horse shovels,' she said. 'Back the night before the wedding, and I will put toothpicks to keep her eyes open through the service. Will you be there?'

'Yes,' I said.

'Promise,' she said. 'For that I came, see.'

'Across my heart,' I said. 'And God love you every step of

the way back, and a little sprinkle of sulphur now and again, for a reminder.'

Weddings I had been to, but that was my first in the Colony, and anything more beautiful you would have to think about. Everybody had worked for it, and all the families in the Valley were riding there, horse, trap, gig and wagonette early in the morning, and the sky a pure, pure blue, and the autumn flowers in riches, and everybody in Sunday clothes, and hundreds singing one song, and hundreds another, all going towards the Chapel through the green shade of poplars and lit by the river's shine.

So many people were crowding round the bride and groom that half of us saw them only when they came past in the carriage laughing at rice and petals. Nobody could get near the Chapel. Everybody from Maes Corwen was inside because they were family, so I had to wait till the wedding breakfast to find the girls, and three broodier hens never were, but looking lovely beyond lovely, whatever.

'A wedding it is,' I said. 'Happy and joyful. Lal, where is the smile with you, girl?'

'We are not in sorts because we had a fight with old Vrann,' Solva said, in the small voice. 'The doctor went to see him. Perhaps the Justice will want to see us.'

'Me, I did it,' Doli said, as if she had been talking about catching a horse. 'I broke a demijohn over him. If he had died we could have buried him, and nobody having a loss, drunken toad, he is.'

'Hisht,' Lal said, as if she had said it many times, and knew it was useless. 'Mr South will have no interest in our business. After today, not much for us.'

'More brothers and sisters, halves, than a farrow from a mongrel sow,' Doli said. 'He will make us three whites among thirty-odd of his spew. Poor Mama should be alive. She would have him, both barrels, or one .45.'

'My father has decided to claim his natural children before the Justice,' Lal said. 'Last night he swore he was coming in today to do it. There was trouble, but we left too early this morning.'

'He was off the floor where I left him,' Doli said. 'I looked to see.'

'Your fault,' Solva said. 'I should have stayed. I would have dragged him outside to the rats.'

'Now, listen, both of you,' Lal said, and weary. 'I am

115

tired to hear what we should have done. We will spoil the wedding, and no luck for life.'

'If I will see a bit of luck, I wonder will I know it?' Doli said, to the sky. 'I have prayed soreness in my knees, but nothing comes.'

'More good will come if you will pick a bit of soreness in your old nose,' Solva said. 'Mama was always in Chapel, and Bible classes, and choir, and readings, and teas. What did she have for it? We have been the same, and getting the same sauce, too. Nothing.'

'We are making a fine day for Mr South,' Lal said, though she had hardly looked at me. 'He will be sorry to be invited.'

'I am only sorry for what I have heard,' I said. 'But could you tell me? Why should he want to swear his children? Conscience for what he has done?'

The three looked at each other, empty.

'Vrann wants us to marry only when he says so,' Doli said, and from the look of her eyes, trying to pretend she was listening to somebody else. 'He wants Solva to marry with Blethyn Rhys. The fat fool, nearly dead with drink, he is. That would bring him all the land to the south. He wants me to marry Iorwerth Probert. Have you seen an old giraffe? That would bring all the land on the north. The land to the east is richest and more than the rest together. Lal would have to marry for that. If we say yes, he will let everything come to us. If we say no, he will bring in the Indios, and the property will go in pieces for each. My mother's property as well, that she left only to us. Now you know as much as us.'

The white flowers in Lal's hat waved from side to side, and the polish of dark hair below sent lights and shadows gold and bronze in the coils, turning, shaking the no into no, no, no.

'Who would you have to marry, Lal?' I asked her, and listening to the words, if they were mine, but I would never have known it.

'Guess, now,' Solva said. 'A fat black calf I will give for a prize.'

'No,' Lal said, and turning in a temper, and eyes big. 'Say nothing, will you?'

'He asked and an answer there is,' Solva said, in the small voice, a child's, and dead. 'Why not, then?'

'All that side belongs to Mr Matithiah Morse,' Doli said. 'He wants to marry her, and he is willing to convey the land. Last night Vrann said so. For that, and a couple of other things, I smashed a new demijohn on him. Smashed, it was. In pieces, there.'

'Now then for you,' Solva said. 'And I gave him a good kick, but I had my slippers on, and I have got a toe with me, so sore to lift from the ground. Matithiah, if you can only think, and Lal. Mrs Lal Matti Mumpo. Mother-by-law to Mrs Nelya Peninnah.'

'A taste in the mouth I have got,' Doli said. 'Every word Mama is saying, I can hear.'

'O hisht,' Lal said. 'You are making us sound like a lot of old Indios, drinking and fighting. Huw, will you come and watch us in the rope and saddle competition? But if you see my father before we do, move. He will be just right to start swearing in front of everybody. We are ashamed to be born, sometimes.'

They went behind the chapel to the dressing tent, and their peons brought the horses, a cream, a chestnut and a bay.

'Where is the black stallion?' I asked Lal, when they came out in riding clothes, each a different colour. 'He is the best I have seen.'

'The best you will ever see,' she said. 'He is in pasture for the racing. Are you going to have a bet on me to win this?'

'On,' I said. 'Ten pesos, even, with old Tibbald.'

'Would he bet against me?' Lal asked, and in a flare.

'On Solva,' I said.

'Best horse, yes,' Lal said. 'He was right. But if you lose, I will pay. With ten kisses.'

'Lose,' I said. 'Win nothing. I will bet on everything.'

A handbell rang and everybody was shouting and Lal held her hat and ran because the competitors were lining up. About thirty horses were on one side, and all the girls were on the other with harness and saddles in pieces in front of them. The winner was the first to put the harness together, and lasso the horse, and saddle the mount, and ride to a post about two hundred yards away.

Silas Ieuan Pendar blew a whistle, and the crowd was in screams, there, and the girls were looking for straps and buckles and fitting them, and dropping a bit, and stamping, and scrambling, and Lal seemed slower than anybody.

Standing there, and I felt somebody push to the side and saw the shadow, and smelling wine strong on the breath.

'A word with you, Mr Morgan,' the little voice said above me, and I knew.

'Very well, Mr Corwen,' I said. 'Here, or anywhere.'

'No more hanging about my daughters,' he said, and swallowing soft, in a run of alcohol. 'Let me tell you, now. Keep away from my place. If not, trouble, me and you.'

'Your place is your own,' I said. 'Your daughters are not property.'

'I will do what is best, and first to the hand,' he said, pale blue in the eye, looking a little to the side, and not firm on his feet. 'They will marry their own kind. Understand that.'

'That is your business,' I said. 'I will do what is mine.'

No sign of doctors or demijohns about him, shaved clean, and combed under a panama hat curled at the sides, and a white jacket and long black bow, and an Indio sash over grey riding-britches, and a thumb hooked in the pocket, and black topboots. A good head taller than I was, and broad, too. And well in drink.

'Make sure you are your side of the fence,' he said, no blink. 'The Widow had to tell you, and put you in the street. I will use no words, remember. Treat my girls with respect.'

'Respect they will always have from me,' I said. 'Big tiddlers are kings in small puddles. Threaten somebody else.'

'Warning,' he said, and lifting a finger. 'Only once.'

The smell of wine comes clear to this day, sickish in the sun.

'Wind,' I said.

'Last night I told them,' he said, and smiling down at me, and tipping forward. 'You, I have told today. Crush you in the earth and no sign after.'

A few had come to get between us, and he went off among friends, and laughing, and the green bottle was busy in the light, and with them.

Gyntaf Glyn nodded at him going away, and looked glum at me.

'Careful there,' he said. 'He will go ten days on the drink and never know what he has done, or where he has been. The girls are having a terrible life with him. Since children.'

'A will of their own, each of them,' I said.

'Not when that one is about,' he said. 'Sober, he is good as gold, see. Very kind. No harm to a fly. But in drink? The

118

three of them he has chased naked from the house before now.'

'I know nothing of their affairs,' I said.

'Nobody else wants to, either, if they have got sense,' he said. 'Lunatic, he is. Everybody keeps an eye open for him. You had better keep two.'

The three girls had gone from the competition, and I looked everywhere. A few people I knew, but most were strange to me because they were in perhaps for the first time that year from all over the valley, and a day to remember for them, with games and foot races for everybody, and a singing festival later. Then, it was, that I saw Tom, Tot, in his Sunday swallow-tail and starched linen shoot eggs thrown in the air, and hit the ash off a cigar in the mouth of Simeon John at the end of the field. With the .45 pistol, there were many to hit the spots clean from the six of diamonds at thirty paces, and the winners had to hit tossed coins. No comfort to me, either, when Vrann Corwen, drunk, was a winner, and cheered by everybody. Mog, Moke, jumped from the crossbar of a gate twenty feet high, and landed on the back of a mare sent under at a gallop, and after, they held a wild colt to be harnessed, and a little coin was put in each stirrup, and they set his boots in place, and let him go. Never mind what the colt did, if he stood on his hinds, or his fores, or turned to bite, or bucked fores and hinds, or galloped and stopped, or jumped and bucked, nothing moved Mog, and when the colt was tired and led in, the coins were still in place under the soles of the boots. The man had not moved an iota.

But he was drunk.

Tom, Tot, was drunk.

Everybody that I could see except the women, and even the youngest men, all of them were drunk or well gone. But they were all happy, and when quarrels started, there were plenty to get between and smooth everything.

'Well,' Jared Perkin said, in the best of humour, and a bottle in his pocket. 'How are you enjoying yourself with us, Mr Morgan?'

'Very well indeed, thank you,' I said. 'I was looking for the Corwen girls.'

'Gone to the City to Miss Kathi's,' he said. 'Vrann has had a drop today, see. They always go to the City then. They would be the first in everything here, foot races or horses or shooting, yes. But not when he has had a drop. A bit handy with the whip, he is.'

I galloped Merri all the way back to Maes Hafod, and thankful for the quiet, and the light of candles, and a chair, and nobody to talk to. A feeling of murder I had for Mr Matti Mumpo, and if silence cannot cleanse the mind, at least it has its peace.

8

A house I wanted, and grazing for sheep and perhaps a few cattle, and a garden big enough to yield the year's vegetables, and of course, enough flowers to make an evening's walk a pleasure. Before I spoke a word to Lal, I swore I would have the place bought and in growth. Funny it is that thoughts come in such a way. The girl first, it should be. But a girl needs a place to live, and a barn is nothing, especially after Maes Corwen, and besides, Angharad was coming.

Tegwyn, Toldo, did her best to help when I went over for the last of my washing.

'A place there is, not farmed these ten years, on the other bend of the river from here,' she said. 'Water, yes, and a bit of salt, but it will take cattle. Have it myself, I would, but I will have enough to do in the Territory.'

Off I went to look, but I was used to the bench and tools, and a stretch of weeds and bushes and pampas for miles brought me to feel helpless.

'The old Maeldrod place,' Rhinberry said. 'The son of a drunkard, and sold it to a Portuguese, and he died. See the Justice and take the titles, and we will have a couple of teams of oxen down there. In a week, you will have to look again. Green it will be.'

It was, too. My name went in the book, and I paid the fees, and Rhinberry and his Indios cleared the ditches and let the water run, and put a plough through the growth, and turned everything. Never will I forget the evening I went out there after work, and saw the huge squares of fresh furrows, and all the land beyond, and wanting to dance high in the air because it was in my name, and at last I could come home to my own place.

'Bricks for the house we will mix and bake here,' he said. 'Bring in trees to plant against the wind and heat, and stone from Port Madryn. Glass and everything else from the Co-operative. I will have the men to work, starting tomorrow. Six weeks, in, before the winter.'

Very simple to say, and as easy to do, and when I saw the stones down for the floor, I was off to Maes Corwen, because I knew from Jones, Price Special, she was there.

'Lal,' I said, at the back of the house, near the harness room. 'I have come to find you.'

'Huw,' she said, and a hand under her heart. 'If my father saw you.'

'Never mind him,' I said. 'You, I have come to speak to. A house I am building, and finished in a month. Furniture I will make. You promised to buy sheep and cattle and look at the land. When will you come?'

'Go you from the house before you will be seen,' she said, and taking my hand and trying to run, but I was holding back. 'Will you let me die before you will hurry? Please, Huw. He will take the first, pistol or knife.'

'But I am speaking to you, not him,' I said.

'Go down to the river,' she said. 'I will be there with tea in minutes. But be sure to go out of our fence. Come here, boy.'

O, and she kissed me. Years, yes, it has been, but the softness is with me still, as then, so now, not a moment of memory lost. If I have lived to carry that, without anything else, there is nothing I have missed.

No page for history, no news to anybody, but between two, only a little kiss, though I will swear nothing was small about it.

Merri must have taken me to the river because I could see only the sun, and to this day it is the light I remember. Lal came with a basket, stretch gallop and jumping the fence, and playing scold because no fire was ready, or wood gathered.

'Helpless, you are, boy,' she said. 'Go down there and bring back every twig and piece of bark, or you shall have nothing to drink except the river. My father will see from the house, so we must be careful with the smoke.'

'Doli and a demijohn are not much,' I said. 'I thought he was murdered.'

'Across the neck she broke it,' she said. 'Still in hurt with him. But a hurt is nothing. He laughs. If I will have sons like him, but thinking different, and not drinking, I will be satisfied.'

122

By yourself, you make many a fine speech to thousands, and everything about love will be easy. But in front of the crowd it will be different, and beside Lal it was no better. Croaking like an old frog. I was.

And she sitting, smiling, lovelier than I could ever think.

Perhaps because when she put a hand in mine, as sweet peas want only sticks to climb, what I had to say began to come easy, and love was in every word but no longer with pain. We are in torture of mind, I suppose, because we are really thinking what we would have to suffer without her, and I am sure that blind though love is supposed to be, blind selfish it really is, and both eyes wide all the time.

'Tell me about the house, now then,' Lal said, after I had talked of moving the shop to Rhinberry's but without a word about the Widow. 'Is there much land for grazing?'

'At the back, as far as the hills, and there is common land both sides,' I said. 'Rhinberry says I could have up to a hundred head of cattle, and perhaps three hundred sheep to start. Forage we have got to put down, and feed for the winter. If I knew more I could do more. But my head is in the shop. My heart is with you.'

'Safe, it is,' she said. 'I will ride over to Maes Maeldrod and see what there is. I have got cattle and sheep of my own. You will need horses. I will send a troop tomorrow. You do your work, and the rest I will do.'

'Thankfully,' I said. 'Why were you so sorrowful about Matti Mumpo the other day, and today no worry?'

With the yellow of the leaves bright behind her, and the shine of the river beyond, she laughed up, at the willows arching deep green over us.

'Solva told Dada she put a special edge in the small axe,' she said. 'Not for him, but for Matti Mumpo, if there is more talk of marrying. He knows she is exactly like him. If she speaks, it is done. There has been no more talk.'

'Let us marry now, and stop any talk,' I said.

'I am ready when I know Doli and Solva are given equal shares with me, and in the bank, or on paper at the notary's,' she said. 'I know Dada. He will say anything, or pretend, or bully and bluff anybody not to part with a spoonful of sand. We have each got a third of Mama's property, but without his consent we can touch nothing. It has got to be protected.'

'Marry, and then demand,' I said.

'There has been too much of that,' she said. 'He would

take us for years through the courts, and the lawyers would have everything. No. I know my father. I will marry the moment those two have got all they are entitled to. And I will come to you with plenty. So be patient, yes?'

'Patient,' I said. 'Everybody here is mad because of property, money, animals, anything except living.'

'Their fathers and their grandfathers worked too hard for it to be thrown to Indios and lawyers, with not a good day's work in them,' she said, and not looking at me. 'We have worked for years on the water, and out in the camp, my sisters and me, too. It is ours. We will have it. Patience, wait, and get.'

She gathered the tea cups, and I splashed water on the fire.

'Have you been in love before, Huw?' she asked me, at the river's edge.

'Yes,' I said.

'But never married,' she said.

'No,' I said, and thinking of Bron, and feeling treachery part of my bones.

'She was married, then?' she said.

'Yes,' I said.

'O,' she said. 'Well. How could you stay so long with the Widow, and knowing what everybody was saying?'

What to say, then, what to say, indeed.

'That shop she built especially for me,' I said, thankful for a fact. 'And lodgings of the best.'

'There is kind she was,' she said.

'She could call me ungrateful,' I said.

'She is calling you more than that, be sure,' she said, wiping the cups, and hanging them on twigs. 'Best to be deaf. Except for one voice.'

'Have you been in love before?' I asked her.

'Yes,' she said. 'With you, since I could think of a picture of somebody.'

'But property first,' I said. 'Papers, and stamps. Love after.'

'You will learn one day,' she said. 'I would go now with you, straight, and never come back. But my father is nothing like Eynon Caerog Evans. Alys has had a lot of help since he came back from seeing them. Do you think my father would help you? Think how we would feel if my sisters came to have nothing. Because I was impatient. I am the eldest. It is my duty. When you are my duty, you will have nothing to want.'

'I know it,' I said. 'But when, when, when?'

A bullet I had heard only a couple of times before, but never near me.

The flat snap! took the hearing out of my head but the leaves fell on me, and Lal was running towards her horse and up, and I saw the man's shadow move through the trees, a quick passing against sunlight on the trunks, and Lal turned in a gallop, bending over the horse's neck to miss the branches, and pulling the carbine out of the holster.

For minutes I waited, and then I saddled Merri, and went in the same way, but though we came soon enough to the pasture, with a view for miles across the flat green, nothing moved, and silence everywhere, such a silence, that you would think you heard the clouds in travel like a hand gentle to smooth silk. Up to Maes Corwen I went, but though the door was open, and fire in the fireplace, nobody came when I called, and after minutes of riding all about, and not a soul, I turned Merri and walked the long way down to the river, but still nobody, and not a sound.

Back to the farm, and Rhinberry waiting for me with tea in the kettle.

'News,' he said, and holding the empty pipe to his mouth. 'We are put from Maeldrod's. The title cannot be bought. It is held in possession, and the Justice sent the police to stop work and have everything off this afternoon.'

'But I have paid the fees,' I said.

'Mistake of the clerk,' Rhinberry said. 'Better to think of somewhere else, and keep the loss. We will look tomorrow. Two families are going to Brazil. If they are not renting, they might sell.'

On that we went to bed, but if I slept I was seeing Maes Maeldrod and my name on the gate, and if I was waking I was seeing everything and my name on nothing, and Matti Mumpo had an arm about Lal.

Off I went next morning to the port of Rawson, a long way on horse, and a poor place made poorer by a big house for the Governor, and little sheds and huts and toldos for most of those he was governing.

The Clerk of Works said he was sorry for the mistake, but a lot of records had to be looked through, and then the rightful owner was found, and out I had to go. Vyrnwy translated for me because it was all in Castellano, and in that language there is no telling what is to happen, especially for one learning.

'Leave it,' Vyrnwy advised me. 'Wheels are within wheels, here. But mark my words, that land will go for years without a shovel in it.'

'Too lazy to work themselves, whoever it is, but not letting somebody else,' I said. 'Who is the owner?'

'The name down there is a Syrian or a Lebanese,' Vyrnwy said. 'Standing for somebody else, no doubt.'

'Please to tell the clerk I want the name,' I said. 'Perhaps he will sell. Or rent.'

Vyrnwy shook his head like a grey old donkey.

'Waste your time,' he said, and went to the door, and the clerk shut the register and took it away. 'It would lead from one to another, and all the way back to the first, and round again. Somebody is sure you will have no place here. If it is Matti Mumpo, millions are against you. If it is Vrann Corwen, more millions. Together, double.'

But when we unsaddled in Dalar Roberts' stable to rest the horses, Evans, Sideways, was at the fire having a maté, and he came, walking slow to where we were, and swinging the belly, hands in jacket pockets and smiling.

'You thought you would be a neighbour, Mr Morgan,' he said. 'The Maeldrod place is bought. Find somewhere else.'

'If you want to rent, I will farm it,' I said.

'Thank you,' he said, and turned the balloon, and walked off.

'More millions,' Vyrnwy said. 'Come to the house for a cup of tea.'

'Where will I look for a place?' I asked him.

'Wherever you look, it will be denied,' he said. 'Whoever you talk to will be warned. Remember that Morwen has got friends, too. He is one.'

'But you are not,' I said.

'I have known her from long before,' he said, and serious. 'Rupert had to drink to be from her. I could have been the second. But I stayed dirty. When she tried to kiss, I was black. So that was settled. She wants what she has got, and a man to worry her, sometimes, when she says so. The rest of the time, she will be beak, beak, beak. Without the beak, no Morwen. A gizzard, not a soul, she has got.'

'Where will I build a place?' I asked him. 'You know the Colony, and everybody in it. Where?'

'Nowhere,' he said flat. 'You have got a bit in the bank, and you will work every day for more. Like me, then. But the work comes from your hands. The people you are up against are having the work done for them. Each little sheep is a moving factory. Every year it will produce wool. Every bullock grows meat. Every hectare brings corn or something else. Peons do the work. Indios look after the animals. These others give the orders, and put the money in the bank. Or the Co-operative. Some are getting more from there in a year by interest than you will earn by the sweat in ten. Where will you find a place?'

'A lot of them work hard,' I said. 'Even the girls.'

He looked at me, long, in pity, and breathed out.

'True, most of them work hard, but how often do you see them?' he asked me. 'They are not the ones we are talking about, are they? And the girls? They work for nothing except their food and lodge, and a few clothes. Most of them, they will have the least their fathers can give when they marry. Some will give more, yes. But enough for years of work?'

'Let them do what they like,' I said. 'A house and a shop I have got to build. Where?'

'You are in the hands of millions,' he said. 'You will never put one stone on another.'

'Did you tell me that this morning when we started?' I asked him.

'Would you have believed me?' he asked me, going into the forge, and smells of burnt hoof, and a dusty warmth of cooling cinders coming about us. 'You could have the shed next door. How long would you last? This is my property. But a talk to the right man, and who am I?'

'Who is the right man?' I asked him. 'I will see if a talk of mine will do good.'

He was laughing in the darkness, and I could hear his hands scraping on a shelf for matches.

'Matti Mumpo is one,' he said. 'Evans, Sideways, and Vrann Corwen will come handy for two more.'

'How about Mr Armon Tudor?' I asked him. 'He would be honest, to say the least.'

'How about his wages?' Vyrnwy asked me. 'One word, and he will be out looking for another chapel.'

'We are thinking differently from our fathers,' I said. 'To them, preachers were of the elect.'

'When they were strict, not in our time,' Vyrnwy said,

127

and lighting a candle, and holding his hat against the draught. 'They are elect for an hour or two on Sundays and a couple of times in the week, and if somebody is dead, or getting married, or having a douse for baptism. A ransom it cost my old man to have me dipped for the kingdom, and he reminded me every day till he died. And still he is grumbling down there, I bet you.'

'You are worse than Rhinberry,' I said.

'Born free thinking outside the chapel, and his father was the same before him,' Vyrnwy said, pumping the bellows and a red eye opening in the coals and coming yellow and bright white. 'My father was a deacon. The Bible I know back to front, and a preacher he wanted me to be. But when I was fifteen I had a baby with an Indio girl. I loved her, yes, the colour of this iron, look. My father sent them off. So to hell, I stayed to make shoes. And be blacker than any of them, and to chapel only to sing and have a cup on the house, after.'

He brought out a bottle and we had a good nip of that to keep out the fever, and a beef sandwich, and lettuce from the patch.

'I will have to go and see Matti Mumpo,' I said. 'Except for Beretroff, I have done nothing to him.'

'Good,' Vyrnwy said. 'But supposing he will not want to see you?'

'He came to see me,' I said.

'Suiting himself, and different when the boot is made for somebody else,' Vyrnwy said. 'Count the Co-operative shareholders and put in the Board and Committee, and you will find if one is against somebody, they are all against. Let me tell you, now.'

Back to the farm I went, and into the candlelight of the barn, and Lal sitting there with a book open, and hat still on, and a smile so beautiful I could think of nothing else. On my knees I went, and resting my head, and smelling the rose-and-sage of her, and holding her dear to me.

'I know about Maes Maeldrod,' she said. 'A bad farm, in any case, so no loss. Water, yes, but a lot of salt, and in the path of the flood, and nothing to save you. Will you go where I want?'

'To China, only say,' I said.

'The troop of horses I will leave here,' she said. 'A girl is getting me coffee. I will have that, and go.'

128

'To Maes Corwen tonight?' I said, thinking of leagues of darkness. 'Let Rhinberry ask a girl to settle a room in the house.'

'Go on with you, boy,' she said, and laughing. 'Three hours is all it is.'

'I will come with you,' I said.

'Where will I wait for you?' she asked me, a little angel, and I thought of her thoroughbred and poor Merri. 'I must be up in the north corral at six.'

'I will help more by staying here, that is what you are saying,' I said. 'Did you find out who was shooting at us?'

'Yes,' she said, direct. 'There will be no more.'

'Vrann?' I asked her. 'Is he such a fool?'

She shook her head, looking at me, but seeing nothing.

'Ask no questions, please,' she said, sadder than I had ever thought possible. 'There was no hurt to anybody, thank God. Leave it, will you?'

'Right, you,' I said. 'In a quiet place like this, and such abiders by the law that are living in it, a lot happens that could sound strange outside, indeed.'

'It would be denied in the bowels by every one of them,' she said, and a smile coming, so I knew we were over the worst. 'What is in the family is kept from everybody. What is outside is common talk, but not for strangers. They hide their eyes not to be asked questions.'

'And what about the Widow and Mr South?' I asked her.

'Known from the start, and a piece of fat business for Jones, Price Special, if it came off,' she said, and laughing. 'A good commission he would have got from her, of course, for sending you there. And from you, too, if you were fool enough. A rich wife is not every day.'

'Who will get commission for you?' I asked her.

'Me, and every bit I will keep for myself,' she was saying in my ear, and nearly throttling me, so that I knew her strength, and thinking of the way she could throw the boleadoras and the lasso, and a lot of other things.

A tap at the door, and she was three paces off before the girl came in with coffee, and Rhinberry behind with a grill of steaks, and loaves, and telling us to eat hearty.

'Somebody is waiting for you in the yard,' he said. 'Beretroff wants to know do you want him to start work. He is ready, and standing very tired with him.'

'I wonder where he left Miss Nelya Peninnah,' Lal said,

teeth in steak, and cutting with an upward slice of the knife, almost taking a piece from the tip of the nose, but not quite, the real Gaucho style that I could never master. 'How long will she leave him alone?'

'Tell me,' I said. 'If he was selling wine to Indios and her father got rid of him for it, why is Nelya allowed to run with him? Why does her father allow it? She is under age. There are police here.'

Lal and Rhinberry looked at each other and laughed without a sound.

'She has been of age for long enough, and no policeman would move further than the nearest maté,' Rhinberry said. 'A joke it is, yes, but a serious one. For her, and for her father, and for everybody near her. When she was little she was running with everybody. Now she is big and she will run with everybody twice. If they will not see her from distance, and ride for life, see.'

'Do you know enough to talk?' Lal asked him, no jokes.

'Who does not?' Rhinberry said, and looking at her straight, for truth.

'Shame to you for speaking,' she said, and looking for salt.

'A question I was asked, and I answered,' he said, not eating. 'Everybody is ready for dirty stories about her, but to talk sensible, no. Very few men ever want to put eyes on her again. I will say that. If a boy will run after girls, one after another, nothing is said. A girl is called everything.'

'You are talking six of one and half a dozen of the other,' Lal said. 'Excusing yourself in the place of somebody else.'

'Listen well, again, Mistress Corwen,' Rhinberry said. 'Sunday school teacher you are, and your mother before, and a strict family. What will you know of Nelya Peninnah? Only what the jokers say? I am giving no excuses. If a woman is free with herself, who will say no? The beauty we will have, and the woman we love. It is the agony of her. Most of us will always run from that.'

'Wait, now, Rhinberry,' I said, because Lal was looking at him as she had looked at me, without seeing him. 'Why not ask Beretroff to have to eat?'

'I will go, first,' Lal said, no hurry. 'He will not stay where I am.'

'Because he has been with Nelya Peninnah?' Rhinberry asked.

Lal stopped chewing to look at him.

'I am unconcerned,' she said, to kill.

'My fault,' I said, and quick. 'Perhaps he can have something outside.'

'He has been eating and drinking well these minutes,' Rhinberry said. 'Nobody goes from this house in want. Will he stay to work, Huw?'

'Yes,' I said.

A lot of shouting had been going on in the yard, and Rhinberry went to the door to see what was the matter, but it was pushed open and him almost with it, and Vrann Corwen came in, straight to me.

'A troop of horses we have tracked here,' he said, in the voice so little and so soft for a man, but with the danger in the tone and the sight of his eyes. 'An explanation, if you please.'

'I brought them, Dada,' Lal said, through a mouthful, and cutting another, no interest.

'They are here, and this man is here, and I gave him good warning,' he said, not looking at her. 'He shall be taught that words have a meaning.'

But if others are very good with pistols and knives, I am the best with any tool in the shop. So when his hand moved, so did mine, and the small mallet I threw hit him exactly on the top of the head and spun off, and he went over backwards, flat.

'O, Dada, my little one,' Lal said, and threw the bread away, and ran to him and knelt, and passed a thumb over the bump. 'No cut, and no blood. Where is the water?'

'Off my property, quick now,' Rhinberry said to the men in the doorway, too surprised to have lost the smiles from their faces. 'I will have you for trespass. Go, you.'

Indio girls came when he called outside, and they lifted Vrann, and carried him out, and Lal went with them, and looked back to me.

'If you have knocked a bit of sense in him, no harm,' she said. 'You very nearly had a horse whipping. But I wish Doli and Solva had been here. A medal you would have had.'

'Pick of the Colony, that one,' Rhinberry said, and shutting the door. 'But before you will have her, Vrann will murder her, and you, and anybody else, too.'

9

Some words will always stay in the mind, and even the sound of the voice, like stones hidden in long grass waiting to be tripped over. They come to me now, said as they were, with the cold still in them, of the unbeliever, one looking at everything as it is instead of believing or hoping for something else better for everybody. Of course, Rhinberry thought I took no notice, but he was wrong, though what more I could have done afterwards, God knows.

A man shouted to me outside Gaiman the night I had the papers with the rights to the farm of Leishon John all signed and paid for in my pocket, and said the horse belonging to Maes Corwen was in the stable of Hywel, Little Bit, and to tell one of the girls about it. I shouted back to him, but he went off in the darkness, galloping. The village was black, except for a couple of windows, and at the house of one I knocked, and Jezrael Hughes came out. Hywel, Little Bit, he said, was a couple of leagues off the road to the City, but unless I knew the path, no use to try.

'Come in, Mr Morgan,' he said. 'A cup, or a glass is ready.'

'I must be in the City tonight,' I said.

'To have the papers with the Justice, is it?' he said.

'The ink is not blotted, and you know,' I said.

'These days we have known, and waiting to give advice,' he said. 'The family going out has had a dispute, see. My wife is his sister, and she has got half share to the property. He has sold to you. Did he tell you about her?'

'Not a word,' I said.

'Then you have not got full title,' he said. 'And there are grazing rights on the land bought and paid for these years. Anything about that?'

'No,' I said.

'And the water is only by permission of the neighbour to

132

the north,' he said. 'No work has been done for years, so the water goes to the neighbour on the south. It passes through. There is no right to fill the ditches. Anything about that?'

'Nothing,' I said. 'But I am thankful we met. I will go back now, and have it right, on paper.'

'Useless,' he said. 'Take the police with you. It is still useless. You will have to deal with your neighbours. It will cost you nothing only money. I am having the same trouble here. Same neighbours as you, because the owners are the same. Take the advice of one who never took advice, and had nothing but pains after. First thing in the morning, see the best advocate in the city.'

But straightway I made up my mind, and instead of going here and there, I went back to the city and got Vyrnwy to come with me to Justice, Dab and Blow, and I talked, and Vyrnwy translated, and at the end, the Justice sat back, with a toothpick busy under the flat of his hand before his face.

'You have got all rights, and none,' Vyrnwy said. 'You have got nothing from the water company to say you may have water. The grazing rights and the sister's half share, Mr Justice will look into. But he advises no building or any further expense, and if you put animals in, expect to lose them. There is not a foot of fence on the place except your neighbours.'

'But the papers say I have got perfect rights everywhere,' I said.

'You have,' Vyrnwy said. 'Clear and perfect except in the most important matters such as water and grazing and inheritance. You could be put from there any time.'

'These papers I have paid for are a fraud, then,' I said.

'No,' Vyrnwy said. 'They are clear title to use the property of that man Leishon John. Did you ask why the family is going to Brazil?'

The man told me his uncle has got a big place in São Paulo, and they are going up to work there,' I said. 'There was not enough land on the farm to live on.'

'But plenty to drink wine and gamble,' Vyrnwy said. 'Did you see the house? The state of the fields? The garden? No wonder they were ready to sell to you. Who else would give them ten centavos?'

'I will go now and have a little talk,' I said.

'Go, you,' he said. 'Next time you feel the money itching in your pocket, see Mr Justice first.'

Well, riding out there in the evening with enough light was a different matter from finding it in the dark from another direction. Nearly four o'clock, it was, when I got there, and I had to hammer on the roof to get the man up. In trousers and shirt, he was, and long hair like a rat's tangle and barefoot and pulling his beard, holding the candle over his head from the draught, looking at me through the crack and steadying the door with a knee.

'No,' he said. 'From sleep I am, and fancy waking the family this hour because you have repented a bargain. Keep what you have got, Mr Morgan, and leave sensible and in peace, and I will keep what I have got, and good night, one and all, here.'

'Every peso I have paid I want back this minute, or I will take you to bits first, and every straw in your den will come down after,' I said. 'Open up.'

He was not quick enough, because my boot was against the door from the start, and I had him by the shirt collar, and in, and over the table, and the candlestick rolling on the earth floor and he had no space in his gullet to shout. But his wife came, and a couple of girls, and screaming to boil old kettles between them.

But I had him, and when his face was purple, the wife came with a box, and my pesos were on the top, and them I took and put on one side of the table, and the papers we had signed I put on the other.

'So it was earlier,' I said. 'Pick up your papers, and I will pick up my money. When your sister has signed her share, and when your neighbours have signed over the grazing, and the water company has given right to use water. I will buy again. And let me thank you for strict education. I am no longer the fool I was.'

Off I went, and they were calling me everything, but I got back to Maes Hafod in broad day, and very happy, and to work, then, without need of sleep. Rhinberry came to get my list of shopping and went in the trap to the city, and I was working on the armchairs for our kitchen and Doli rode in breakneck and stopped outside the door and slid off the saddle, it seemed, in one move.

'What is this message you got about a horse of ours at Hywel, Little Bit's?' she shouted to me, coming in, no Good Morning and no smile, either. 'How did you know?'

Well, I told her about the man shouting to me in Gaiman,

and not seeing him in the dark, but she stood frowning as if I had the horse in my pocket.

'How did he know you?' she asked me. 'Dark, too?'

'I have never thought of it,' I said, in all truth. 'But he had my name right.'

'How many do you know in Gaiman?' she asked me, still frowning.

'Two or three to nod, and if somebody passes, one to talk to,' I said. 'To say everything right, nobody.'

'But he knew you,' she said, looking into the sun of the farmyard. 'Your name, and Maes Corwen. And the horse was at Hywel, Little Bit's. I found him this morning. If Solva had not got your message from Jezrael first, and my father had got it instead, he might have come here again.'

'He would find everybody to welcome him,' I said.

She looked all the way round, ready to drop with impatience.

'I am not here for a joke, or to pass time with a cup,' she said, to the racks of tools. 'Lal will be here this afternoon. Say nothing to anybody about the horse, will you?'

'What is the importance of one horse?' I asked her. 'You have got hundreds.'

'Tanfl has never lost a race,' she said. 'He is the best in Patagonia, and we love him. How he got loose, or who took him would be good to know. Good-bye now.'

Off she went, not another word, and left behind the colour of trouble almost to be seen in the air, like a pink smoke.

Real trouble started that afternoon, when Morris, Carpenter, and Harries, Sawmill, stopped the trap. They got down, knocking the dust from themselves, and gold flying from Harries' white beard, and Morris came, wiping his face.

'We have both come over for a word, Mr Morgan,' he said, and looking to see if anybody was near. 'Listen, then. What is this we are hearing about you attacking Leishon John, and assaulting his wife, and stealing their money in front of the children?'

Both of them were listening, and looking, and wiping sweat and dust in between while I told them, but Harries, Sawmill, shook his head and put his hat on straight.

'That will do for everywhere else,' he said. 'But not here, no indeed.'

'You will go in front of The Twelve if you are not very careful,' Morris, Carpenter, said.

'Not only that,' Harries, Sawmill, said, in his bubbly skim-milk voice. 'It will come to a question if we can afford to deal with you. We have done good business together, and I have done my share to promote your success among us, you cannot deny that, can you, Mr Morgan?'

'I am denying nothing,' I said. 'I took what was mine after fraud had been put on me. How does this concern if you can supply me?'

'We have both come over to decide that,' Morris, Carpenter, said, and wiping his hat very careful over his sleeve. 'Look here, there is very strong criticism about you in the Colony. Nothing about your work, no. It is the moral climate you are moving in, see. The way you treated poor Morwen Glyn, for one. Coming to live here after, when you know what this man is. Indios about the place day and night. Running with this one and that. And now this, with Leishon. A drinker he is, and having hard luck, yes. Three young children in a year gone to their rest, see. But it is no excuse, Mr Morgan.'

'You are in no chastened frame, either, that I can see,' Harries, Sawmill, said, and looking at me as though he wished he had a magnifier to see better. 'We cannot have business with somebody behaving like this. A good book of past orders, yes, and a lot on order now. But I believe I will have to alter my mind, here.'

'A loss, no doubt, but respect for the peace,' Morris, Carpenter, said.

They both turned to the sound of a gallop, and Lal came through the yard, and slid off before the horse stopped, that I was never able to do, and I have bruised the bone trying.

To hear them greet her, you would think we had been standing arms about each other and making gifts, but Lal saw from my face that a lot was wrong.

'Well, Mr Morgan, take care then, yes?' Harries, Sawmill, said, and bowing to Lal, and going to the trap. 'Good day, Lal, and kiss your sisters, and compliments to Vrann when you see him.'

'Only for a minute we came,' Morris said to her. 'A word with Mr Morgan about business, and everything settled, yes.'

'And a word from me,' I said. 'If you want to supply me, you shall have your money and your profits. But no nonsense about moral climates, please.'

136

'Not nonsense,' Harries, Sawmill, shouted from the trap. 'A good talking to, it was. If you want to make it open before Mistress Corwen, very well. She will know soon enough. We will do no business with people like you, Mr Morgan. Final, from me.'

'Final, me, too,' Morris, Carpenter, said. 'Nothing more of any timber of mine. And good day.'

Well, I had to start again to tell Lal, but she knew.

'It was at the house first thing with the drovers,' she said. 'They heard you had murdered the family and burned the place. Solva went to the dam, and Doli went in to Gaiman, so I had to wait till she came back. What will you do if they refuse to sell wood?'

'Get it somewhere else,' I said.

'Easy to say where you have come from,' she said, and going inside, and falling in the big chair, tired. 'Who else will supply you here?'

'Where Harries gets it from, I can get it,' I said.

'The Co-operative supplies him and Morris, too,' she said. 'Have you been to the Co-operative lately?'

'No,' I said. 'No need. I have got plenty of supplies.'

'Go,' she said. 'Then you will know how you are placed. What was this man like, the one who told you the horse was at Hywel, Little Bit's?'

'I told Doli,' I said. 'It was too dark. He called my name. He must have known me.'

'A mystery,' she said, and miserable. 'If my father knew, he would go raving. He is at the dam, thank God, and Tanfi is in his stall with three, day and night, to watch him. Racing on Saturday, he is. Hywel, Little Bit, had no idea which horse he had. Too lazy to go and see, and a peon put him in the sheep corral. Sheep, mind you. If my father knew.'

'Who would try to steal him?' I asked her.

'A guess, nothing else,' she said. 'Go to the Co-op first thing. See what they say. Then tell me with a letter. I have never had a love letter. Could you write one to me, Huw?'

'Come here, girl,' I said, and rested my arm easy about her. 'I will tell you a love letter, and if my hands were not all glue and sawdust, I would stroke your hair, and each one would be a lighted silk to thread the words prettier than Tehuelche beads, and those I would put about your throat with love, but instead to tap together when you moved, they would call out with my voice, but only you would hear. And

137

I will write to you, too, but how will you have the letter?'

'Send a peon,' she said, and her face close, and whispering. 'There is nice to be in love, and if with beads or not, I shall hear. Different I am feeling. Wanting to die with you, and hoping to live and praying for sense. Not to be like Nelya Peninnah. And wanting to be.'

She pressed herself against me, and quick away, and out of the door, and waving her hat and crop, and whistling for the horse. But through the hedge of tamarisk I saw a man, young, and hair black and cut square above the eyebrows and eyes very pale, reminding me of somebody, but his skin in shadow was dark as an Indio, and he was watching Lal, and then he had gone. Thirty paces are nothing in the run I made, but though I went through the hedge like a bullock, and out the other side to the kitchen garden without cover except for cabbage, nobody could I see and nothing out to the front or up and down the road, nobody.

'Did you have a twitch, boy?' Lal said, riding out. 'For what were you jumping like an old spider with you and the hedge in ruins, look?'

'Did you bring a peon?' I asked her. 'Pale in the eye, and big, and black hair cut with a basin?'

Her face changed colour though what colour I am not sure to this day, but I saw the change and my neck came with tickles to see it.

'I brought nobody,' she said, very ordinary. 'One of Rhinberry's, perhaps.'

'Not that I have seen,' I said. 'He was looking only at you.'

She turned the bay, and gentled him, and looked back.

'I will come the moment I am wanted,' she said. 'If you want me, come to the fence on the south corral, and find the fenceguard. He will come for me. My love till then, and think of nobody, only me.'

All I wanted was in her voice, only above a whisper. For minutes I watched her galloping over the pasture, and clean land all about, but I saw nothing else move, even when she was only a dot of red going into the willows to cross the river.

'Have you got a tall Indio with grey eyes?' I asked Rhinberry when he came back.

'No,' he said. 'Funny kind of Indio, him, indeed. Only the Tehuelche is tall. Araucanos are shorter than us. Black eyes all of them have got. Unless a cross, see. A crossbreed might run grey eyes.'

He went out after I had told him, and did a bit of tracking, and seeing marks in the ground that had no meaning for me, but to him, a newspaper.

'Tehuelche,' he said. 'Came through the orchard from the path to the river and left two ponies and a dog under that old poplar. Who would that be, now?'

'After one of the girls, no doubt,' I said.

'For every one of those girls a wedding there will be when their men come from the camp to be paid,' he said. 'Never mind who he is, if another man misbehaves about them, he will have his stomach opened, and the dogs will eat his entrails while he lives. Indios are strict about their women. They worked for my girl up by there, so I am strict for them, too.'

He went back to the house calling, and I went on with work, and the girl came to say supper was ready, and behind her was Mr Armon Tudor, and a man I had never seen before.

'Mr Prosser Vaughan,' Mr Tudor said. 'Pity it is, Mr Morgan, but I felt it my duty to come to see if I could be of any help.'

'In what?' I asked him.

'You are in bad odour here,' he said. 'I am sure there is a good explanation.'

'No bad odours anywhere, except those brought in from outside,' I said.

'But after this business with Leishon John, the whole Colony is seething, no other word,' he said, and looking at Mr Vaughan. 'Seething, then.'

From the way he hissed and drew it out, I could see froth coming from all of them, busybodies, cackles, gossips, old, young, no difference.

'Look here,' I said. 'When their horses were stolen, they were off with pistols, and they were back here with prisoners tied face to tail like poultry. Who said anything?'

'Cattle thieves, that is different again,' Mr Prosser Vaughan said, in shock to think of something new. 'A family assaulted in the small hours, and women pulled from their beds, and the father strangled to whispers, and in front of the children? What is the effect?'

'A good lesson for all of them,' I said. 'Did you use your nose near them?'

'You were willing to buy the place,' Mr Tudor said.

'And build at distance after putting a match to what was on it,' I said. 'He is a thief long past the making, and many more times than once. Future business will be through a lawyer.'

'If you have the chance,' Mr Tudor said. 'You might be put from the valley.'

'Name who might,' I said.

'Everybody here, and especially those in my congregation,' he said. 'Remember that moral fervour is a bad enemy here or anywhere else.'

'Where am I in this?' I asked him.

'To condemn somebody else is to find salvation for the moment,' he said. 'Many are condemning you. That is the reason I have come here, to help.'

Rhinberry was shouting outside, and an Indio girl ran in with her eyes like stones in fright, and Beretroff came in sliding his hands on a pickhelve, and Donato behind with a fence post.

'Wait,' I said.

But a score were running behind them, and pushing through the door and only stopping to see Mr Armon Tudor, and he slipped off his cape and showed the frock and collar.

'O, sorry, indeed, Mr Tudor,' an old one said. 'This one, here, we came to see with Hywel, Little Bit. About a horse, stolen, it was.'

'I know about it, and I was told about you, and that is why I am here,' Mr Tudor said, and walking between them and me. 'Please to keep your distance, and remember there is a law, and I am witness. Was your wish to make an inquiry, Mr Hywel?'

'Well, yes, in fact, Mr Tudor, little bit, yes,' Hywel, Little Bit, said, and a little bit of a man he was, and a little bit of a head with a little bit of black hair in front. 'He was saying a Corwen horse I had in my stable, see. But every peon I had before me and not one knew a little bit about it, no, not one.'

'Mischief making, and a good leathering will teach him to have respect for others, yes, and women, too,' Mostyn Rees shouted. 'Have them all outside here, boys, is it?'

'Outside, everybody,' I said. 'Three of us will leave a few marks on some of you.'

'Wait you,' Mr Armon Tudor said. 'Nothing will be gained by more misbehaviour. Mr Prosser Vaughan has something to say, too.'

The crowd turned to see him, standing under the timber racks, and they were quieter even than when Mr Tudor spoke to them, and the air seemed to empty.

'As the Caller for The Twelve, I am here,' he said, and taking an envelope from his pocket. 'I am instructed by decision of the Senate. Huw Morgan, you will attend the meeting on Saturday, at midday, in the school, side entrance, and nobody accompanying, or representative, legal or other. Until then, your person is inviolate. Is it understood?'

'Yes,' I said.

'Clear off, the rest of you,' he said. 'Every name is down here, with every word said. Any trouble, and I will order you to immediate arrest. Out, quick.'

They went.

10

Custom came better that week than it had for a long time, perhaps because everybody wanted to see who was going in front of The Twelve. If the Widow Glyn, or Harries, Sawmill, or Morris, Carpenter, thought they had finished my business, they should have looked at my orders, all cash down, for that week alone, and they would have seen that I had months of hard work in front of me, and still plenty of stock left. But I remembered what Lal had said, and when I had the chance, in I went to the city and a talk with Mr Rhos Phillips at the Co-operative.

'Very regretful I am to say it,' he said, glasses on, and ribbon looping past the whiskers down his cheek. 'You are not a shareholder, so I can make no exception. We are having great trouble to bring in timber because of the shipping situation. So all we are getting can only go to the older co-operators, and none anywhere else. If they want to sell to you, well and good.'

'What about my other orders?' I asked him. 'A list went to Jones, Price Special, only a week ago.'

'The fashion of nicknaming is an abhorrence,' Mr Rhos Phillips said, and taking off the glasses with a pinch to the nose. 'Mr Jones showed the list to me, and regretted that the items were not to be got. Not, at any rate, among our suppliers. You might have your own sources, Mr Morgan, if you are so fortunate.'

'They will be found,' I said. 'And about credit?'

'Your credit is complete,' Mr Rhos Phillips said. 'The state of finance, at the moment, does not permit extension, unfortunately. The flood, and the hundreds of loans have almost exhausted our reserves. The cashier has been notified to ask for payment on the outstanding accounts. Current purchases will be for cash, of course, otherwise no sale.'

'Of course,' I said. 'One more customer for the Italians, the Arabs and the Turks.'

'Shrewd people, too,' he said. 'But you will have had practice with a Slavo and a Basquo for helpers. You will take their advice, perhaps?'

'Often I have wondered how they and all the others arranged to live without the Co-operative,' I said. 'Now I will find out. Perhaps a day will come and everybody will.'

Mr Rhos Phillips sat back, and the draught from the window blew the ribbon loops across his mouth open to laugh, and he coughed instead.

'A statement of our holdings and reserves is to the side of the cashier's desk for your perusal,' he said. 'On the right as you leave, if you please, and good day, Mr Morgan. '

Out to the desk, and I paid, and got my receipt folded, and went into the sun with the place behind my back, and never again did I turn towards it for so much as a tack or a leaf of tea.

'I will see Phillips, Finger and Thumb, myself, him and his nicknames,' Lal said. 'Shareholders, is it? Give me the list of what is wanted and I will have it at the door tonight.'

'If it would save your life, no,' I said. 'Nothing more to do with them. They can rot.'

'How will you have stores?' she asked.

'Plenty, and cheaper by a quarter,' I said. 'Bellini and Hassan have both got good shops. Moishe Levy is getting me better woods, and bringing more from the Andes. Never fear, I shall want for nothing once I have got you. When, now?'

Wednesday morning, and in for shopping she was, in a white dress with lace, and a white hat and pale blue flowers, and only to know that soon she would leave me again, I felt lonelier near her than when I was at Rhinberry's and she at Maes Corwen. At the back of Rhys, Saddler, in the shadow of his stores, we were, not to be seen by anybody because she was afraid her father might come to know.

'But look here,' I said. 'A girl under age and afraid of her father, yes, I understand. But girls of your age, over twenty, Doli and you, why? Father, yes, and authority, yes, but why frightened?'

'Not frightened,' she said, soft. 'Only we would rather not have trouble in the house always. When we have got our shares we shall be freer. But till then, best to keep on the safe side. What will you say to them on Saturday?'

'Let it come first,' I said. 'When will we be married?'

'When we have got our shares,' she said, close, and I could feel her heart, because she wore no corset and a surprise that was, too. 'If Tanfi wins on Saturday, perhaps we shall have everything, and more than we thought. Vrann has left the bottle, and Solva has bet him a win by one round of the track.'

'If he is racing a horse, how could he bet against himself?' I asked her.

She looked at me with one eye, a world of smiling brown, too near to see the eyelashes.

'Vrann is a gambler,' she said, as if we were both going to sleep, and I was quite willing. 'Solva is like him. They will bet anywhere, for anything, only to bet. Doli told you about wanting us to marry the others for the land? Well, all that land was ours. He lost it in gambles. Through us he would have it back. If Tanfi wins, he will be the richest man in the Colony.'

'But if the horse is so sure, who is betting against him?' I asked her.

'Everybody with a horse in the race, or outside,' she said. 'Vrann has taken every bet.'

'Supposing he loses?' I said.

'Tanfi will be back in his stall when the others are only halfway,' she said. 'Nothing to beat him, even if you tie his fores. Five races he has won. This one will be the biggest. Then Vrann will take him to Buenos Aires, and perhaps to Europe. By that time we will be married, yes?'

'Sooner,' I said. 'But where are we going to live girl? The families off to Brazil have got the same kind of place. Falling to pieces, every bit, and nothing tidy, not even the potato field. Lazy, they are, and the rights are not worth the paper. Nobody else wants to sell.'

She moved away, far enough to hold my shoulders to look at me.

'What will you say to The Twelve?' she asked me again. 'Supposing they tell you not to work again in the Valley?'

'They have no authority,' I said.

'Authority enough to tell everybody not to give you work, or supplies, or anything else,' she said. 'Authority to put Beretroff and Urrisbiscaya from the country by the first ship. You, too.'

'The Government would never allow it,' I said.

'The Government will take their advice,' she said. 'Everything is done quietly, but it is done.'

'I am surprised if they have got so much power,' I said. 'The three of us are on Rhinberry's property to work, by his invitation, on payment of rent.'

She sighed ha! in the air, from sadness.

'The floods took Rhinberry's other farm and everything on it,' she said. 'The one you are in now was in his wife's family, and a brother and two sisters to share. He has paid them off since she died. But he owes most of the loans. I have been afraid they would foreclose since you went there.'

'The Co-operative,' I said.

She nodded, putting her hands together, and for the first time I saw her as though in a storm, without shelter, and helpless.

'If he is told to send you from there, where will you go?' she asked me, and worry changing bright in her eyes. 'Not from the country, Huw? I would follow, yes. But I want you near, where I can ride, and kiss, and talk about something more than old dams and canals. Promise me you will stay somewhere close.'

'They will have to throw me out with the police,' I said. 'But if they foreclose on Rhinberry, I will have to go. Where?'

'Let me think between now and Saturday,' she said. 'I will be outside the school, and look for the trap round the back of the garden. I will whistle and you will follow, yes?'

'And give you more like this,' I said, and bent her, and the woman of her answered me, and her arms were strong as mine and we could have melted in one piece but she held away, looking towards the back of Tibbald's shop, among the pile of crates and rubbish. But I had seen the man, too, with the hair cut with a basin, and too tall to hide.

'That one with the leather blanket,' I said, when she looked at me. 'The same Indio. Why should he follow you?'

'Why is he so careless to be seen?' she asked me, to the sky and herself. 'If he wants to speak, why not come close?'

'Kankel will tell you who he is in a moment,' I said. 'He knows everybody.'

Lal laughed at me, soft, as if I was a small one tumbling over himself.

'Kiss me, first, and go you and ask,' she said. 'See what he says, and come to Tibbald's, is it? But if my father is there, say nothing. Not a sign. Mind, now.'

It took a few minutes to get Kankel away from the idlers, but either my Welsh was too far to the south for him, or the Castellano beyond him altogether, but I could get no sense. Back to Tibbald's, I went, and he told me Lal had gone home with her father and left her love in a whisper, with a new silk tie in soft paper and a box from Paris for Sunday.

Volde was coming over the river when I got there, so we lit a fire and grilled a steak on the bank, and he told me all about James and Alys, and how happy, and what rich place they had found halfway across the Territory on the south bank of the Camwy. It surprised me that it went so far, but he said it went all the way to the Andes, and well worth following to choose a piece and settle. But it was at least ten days' hard riding from the city, and they would soon have a flock of a couple of thousand sheep, if they could have peace from thieves, and enough money to fence the land entire. After that, he was helping them to build a house, and then he wanted to go on because he was tired of the pampas, and sick for the sight of a mountain.

Well, indeed, coming to think, so was I, but there was always too much work to spend time on it.

Off he went to Tegwyn, Toldo's, and I rode down to the new bridge, and crossed beside it. A good strong piece of work, it was, and a credit to the carpenters, but still I thought the baulks were too wide and giving too much surface for the current to push against.

Several families had called while I was away, and left orders for bedroom suites, and a dining suite of eight pieces for one, and chairs and tables for others, and the money down for all of it. Out with the box to count the money in, and open the book to note the orders, and I was looking through the door to fix a day when the pieces would be ready, and I saw Beretroff stop work to look at an Indio girl. Looking at him, she was, black eyes sideways, and shining whites, and black hair half to her waist, and the sun busy in ink silk, and she stood, waiting. Solva came first in my thought, and then Nelya Peninnah, and I wondered what they might say if they could see what was so clear to me.

'Beretroff,' I shouted. 'No familiarity with the servants. I am responsible. Do we agree?'

He put the plane down, and came towards me, waving the girl away.

146

'A man becomes used to the touch of a woman,' he said.
'Good,' I said. 'But not here.'

'They stand,' he said. 'An hour. Two hours.'

'Send them off,' I said. 'Throw something. Tell Rhinberry.'

'If he is here, they are careful,' he said.

'Be careful if he is, or not,' I said. 'If there is trouble, out you go.'

He shrugged, and his shoulders stayed up and he held out his hands.

'A man can do so much, more or less,' he said. 'For how long? How many days? These, they are like the cats. A time comes and they howl. They have the nature.'

'Excuse yourself or them,' I said. 'Behave yourself, or go.'

'Perhaps I marry with one,' he said. 'Then everything is correct.'

'You are a first-class workman,' I said. 'You could have choice of the best girls in the Colony.'

'It is true,' he said, and looking towards the pasture, and smiling. 'One day, perhaps.'

'But why would you think of marrying an Indio?' I asked him.

'Because then, there is nothing to molest,' he said. 'No more worry. A house, children, work. Finish. If other Indios look, my Indio takes a knife. After a time, I take another Indio. After that, more. Or how many I want. It is simple. They live better, I live better. We have tranquillity.'

Thinking of ink silk, I knew half of what he meant, though a quick notion of Lal made me aware that danger is in the curiosity, not in the act.

'But listen, Beretroff,' I said. 'Why should a European mix himself? You produce children. What of them?'

'I come to America to make my life better,' he said. 'I find everything worse. No shops. No cities. No cafés. Nothing. But the country is new. The Indios, they are the people of the country, no? You are not. I am not. It is their country. If we are European, we make it better. With children, and the school, we make them better.'

He laughed, and shook his head, and his moustache curled up in the breeze.

'But I think not,' he said. 'We make them worse.'

'With wine?' I asked him.

He turned his eyes to me, and sunlight in a slant made them a shock of pale red.

'We give them wine to take their land,' he said. 'With the land, what do we do? Everything in the pocket, nothing for anybody. Where is the school for the Indio? Where is his house? Who is he? What are these women? For anybody.'

'But you will take an Indio to marry,' I said, not a word about Solva.

'That way it is easy to live, and they are good people,' he said, and off to the bench he went, but women were screaming out in the garden, and he ran, and so did I. Somebody had left the gate open, and a ram and a few sheep were eating the cabbage and lettuce in bites of big teeth and taking no notice of the girls flapping cloths. In went Beretroff, and picked up the ram by the fleece, and threw him fourlegs over the fence and one by one the sheep, and slapped his hands, and walked out, and the eyes of all the women went after him. I can see them now, big and black and the whites in a glisten. But nothing was in their faces, not a line, but saying far more than all the words said loud.

Standing like that, a great darkness was over me, and a halloo! and Lal jumped a five-wire fence and landed about a yard away on the path, and looked round, laughing at me, and cantered down to the gate and cleared it without a run. A vault I gave it, but only just, and I had her close in a moment.

'Listen to me, boy,' she said. 'A beautiful place I have found for us. Only wait till Saturday, and after the race we will go together. Listen again, a house of furniture is wanted by Clydach Evans, up the valley. Go to see him before Saturday. On the way back, go in the chapel at Gaiman. Choir chairs and a lectern they want, and a chair for the bard this year. How much is my commission?'

'More like this,' I said, but she was away, towards the barn, and running fast enough, never mind the long skirt and riding boots.

'Wait now,' she said, when I had her again. 'Ruin me after we are married, not before. She will come with the tea and tell everybody we are acting like lords, here.'

'If lords are like this, there is nice for them,' I said. 'Listen to me. How did you get all these orders, and how much of your own work have you done today?'

'Twice I went round the track with Tanfi and helped to choose the jockey with my father,' she said. 'This afternoon I went to see friends, and I got the orders. Tomorrow and

148

Saturday, the races, and looking after Tanfi. Sunday, back to the dam. I will come back Thursday or Friday. If my father is not at Maes Corwen, will you come to meet me? I will send a peon to tell you.'

'Supposing the peon told your father?' I said.

'They are mine,' she said, and smiling. 'Doli and Solva have got theirs. I will give a thousand pesos for every word to be got from Tamaño, Tampoco or Tambien without my permission.'

'Indios?' I said.

'Pure blood,' she said. 'Gauchos, every one. Good boys, they are. They have been with me since I was little and working.'

'How old were you when you were little?' I asked her.

'With Mama, I was seven,' she said. 'Doing only what she told me. But she died when I was ten. In the summer when I was twelve, my father was in bed months with typhoid. So I took charge. As Mama had done, so I did. I have worked ever since except for the time away at school.'

'When can I come to the dam with you?' I asked her.

'When Vrann and his friends are somewhere else,' she said. 'But if we are married, we can go for picnics, yes?'

The girls came with tea, and we talked with a couple of yards between us because the girls stood there to serve and to look at Lal, and she knew it, and to please them she spoke in Castellano and taught me a little more of the language, if not of social usage.

'If we speak anything else in front of them, we put ourselves from them,' she said, when we were going out. 'They never speak Araucano in front of us. They want to be as we are. It is our duty, too.'

'Only a few think so,' I said.

'The few will be fewer, and soon,' she said. 'We should stop talking Welsh, as well. Except for ourselves. The churches are filled with Indios because they understand Castellano. How many Indios are in chapel? Even if they were allowed in?'

'I can see somebody else in front of The Twelve before long,' I said.

'All the proof they want they shall have,' she said. 'Huw, when will you buy me a ring?'

'What sort of stone will you have?' I asked her, still apart, because a dozen girls were around us.

'O, no stone, boy,' she said, closer. 'Something to see, and think of you and touch. Cut a piece of wire and give a twist. It will be yours and mine. Think of me, feel my heart, with blood only for you.'

And she was up in the saddle, and riding before I had my wits, and my hand warm from the place under her breast. Slow I was in those days, yes, but getting quicker, and learning more with the hours.

To the shop of my friend Mr Tibbald I went, and through the half door, to the darkness, and the jumble and the dust. That place would have to be seen. Little tables he had everywhere, and a long counter on three sides with a space for a door to the back, and shelves to be reached by a ladder all round except for the front door. Books were in piles on the floor, on benches, and pushed on the shelves and stacked in the window high enough to block light. Newspapers in every language were on the counter, with ink and pens and rubbers and pencils, and flat irons and toasting forks and saucepans, and cards of buttons, and rolls of lace and bobbins of ribbon and reels of cotton and balls of yarn, and spares for sewing machines and teapots and caddies, and coffee services, and sets of china, and everything under the dust, and everything else on top. A day could be spent going from place to place, and turning this over to find that, and the next turning that over to find this, and everybody turning everything over to find something for somebody else but never finding anything for themselves. If ever a husband lost his wife in the city, or if mothers missed daughters, or friends were parted, to Tibbald's they went, and if they were not all in there, it was a miracle, and you could tell who had been in there by the dust all over them. Sneezing, then, and a good cup of tea, quick.

A good place, though, and plenty to see, and a marvel of luxuries to buy, because he knew the captains of all the ships, and they brought him cases of goods from all over the world. French soaps and perfumes he had in the back with women's hats from Paris and London, and raw silks from Hong Kong, and patterned silks and satins from Italy, and Irish linens, and English cloths, and tweeds from Scotland. The hats he had in boxes, if he had time, but women had them all over the shop, with this one trying, and taking it off, and picking up another, and two more waiting for the first, and twenty waiting when they were finished, and Mr Tibbald sitting in his big chair and letting everybody help themselves, and if they wanted to pay, he put the money in his trousers pocket, and if not, they called out what they were owing and he waved good-bye. The pioneer families, of course, had the run of the place and Mr Tibbald knew everybody by name from when they were young together, and all the children from their christening.

Behind the chair I went, and spoke in his ear about a ring for an engagement.

'Ah,' he said, and took out his spectacles, and put them on, and got up, and pulled himself into his long shop coat, and pointed towards the door at the back. 'Do me the very great pleasure, Mr Morgan, if you please.'

The room at the back had a window in drapes with cobwebs and the dust of his time there, and nothing to see outside except piles of crates and paper not yet blown away, but it was light enough to see. The walls were all racked with drawers, and from one he took a key, and went to the safe and opened it with a twist, and came back with a tray filled with rings, and very pretty, too. But the one I wanted cost too much and I said so.

He took it out, and brushed fluid on it from a bottle, and opened the table drawer and chose a small box with peach velvet and put the ring in, and put it in front of me.

'That is your property, sir,' he said. 'The question of payment will arise when you consider the circumstances most favourable.'

'It might be a long time, Mr Tibbald,' I said. 'Except the little I have got, I have got nothing.'

'But you see, Mr Morgan, when I first came here, I had nothing,' he said. 'No means, no ability. Not strong enough to ride a horse or sweep a street. Somebody of your name put up the capital for my first stock of books, and here I am. Very well established, I believe, and fully paid up, I assure you. And I shall venture to offer my felicitations, if I may. A perfectly lovely creature, dear Lal. She's always been that to me, of course. Her sisters as well. But that radiance of hers was very marked even as a baby, when her dear mama brought her in for her first bonnet. Mistress Corwen was a charmer. Very beautiful. Old School. The father, Vrann? A complete blackguard, I should say. Often happens. Nice woman. Swine of a man. Do you think?'

To hear it in the gentle voice, with that confidence, and

looking at me with the smiling, peaceful eyes, well, I could only sit.

'You may not have had much to do with him,' he said. 'Just as well, perhaps. Allow me the liberty of suggesting that you take especial care of yourself between now and the wedding.'

'It is unpleasant to think that,' I said.

'This is still, in quite a number of respects, very much an ancient community, you should never forget that,' Mr Tibbald said, and going to stand at the window. 'When I came here first, this little city was merely a turning off a path leading along the floor of the valley. The style of living was a mixture of the old Welsh farmer, and the Tehuelche and Araucano hunter. The Welsh survived, you know, by the help of the Indio. Almost everybody lived in a small barn of mud bricks and a rush roof, with their lodgers, visitors, and anybody else who came along. Hospitable to a fault. Naturally, because they knew the meaning of hunger. Very hard years they were, too. But that sort of public living, without a moment of decent privacy leads to a state of mind and behaviour which some of us might be tempted to describe as simply deplorable. A lot of it has gone with better living conditions and more money, of course. Some of it persists. That's certainly to be said of the top of the valley. Their women are used like beasts of burden. Rights of the squire, and so forth.'

'He keeps the girls working very hard,' I said. 'He will find it difficult to replace them when they marry.'

'Exactly what I have been trying to say,' he said. 'Those girls work that place almost as second nature. Where would he find three men to take their places? Would as much get done? Could he live the life he does? Would he be able to hound at will? There are men, you know, who own. They own land and horses and cattle and so forth. Their fathers owned before them. There was never a time when they were not owners. Their outlook is that of the owner. That fellow Corwen is one of them. He owned his wife. Poor soul was treated like a chattel. He owned his Indio women. He owns his daughters. He does as he pleases because he owns them. When they marry, you say? Highly probable, if he were permitted, he'd far rather marry them himself, all three of them. That's why I say, be extremely careful, won't you?'

Light.

Not the light from the diamond in the little bump of peach velvet.

But light, yes, pity enough, and I knew why Lal would never marry until her sisters were from there. I wanted to go to her and hold her gently, gently to me, and tell her that I knew.

But better still I knew that I would have my answer.

11

Donato came on Saturday morning early, and asked me to come to his shed behind the barn. Ever since he had started work I had paid him regularly but I had never asked questions and he had never invited me to see what he was doing. That way I am sure a job is done better, because if somebody is in squints over your shoulder all the time, nervous you will be of testing, or doing something new in case to make a botch, and it will end either in a down-tools and telling everybody to go and scratch, or else in a bit of a thing without heart or thought.

But my heart and thought was in the two-wheel trap he made for me.

Slender the wheels were and spokes barely of a thickness to be seen from the side, and a body of steel and ply, and red leather cushions and panelling, and shafts like pencils, but strong with brass binds, and all shining in a sand enamel and cream lining not to show the dust, and sprung to bring Eos with smiles from her worst morning temper.

Never was anything prettier pulled by a horse, and I knew I would lose it in the moment Lal looked.

'Well, Donato,' I said. 'Words are not in my mouth, man. Every moment and every penny is well spent.'

'Five more are ready,' he said. 'If I make one, why not six? This is the best.'

'It will be a pleasure to show the grace of a craftsman,' I said. 'This is the real work.'

'I shall work for you until you tell me to go,' he said.

'Never,' I said. 'Those other five I will sell, and we will share the profit half and half. From this morning you have got your own business.'

'Half and half with you,' he said, and we shook hands, and the years were signed between them, and never a word to paper.

A new mare I had from Rhinberry, a lovely roan he had trained without my knowing, and the two together with a harness of rawhide plaited by Orkiki and his Indio brothers, and I never had a pleasanter drive in all my life than that Saturday in autumn, with showers of leaves rustling gold to fill the road from every breath of El Pampero among the poplars, and farmers standing in their wains and carts to see me pass, and horsemen riding alongside all the way in to be part of the show. Early I was, so I went for a cup of coffee, and not fifteen minutes after, I had sold every one of the five traps, money from the pocket, cash down, and within the hour, orders for ten more, and I had to stop because there was a year's work complete, and Donato had no helper.

'This rate, you will have your first million while the rest of us are looking,' Idwyn Thomas said. 'When will you come to the Andes? Furniture, traps, everything else we are needing there.'

'If The Twelve decide against me this morning, I might be there with a toe behind me,' I said.

'You have got plenty of friends here, so be calm, and have patience,' he said. 'If anything happens, put everything on the wagons and come back with me, and have a fat trout for breakfast.'

'It is news to me there is a trout over there,' I said.

'Then come you, and eat a bit of news from the grill,' he said. 'I will be waiting.'

Outside the school it was easy to see who was a friend. Two groups filled the space in front of the cemetery next door, with horses by the hundred tied along the street and traps blocking the lanes and yards at the back. In for the races most of them were, and doing the week's buying in the morning to have it out of the way, and to see the show as well. Leishon John stood in the middle of one group with Evans, Sideways, and some of his relations, and Hywel, Little Bit, and a lot of their friends I knew by their faces, and the Widow Glyn sat in a wagonette with Mrs Roper Hughes and a couple of other women at the back. On the other side was Vyrnwy Beris, with Jezrael Cadfan and Box, Quiff, and Asaph Hughes and a lot more, all smiles and waves, and a good shout to raise the heart.

And a nice, wide space in the middle, and down that I went, to the side entrance just as the doors opened, and Mr Prosser Vaughan stood there looking at his watch.

'Very punctual, Mr Morgan,' he said, with his hat half off. 'Please to sit until your name is sent out.'

So I sat in the little room, looking at children's drawings of flowers in crayons, and houses and birds in water colours, and all of them as I remembered from school, and I was back, listening to Mrs Tom Harries, and to Miss Cash, and having a smack on the head for using white from the tube to bring bloom to the stalk of a carnation.

'Mr Huw Morgan, cabinet-maker, of no fixed abode, living at Maes Hafod,' Prosser Vaughan called down the corridor, and the echoes chasing themselves. 'Present yourself for the judgement of The Twelve, elected from the free citizens of the Colony of Camwy, and cleanse your soul with a prayer.'

A blue curtain was over the board at the end of the classroom, and white curtains hung from the other walls and net over the big windows. A long table was in the middle with five chairs each side, and one at each end. Banner Prichard, the clerk, was at a little table to the left, Prosser Vaughan at the right, and at the foot, Iolo Tudor and Uryan Rowlands, but what they did I never came to know.

Tynant Lewis, the president, came in while we were standing.

A short, strong man, he was, with a head of white hair and a clipped beard, and wearing a good tweed swallow-tail, and breeches with thick woollen stockings, and a grey square-crowned bowler hat. He put his staff of cherry wood in the corner, and sat, and picked up the paper.

'First member of the Senate, Silas Ieuan Pendar, on my right, please,' he said.

Silas Ieuan Pendar, tall, with white hair shining, in black with a high collar, sat.

Enoch Humphrys, Rhyader Owain, Maldwyn Glyn, Plenydd Bala, Rhys Bryn Gilfa, Jenkin Taft, Morgan Thomas, Aaron Caerog Evans, Rhydderch ap Afon and Talban Llywarch all sat where they were put, to the right or left, and when the clerk gave another paper to Tynant Lewis, all the faces turned to me, and I saw where the Colony had its strength, and I knew then that most of the people I had met were the smallest of very small beer.

'Mr Morgan, we shall waste no time,' Tynant Lewis said, and very civil, and not in a big voice. 'A series of complaints were made against you, and we thought it our duty to review

156

the bill, and find out the facts. The matter of Leishon John may be dismissed. He smallholded for me for some years. A more useless lout cannot have infested the Colony. We shall be happy to subscribe to send him and his litter wherever he pleases. Vote.'

All hands were raised, and the clerk said Aye, and wrote.

'The second matter concerns a horse presumed to have strayed from Maes Corwen,' Tynant Lewis said. 'You are supposed to have said that the horse was in the stable of Beynon Hywel. You cannot tell us the name of your informant?'

'Unknown to me,' I said.

'Very unfortunate,' Tynant Lewis said. 'You are a newcomer, we know. You are acquainted with the Corwen family. You had a quarrel with Vrann Corwen. Were you aware that there was bad feeling between Hywel and Corwen?'

'No,' I said.

'This may sound rather strange to you,' Tynant Lewis said. 'But try to imagine what might have happened, and Corwen and Hywel not on friendly terms. Tempers are short. The horse is a most valuable animal. Supposing an argument had got out of hand. Would you account yourself responsible?'

'Perhaps the Senate will tell me what I should have done,' I said.

'The best thing would have been to send a peon to Beynon Hywel to say that somebody had said a horse was straying near his place, and let him find it himself, and send one of his own peons with it back to Maes Corwen,' Tynant Lewis said. 'It often happens that a man will never see his stables for weeks on end if he is ditching, or clearing land, or serving his time up at the dam. Uncertain situations like this have to be handled delicately, because these men are not nearly so docile as you might think. A small act of violence can lead to something much worse, do you see?'

'I shall be more careful,' I said.

'The third matter concerns Mistress Morwen Glyn, a widow with whom you lodged,' Tynant Lewis said. 'Her complaint is, that by agreement, she spent considerable sums on alterations to her property for the purpose of housing your business, but that you left without reimbursing her.'

Glass at the window smashed while he was turning the

paper, and the net curtains flew in the room and an arrow with blue feathers stuck through the curtain of the far wall and stayed in the wood. Everybody looked at it, but nobody moved.

'A boy is playing out there in the cemetery,' Tynant Lewis said to Uryan Rowlands. 'Find him, and take him to his father, and tell him from me that he is to have a sound thrashing, and I will make sure it was done.'

'I would like to see the boy,' Rhys Bryn Gilfa said. 'I can use a bow, too. He will have to be very strong in the arms, yes.'

'If he is older than ten years of age, bring him here,' Tynant Lewis said. 'There is too much idleness. It will be stopped.'

Uryan Rowlands hurried out, and Tynant Lewis looked at me.

'Apart from that, there appears to have been a promise to marry, which, by your departure, exposed her to ridicule as a jilt,' he said. 'Any foundation?'

'I was asked to leave by noon of the following day, lock and stock, and I did,' I said. 'There was no promise to marry.'

'In a matter of breach of promise, it would be as well to find out if you were at any time in a relationship approaching the connubial?' Tynant Lewis said.

'Approaching it, no,' I said, with sounds of running and shouting outside.

'The gravamen of the complaint seems to be that in taking advantage of your place as a lodger, you lowered her in the eyes of the community,' Tynant Lewis said. 'On certain promises, in other words, you adopted familiar ways, even to sharing her marital bed.'

'I never slept anywhere else except in my own bed, in my own room, every night I was there,' I said. 'I never went in any other room in the house, except the parlour and the kitchen. Nobody could be familiar in either of them.'

'Inhospitable furniture is often no bar,' Tynant Lewis said. 'What would prevent familiarity?'

'Too many photographs of the dead and gone for me,' I said. 'Besides, the maids sleep in the scullery and no door between. The upstairs parlour is filled with wool bales, floor to ceiling, for carding in the winter. Try to get in.'

'Did you try?' Tynant Lewis asked.

'To get the machine to mend it for her,' I said. 'It was under too much. It is there, still, I expect.'

'While you were trying to find the wool machine might there have been opportunity?' Tynant Lewis asked.

'Sharing the marital bed, she says I did,' I said. 'Nobody with sense would share a bale of wool.'

'To end the examination, you never had carnal knowledge of the complainant,' Tynant Lewis said.

'No carnal knowledge in any marital bed, because I was never in anybody's bed but my own that I paid for, by the week, laundry and sundries extra,' I said. 'Let Mistress Glyn deny it.'

'The sole reason for the existence of this Senate is a rare, and I believe a unique privilege which we greatly prize,' Tynant Lewis said. 'It was granted by the Government of Argentina to our fathers, for the purpose of hearing evidence in the Welsh language, and deciding by a majority vote whether there was a case to send before the Argentinian Courts. Until recently there were no police here. They were unnecessary. They came to protect property when the Indios misbehaved themselves. There has never been any trouble. This complaint of Mistress Morwen Glyn's could result in a suit-at-law if certain facts were proved. I doubt if they can be, since she refused to make her statement on oath. Move to strike out the Glyn Motion. Vote.'

Seven hands up, five down, and the Clerk said Aye, and wrote.

'There are a number of minor complaints here,' Tynant Lewis said, looking at the paper. 'But you must have realised by now that this part of the world is not Glamorgan. Argentinian law is very much as it was in the Middle Ages. A man can be put in prison here without a charge. There is no Habeas Corpus. You see the risk we run. A small infringement of the law might mean a long time in custody. That is the main reason for the existence of this Senate. To protect the individual, first. Secondly, to defend the peace. Third, to uphold the good name of all of us in the Colony. Remember, we are trusted, virtually, to govern ourselves. We must conduct ourselves accordingly. The Senate therefore admonishes, and delivers reproof, in the case of Leishon John, and urges recourse to legal authority at all times. The complaint of Morwen Glyn is dismissed, but it leaves an impression of looseness. The matter of the Corwen horse is a mystery, but

159

it was probably a joke, though the consequences you will take to heart. The other complaints, of making coffins for unbelievers, and living an unruly existence among the infidel and Indios, cannot altogether be ignored, because they give rise to adverse comment, which seems to be an expression of bad feeling somewhere. That in itself might stand as warning that there are more suitable places and companions. Your appearance here, I believe, has made a favourable impression. We are sure that Mr Morgan will remember his responsibilities and ours, and we wish him all success among us in the future. Vote.'

Eight up, and four down, and the Clerk said Aye, and all the chairs were pushed back and the members went out behind Tynant Lewis' square-crowned bowler and the thump of the cherrywood staff, and through the open door was a sound of bottles becoming friendly with glasses.

'You came well out of that,' Prosser Vaughan said. 'Some of them were after your spare ribs, I can tell you. But the Widow Glyn would put nothing on paper with an oath and signature. What did she expect? Marital bed, goodness gracious. That old couch in the side room at the back, it is.'

'How do you know?' I asked him.

'Same as everybody else,' he said, and going to meet Uryan Rowlands coming in breathless, and wiping sweat from his neck.

'Nobody saw any boys near the cemetery and the gate is locked,' he said. 'We went in there and looked over every inch. Nothing. But the shaft came in straight. No boy will pull a string that far, look.'

'Tynant will have a currycomb through every house in the place,' Prosser Vaughan said, and turned to the room where the bottles and glasses were still doing the talking. 'Good day, now then, Mr Morgan. You know your way out?'

I did, yes, because I had looked for a side door to the garden where I would be safe from friends and everybody else, and out I went, along the wall, and Lal was dreaming in the trap under the trees, and in a kiss almost before she could turn. Happy she was, and glory in her eyes, and the beauty alive in her face, and I knew well why men built temples to a woman. Cathedrals they should have when they look like that, and a cathedral will give you the same feeling.

'I will give Uncle Tynant a kiss for being nice to you,' she said. 'He promised me he would. We have got a little asado with chicken at Miss Kathi's in the school. We will go in the trap, and I will drive, and it is yours only for a lend, after. Mine, it is. Remember, now. Mine.'

Back we went among the crowd, and cheers and hats off all the way. But El Pampero was blowing too hard to eat in the garden, and we all went in the big kitchen of red tiles and willow-pattern china on an applewood dresser, and a table axed from a log, and chicken in varnish of gold from the spit, white and fat and filled with thyme, and the taste is with me still. Red-currant tarts and cream next, and I was looking for a handkerchief to take the syrup from my chin, and a man pulled a horse to the window and said the races were cancelled because El Pampero was sending the little stones in showers to cut, and the horses were jibbing, and the dust was too high to see through, and Tanfi's jockey was drunk as the rest.

Solva laughed, and red-currants in her teeth, but Lal was looking at Doli, and if fright was not in their faces, it was near.

'We must go up there,' Lal said to me, and putting her plate down. 'My father will do harm to that jockey. More trouble, again. Be sure not to let him see you when you come up.'

'Right,' I said, and glad not to be going because the dust was thick and full of grit, and the enamel on the trap would have scratched. So we think, at times, and lash ourselves later. But when the peons were bringing their horses, Tynant Lewis walked in with little dots of blood on his face where the stones had cut, and the girls kissed him, and he spoke to them with their arms round him, and Lal blew me a kiss through her veil, and up in the saddle, and off in front of Doli and Solva, and Miss Kathi said to come in, everybody, before the house would be filled like the desert.

'A disagreeable experience this morning, Mr Morgan,' Tynant Lewis said, and waving off the girl ready with a towel to bathe the cuts. 'Do please get rid of any notion that the Senate is a parochial busybody. If there had been substance in any of the charges, you would now be on your way to trial.'

'The charges were small enough,' I said.

'Not here,' he said. 'People feel very strongly. Word is going about that you were treated leniently because we no longer possess the power of condemnation. If we can find whoever shot that arrow this morning, we shall see if, or not. Obviously somebody brought up in the Territory with the Indios. What is worse, those blue feathers are Manzanero. The fighting tribe of the Tehuelche, mostly. This man Winn is not a Christian, I know. A rarity here, of course. Tell me, then, what sort of Indio does he allow at his place, there?'

His frown came after my grin, but I could have raged to think of the un-Christian Rhinberry, with sacking round his bare feet, and in rags of years because he was always giving everything away, even the shirt off his back, and the eyes that looked straight and grey into one of yours, first, and in the space of moving to the other, flashed the light of his smile to let you know that he trusted you to the rock wall at the back of your soul, and loved by the Indios because he treated them as if they were brothers and sisters and not some old rubbish, and this one, an Unbeliever, yes, un-Christian, and held to be suspect.

'More colours and piebalds are among the Christians than in fifty generations of horses,' I said. 'To find out what they believe would be a good puzzle, too. If you saw the way he works, you might think again. The Indios are mostly girls and a lot of mothers and babies. The late Mrs Winn kept a sort of little hospital, and a school for infants. Nobody is idle, there. They all wear ordinary clothes, men and women. No blue feathers that I ever saw.'

'There is a lot of restlessness among the poorer sort of Indio in the Territory,' he said. 'Thieves are multiplying. A great deal of fault is with us, too. I understand you are looking for a piece of ground for a house and your business. Will you marry Lal?'

'Yes,' I said, direct at him.

'Good,' he said. 'Her mother was a boyhood sweetheart of mine, so I have a special interest in the family. Lal said you wanted something with suitable conditions for a garden. I can offer you a piece of land fronting the river on the other side of Gaiman. We will sign when you publish the notice of marriage.'

'I will speak to Lal,' I said. 'Only she can say when.'

'That was why I came here,' he said. 'I called at the Widow Glyn's on the way and went up for a look at the parlour. You were correct. The machine is still under the bales. And as for

162

that kitchen, those pictures would put the daunt in an old ram, indeed.'

He went to join Miss Kathi, and the room was full of friends talking and laughing but I was too much of a stranger to know many of them, and I stood at the window, and looking out at the earth blowing thick off the road. Then, it was, I saw the Indio with the hair cut straight above the eyebrows, standing on the corner of Vyrnwy's place and looking over at the house, and turning, then, and the dust hiding him. Nobody was noticing me, and out I went, into the deep howl of El Pampero, and pulling up my collar and crushing my hat over my eyes, and over where the Indio had stood, but the streets up and down were empty. Along the way to the racecouse I walked, head down, trying to see the path without falling in a ditch, every minute trying not to breathe dust, and to cover my face from the showers of little stones that chipped the skin like the point of a knife. I got to the long fence and walked close, out of the blow, to an open gate, seeing only one path, to the stand of planks and I stood behind, in the quiet, with the dust and grit blowing on both sides, and listening to the thrash, and the creak of the timber, and asking myself why I was such a fool as to leave a warm kitchen and smells of roasting chicken and redcurrants and fresh pastry.

But the mist lifted, and El Pampero drew breath to blow again, and the sky was blue and the rails were white all the way about an oval, and a black horse was coming on the far side at such a run that I thought I was dreaming, but the red coat lying flat on his back I knew, and I ran to the rail and shouted, and others were shouting somewhere, and the horse was leaping, not running, and coming along the curve and there were other horses a long way behind. Solva was screaming somewhere, and I could hear Doli's voice in rags but not what she was shouting, and men were running from the stand, and when I looked again the horse was passing me, and Lal was over his neck and her mouth was moving and her eyes were laughing and they passed me in silence because El Pampero started again and dust came off the ground like a shaken carpet and in a moment the grit struck, and the howl was as loud, and I had to go for the shelter of the stand, face in hands, and the stones cutting, to another path, and at the end, a stables with a high wall. A crowd was in there, and Lal in the middle, and Vrann Corwen crying and laughing

163

and the men holding her back to put flowers round her neck.

But she saw me and pulled away, and ran, and we kissed, there, in front of everybody, with the dust like dirty curtains about us. Out with the box from my waistcoat, and a press for the stud, and I took the ring from the little bump of peach velvet, and put it over the knuckles of her finger with a bit of help from her, to be sure, and if you could have seen her face.

'Huw,' she said, and no voice.

No use shouting in that noise, and we kissed, and El Pampero prayed silence for us.

'A fortune,' she said. 'Beautiful beyond sighing.'

'For one breath, only one, what is the price?' I said. 'Who will pay?'

'In my breasts for ever, and your children shall be in me,' she said, and we were tight held, and El Pampero all round us, blowing hair, and hats, and chipping with grit, and putting sand in our kiss, and us careless.

But when the howl stopped and the dust was gone, Vrann Corwen was standing a couple of yards off, pale blue and shining in the eye, not frowning, only seeing, and I remembered Mr Tibbald.

'Lal,' he said, in a whisper from shouting. 'We must drink a health to Tanfi.'

'Yes, Dada,' she said, but leaning against me, and holding my arm about her waist. 'Huw will come with me.'

'Certainly,' he said, as if it was ordained from beyond. 'The bottles are only now from the well, and cold, and Solva is getting the glasses.'

'You promised,' she said. 'He is mine, and the ring is here, look.'

'Yes,' he said, and turned in a swing, and walked to the cheering men, but if there was anything of a winner about him, it was only Tanfi's number pinned on his back.

'Stay close to me,' Lal said. 'Never mind what anybody says, stay close, boy. Did you see me win? Only to shame the jockey. These horses will run in anything, only show them you know. We will have the real race next. But I won plenty from that one, too.'

Doli served at a table with glasses and trays of pies and sandwiches, and laughing, but in so much noise, not to be heard, and Solva was pouring here and there and throwing the empty bottles over her head, and all the men were cheering. Vrann stood on a box, and shouted but if his mouth opened, nothing seemed to come out, and everybody was pushing the next and nodding towards him to have silence.

Vrann raised his glass high and his mouth said words nobody heard, but there was no need because everybody drank, and shouted against El Pampero, and went back for more. Lal was lifted to the table, and the drinks went round again, and Vrann climbed up beside her, and more mouthing and nothing heard, and glasses up, and the bottles pouring, and the dust in brown clouds outside, and the rattle of grit against corrugated iron and the howl of El Pampero almost louder than Tom, Tot, shouting up into my face, but what, only he knew.

Everybody was turning towards the far door, and Lal was looking for me, and I pushed nearer until I could reach up for her hand, and she looked down at me, and I up at her, and we twined love only in a look, and El Pampero dropped his voice, and a Maes Corwen Gaucho was shouting and hooking his fingers and bending his knees with the words, and his eyes pointed to the door and back, and when there was no sound his voice was high, like a girl's, and then in whispers.

Vrann jumped down to shake the ground, and ran, and the crowd pushed to be with him.

Lal put hands to her face and closed her eyes.

Up on the table I went, and she put her face in my shoulder.

'Lal,' Doli was shouting over the heads. 'Lal. Answer me. What did he say?'

'No,' Lal was whispering, as if a knife were turning. 'No. Tanfi. No.'

'Lal,' Doli shouted, and hitting fists against her boots. 'Tell me, girl. Tell me.'

'Not true,' Lal screamed up at the roof, and shaking me. 'Not true.'

She was down and running, and Doli after, and I jumped, and in the crush I was next to Caedmon Phillips, the drover.

'Vrann will lose much more than a million, today,' he said. 'Not the first time, but enough, no?'

'But Lal won,' I said.

'Owner's stakes,' he said. 'The big race is still on, so far.

165

He will lose his bets.'

'How can he, and the race not run?' I asked him.

'They say Tanfi has bled to death out there,' he said. 'His tongue has been cut.'

12

Looking into this candle and seeing the red point of burning wick, and remembering what little light or time is left for us both, it is not easy to go back to the days of that autumn, and yet if I think of the poplars and driving down tall gold avenues from the city, everything is clear and I am turning Anwyl's corner to go into Rhinberry's, and even with this stench of coal's ghost all about and the stale of waters unused these years, I smell the scent of the clover ricks, and the green of the garden when the leaves have warmed, and the creamy breath of cows in morning milk.

Gwenonwy James came in one afternoon, and so hot from walking that I had to clear a place in the shadow of the chrysanthemums and go to the pump for a jug of cold water. She walked all the way from the James' place only to ask me to make a wagonette, and she had the measurements on paper and the money in an envelope for the half payment. If it had been anybody else I would have said no. But thinking of the baby she had left with her mother and the long way she had walked, I had to say yes, if Donato agreed.

But he looked at the drawing and gave it back.

'Only a light one I want,' she said, and almost afraid to raise her voice. 'Two good horses I have got, but not strong enough to pull a full-sized wagon where I am going. The country is rough, and I have got a lot of things to take.'

'For the roads to the City and to Port Madryn you will not need so much,' Donato said. 'What you have paid is enough.'

'But I am going past Indio Crossing on the Camwy,' she said. 'I shall not be back in the Colony till next year. There are no roads.'

'You are going alone?' Donato asked her, and his eyes came alight with surprise. 'You, with a baby?'

'My baby will live on the land his father left him,' she said.

Donato took the paper from her, and looked at it.

'Very well,' he said. 'It will be ready in ten days.'

She put her hands under her chin and smiled a prayer.

'I can be out before the rains,' she said. 'Thank you, Mr Morgan. I will be here Monday next.'

No cup of tea, no loan of the trap or a horse, nothing she wanted and off she went, and her long skirt held, and a parasol, and a wide straw hat with a black ribbon, and fair hair bleached by the sun in a tie with a black bow.

'They have courage,' Donato said. 'I kiss their feet.'

Towards evening, while I was washing at the pump, Rhinberry came out of the house with Tynant Lewis and two police officers, and very serious all of them.

'Mr Lewis wants to know have we ever seen Manzaneros here,' Rhinberry said. 'Indios they are, from the Andes, and always with the blue feather.'

'Informers have said that one or two have been seen here only recently,' Tynant Lewis said. 'We are prosecuting a search because of this tongue-cutting affair. These officers are giving warning that the culprit will be shot on sight. We are very worried about this, and the arrows. Somebody shot one in the Justice's office yesterday. Did Gwenonwy James come here?'

I took him down to the shop at the back, and when Tynant Lewis asked what he was doing, Donato said he was making six wagonettes.

'But Gwenonwy wants only one and I told her to come here,' Tynant Lewis said. 'Why six?'

'In the time I make one, I make six,' Donato said. 'The same work for one, six times. I make six.'

Donato, Make Six, he was from that minute, and next morning the first buyer arrived just after dawn, and before the breakfast coffee was on the table, every one of the six was bought and paid for.

But before Tynant Lewis went he spoke to me about the piece of land.

'Vrann is still in bed,' he said. 'He took it very hard. A big loss, and no replacing. Poor Lal. Have you seen her?'

'Not since she took her father back,' I said.

'Thin, she is, and not the girl she was,' Tynant Lewis said. 'I saw her at the dam yesterday. Go out when she comes back, and marry her. Why not?'

'That is what I want,' I said. 'But she refuses till her sisters have got their proper shares. She is afraid her father will make his Indio children legitimate.'

'There is no such thing as an illegitimate child in this country,' Tynant Lewis said. 'If a man wants to acknowledge them, they share his property, yes. I would have a word to say, there. Tell Lal from me. Vrann will be told no later than tomorrow.'

Before dawn I was riding to Maes Corwen and I was there when the hens were still in a cackle and a lovely smell of fried bacon coming across the meadow, and Gwilym Martin cooking breakfast after bringing the cattle back from the river.

'Vrann went with a tracking team only a couple of hours ago,' he said. 'Mistress Lal is in the Territory for the sheep, back tomorrow night, and Mistress Doli is at the dam. Mistress Solva went into Gaiman for the shopping. Will you have to eat? There is plenty.'

So I had eggs and bacon, and very good, with all the autumn flowers and the leaves red on the ground, and Gwilym told me that Mathias Watcin and Rhidian Bala had followed tracks after a dead mare had been found at Maes Watcin, and they had called out others on the way.

'About twenty went through here this morning,' Gwilym said. 'I would have been with them but I have got the cattle here. So no luck.'

'Is there chance of catching the Indio?' I asked him.

That look across the fire has always been with me, so much of a cold in a smile.

'No Indio uses a knife like that,' he said. 'They cook the tongue, see. But it is cut from the back. Every one of these is cut across, nearly the half left in. They will take out his tongue by the roots and nail it to a post if they will catch him. I would show them how to use the knife, there, too.'

I left a note for Lal and back to work I went, and I was crossing the river, and I saw the long line of men on the other bank, dogs in a run, with Mathias Watcin and Vrann and a couple more in front, and the rest in a wide fan behind, all looking down at the ground. I got near enough to speak to Brychan Deri and he said they had tracked since early morning, and whoever it was had doubled back twice, but his dogs were leaving scent enough, and whatever he did, he would need wings to get away.

Looking at their faces, and the slow advance of the horses,

stopping when there was doubt, moving on at a whistle, I was sorry to think of him they were chasing, and glad I was from it.

Rhinberry had a lot of papers when I got back, and reading them one by one, and putting them on the fire, and I saw the Co-operative heading.

'They are coming after me for a funding,' he said. 'They know if I have another good year I will be free of them. But I will sell by myself. There is plenty of good profit to be had somewhere else, without worry.'

'I will give you any money you want,' I said.

'You cannot give me a peaceful head,' he said. 'Plenty of people will lend. But there is no sense in borrowing to keep a worry. This farm is on salt land. It will graze in places, but nothing grows. I kept it to please my girl, but she is up by there. Useless to you or I would have offered it before.'

'Give me a day or two to find another place,' I said.

'Day or two?' he said, and laughing. 'In the spring I will go. But I will sell, cash, and pay the owings. The rest will buy animals and tools.'

'Where will you go?' I asked him.

'I will follow the river to the Andes,' he said. 'Peace I will have, and Thomas, the Peak, has found gold. If I will find a bit, we will live comfortable.'

'What about the Indios?' I asked him.

'They will come with me,' he said. 'I will put them to good work, and have a teacher for the children. No child shall go from this house thin, or without letters.'

Donato was ready to go if I went, and we had a good talk about it while we were having an asado, there. Work there was for both of us for years where we were, and we knew it, but we had no comfort. Single we were, and wanting to be married, me with an eye on Lal and the ring on her finger, but Donato had seen a lot of girls without choosing, because until he met me there was nothing in his pockets.

'I would ask that girl,' Donato said. 'That one with courage.'

'Take the horse,' I said. 'Go you, and ask her.'

'She will come for the wagonette,' he said, and smiling. 'But I could do no business at Indio Crossing. It is the desert country. She would have to come with me.'

'She is the one to talk to, and I believe you will have more success if you will put your face in the boot of that trap by

170

there, and talk yourself dry and black,' I said.

'For that reason I wait,' he said, and laughing. 'If not, I would go now.'

Only a moment after he had gone, and a shadow was over the door. I looked up but I saw nothing, and thought of a bird. But I went out to see, and in the bushes of chrysanthemum, the Indio was looking at me, and holding a dog in his arms. He put his hand across his mouth, and held it out, flat, to me, and wanting help. I looked down to the house and all round, but there was nobody, so I pointed inside, and out he came, twice as big as me, with leather round his middle, and a leather blanket and nothing else.

He pointed outside the farm and cut his hand across his throat, and I thought of the trackers.

'Up there,' I said, looking at the ladder to the loft where my best timber was stacked.

He went up with the dog, and I took the ladder to the other side, where I had all the racks of small stuff, and back to the bench, then, and going hard with the plane, and in walked Vrann Corwen and half a dozen, but so quietly I heard nothing till they were there.

The dogs sniffed at me, and went away, sniffing at the shop, and out.

'Where is he?' Vrann asked me. 'Quick with your answer.'

'Where is who, and what manner is this of coming for a cup of tea?' I said to him.

'There is an Indio here, and we will burn the house and everything in it to find him,' Vrann said. 'Where is Winn?'

'About the farm somewhere, I expect,' I said. 'There are plenty of Indios in the house.'

'They are all in the road outside,' Vrann said. 'Where is Beretroff?'

'Coming back from Port Madryn with timber,' I said. 'Donato Urrisbiscaya is in the back and working.'

'Outside, you, and stay there till we have searched,' Vrann said. 'Take him out.'

'No need,' I said. 'Once before I gave you a mallet, and I would give you another. Anybody putting a hand on me will get worse.'

'If the Indio is here, you will have the same as him,' Brychan Deri said. 'No wonder you were near the river today.'

'No talk,' Vrann said. 'Search every centimetre.'

Outside I went, hoping the Indio had gone through the barn loft and out to the granary where no tracks would show. I was standing in the shade, and listening to them pulling everything to pieces in there, and Solva came from the house, so pretty in a long dress of pink and a pink hat with red flowers that I was looking with a mouth open to swallow anything flying.

'Are those fools here?' she asked me, in the little voice. 'Rhinberry has got four round him, and the poor Indios are cowering out there. To Gaiman I have been and going back home, but Lal asked me to say not to come to the house, and she will come here, and good news she has got, with love, and to give you this.'

She kissed my cheek, and looked up at me.

'They said Beretroff is out somewhere,' she said. 'Dressed specially I am, for nothing. Have you seen that house? A swine would think of it in tears. Does he live in by there?'

'No,' I said. 'He is at the back with Donato.'

'I told Rhinberry I am coming here for a week to teach those Indios,' she said. 'To their old bottoms in grease, they are, all of them.'

Vrann came out, and stopped when he saw us, and walked on.

'Dada,' Solva said. 'I will stay here till next Friday, tell Doli. I will put some shape in the house.'

'What you like,' Vrann said, not turning. 'I am off home.'

The other men were coming out, all covered in dust and straw, and beating themselves, and not one looked at me, and Solva followed them, and I went back in the shop.

Everything was in its place, every tool in the rack, and up in the loft, it looked even tidier than before. Donato waited when I came down, and looked out in the yard, and made sure we were alone.

'The Indio is in the trap,' he said, in whispers. 'The big Indio. Under the seat.'

'Good,' I said. 'The best thing, now, is to forget him, isn't it?'

'What you say, I do,' he said, and went.

The Indio must have gone while Solva came with the supper, and a better meal you would have to ask for in shame. She had those girls running, with a table and chairs, and linen, and cutlery, and salt and pepper, and one after another, dish after dish. Rhinberry came at last, very quiet, and no smiles.

'If that Indio had been found here, I would have lost my place and everything in it, and prison for me and all these innocents,' he said, when we had finished. 'I wonder if he was here, and why?'

'Perhaps the Indios know,' Donato said.

'No,' Rhinberry said. 'They all looked at me in the eye and said no. If they were not with the truth, they would look anywhere, and say nothing.'

'Rhinberry, let me tell you,' I said, and looking to be sure Solva was in the house. 'You have always been a good one with us. It is no use to be less with you. The Indio was here, and I let him hide. Killing somebody is far from any work of ours.'

The big smile on Rhinberry's face, so sudden, and different from the long one before, put Donato in his quick laugh, and us in our own.

'If they had tracked better instead of letting the dogs tell them, they could have had him,' Rhinberry said. 'I saw where he had been. They have forgotten what they were taught when they were little boys. A cattleman would have put the rope on him hours before. A Tehuelche, he is. Grey eyes, you said?'

I made no answer, pretending to chew.

'The same one you were asking about before,' he said. 'A crossbreed. Barefoot, wearing hides, and carrying the dog.'

'How do you know?' I asked him.

'I saw his track,' he said. 'Wearing hides because he went through the posts and took splinters without leaving a hair, and carrying the dog because the other dogs lost the scent down by the river. Whether you know him or not, he knows you and Donato, now. So you have got a blood friend for life. If he was chopping a bit of ice at the South Pole and he heard you were having it rough, he would be here. The best friend in the world is the Tehuelche.'

'You must have some in you,' I said.

'I would be a better man,' Rhinberry said. 'Not a word anywhere, is it? They would have us all, and no trial.'

'But who is he, and why come here to us?' Donato asked. 'Because he knows you are kind to Indios?'

'Araucanos, most of mine are,' Rhinberry said. 'Araucanos and Tehuelche have been enemies always. If a Tehuelche

173

gets drunk, he will look for Araucanos. Murder, then. But this one, now, and his grey eyes. He might be one of the crossbreeds from the Territory. We threw good seed out there like a scatter of corn. Some good ones came from it, too.'

'Good ones, cutting the tongues of mares?' Donato said. 'The lowest would never do it.'

'A mare's tongue is the pick of the best they can give you,' Rhinberry said. 'Like roast turkey, or a sucking-pig with us. One horse is like another to them. Every Indio has got plenty of horses and mares. Do we worry about slaughtering cattle or sheep? Poor Tanfi was different, mind.'

Solva came back to say that nobody was allowed in the house till she said so, and Rhinberry went to get his sheep-skins to sleep in the back. We waited for Beretroff, and when the night was coming, we strolled out on the rise to listen for the wagons, but we could hear only the choir from the chapel coming on the lowest breath of El Pampero, and sounding as if all the world was at prayer. Donato went to his knees and the little black necklace was passing through his fingers, and his face was peaceful, and he prayed, quiet, a child.

Rhinberry walked farther, and stood black against the sky, not day, nor night, looking towards the place where his mind went always.

'He will not suffer thy foot to be moved,' he said, in whispers above the singing. 'He that keepeth thee will not slumber. The Lord shall preserve thee from all evil. He shall preserve thy soul.'

'Well, Rhinberry, my little one,' I said. 'Who will call you an unbeliever, then?'

'What does it mean, unbeliever?' he said, and looking at Donato. 'Meirion Tudor has got two rooms to the roof with books. Every one of them is the Bible of somebody, if it is Mohammed, or Buddha, or who. Every one of them is an unbeliever according to some. Will it harm if I am one more?'

'Who is Meirion Tudor?' I asked him.

'A scholar in Latin and Greek and Hebrew and Arabic,' Rhinberry said. 'We will go to see him.'

'Has he got students?' I asked him.

'Students?' he said, and looking at me with eyes in the

174

shine of night. 'Who is here to be student of what, except to put a peso in the bank?'

El Pampero was rising, and the voices were stronger, and the hymn I knew well, and I was humming, and back with the family, twisted in the heart to think of them, and my father opening the hymn-book careful to the number and resting it flat in the palm, but never once looking at it to sing eight verses at the roof, and my mother picking down the front of her blouse not to be seen, because when she breathed deep it wrinkled with her and she said she was looking like an old pouter there, and Angharad trying to open her mouth to have a high note and teeth stuck tight in peppermint toffee, and Davy pulling out a handkerchief because my mother was giving him a look not to sniff, and every marble in the world bouncing over the floor. In a moment, among the voices, they were living with me, and I with them, and taking Bron's hand to walk two by two back to the house, and waving at everybody on the way, and the girls going in the front with my mother to have the dinner ready, and the boys round the back with my father to be from under their feet, and a squeeze of the hand from Bron before I left her.

Even now my hand is with the warmth, and the pressure, and I am alone with her beauty.

So much, even with a thought, can a woman do.

The wagons were almost in when we heard them, because El Pampero was blowing a good whisper in the poplars, and they came on an earth road, so we were late to meet them, and Rhinberry went to look after the oxen, and Donato took charge of the wagons and led the drivers to the asado pit. Looking for Beretroff I was, and I heard him laughing in the kitchen, so up I went, and through the sprigs of honeysuckle black round the window I saw him lighting more candles, and nearer, Solva reaching for the maté, and in the pink dress, pretty to peel paint.

'I am a fat man,' he said to her, leaning on the door, with a beard of days, and the rest of his hair in a thatch of dust round his ears, and enough earth on the rest of him to plant. 'Who loves a fat man?'

'A lot of people will love a fat old baby,' Solva said, watching the kettle, and pulling this pot to slop, and giving that one a good push. 'What is the matter with a fat man?'

'Fat men eat much,' he said. 'It is disgusting, no?'

'Good food, there is nothing disgusting,' she said, and more pull and push, and a clout for the stove lid. 'Only bad food is disgusting, see. Old rats roasted, with a knob of garlic. Or dead dogs and toadstools. Would you eat them?'

'If you cook, I eat,' he said. 'With this, I become thin.'

'No taste to bones,' she said, and still, with her back to him, and hands to face. 'A fat husband is a credit. If he works.'

'I work,' he said. 'Also I am bald.'

'Babies are always bald,' Solva said, in the little voice. 'They grow, and hair comes, and when they are old enough, it falls off them. What is the odds, bald or not? Babies they always are.'

'It is true,' he said, and very serious. 'But whiskers. That is not a baby, no?'

'Salt in the butter,' Solva said. 'No salt, no savour. Go and wash, now, and I will send a maté before supper.'

'Many, many thanks,' Beretroff said, holding up his hands. 'The bombilla burns my tongue. Many mouths on one pipe, no. For Beretroff, no maté. Coffee, very good.'

'I am glad,' she said, and putting the maté up on the mantel. 'It will never come in my house, either. Tasting somebody else's old spit, ach y fi.'

'One cup, one glass, one razor, one comb,' Beretroff said. 'For me, only one.'

'How many women?' Solva asked him.

'One,' he said.

'Who?' she asked him.

Leaning in the door, he was, a couple of yards from her, and looking down at her feet, and seeming to slide lower, and he fell on his knees and little puffs of dust came with the bump.

She ran to him, and he took her hands and kissed, and speaking in his own language, and she looked up, and strained him to her, tight, O tight, the dusty head, close held and mothered.

And the sound of his voice was in me, and hard in the throat but without words, and I went from there.

13

The morning I remember well because the quiet woke me, and I knew we would have a storm. Clear, and blue, with rose in the clouds and red in the tips of the poplars, and gold shining from the last leaves, and not a sound, no bird, or dog, not even the splash of a frog from the ditch or a little drip from the pump. Not yet five o'clock and nobody out, but I was thinking of a fire and a cup of tea, and I heard a move, as if somebody was tiptoeing. Indios never moved like that, and none of us would, so I waited in the blankets, watching the doorway come lighter with the creep of the sun, and a tall man came to the side in shadow, and looked in, only half his face, and crafty to make you itch.

Vrann Corwen's older brother, Clais, it was, and I knew him from the Widow Glyn's because he was always coming drunk from Trodd, Split's, and saying he would have Vrann skinned in the butchery and the joints hung to smoke. Nobody took notice because it had been going on for years, and the Widow told me he had been put from the house when he was only a boy because he was selling sheep and cattle on the sly to buy drink, and pay Indio girls, and going off for months to live with a tribe and coming back in rags and nothing to show. So out he went, and when old Tanfi Corwen died, everything was left to Vrann, because Clais was a rascal and not fit.

'Good morning, Clais,' I said. 'While you are up, why not fill the kettle and start a fire?'

If I had been Dan, Three, and able to put three knives one after another in the same place, and an inch from his nose, he would not have hopped more, but he came quick with smiles and up with the kettle and out to the pump, and before I was dry from a wash, the water was on the boil, and in all that time no word from him. From me, either.

'Well,' I said, when the tea was poured. 'Have you come

to pay respects, money, or give me an order?'

'No,' he said, in the same voice as Vrann, but littler from drink, and speaking as the Indios. 'I want to take a horse if Rhinberry will let. My mare is lost. Not a mile from here. Sleeping by the river I was. First time in since the shearing, and look. I am thinking if she is cut.'

I ran to the stable, but Rhinberry's peons were at work and Merri and Mil, the bay mare, were pulling hay with the others, and I went back thankful, and Rhinberry was at the pump, and talking with Clais.

'Find the mare, first,' he said. 'If the girl will put a good beef on the spit we will have breakfast when we come back, is it?'

It took Rhinberry no time to see where Clais had come across the orchard, and all round the house, and out, off the path, down to the river.

But no mare.

Clais was running his thinness and flapping tails here and there, and showing the pink of feet through the soles of his boots, but Rhinberry stood where the grass was crushed, and looking and saying nothing, and I asked no questions because then, and now, too, tracking is far beyond me.

'Enough is here for a good debate,' he said. 'Four horses, three people with boots, and somebody else in rope soles. But if the mare was cut, blood there would be by the gallon. Not a drop, look. Not one.'

He circles his mount about the place, and had a good walk all the way round, and pointed where they had crossed the river, as if I could see, and said we ought to go back for breakfast, and I was ready. A good steak at six in the morning is a pillar for the day, and I was eating and Donato was cutting from the fillet, and I heard a smack! and Clais was on the ground, and Rhinberry standing over him.

'Now,' he said. 'Before you will push another bite between your jaws, what were you doing this morning? Two were with you coming in, and three more after. You had no mare. Speak, before I will open you at the liver.'

'Wait, Rhin, wait,' Clais said, in the little voice, and eating. 'Nobody was with me, look.'

'Stinking from every pore with wine, you are,' Rhinberry said. 'Your rags have not been from your back these months.

178

Open your mouth, or I will sink a boot in your lungs. Who, and why?'

'Hywel, Little Bit, said if I would help him, I would have money, and I did,' Clais said, still on the floor, and picking at the loaf and meat fallen in the dirt, and eating to show the teeth, like a dog. 'Money I wanted. Clothes and boots I have got to buy, no?'

'Who was he in the rope soles?' Rhinberry asked, and eating, without a thought, or so it seemed.

'Some old peon,' Clais said, and tearing meat from a rib.

'Of whose?' Rhinberry asked, and cutting a piece.

'Who knows?' Clais said, chewing a crust.

Rhinberry kicked the loaf from his hands, and put his foot in Clais' face, and pushed him flat.

'Whose peon?' he said, and holding the long knife between finger and thumb and letting it swing.

'His name,' Clais said, and looking sideways at the knife, and trying to reach for the crust of loaf. 'Wait you, Rhin. No, I never heard his name.'

'Who sent him?' Rhinberry said. 'I will put your bare feet over the fire.'

'Hywel, Little Bit, knows who he was,' Clais said, and putting in a mouthful of bread. 'Will I have a drop of wine to wash?'

'Water you shall have by the bucket, but after,' Rhinberry said. 'Hywel, Little Bit, told you what to do, yes? Tell me, before I will call the men to skewer your ears and hang you to dry.'

'No, Rhin, no,' Clais was saying, and tearing bread, and pulling meat from the bone, and still in the dirt, and dirt all round his mouth. 'Wait you. Mr Matithiah Morse's peon. I believe he was, and orders to do what Hywel, Little Bit, wanted.'

'Him in the rope soles was Matti Mumpo, then,' Rhinberry said. 'No peon of that weight I have seen. He was a foot in the ground every time he stepped. What did he want you to do?'

'The farm is bought, no?' Clais said, kneeling and eating. 'Wheat you have got. The wind was right. Pasture is very dry with you.'

'And a little match, and my herd would be an asado in two minutes,' Rhinberry said, eating, and no worry. 'My wool is in the barn. The flock is on the other side, but fire would reach them soon enough. This shop and everything in it would burn beyond ashes. Us, as well, and no chance. These poplars are snap as the devil's whiskers.'

'Well, Rhinberry,' I said. 'You sold to Matti Mumpo? And he would burn what he bought?'

'I sold for a good price and cash down, and more to pay when I moved,' he said. 'But if I moved from smoke and ashes, how much would I get? What else would I have? How much would you have?'

'Not enough to employ Beretroff,' I said. 'And where is he?'

'He went early,' Donato said. 'Before I woke.'

Rhinberry kicked Clais in the chest and put him flat again.

'Come on, you,' he said. 'What is the story of the mare?'

'I came to see Solva,' Clais said, and his teeth biting scraps from the beef rib. 'A niece, yes.'

'Ah,' Rhinberry said. 'Somebody told you she was here, then? It was you crawling about the place last night, was it? And somebody with you through the orchard and over the potatoes this morning. Rope soles speak as loud as boots. So Mistress Solva found the three of you down there, is it? And Beretroff was with her, yes?'

'Yes,' Clais said, over the chew. 'I am in famish for a drink, here.'

'In the river you shall go, now just,' Rhinberry said. 'And Beretroff went for old Matti Mumpo, yes?'

'Yes,' Clais said, and reached for bread, and had his fingers stepped on.

'Before I will break the bones in your hand, look up at me,' Rhinberry said. 'You were there, and a peon of Hywel, Little Bit, and Matti Mumpo, is it? Three of you.'

'Yes,' Clais said, and sideways with the little eyes to watch the boot crushing his fingers in the earth, but chewing still.

'And the fight was between Beretroff and Matti Mumpo, yes?' Rhinberry said, and bending to put the point of the knife between the bones of Clais' hand. 'Two big men fighting, and no blood, yes? Speak, or feel this blade slit you to the elbow.'

'Wait,' Clais said, watching the dent of the knife in his hand. 'Not Matti Mumpo.'

'And not Beretroff,' Rhinberry said.

'No,' Clais said, and rubbing his hand and reaching

straight for the loaf. 'A drop of wine would sop the bone of my throat, yes.'

'Half a demijohn you shall have to yourself,' Rhinberry said, and taking another loaf and cutting more meat. 'So it was not Matti Mumpo then? He was not there. Nelya Peninnah was in the rope soles, yes? And Mistress Solva, it was, who had the fight with her, no?'

'The truth,' Clais said, and standing. 'She was hitting, and Beretroff pulled by the hair. They crossed the river. Nelya Peninnah told me to cut the mare and give them the blame if they were followed, see. With Hywel, Little Bit's peon, she came, for him to show her where Beretroff was.'

'Once to be warned, three times to be careful,' Rhinberry said. 'The men will sleep in the other barn from tonight. The fields will be cleared today. The herds will move to pasture. The flock will go to the hills. The dogs shall go loose. They have been in the big corral because they worried the girls, here. They will have to be worried, then.'

'How did Solva know about Nelya Peninnah?' I asked him.

'She has got her peons with her,' Rhinberry said. 'Perhaps Clais came to the house to talk to them, eh, Clais? You have known them from a baby, see.'

'Yes,' Clais said. 'One went to call her in the house.'

'And why did you come creeping about the yard?' Rhinberry asked.

'I waited till they had gone,' Clais said, cutting more meat. 'I looked to see who was here.'

'To see what would go in purloin,' Rhinberry said. 'Have you spoken with Vrann?'

'No,' Clais said.

'His tracks were this side of the river,' Rhinberry said, and kicked, and the bread and meat were out of Clais' hands. 'How much were you paid, for what? Turn out your pockets before I will burn every rag.'

Clais felt inside his shirt and showed a roll of hide tied with thongs. Rhinberry pulled it from him, and let it run out, and took the notes from the pocket.

'Seventy pesos,' he said. 'Enough for many a good skinful. Only to light a fire, is it?'

Clais chewed, and stuffed more bread, spitting crumbs, and looking anywhere.

Rhinberry called up the yard for his peons, and they came running, as though they had been listening round the corner.

'Get the kerosene,' he said. 'Poor Clais is thirsty.'

'No, Rhin, wait you,' Clais said, and spitting out a mouthful to speak clear. 'Every word I know you have heard.'

'A sluice of kerosene down the throat with a funnel,' Rhinberry said. 'We will blister it from you. Tell, or gargle.'

'Rhin, look now, Vrann is my brother, see,' Clais said. 'Before he will have a daughter married, he must see the husband and make a contract, no?'

'Who told him Mistress Solva will be married?' Rhinberry asked him, and signing the peons to come close with the tin of kerosene. 'Who would know?'

'Everybody,' Clais said. 'She put notice with the Justice yesterday.'

Rhinberry threw the meat in the fire and the loaf went to the hens.

'Enough,' he said, in disgust. 'We could have known in the beginning, and no need to guess who anybody was. Clais, you have got one minute to go from here. If not, the kerosene will go over you, and I will put the match, and you will travel faster than on wild mares. Go, you.'

'Half a demi you promised,' Clais said, watching the kerosene tin.

'For not telling us, no demi,' Rhinberry said, and picked up a pebble. 'Go, and I will tell my peons to throw at you till you are over the fence.'

Clais ran, and the peons after him, and for minutes we could hear the shouts.

'So that is a Corwen,' I said. 'How to think that Lal comes from the same blood.'

'Or Doli, or Solva,' Rhinberry said. 'Father and grandfather of the highest and best. Look at the work at Maes Corwen. Clais was in the Territory riding before he could walk. Fourteen, fifteen, he was father of half a dozen children. Then he was living out there. After that, lost.'

'Vrann was better, then,' I said.

'His father favoured him,' Rhinberry said. 'Clais was always silly. A girl took him young. A baby with a white, and they are settled for life, above the others. '

'They live a difficult way,' Donato said, coming down the ladder. 'But from good trees, good fruit, no?'

'It will depend on the weather, and pest,' I said. 'I have seen many a good garden eaten, leaf and stalk. If a boy is caught young, and he can do as he likes, he is finished. He

182

will have no life in him to do anything except what others are wanting.'

'Gwenonwy comes for the wagonette, today,' Donato said. 'At four o'clock it is ready. But no paint.'

'A good excuse for her to come back again,' I said.

But towards noon the clouds were passing the poplars like blown steam, and not a sound or a move from El Pampero, and it was hot, and the sweat would go in trickles only to stand still. Midday, there was nobody else in our world except us two round the fire to eat, but the grey skies and heavy air were no use for appetites and we had brown bread and cream cheese and salad from the garden and only a bite or two, if that, and back we went to work. After two o'clock, and no sound, and I heard Donato shouting, and I ran out round the back, and a wind caught me and I was thrown to the wall, and while I was trying to think, the rain blew down and filled a boot while I looked, and there was no breathing in the force of it, and I crawled round the corner, and sat to have my nose free of water. In those little minutes the yard was flooded, and the flowers were all down, and branches were breaking from trees. I stood to feel my way to the door, and then it was that I heard El Pampero as others had told me, that I had never believed, but standing there, spread and pressed against the wall, I was taught that wind and rain could hold me against my strength. I was flat, and face held to the logs, and not a move in me.

El Pampero I heard at his best that day, indeed. Every little chink in the barn he found, and through it he blew the water, because torrents are not rain. Trees he threw down, the garden was part of the ground, every path was a river, and the ditch was a froth going a foot or more through the house and carrying everything in whirls, boxes, hen houses, kennels, wheels, logs, branches, and the poor poultry sitting on the top of anything to float, and twisting their heads to look with one eye up at the rain and the other eye down at the flood, silly, to us, but we were just as helpless.

Inch by inch I worked to the doorway, and once in, I fell on the bed, only inches above the water, to stretch and have my breath. Donato sat in the loft with his feet in a dangle, and letting the water drip off him. But neither of us tried to speak because the voice of El Pampero was strong enough to smother any sound ever made by a man. In those minutes I understood what a small lot we are. A couple of yards from

183

the door there was nothing except driven silver and the bits floating past, and the house and everything else was hidden.

But a shadow moved and Lal was in the doorway, sopping, and laughing to be helpless. I pulled off her boots, full of water, and lifted her to the ladder, and she went up, and waving to Donato, and I opened my chest and took a towel and dry clothes, and reached them to her. In she went to the tool racks behind the open doors, and out she came drying her hair, and wearing my shirt and coat that were big enough to go twice, and a blanket wrapped for a skirt. Still nothing to be said because of the howl, and the roaring of rain on the roof, so I lit a fire from shavings and dipped the kettle in water to my knees, and Donato came back with the tea tin and cups, and we put planks across the work benches and boxes on the planks, and a yard off the floor and the water only inches beneath, we sat comfortable.

Whether cold rain gives the skin another taste, or if El Pampero's rough brushing sends rarer blood, I might argue, but the kiss I had from Lal when she put the towel away was far from ordinary, even if any kiss from her could be called that, and it was then, I think, in all the noise and battering that I came to know the power of the lips. Before, kissing was only for the family, and in love, of course, the kiss was naturally in pair like bread with cheese. But to feel the life of somebody coming into you from the mouth is an awakening, and to feel yourself pouring out with nothing to stop it, not even will, or want, but only to drink and to flow, to give out, to accept, as if ages had made it right, and it was written, that truly is a wonder, and a beauty then, ever more.

From her eyes I knew there was no need to speak.

Always I had been near women with the family, and Bron for years, and others to speak to, and memories of more. All of them I knew as I knew a daisy from a buttercup in the fields. I never knew the woman herself, even Bron. By sight, and the sound of their voices I knew them, if that is knowing.

But a stranger to me was Lal. I saw her, and I was in love, whatever that is. I was dreaming of her through the day, and food would dry in my mouth to think of her, and thirst would only bring her closer. But who she was, beyond Vrann Corwen's daughter, or how she thought, or what she imagined, or if she dreamed, or where her mind went, or how she grew, or even if she put rags in her plaits, or how she

184

brushed her hair, or if she would wake in the morning and throw off the blankets and feel for her slippers, or go out tiptoe, and look for slippers after, I knew nothing.

Only that I loved her, strength and sweet together, if love is the choir that makes anthem in the veins, and sleep with no dream of her not rest, but waste.

But the storm got worse, and the skies were almost like night, and the fire lit the dripping water into little ropes of gold, and while the kettle boiled, Lal had her mouth to my ear, and shouting that Solva was trying to be married by the Justice without trouble from Vrann, and Nelya Peninnah had a big nose and limping with her, and Vrann had gone, nobody knew where, but what he could do with legal notice called, only he would be fool enough to try.

We were having a cup of tea, and Lal pointed outside, and Donato was up to his waist before we could move, and jumping splashing strides outside, and putting his arms round Gwenonwy James and lifting her to bring her in and she sat up there like a bird, smiling at everybody and wet as the rain. Another one for the ladder and a change, and Lal went with her, and while they were up there, Donato and I went up to the house. Rain was still strong enough, but less wind, and the water seemed lower, just above the waist, though I remembered we were on high ground.

Rhinberry was lucky to have laid bricks on stone, because the mud walls of the outhouses were all down, and the roofs had gone, but the farmhouse stood solid, except for a tree that had fallen on one corner, and water to the window-sills inside.

The Indios were sitting on the tables in the kitchen, about a dozen girls all squeezed together, knees to chin, and looking with big eyes at nowhere. Nothing was broken, and the roof held, so there was little to be done, and we went to the stables and found Merri and Mil standing in water almost to the girth, and gave them some oats to keep them in courage, and back, through the poor garden with nothing, not a leaf, to be seen, and to the barn.

'The river is running high,' Lal said. 'We ought to start thinking of higher ground if the water is still rising. Gwenonwy had to swim here.'

'You took a risk to come,' I said.

'I told you this afternoon, so I came,' Gwenonwy said. 'A lovely wagonette it is, too. But you will have to take the money, Mr Morgan. He says he is paid.'

'If he says so, paid it is,' I said. 'He is in charge of his own business. We had better set everything ready and have the horses where we can reach them.'

Lal came with me to the stable, and I told her about Clais, and the search for the Indio, and she listened in frowns, and stood still in the water, and got up in the trap while I saddled Merri.

'About old Uncle Clais, there is nothing more to do except to be sorry and give him a few pesos to go off and drink,' she said, after a long time. 'We have argued, pleaded, prayed, beaten, but no use. He will have to die, and that will be the end. But about the Indio I am worried to my soul.'

'Why should you have to worry about an Indio?' I asked her.

'It might be him my father is after,' she said. 'If he finds him near a cut tongue, he will kill him.'

'But it was Gwilym Martin told me it was not an Indio,' I said. 'Somebody is clumsy with the knife.'

'Enough is out to eat,' she said. 'If only I could kill him myself.'

Tears were quick in her eyes, and I went to her.

'But Lal, flower of my heart,' I said. 'Why are you so upset about an Indio?'

'You would have to find out,' she said, cold as the water. 'He will be here again because now you have been a help to him. Even from a little boy he would do anything for me. But always very shy. Him, it was, shot the arrows, fool he is. His inheritance he wants, and for his brothers and sisters. His mother was Tehuelche. Vrann was his father. My half-brother, and older than me. Ithel, his name is. Think of it.'

In my mind I still saw him, a big shadow in the dustcloud, waiting on the road to the racecourse.

'Would he have cut poor Tanfi?' I asked her.

'No trouble for an Indio,' she said. 'For that my father is after him. But a father killing a son is terrible. Even in the Bible it was stopped. I would be happy if only I could kill him myself.'

14

Memory with me is a picture, and if I can see a face I will
hear the voice, and if the words are not exact they will have
to do. Strange it is that important times are nearly always in
fog and without a word, but small things, like breaking a
bootlace or the way a woman held her skirt will stick with
you as if in the moment. Everything to do with Lal is clear
because I can see her eyes warm with the heat of her spirit,
and her voice is always with me, and the two together will
bring memory solid as statues, and often the time of day
from the place of the sun in her hair, or where we were from
the way she was dressed.

Coming back from setting the lectern in the chapel, I was,
and I met Evans, All Shapes, outside the city, and jogging
himself senseless with a knee here and one over there, and an
elbow back and one out, and stirrups dancing like a pair of
old clogs and trying to hold his hat on, and keep to the
saddle, and the string of a parcel between his teeth, and his
mare taking no notice of curse or cajole and changing feet
every moment, poor man.

'Well, the very one I wanted to see,' he said, and pulling
up. 'A wagonette like that one you made for Gwenonwy
James is what I am wanting, and sooner the better, yes. I
have gone very tired of this old thing, indeed. I am in
dangers of my life to be up here, look. Could you take an
order, Mr Morgan?'

Well, no sense to turn business, so I booked the order, and
cash to the centavo he paid me, and I told him when to come.

'Bad news in the Colony,' he said. 'The river is over banks
again. If the rain keeps on, we might have another flood, so
everybody is going out in the camp for a week or two. And
did you know that Nelya Peninnah has got Beretroff back?
Solva has gone to Maes Corwen. Have you seen any of
them?'

'No,' I said. 'They were up at the dam. We have had all the work we wanted to knock a bit of shape in our place.'

'You should have seen ours,' he said. 'Two barns we lost. Not a plank to show for both. Come back to the house for a small one. A minute, it is.'

More luck that I went there instead of saying no, because a crowd was in the yard and Mrs Evans, All Shapes, was busy with the asado, and Mr Matithiah Morse was speaking, but he stopped when we came in, though I am not sure he saw me, because I stayed at the back and Evans, All Shapes, pushed through.

'There is a nice surprise,' he said. 'Has everybody got a glass, and comfortable?'

'Everybody,' Matti Mumpo said, and laughing to himself. 'We came this way and we are going on to the city. The tongue-cutter has worked through the north of the valley, and in the last few days he has crossed south and coming this way. Last night poor Davies, Tom Tiddler's, lost his brood mare. Five leagues along the river, now. If he works as he has, he will be here, or near, very soon. The Colonel has got a map, look.'

Everybody crowded, and the police officers went in the middle, and I could see their caps and no more because as I thought then, it was not my business. So I slipped out, not in any way afraid of Matti Mumpo, but not wanting to speak to him, and for money not wanting to hear that laugh.

Merri took me home, and Rhinberry met me at the stable. Everything was off the farm, but most of the Indio girls were still working, and waiting to be married though nothing was certain when the men would be in, or how many couples, but we worked every night on a table and four chairs as a present for each couple, and crates of dishes and kitchen pots were stacked ready in the hayloft.

Nearly midnight, and taking off my boots, I was, after working, and a tap came to the door.

Strange, yes, but even with the knuckles some people can present themselves, and I knew Beretroff was outside.

'Come in, Anton,' I said.

A couple of moments went, and no move. But the door came open, and Beretroff stood there, so dirty, so worn, so lined in the face with sorrow that I had nothing to say, and I pointed to the bench and he nodded respect, and sat, weary.

A pot of coffee I made, and put a cup for him, and sugar,

but his head was down, and I had to hold the sugar bowl.

'I offer my life for something you can do for me,' he said, down at the floor.

'I have got my own life,' I said.

'Ask my Solva to permit me to go to her,' he said, in whispers.

'Go yourself,' I said.

'She would kill me,' he said. 'She would kiss me with a knife.'

'No business for strangers,' I said.

He nodded, and put down boiling coffee in a gulp, and no effect, not even a lick of the lips.

'That other one,' he said. 'The father promised to ruin everybody here. No more work. No materials. No place to live. The daughter promised to ruin Solva and her sisters. Take the property. Everything.'

'But why did you leave Solva?' I asked him.

'She left,' he said. 'She was very jealous.'

'If you were together, why should she be jealous?' I asked him.

'Every day Nelya Peninnah sent chickens and cream and butter, and sweet pastry,' he said. 'Every afternoon the peons came, with the basket and the wine.'

'You drank the wine,' I said. 'For that Solva left you.'

'She found Nelya Peninnah with me,' he said. 'Yes. It is correct. I cannot remember. I am an abyss. I have no place.'

'How did Nelya Peninnah know where you were?' I asked him.

'She followed,' he said. 'Every day she watched us. The peon said so.'

'The devil spawned a few here, too,' I said. 'Do you want to work?'

'I came to tell you what Nelya Peninnah told me,' Beretroff said. 'Her father has bought this farm and all the land on every side. Soon you must go. But wherever you go, the doors will close. For Rhinberry, for you, for Donato, for me.'

'Do you want to work?' I asked him again.

'Yes,' he said.

'Go to your bed, and start in the morning,' I said. 'Work we will, until we are stopped.'

Rhinberry said nothing when I told him, and he was away for a couple of days after, so except for the other two at meals, and the Indios coming to clean and make the beds, and a few customers, I saw nobody and work went all the better, especially after I had finished for the day. Then I pleasured myself with the furniture I was making for our house, and I took plenty of time because in every millimetre was a thought of Lal. The dining-room was after Hepplewhite, in teak, very hard to work but giving back a bit of beauty for every moment, and the upholstery was in deerskin brought from the Andes by Idwyn Thomas, and worked by Orkiki, a Tehuelche from the Territory, and a touch with him that made leather like silk.

Often I worked well into the night, because time went without help from me, and if a few minutes longer would bring more smoothness, or a better shape, the minutes were taken and I went to bed and slept happy, and if there is more to be felt than waking to see good work from the day before, I would like to share it.

Like that it was one night, and the puppy I had from Rhinberry put his ears up, and the hair on his neck stood, but he was trained never to bark, and there was no sound from him. Down he got and went to the door, lips over teeth and ready. That sort of sheep dog will kill a fox, so it is better to stay on the safe side with them, and if they nose you, to stand still while they are called off. Into the timber room I took him, where it was dark, and through the window he went, and no sound.

Only two moments after and I heard the shouts from the stables, and out I went with the lamp and Rhinberry's gun, and inside, but the noise was from the other end, away from the horses, and they were looking at me, poor old things, too, and very thankful and having a whicker. The lamp shone on the dog, teeth shining, and a big peon, with his baggy trews hanging in bits and his shirt in rips, and behind him, Miss Nelya Peninnah Morse.

'Call off the dog, will you?' she said, and very angry. 'Such animals, indeed. Visiting, and only a little later than usual we were, and having this. Nowhere else in the Colony will a dog be set on visitors. Disgraceful. My peon is ready to give you an account to pay for clothes.'

'Both of you, outside,' I said. 'No words. Out.'

I had the dog by the scruff, and out they went, and I took them to the barn where there was more light.

'Mr Winn is from the house,' I said. 'Have you got business with me?'

'For your employee,' she said.

'Not from you,' I said, quick. 'Go from here, and never enter again.'

'It is not yours to order anybody,' she said, nose back and pale eyes slid sideways, and a tone from the haughty if her voice had been equal, but she was still shaking from fright. 'You will be from here soon enough the moment my father hears about this.'

'Be first to tell, and we will wait till then,' I said. 'Before you go, what were you doing in the barn?'

'We lost the path,' she started to say, but she turned to the peon, and whispered, and he ran from there, and she looked again at me, softer, and breathed, and threw off her cloak, and the blouse of pale blue I can see to the detail this moment, loose, with lace at the collar and cuffs. 'Mr Morgan, please to listen, now, will you? Friends we are, and no quarrel, yes? My conscience is in pain with me because of poor Solva and that old Beretroff. A drunkard he is, and blaming me, and I wanted to tell him, straight. I am going with my father to B.A. soon, and perhaps I will never have the chance again. For the sake of poor Solva, yes?'

'You will do no talking to Beretroff tonight,' I said.

'In the morning, then, and I will sleep here, yes?' she said and went to the bed, and sat to toe off her shoes. 'Tired I am, and a day to shudder, then, and trying clothes and nothing to look nice, see, and in a search everywhere to find where Beretroff was.'

'Wait,' I said.

'No, no,' she said, and unbuckling her skirt to show her riding trews, and stepping out. 'Listen to me, Huw, is your name, no? Nothing is lost if I sleep by here. Nobody will know. Lal is at the dam, and Dada told me he saw her, so nobody will be the wiser, yes?'

Off with the blouse over her head, and nothing underneath.

Nothing.

Any woman without clothes is beautiful, but some women have got less here, and more there, and some have got more of everything everywhere, and others less, but Nelya Peninnah had everything a little more than that, and if you could dream anything as lovely you would be a fool to wake.

'Come on, now, Huw,' she said, as if everything was settled, and nothing more to be done. 'Out with the candles and these old lamps, is it? You have seen me enough. You are dragging, man. Come near, and look closer, and long as you want.'

But I could see the Widow, and at last I could be thankful for a lesson.

'Two moments you have got,' I said. 'After that, I will drag you outside, and well down the road. On with your clothes, and quick.'

She lay straight in the middle of the bed, hands by her side, looking at me down her nose.

A big girl she was, too.

White.

As if he had spoken, I heard Mr Gruffydd saying I would find out if she put her claws in me, and in the same moment she seemed to know. She got up, and walked slow to me, and I was sorry for poor Beretroff, because Solva, of course, yes, lovely indeed, but Nelya Peninnah was beyond thinking, and everywhere.

And me standing there with the lamp in one hand, and the gun in the other, eh dear.

'Huw,' she said, and soft. 'Stories you have heard about me, is it? Well, it is true, yes. No use to deny. What do these fools know outside here? What is a moral? Will you tell me? Hours they have talked. Prayed on their old knees, too. I have got pains with me, I tell you. Pains. Who knows what is pains? Cut it from me and put a moral there. Never mind them outside. A bull I am wanting. A bull. Be a good bull with me, Huw.'

I felt her claws, as if with hate, with teeth, and froth on her mouth, and her eyes wilder than a drunkard's, and dry, and I remembered Rhinberry telling of a woman to love, and the beauty, but wanting to run from the agony.

If to drop the lamp and the gun, I was thinking, but I felt the cold from the doorway, and the candles blew, and a couple went out, and Nelya Peninnah stood, hands behind, and laughed.

Exactly like her father.

He was standing in the middle of a dozen or more, and one of the men held the bar he had taken off the door, and another had my dog with a thong round the muzzle.

Laughing at each other, father and daughter.

192

I stood in front of the lamp, and the men turned their backs, and she went in deep shadow to the bed and started to dress.

'Well, well,' Matti Mumpo said, still laughing. 'Changed you have, again, then? Different, every day, a new one.'

'Mistress Morse came for a moment,' I said. 'I was taking her to the road.'

'Address your remarks to somebody with interest,' Matti Mumpo said. 'How are you, Nel?'

'Very well, Dada, but tired, yes,' she said. 'Did you come for a reason?'

'For the fresh air,' Matti Mumpo said, and laughing, and wiping his eyes. 'Who would think to find you here, then?'

'Yes, indeed, who, no?' she said, and standing up to button, and feeling for her shoes. 'You are far from the house, and nobody home, is it?'

'Empty, yes, when I came away,' he said. 'When your mother was live and well, it was always to the doors, and in crowds.'

'Well I remember,' Nelya Peninnah said. 'With nice men always. Not old peons.'

'I thought you would know better than to come here,' he said. 'Other places there are, indeed.'

'Yes, but men are here too,' she said. 'Why did you come?'

'We are rounding up for the cutter,' Matti Mumpo said, and dabbing at his eyes up at the roof. 'The last I want is to lose a good mare or two.'

'Will we go on a little bit, Mr Morse?' Hywel, Little Bit, asked from outside. 'The moon is coming, see, a little bit, here.'

'Go, you,' Matti Mumpo said. 'I will be there with Nelya Peninnah, now.'

'No,' she said, and loud. 'I will go by myself, or not at all. Now then, for you.'

'But Nel, my precious, come with your dada only till the turn,' he said, in a giggle, if his eyes were from the Pit. 'The night is dark, see.'

'Dark nights I have known before,' she said. 'My way I found here in the dark, no?'

'Be quick, wherever you are going,' I said. 'I want you off this farm.'

'Keep silence, I have told you, or you will be put from here tonight,' Matti Mumpo said, and shaking laughing. 'Mistress

Morse will stay for as long as she pleases on my property.'

'Go from here before I loose the dog, to start,' I said.

'Perhaps the men have gone too far to call back,' Matti Mumpo said. 'Tomorrow, you can expect to be thrown from here. There is nowhere for you to go, either, I have seen to that.'

'Everybody says so,' I said. 'Now I shall wait.'

'I will say a word to Beretroff,' Nelya Peninnah said.

'You will have to go to Clydach Evans,' I said. 'He is there, fitting shelves.'

'What is to be the end of this, God Himself knows,' Matti Mumpo said, and for the first time I was sorry for him, because if a heart he had, every word came straight from there, but he was still in fits with him. 'I will get rid of you and that Beretroff in the morning, anyway. That is two less. And when I am finished, you will have to go very far from here to find them, yes, Nelya.'

'You have said that before, Dada,' she said. 'About everybody you say it. But they are all still here, and where they are, there I will find them.'

She was looking at the furniture and walking from piece to piece as if in a shop to buy, and talking over her shoulder. Gently, in their family voices, they spoke to each other, and no notice taken of me, and nothing to tell anything out of the ordinary, except that in the tone of both was something not true on the note, as cats hum at each other, quietly, before the claws and teeth.

'If you want to examine the furniture, please to come in the day,' I said. 'I have got work tomorrow.'

'Nothing you have got tomorrow except a journey,' Matti Mumpo said. 'Nelya, will you come, now then?'

'To the corner, yes,' she said.

Out they went, and no other word, and a peon had their horses and I waited until I heard the gate swing shut, but for moments after I could hear Matti Mumpo laughing, and shivers were in the sound. Back to bed I went, and thankful, but if I thought of Nelya Peninnah lying there or not, I cannot remember, though I doubt if I had closed my eyes, and the dog was up, and the tension of his fix was making the bed shake with him. By the scruff I took him, and wrapped a blanket, and opened the side door.

Somebody was calling out there, beyond the gate, so I went for trews and a coat, and by the time I was in the yard, the Indios were out of the house and talking, and I sent them back to light a fire.

Tegwyn, Toldo, was out there, carrying the girl, and dragging the boy, and a great load tied about her shoulders, and ready to drop.

'The river is in the kitchen garden since this evening, and coming up every hour,' she said. 'Could you help us, Mr Morgan?'

But she refused blank to set foot in Rhinberry's house.

'No,' she said. 'It would call trouble on the children. He is an unbeliever, and smoke he is burning to the Indio gods. With you, yes. Him, no.'

Nothing to be done, so into the barn, us, and the Indios went away, and doors shut, and the moon shone.

'Wait you, now,' I said. 'The children will sleep in the chest. With the blankets I will sleep out in the timber store. You take my bed.'

'For you, I am a man,' she said, and so tired not to have the words clear from her mouth. 'For me, you are a woman. We will sleep in this bed, one and one, and the children in reach. If not, I will go from here.'

Poor girl, if she finished speaking it was only seconds, and her eyes shut, and she was asleep like her children, and not a sound. So there, in one bed we slept together, and I woke up to the best alarm clock of all, a whiffing of bacon and eggs and new bread and coffee, and everything ready, and the children washed and dressed and out playing in the yard.

'A wonder, you are,' I said. 'You must have been working all night, girl.'

'The soundest sleep for years,' she said. 'Up only a few minutes I have been, see. But everything was ready to hand. There is a lovely place you have got here, Mr Morgan. A good job the toldo is under the river. I was used to it, dirty old thing it was. No more.'

'Stay for as long as you please,' I said. 'Find your own corner, and I will use a hammer and nails to have everything comfortable. Rhinberry will be here tomorrow and you can make terms with him.'

'With you,' she said. 'Not with an unbeliever. It will bring bad luck, sure. The Widow Glyn blames everything on him. Everything was happy and going lovely, and then you made the coffin. From that very moment, nothing only trouble.'

'Daft, you are, girl,' I said. 'Rhinberry has been the best of friends to me.'

'To make up for the loss,' she said. 'No. I will stay here till there is a chance to move, if you will let me. In the stable is dry and clean.'

'In here, and I will sleep in the loft,' I said. 'Take care of everything as you would in a house. Keep the children from the shop. Have no more worry, Teg. Live quietly.'

All day I was waiting for the police or somebody to come and put us out, but when it was dark, we had not had a visitor, and I was thinking it was time for the children to be in bed. Then it was that I remembered they had gone after supper, and no sound from them or Tegwyn after. I looked all round the place quietly, but like a hen with her chicks, she had found a place somewhere, and I knew it would be hopeless to try to find them.

Pitch black when I woke, and I could hear the children, and the matches were anywhere except where my hands would find them, and by the time I had a lamp alight, and trews on, and a blanket, and the gun, it was endless minutes, but I will bet I broke records getting round there. In the stable it was, and Teg looked down at me from the haydrop over the horses.

'Somebody was in here,' she said, holding up the pitchfork. 'I tried to put the prongs in him, but he was off too quick. Was it the tongue-cutter?'

Merri and Mil, and two of Rhinberry's horses were in there, none of them showing any harm, but when Rhinberry's peons came in coughing and spitting from sleep, one of them said Merri's halter was cut, and showed the pieces.

'Sleep in the manger here,' I told them. 'Bar the doors. Until Mr Rhinberry comes back, you will sleep near the horses.'

'It was I told them to go from here,' Tegwyn said. 'How can I sleep, and peons near us?'

'Take the gun,' I said. 'But I would be sorry for any peon who climbed that ladder, indeed.'

'Two of them,' she said. 'And sleep is sleep.'

'Right,' I said, and threw the blanket in the manger. 'Here is comfortable as anywhere. Good night, you, and sleep well.'

'Good night,' she said. 'Now I can sleep safe.'

'Safe as you slept last night, too,' I said.

'Yes,' she said, and her eyes the wild, bright blue between the pitchfork's silver prongs. 'Safe from nasty old people, I meant.'

15

The night I learned much more comes to my mind because of Tom, Tot. Twice a week I went in to help with the English lessons at Miss Kathi's school, and the rain was pouring and the paths were to the hock in mud, and I met Box, Quiff, on the way, and he told me that Lal, Doli and Solva would not be coming because they had gone up to the dam with all the other families and breaking their backs to keep the water from spilling along the valley.

'Did you see Lal?' I asked him.

'Well, of course,' he said. 'If they let the water spill, the Maes Corwen canal will never hold the pressure. So you should listen to her saying a few words. Not to mention Doli and Solva, mind you. But nobody has seen Vrann. Off on the bottle, I expect.'

We went in late, and Miss Kathi was in the middle of the Subjunctive, and Box, Quiff, went to sit in the class, and I sat beyond the blackboard. Most of the students, of course, went to the lessons because it was a good excuse to be out of the house to meet each other, as I did with Lal, but we all had to learn, like it or not, even Tom, Tot. English he spoke well from being a soldier, so he was always first with the answers, and nearly always right, and turning very cocky with him, some said.

'This week I am being sixty-five, but next week I shall be being sixty-six,' he said. 'Present progressive is the first, and future progressive the second.'

'Correct answers,' Miss Kathi said. 'They will do for exercises in grammar. But neither are examples of good English.'

'The Drill Manual I knew page by page, and the Small Arms Training, too, and no marks against me,' Tom, Tot, said. 'If you tell me I am wrong, I will show you the page in this book, Mistress Jones.'

'I am sure,' Miss Kathi said. 'But if you knew the Drill

Manual, you still had to put the instruction to practical use.'

'Well, yes, practical, certainly,' Tom, Tot, said. 'But the words and the drill were the same. Here, you are saying the answers are correct, but not in good English. The book says it, and the book is English.'

'Put the book away and listen to me,' Miss Kathi said. 'Next week I shall be sixty-six. It tells everybody that now you are sixty-five without saying a word. Good English is fewest words to tell most. Grammar teaches you how to use your mind before you use the words. To think, first.'

'Well, indeed, I never think how to say anything,' Tom, Tot, said. 'I say it.'

'Now we are knowing,' Jones, Price Special, said, from the back. 'I often wondered, yes.'

Tom, Tot, was out of his place and up there, and a fist in a short right to hit Jones, Price Special, over the bench and nerveless.

'There is a fine state of grammar for you, aye,' Tom, Tot, said, and looking back. 'An English of the best, not even with a few words.'

Miss Kathi looked at him over her spectacles, and by lamplight in her black dress against the blackboard there was only to be seen the silver buckle of her belt, and the gold bow of her watch, and her face almost white as her hair.

'You should have asked permission to leave your place,' she said. 'Any punishment in the school is my prerogative. If I were a man, I would thrash you soundly.'

'Lower than the little things crawling in the belly of a dead fox, I am,' Tom, Tot, said, in a bow, and red and very quiet. 'I lost my temper, Mistress Jones. If you would hit me with anything, I would raise no hand or whisper. Old, yes, but not beyond learning a lesson, I am.'

'Take your book, and be seated,' Miss Kathi said softly, because Jones, Price Special, was rubbing his face and sitting straight, and trying to blink himself into seeing less than two of everything. 'Mr Jones, you were in the middle of explaining everything. Tells us, will you?'

'Up early I was, and no siesta,' Jones, Price Special, said, and looking round, and everybody very busy with pages. 'I could swear I was having a punch from somebody.'

'Your swearings are not our responsibility,' Miss Kathi said. 'Do you feel well? Would you like a headache powder?'

'No, good God, no,' Jones, Price Special, said, and very

rough, because Siriol Mathias was there, and he knew he had some ground to cover with her. 'I would like to know how I had this swelling, though. Can I dream so much?'

'You can,' Miss Kathi said. 'You should ask if you may. Mr Morgan, please read to us from Mr Charles Dickens.'

We had a page or two from *Bleak House* and Miss Kathi put some of the sentences on the board and parsed them, and showed how the language was used.

Tom, Tot, put up his hand.

'Words there are, and telling a story,' he said. 'But no grammar, only when you are asking subject and predicate. I never heard of them, before, no, and fourteen years solid serving with the English.'

'Perhaps,' Miss Kathi said. 'Ask yourself how you speak Welsh without knowing Welsh grammar?'

'Well, indeed a surprise to me if we have got some,' Tom, Tot, said, and looking round the class. 'I never had a word, or my father before me, and I wonder did anybody else?'

'Grammar teaches us how to put the words together, and why,' Miss Kathi said. 'How else can a language be learnt?'

'Indios and Turkos and Basquos I know, and speaking good Welsh,' Tom, Tot, said. 'If one of them has heard of grammar, I will put a rope on Orion, yes. Kankel, at Dalar Roberts' stable, will speak Welsh with the flower of us. But not a word of grammar. I asked him.'

'He picked it up in the house,' Rhidian Prys said. 'Easy for him, too.'

'Welsh is not easy for a Tehuelche,' Evan John said, from the side.

'He is not Tehuelche, pure,' Rhidian Prys said. 'He is old Tanfi's son. The eldest. He, it is, ought to be number one at Maes Corwen, not Vrann, or Clais, either.'

Miss Kathi took the cloth and rubbed the sentence off the board.

'Because you are grown up, you dare to take liberties,' she said. 'Mr Prys, if you speak without permission once more, you shall go from the school.'

'Mistress, your permission if you please,' Jones, Price Special, said, standing up. 'A lump in the mouth I have got, here.'

'Poor boy,' Miss Kathi said. 'Come into the house, and I

will give you a rinse of permanganate. Read Chapter Fourteen, the remainder.'

Jones, Price Special, went down the steps of the class and stopped at the side of Tom, Tot.

'If I thought you put a fist on me, I would fold you in the stove,' he said, bending to see better. 'I am not one to hit an older man.'

'Mr Jones,' Miss Kathi said, high, from the door. 'I am waiting.'

'Go, you,' Tom, Tot, said.

'Not when you say so,' Jones, Price Special, said. 'Talking from a hole in the floor, you are.'

'Go now, before I will put you in one,' Tom, Tot, said, turning a page.

Jones, Price Special, snatched the book.

'Put who, where?' he said, and bending, with his nose next to Tom, Tot's, but only a little move, and the short left hit him below the ear, and down he went, legs and arms, flat in front of the class, again.

'No siesta,' Tom, Tot, said, and picked up the book, and sat down. 'Sleepy, and full to the chops with grammar, aye.'

A few of them carried him out, and Miss Kathi called somebody from the house to get the medcine chest, and came back in the room and shut the door.

'I have never witnessed such behaviour,' she said. 'What is the Colony coming to? Even fists in the classroom in my presence. No discipline. No courtesy. We are catching the habits of common Gauchos. The class may dismiss. I shall make up my mind if I wish to continue.'

Out she went, and we all looked at each other, and some of the girls went crying after her.

'Your fault,' Colwyn Evans said to Tom, Tot. 'You should have had him outside.'

'He has been sniffing about the house while I was at the dam,' Tom, Tot, said. 'I had a little account with him, see.'

'Pity to pay in here,' Gil Martin said. 'If she stops English, who will give it to us?'

'If there is one here to be taught, she will teach, so no worry,' Eiluned Morris said. 'None of us are in comfort with Mr Price Special, not only Mrs Tom, Tot.'

'O?' Blethyn Kylsant said, tall beside her, and frowning down. 'Forward with you, Eiluned? It has taken you a bit of time to say so.'

'If I run to tell every time Jones, Price Special, or anybody else was being forward, I would be purple, and not a breath,' she said, and laughing, and a pretty girl, too, and red hair in plaits. 'But some are only joking, see. Jones, Price Special, is always business.'

'Right you,' he said, and looking as if he had filled a note-book. 'Shipping manager, and a straw hat and collar and tie every day, and no time to go strolling when the men are out of the house. No siesta, he said.'

'Working somewhere else,' Ben Rhys said. 'A plumber, perhaps. Fitting a bit of pipe, man.'

'A name you are giving to women,' Siriol Matthias said, from the back. 'I have been coming here with Mr Jones. Have you got something to say to me?'

'Only watch out,' Tom, Tot, said. 'Too many are pretending to be Nelya Peninnah. She has got the money to afford it.'

'Shame on you,' Siriol said, and pushing books under her arm. 'Miss Kathi is right. More like the Indios every day.'

'Act less like them, then,' Blethyn Kylsant said. 'Habits of Gauchos, yes, but without the usefulness, and not fit to saddle a good pony.'

'Some, not all,' Tom, Tot, said. 'You are come very high-spoken for a sudden, isn't it?'

'Eiluned is listening to him,' Gil Martin said. 'Pity for Nelya Peninnah if she meets the Corwens. They called her father all the animals yesterday up at the dam. He laughed at them. But they had to hold Solva.'

'If I had to run after a Beretroff, I would stay single,' Eiluned said. 'Not a cup of tea for nobody, and no wedding dress, either. And no presents. Well, well.'

'Not a marriage, but only notice with the Justice, it was,' Tom, Tot, said. 'None of mine will do that to me.'

'If she had a different father, no need,' Iolo Deri said. 'Everybody knows what is going on up there.'

'Perhaps you would share what you know?' I said.

'No, wait you, family business, that is,' Tom, Tot, said, and shaking his head at Iolo. 'The poor girl was driven, no doubt. But Nelya Peninnah rotted the man, see. She will go on rotting till she is prevented.'

'And what will prevent?' Gil Martin asked anybody. 'Come from Damaglou's, and she will be waiting for you. Or me, or him. Come from Trodd, Split's, she is in the back, by the horses. Or behind old Tibbald's. Or knocking at your window.'

'Come on,' Blaina Hughes said, and got off the bench. 'Everybody talks, I notice, but they all know where to find her, and she knows where the windows are. If there was not weight both sides, nothing would be in balance.'

Sarah, Buckets, came to the door and knocked her wedding ring on the jamb, a sharp rap I can hear to this moment.

'Will you be planted there all night then, or off?' she said. 'People have got to sleep. Work there is in the morning. Your voices do rattle in the boards, mmmmm, like old bees, with you.'

'Women we are talking about, Sarah,' Gyntaf Glyn said. 'We were saying there is a pity you are not thirty years younger.'

'If I was, you would be to the neck in the bog this minute,' she said, and such a temper. 'Thirty years ago you would not rest your eyes near me, never mind open your mouth. Go from here.'

The girls went with her, and trying to put an arm about her waist, but she threw them all off and stood behind the door waiting to close it after us.

'Poor Sarah, too,' Tom Tot, said. 'Husband gone in shipwreck, and looking along the shore for years, here, trying to find him, and calling over the sea. Then she carried buckets of water from the river to the houses for pay, and Miss Kathi found her outside, too weak to lift more. Now she cleans the school. Good old girl, but hard in the tongue, yes.'

'Muscles like a man, my father told us,' Moelwyn Pugh said. 'He saw her swimming. Nothing to say she was a woman till she came from the water.'

'How would he see when she was under?' Tom, Tot, said. 'Long hair?'

'Short,' Moelwyn said. 'That was why he stayed quiet to fish?'

'On the other bank he was, then,' Tom, Tot, said. 'I have been unlucky like that.'

'In the boat, he was, down there near the reeds,' Moelwyn said. 'We have got it still, and him gone these years. A tree trunk, hollow with an axe. I would never have the patience.'

'And where would he have a tree, then?' Gyntaf asked. 'The willows are no good.'

'The Andes,' Boelwyn said. 'One of the first to go, but

my mother was unwilling for him to go again. Seven children, and nobody to work the farm. But I am off when we have sold the harvest. Seven parts after Mama goes, there will be nothing worth for me to work.'

'My place will be cut in sixteen when I go,' Tom, Tot, said. 'If all of them have only seven children each, what is left for their grandchildren? Penny stamps?'

'Look at this water,' Eiluned called, from the dark, where the horses were. 'I have never seen it so high. Will we get home?'

'Go over the other end of Idris Ebrill's,' Box, Quiff, said. 'Let me go first.'

Horses I have always been fond of, but never more than on that night, because without them we could not have started, and it is sure we would never have reached home. Merri found the way by herself, and walked when she could, and swam when she had to, and all the time I saw nothing except darkness and the water falling from my hat, and heard only the splash of rain and the howl of wind almost as loud as from the mouth of a beast. But it was all the same to Merri. She went in her turn with the others and never paused except on the river bank to find a steady place for her foothold, and in she went, and out on the other side, and up the steeps, and down the slopes on her hinds, and across pasture sinking in mud, and pulling herself out leg by leg, and waiting, then, to have her breath, and on again, and all the time I was thinking that if I could have given her a hot bath, and rum and lemon, and put her to bed in blankets, indeed I would. But a horse needs only a good wipe down with straw, and a blanket, and half a bucket of oats, and no king warm in his ermines is more comfortable.

Couples had turned off on the way though I had seen nothing, but down at Anwyl's corner, Box, Quiff, shouted that he would take Blaina Hughes back to her place, and pointed along the path to Rhinberry's, and said he would be there to sleep. Merri found the stable by herself, and I gave her a good rub down, and the best blanket I could find, and a bucket of oats, and a good pat, then, and back to the house.

Tynant Lewis stood at the fireplace with his coat steaming on a chair, and the girls were laying the table, and Donato had his special pot to make good coffee, and a lovely smell of beans roasting in a tin in the ashes.

'I was on my way back from the dam,' Tynant Lewis said.

204

'The water was too high for the coach, so I will sleep here. I am very worried about the people up there. Nothing will move them if those Corwen girls stay.'

'What is it they all are doing?' I asked him.

'In the time you have been here you have spoken to a few vegetable mongers or cattle drovers,' he said. 'Tipplers or chatterers down here are nothing. Go up there and see the soul and the spine. Perhaps you will understand better what is in our people. Then talk. Especially about Lal and her sisters. Three for pride, there.'

'Perhaps you will tell me, then,' I said, because Donato was outside. 'What is this whisper I always hear about Vrann Corwen and the girls? Everybody seems to know. Using the whip. Driving them naked. If there is truth in it, where are The Twelve? You were quick enough to have me in front of you.'

'Where is gossip under control?' he said, and looking at the fire. 'Where will you find proof? From Vrann? From the girls? Who will speak? Who would dare? What questions would you ask? On what evidence?'

Strange feeling it is to look at a man and know that more is in his brain than he will let from his mouth. Even so, I knew that a lot was to be said, and he was in defence, but those moments told me he was a friend, and they are as clear today as then, and the sorrow of his eyes when he looked at me.

'Everybody has got a reason for madness,' he said. 'A man lives only a little while as a man. He is a boy first. Then his voice is breaking. Then he has got years of trying to learn his business. He is a man when he has got children. After he has passed having children, what? It is then he thinks of other times, and other lives he might have lived. Or other things he might have done. Other women, too. Why not? Is he prisoned? After all, we still read the Word. We accept it for the truth. The best examples are there.'

His voice I can hear now, low, and so sad, that you might think he was a peon speaking of long years of wasted money, and drunken nights and sorrow for wrinkled flesh and slack sinew. But he was the first man in the Colony, and president of the Senate, and the biggest landowner by far and more in the bank than any two.

And having everything, sad.

'If I had a good excuse I would go up there,' I said, and

205

kicking the fire to loose a few sparks. 'Lal asked me not because of her father.'

'If you want an excuse, they are in desperation for a carpenter,' he said. 'Rough repair, no more. My peons will go with you. Your stores will go with the pack troop. Good excuse? They will think you are come in the midst, without wings. When will you marry Lal?'

'The moment she will come by the arm instead of by the hair,' I said.

'There is property waiting for you,' he said, at the door. 'Remember it, I will tell the men.'

Tegwyn, Toldo, put her head in the window while he was going out.

'Too many in the stable to sleep comfortable,' she whispered to me. 'I am taking the children to the loft, if you will please to let me.'

'Go, you,' I said. 'But you can sleep comfortable here, in the house.'

'Never,' she said. 'For the children's sake, no.'

A peon came through the rain to ask shelter for his employer and two more, and the girls put more meat on the grill, and I went to the barn to make sure that Tegwyn and the children were safe. They were above the tool racks under the beams, where even the robins could not have reached them, and the three heads came from sheepskins up there, and I thought of the Child in the Manger, and their smiles and Good nights were little blessings like shining lights about the place. Out in the back I could hear Donato, but no Beretroff, and his bed was still bundled on the bench. To the stables, then, and a look at Merri and Mil, and mist over the lamp from the sweat of horses, and the mangers full of hay, and the floor at the end deep in straw for the peons. A pack troop was unloading, and I went round to the kitchen, and half a dozen in there, and Mr Gruffydd talking to Tynant Lewis, and for minutes nothing but handshaking and shouting.

'The last you expected to see, and the last to expect to get here, too,' Mr Gruffydd said, and like a boy with him. 'I never saw weather like this in my life. Did you get Angharad's letter?'

'No,' I said. 'Rhinberry has gone in for the mail.'

'A peon comes express to me every time a ship is in,' he

said, and opening an envelope. 'They will arrive in Buenos Aires about the fifth of next month. The day after tomorrow a ship goes up from Port Madryn. I hoped you would be with me, but Mr Lewis says you are off to the dam.'

'Before light,' I said. 'My love to her, and say I will bring a wife to meet her. I suppose they will stay in Buenos Aires.'

'Yes,' he said, but not much lift, either.

'He will do better to go up there,' Mr Lewis said. 'If he is going to be one of us, he will do his share, and everybody will know it.'

'Call at three-thirty,' I said, to end any doubt. 'Angharad will understand. Besides, where is there room for them here?'

Talk, then, about livestock, and thieves in the Territory, and the price of wool, and a prayer from Tynant Lewis to be held in the Keeping, and a lantern for everybody, and to bed we went. But I was wondering about Angharad coming such a long way, and what she would think of me for going somewhere else, for any reason, instead of meeting her. But a thought of Lal was stronger, and I knew Angharad well enough to know she would say Be off with you, boy, and give me a little push to be there quicker.

Box, Quiff, I had forgotten, but when I heard him shouting I thought he was drunk, and got up to take him out to the barn, not to disturb. But he was stone sober, and in the eyes, a stranger.

'Huw,' he said, and almost without shaping his mouth, 'Sorry, boy. I put my mare in, and next stall I saw. The tongue is cut from one of them.'

I ran, but poor Merri was lying there, and her mane dripping with blood, and mouth open and bubbling red, and one hoof in the air and the foreleg curved, like a hand she was holding out to ask why, and drooping, then, from pain and tiredness.

Standing there, only to look while they lifted her, I was riding again the hours in green shade, and seeing her shadow in the blue shine of the river, or black in the heat of sand, and turning among the pampas, or climbing the rocks, and swimming cool, and feeling the threat of her muscles working under me, and knowing she would go where I wanted and keep on till she dropped, and never with a bite or kick, but only a soft muzzle, and a pelt like velvet and a mane combed, and hooves scraped and the sides of her shoes filed bright. Rage, yes, to shake, but drowned only to think of the way she spoke with the points of her ears, and turning to see where I was, and eyes rolling, and stamping very dainty to be gone, and a whinny and a blow down the nose when I gave her sugar from the palm.

And now with a head turned, and an empty mouth, and a hoof held out to me, and pleading, and O, Merri, old beauty you were, nothing to be done.

Tegwyn, Toldo, sewed the sacks, and a little muzzle, and after Merri was buried we cleaned the tools, and she had a cup of tea ready for us.

'Look here, Mr Morgan,' she said, and metal hard in eye and voice. 'I would say nothing, but I must, see. Nelya Peninnah I am sure I saw down there in the shop, and running, her and somebody else when I was on the ladder.'

'Here the other night, and looking for Beretroff,' I said. 'No interest to me, then or now. Never permit her to enter the place. Tell her if you see her again.'

Three-thirty to the dot, and the troop was in harness, and I was up on Mil, glad to be going.

No rain, and moonlight over the clouds, and Mr Gruffydd came to the gate, quiet, wrapped in sheepskins, and stood till the troop was out, and I was last.

'Huw,' he said. 'Listen, then. Last night I could say nothing. But you know Olwen is with Angharad?'

'I expected it,' I said. 'When they know, they will forgive me. I have tried to build, but I need more time.'

'Of course,' he said. 'But there is something else, too. I know how upset you are. I would do anything to save you worry. But I was asked to give you a particular message from somebody. Bronwen is with them.'

In the name I heard my mother's voice, and all the life of the Hill, and my father singing with the boys out in the bath-house, and we were coming home to a good supper, and clean clothes smelling of gorse on the mountain, and a chorus in the kitchen, and sleep of the sweet, and candles in all the windows at Christmas, and holly everywhere, and mistletoe over all the doors, and a smile that was not a smile, and tears gold in the firelight, and a whisper to go from there.

So much there is, only in the sound of a name.

No use to speak, and I shook hands, and kneed Mil, and I heard the blessing, but I knew the curve of Merri's hoof, and in the shape was sound of Sarah, Buckets, calling for a lost one over the sea.

16

In a darkness of closed eyes, the bright sparkle I always see is the lantern Lal held up as if to light me through the rainbow. Never had I heard of one at night, but coming from the stones and out to the open, I saw the arc, pale grey over, and shining white in the middle, greyer then, and dull grey going to night below. But a rainbow, and the Indios with me shook their leather blankets like little thunders, and galloped for the lantern, and poor Mil tried to follow but she was tired, poor girl, and so was I.

Twenty hours in the saddle, and a few rests for the horses, and about an hour to cook a meal, and bullied the whole time by rising water that put out the asado fire in one long hiss only moments after we were mounted, and the tide coming white, unlike any flood I ever saw. But I had never seen a real flood. Our brook at the back of the house here came up a few times, and the sewers filled, and kitchen was inches under water, and my mother was in tears for the furniture, but a few shovels and a couple of ditches, and the water went.

Not the Camwy water, though.

It was not to be seen.

Hours we were riding, and dry wherever we looked. Suddenly it was there, white, under grey sky, nothing moving, and water coming as though from the ground, in a wash above the hooves, and the horses going on their hinds and splashing down, and whinnying, and turning away, and nowhere to go except up, among the stones and the sand, and in and out of the dips.

And the hours going in walking over miles of stones.

And out, to a lantern, a bright spark under a grey rainbow, and night all round.

Lal knew it could only be me, because nobody else would have been such a fool as to come by that way, and she slid off her horse still with its shovel harness coiled, and walked with the lantern, slow, to meet me.

Tired, she was, and I put my heart under each foot, to cushion.

'You are here at last,' she said, and leaned against me, but I should have been leaning against her, and I did. You can feel how a woman feels when she leans against you. She could be a thousand times stronger, but she will lean if she needs to know there is somebody.

'There is dirty you are, girl,' I said.

'Well, Huw, my little one, my heart, is that all you have got to say to me?' she asked me, in whispers, and leaning, arms at her sides, and her hat in my face. 'Dirty, yes, because there is nothing except water, and old horse shovels, boy.'

Laughing we were, quietly, leaning one against the other, but I knew who needed it most, because if she had moved, I would have fallen, flat, and if you have never had pins and needles after riding all day, you are not free to talk.

'Lal, I have come to take you down there,' I said. 'Money I have got in the bank, enough for years to come, and work in the shop for two years at least. The furniture is all made. Cows and sheep I have got. Chickens, geese, turkeys, I have got. The practical side is all done. There is a ring on your finger. Every drop of blood I have got is yours. Every dream I have had, you are in. What shall I say to an old hat with a piece of torn old ribbon? Raise your face, girl.'

She shook her head.

'I must stay here,' she said. 'There is work!'

'You are gone dull with it,' I said. 'Saddle, now, and come with me. You saw the rainbow. A sign, and given to few.'

'Noah had the dove, and a leaf of olive in the beak,' she said. 'I have got the rainbow in darkness, and you are here, God knows why.'

'And this shall be a sign,' I said.

'Enough for me,' she said. 'Faith, and work.'

'The pack troop is ready to take all you need,' I said.

'Nothing to need, nothing to take,' she said. 'All I have got is on me. Extra, two sheepskins, and they go on my saddle. Come, there is work for you, as well. Did you bring tools?'

'I thought a few might be useful,' I said. 'Our wedding could be on Saturday.'

'No,' she said, and standing straight, and turning. 'Not for many a Saturday, either. If this dam goes, everything in the valley will be gone again. If everybody got married on Saturday, nobody would have standing walls for Sunday. Where is the use in that?'

'I was only thinking of us,' I said.

'Up here we have got to think more,' she said. 'It is nearly time for our turn. Doli and Solva are sleeping. Have you seen Beretroff?'

'He has gone again,' I said.

The rise where Lal had been standing was highest of all, and there I stopped, and my mind is always going back, and in every sense I feel the pride and the shame and the pity that was in me then, and the wonder that I could listen to all the talk, but never, no, never dream of what was real.

The moon lit white above clouds throwing shadow over miles, and water in waves down all the middle, silver, wide as a sea, and pouring into a channel of rock, and out on the side nearest, and tipping over and spouting through stones built in a sloping wall. Men and women were piling rocks and sacks of earth, and children were filling the mouths of ditches cut from the canals, and others farther on were digging overflow trenches. Down near the river, lines of men on horseback were skidding boulders along the pebbles for others to push and lever on top of the wall, and teams of bullocks were hauling bigger stones and cartloads of sacks. Lanterns hung on sticks everywhere, and torches were alight and dragging long flame, and logs were burning high near the dam, and all across the slopes, hundreds were asleep in sheepskins in rings about fires, like ragged petals, pale, with a red centre. Over the land there seemed a breath, an act, a lifting of prayer. While I stood, a voice began a hymn I had never heard, and others sang, and more beyond, and the rest came in, and the night wind took gentle hold and laid the sound across the water, and a man dragging a rock on a rope lifted his head to sing up at the clouds, and when it was done, putting fists and shoulders and tramping legs into pulling weight towards the dam.

Down to the hut I went, and in lines and piles outside the door I saw my work. Horse shovels were new to me, of steel, and about two yards wide by a yard deep, and the same shape as the pan my mother used to sweep breadcrumbs from the table. A horse fitted with one to clear sand, or earth, or rock, would do the day's work of any dozen men, but the shafts were first to go, and timber was scarce. Out with the tools, and deciding what to repair, or throw away and make new. But there was nothing to throw. The only sound timber was in the couple of huts, so the posts had to come down, and many went in pieces behind a horse, and nobody said a word because they knew it was that or nothing, and in any event, they were hard to any sort of loss.

Well I knew the soul and the spine of my people.

Even I felt I could understand Vrann Corwen.

Every one of those women I loved, from the bare feet of most, to the split boots of some, even to the twisted string of their hair filled with dust, and greasy with the weeks of sweat and sleep.

Beautiful with work, they all were.

Lal, of them all.

Doli and Solva came down the path stretching, and making noises as if they had slept for a hundred years, and they looked as if another hundred would do them good.

'A nice cup of tea,' Doli said, in a voice thick from a pond with her. 'I have slept on a leg, see. Nothing I can feel. And I got pushed over yesterday. An old ox, coming down, and me coming up. I am bruised a bloody paintbox, here.'

'Well, Mistress Doli, such an expression, yes,' a man said, from the shadow behind the hut. 'Give thanks to be whole, and go, without unwomanly words.'

'I am the one to give thanks, and no advice from you, Selwyn Rees,' Doli said, and trying to see in the dark. 'Be squashed by an old ox, and you would have more to say, and I have heard you. Hell's damnation you said the other day when you scratched your old thumb with you. Blue, and green, and turning to mildew, and hurting to cry with me, I am, and shall I say There is pretty? Solva, you are standing one leg, girl. Where is the kettle with you?'

'To hell with the kettle,' Solva said, in the little voice. 'I am scratching lovely, look.'

'The tin is coming to boil, now,' I said. 'The tea is in my bag by there, and fresh bread, and bacon, and eggs, and a side of beef in the other bag. Choose which.'

'Beef,' Doli said, and pulling out her knife. 'A cup of tea, and a beef, and I will mend the dam and no help.'

'Is Beretroff with you?' Solva asked me, in a whisper, and

her face like milk in the light, with silvery hair, and the eyes of a baby, wide and hoping.

'I only came up to see Lal, but she wants to stay,' I said, and talking to talk. 'Beretroff is doing some work, somewhere, I believe.'

'Only wondering, I was,' she said, and off to help Doli, and not another word.'

Morning was full when the asado was done, and people on both sides of the river were eating round the fires, but as many were still at work on the dam, and after the knives were wiped and the mugs swilled and the matés emptied, the fed went down and up came the hungry, and more meat on the grills, more water for tea, more yerba for maté, and nobody asking questions or who would do what, but everybody doing something to be done the sooner to go back again.

Tireder people I never saw, and quiet, and red copper with sun and the scorch of El Pampero, and thin, eating only meat, and little bread because women had no time to bake, and drinking tea or maté, or where there was enough, wine in spurts from the goatskin bag. Only one barrel I saw, and that was filled with spring water for the children.

Through the day I worked, and worrying because there was so much to mend, and no spares, and more men and women came with broken shafts, and asking with their eyes if I would please be quick. No need to ask why because only to look up at the water would tell, even if the sound was not enough.

Rain came down, not in sheets or torrents, or any ordinary way, but falling to splash on the ground, like a tap filling buckets, endless, and hitting the shoulders not with pats or drops, but like the hit of a hand, and making everything in front a grey fog, and people passing only a few yards away, moving shapes, a darker grey, and a sound like somebody thumping an empty cask always on the corrugated iron roof. But over everything we could hear the river, and when people came in to get their shovels, or leave the broken for repair, their faces turned to the sound, and their eyes said all their tongues would not.

I understood how they could forget themselves to work together. After only that morning I had no wanting to go back to the shop, but only to stay to see the dam strong, and the river held, and the water beaten, and the canals flowing quiet to the valley.

Rain stopped in the late afternoon and Lal came to the hut to sleep. All day I had seen her between drifts of rain, either on the dam or going to it or up the slope loading, but except in the heart never close. Thin to wasted, she was, but her eyes were live and always the tender red-gold brown, and shining, even when she had to think to keep them open. In the back I put her, and a couple of planks, raised, to be out of the damp, but she laughed at me.

'This hut is for feed for the animals,' she said. 'I am here only to be near you. Or I would be up on the slope with the others.'

'Why not build sheds, all of you, and have a bit of comfort?' I asked her. 'In these years, you could have had a little town?'

'Too glad to go from here,' she said. 'If there was comfort we might stay longer. Besides, what use would a town be up here? And what would happen to the farms down below? Peons in comfort and us in Edom?'

'Send the peons up here,' I said.

'How many would stay?' she asked me, and laughing, and too tired to take off her boots, so I had to help her. 'Peons are useless. Only those with something to lose would work like us. Did Beretroff ever say anything to you?'

I said what I knew, and she wanted to know about Nelya Peninnah, and I told her, and if I had seen Vrann, and I said no.

She lay down in the sheepskins and looked at the roof, and sideways at me.

'If only I knew where he was,' she said. 'Solva is worry enough, but he is worse. First time he has been away. He was always first here, and last to go.'

'Did he go without saying anything?' I asked her.

'He will find who cut Tanfi,' she said. 'He has never been well since the day. He was from his senses one night, and off he went. No peon, nobody.'

'If the police catch whoever it is, they will shoot him on the spot,' I said. 'Tynant Lewis said so.'

She patted the sheepskins beside her, and opened her hand.

'Sit beside me till I sleep,' she whispered, nearly sleeping then. 'Always I have wanted somebody near before I slept.'

I lifted her shoulders and kissed, but she was sleeping

before I put her down, and the lids of her eyes seemed blue, and her plaits hung, and I kissed all four, and put them straight beside her, and I kissed her forehead, and she turned in a sigh, and Gabriel could not have wakened her.

But when all the lamps and torches were alight, and night was black, just as many were at work down there, and as many were sleeping like petals round the fires on the slopes. On my bench I slept and woke shivering before dawn, and got a fire going, and water on, but they were still working down there, and fire flamed along the hillsides, and mules brayed and horses were neighing, and El Pampero brought the crying of babies, and the men driving the bullocks were calling and urging them in voices that sounded like the agonies of the last on earth.

Lal slept.

In the quiet of the little hut, full of wood chips and rusted pieces of iron and broken harness and empty boxes, and forgotten coats on nails, she slept and my heart was with her, and about her, and under and over and around her, and I held, and cherished, and nothing more than the sleep that she needed more than I needed air.

Doli and Solva came up with hot coffee and bacon sandwiches, and we sat outside under a roof of odds I made, and we had breakfast without a sound, though the river was with noise enough, and if you spoke, it would have to be in the ear of somebody next to you.

It was a noise like the silence of an empty house, that you would never notice till you listened, and then you would be frightened because it got louder with the moments till there was nothing else to hear.

The sound of that river was more than water spreading to the horizon, and more than a white shine between the hills, and not only the boil in the cliffs, or the smooth greenish run over the rocks of the dam, or the spouts between the stones, or the waves and spray near the canals.

It was a true voice of natural warning, and nobody taking notice.

Doli was no more than half from sleep, and Solva not quite awake, and eating only to put something in their mouths, and drinking because the coffee was keeping the cold in its place. If they had washed, it must have been a week before, at least, and if they could have got a comb through their hair, it would have lifted every root, and their clothes were

215

in rags and part of the earth, and barefoot, both.

But to see them in the city, you would never know and so with the rest of them. Pride was in thought of it, and pity, too, that it had to be or there would never have been wheat, or grass, or flocks and herds, much less a roof or a street in the Colony.

Shame I felt again for any unfriendly notion I had ever had about any of them, for any reason. Even the Widow Glyn had served her years from childhood, and looking about, I could almost see her working, and all the women of her age, riches or not, and I said so to Doli when they were going back.

'Nelya Peninnah has never been up here,' she shouted, but it was only a little whisper. 'If she did, she would go in the dam, bitch of a bitch's bitch, she is. Her father is here only sometimes to look. One hour's work would kill him.'

Through the sound of the river I heard him laughing, and he was in the hut before I could turn to throw him out, and if it was her time to awake, or if she had heard, but Lal opened her eyes, and saw him, and he tried to go to her, but I stood in the way.

'This is my property,' he said, laughing to put teeth on edge. 'If you were not some use, I would order my peons to put you in the water. Out of the way, now then.'

'Outside, or I will boot you there,' I said.

But between us came Lal, and binding the plaits.

'Enough,' she said, and sleepy cross. 'Go from here and leave him to work, Mr Morse.'

'I am here with a message about your father,' he said, and laughing, and out with the handkerchief from inside his shirt. 'Mr Prosser Vaughan has sent a peon, now just, and he says Vrann has brought in twenty or more of his children to swear for his own. The Senate of Twelve requires you and your sisters down there, and Mr Tynant Lewis sent a message. Personal, yes. You are to be there without fail, or he will come up here for you.'

Lal had closed her eyes, not a line in her face, and put her hands together and pressing till the lids were trembling.

'Call Doli and Solva,' she said. 'I will get peons to find the horses.'

'Now you know where he has been, yes?' Matti Mumpo said, and drying tears with dabs, and laughing breathless. 'Rounding up his flock in the Territory, no? A terrible thing to do to you girls, mind. Nothing you will have for all you have done. Your poor mother's property, too, yes. And Indios sharing, and doing nothing in their lives, never.'

Bending double for the joke and if ever I wanted to use a boot, then it was, but Lal knew, and she put a hand out, and looked at me, a look I will always see, that made me think of the little bit of bright water between the ship and the quay, and everything going away, and nothing to stop it or bring it narrow again.

'They need you here,' she said. 'You have made friends, too. Will you wait till I come back?'

'A moment with the Justice and we could come back married,' I said.

'No time except for this, of The Twelve,' she said, and impatient, and looking at Matti Mumpo coughing fits into the handkerchief. 'Straight back, after. There are more important things.'

'The dam and your property,' I said.

'Without the dam there is no property,' she said, and throwing the sheepskins together. 'Without property, why any work at the dam? What use to think of anything else till what we have got is safe?'

'You said you had to think for everybody,' I said, feeling like a little one answering his mother.

'Think and help, and they will do the same for us,' she said. 'What, if not? Is there virtue in being beggars? Like Indios? Is my property going to them, and not a word from me? First, I will have my share, and my sisters, and then back here to protect what we have got.'

'Good girl,' Matti Mumpo said, and laughing helpless at rusty iron. 'Every word right. Only say, and help you shall have.'

'Not needed,' she said, and strapping on the pistol belt. 'Help if you can, Huw, and proud I will be to think it was for me you came.'

'If there was other shelter, I would go not to be near this one's property,' I said.

'It is everybody's, and for everybody you are working,' Lal said, and swinging up the pack. 'I am not sure which day I will come back. Good-bye now, and remember me every minute, and I will remember you. Put your hand strong in mine, and like that I will go.'

Strong in the hand I held her, and her mouth was a rose,

217

and she rested, and the tears came from her throat, and a fist on her mouth to stop, and running, then, and gone.

Only Matti Mumpo laughing to take her place.

'Well, you will have less than you thought, no?' he said, from the door. 'Not a third of Maes Corwen and a third of her mother's property with Lal, but only a little piece. Enough to grow a couple of spring onions, yes? And a family full of crosses. Nice, no?'

'Better than everything owned by Morse, and that female sewer put to use by every toe-rag in the Colony and outside,' I said. 'Go now, before you will have this hammer.'

Too weak in a fit, he was, to lift the handkerchief to his eyes. With light in a bright line all round him, and bent nearly double, he breathed, breathed and breathed himself upright.

'Ah,' he was saying. 'Wait. Sewer, yes. Wait you. Ah. Wait.'

In the scurry of a rat, quick, and legs going so fast you would think he might trip, but never, he went from sight in the same way, a big man, and fat, but light as fluff from a dandelion.

Later that afternoon Webber Thomas came in.

'Words you had with Matti Mumpo,' he said, and a different eye, and a different voice, and a different sort of man. 'He has been told that if he comes near here again, he will go in the dam, and a louder splash than a stone, see, and no move after.'

'I will do it, and no help,' I said.

'It will be done before you are in plague with him, swine from Gomorrah he is,' he said. 'If you are wanting pay for your work, keep account and you shall have it, cash.'

'No account, so no pay,' I said. 'Are you one from the top of the valley?'

'Yes,' he said. 'And while any of us have breath, you shall want for nothing. The girls will attend to your fire. Your food will come up same time as ours. Moishe Levy is sending timber, but his wagons are too heavy to cross the mud. We are waiting for a pack troop big enough. You have done marvels with nothing, and nobody knows how. Go, you.'

After that I was feeling better than for a long time.

But without Lal, lonely and hungry, and in pain of emptiness.

Every day was the same, and getting up and working, and having to eat, and working, and going into the sheepskins

218

and sleeping, and up again to work, and eat, and work. But for others it was the same, whether man, woman or child. Six years of age, they were carrying a sack of sand down the slope to be piled on the dam. The two little girls looking after me were not older. They lit the fire before I was awake, and brought a maté, and when it was empty, brought another, and one rolling the sheepskins, and the other watering the floor to sweep out, and one coming with coffee, and the other with a beef or bacon and eggs, or later in the day, soup and boiled meats, and always tea. Both of them I remember well, but not their names because they never had time to tell me.

Strange that a grown man could not be kinder to two little girls, and sit even for a moment to talk and ask their names and where they came from. But every moment and word and feeling was in the dam, and nobody had time to waste and the children had no time to play. So the little ones came and went like a passing of angels, and I was fed and the hut was clean, and work came in and out, and I believe I slept on my feet, like the rest, and the dam swallowed stones and sacks and sand, and the river carried most away, but fast as it went, more was put in, and night or day nobody told anybody what to do.

Only the water spoke, and in a voice to frighten.

Late one night, in a storm that would make you wonder could anything move, a black pony with a white mane and tail was under the plank shelter, and Michaye came in. The girls had sent her to look after me, she said, and stores came off the pony, and I had a soup, and a roast, and stewed fruit and coffee, and no talk of questions, or noise from her, and nobody happier, or fuller, than me.

She put her saddle and sheepskins on the other bench before I could think to say no. Not that I wanted her out of the place.

Shame above everything, but I was thinking of ink silk.

But whatever I was thinking, Michaye went into the sheepskins before me. Out came the pink sash, and the blue blouse, and other things rolled for a pillow, and no sound except the rain. What there is in a little thing with long black hair, and a dark skin, and black eyes, and not a word to say, God knows. But never mind Lal, or anybody else, I had to call myself names to have my mind free of her, and even then she was there, in a shadow, and a beckon, and I knew what those men had felt out there in the Territory for months on

219

end, and nobody to see day after day except a Michaye and her sisters, and little else only sheep to think about. Clearer, then, what Beretroff had meant about a man becoming used to the touch of a woman.

Wondering, I was, how many nights I could be next to her, knowing her so near, and no move.

But sleep can be a good friend, too.

She was up before light, and breakfast ready. But guilty I must have felt, or glad I was dressed and working, because I puffed relief to see Mrs Roper Hughes coming along the slope and looking friendly, but ready to take the smile from her face, too.

'Have you heard about Maes Corwen?' she shouted when she was near. 'Safe it is, for the present, there. I saw the girls, yesterday.'

'Good,' I said.

'Till Vrann goes, anyway,' she said. 'Then there will be a fight. The girls against all the Indios claiming shares. And my eldest sister, the one you met, remember? Mari Ann Gwythir, yes, she came back on the same ship with your family. Sisters, is it? In B.A. she left them, now just. Very nice, she said they all were. Very rich, too. First class, all of them, and the best of everything. You have been hiding yourself, Mr Morgan.'

'Behind tools and a bit of timber,' I said. 'How did you leave the girls?'

'They were going from Miss Kathi's,' she said. 'They found Vrann drunk in Trodd, Split's. Losing at cards in thousands and thousands, there. Tynant Lewis was very strict with him for false witness. Most of the Indios were not his children, they say. Mark my words, one of those girls will kill him.'

'Let us wait for the day, and pray against it,' I said. 'Did you bring stores?'

'Only food,' she said. 'Moishe Levy sent to tell Webber Thomas to load all the timber he wants, and Webber said for you to go. The pack troop is big enough with ours, see.'

If she wanted to say more to me or not, I was off, because Rhinberry was leading a string of ox carts down the slope and he saw me, and waved, but no smile, and Tegwyn, Toldo, left the children, and ran, skirts tied up, and crying, helpless.

'O, Mr Morgan,' she said. 'We had to leave, see. I told you there was a curse on that old place. I told you. Yes. I knew it.'

220

'Go back to the children,' Rhinberry said. 'You are making everything worse when you are crying like that, girl.'

'Crying for what?' I asked him.

'Beretroff,' he said, and trying to stop Tegwyn, Toldo, from her tears. 'He went back there and slept a couple of nights, I suppose. He must have had something too with the Indio girls. Somebody opened him and let the dogs in. We found him yesterday.'

'Opened him?' I said.

'Across the muscles of the stomach,' Rhinberry said. 'The dogs did the rest. Times enough he was told, but no notice. A good cup, yes, Teg, my little one? Dry your eyes, girl. One like that, who can tell him anything? Yes, Huw?'

But I was remembering the light in the hut, and bare arms pale against sheepskins, and a longing for the touch of ink silk.

17

Everything Under The Sun, Twice, was the name Moishe
Levy gave to his sheds at the top of the valley, nobody could
say truer words. It was a big Tibbald's in the open air, but
doubled and redoubled, and if you could find what you
wanted, good, but if not there was no help from Moishe,
because he was always too busy trying to find something for
himself, and cursing everything he had to pull out of the way,
though he had never been known to find anything, and people
used to say it was Lost In Moishe's when they meant it was
there, somewhere, but it would take the Devil himself to put
claws on it.

Wheels leaned against the fence, and rims, axles, chains
and heaps of every kind of scrap iron were red in rust among
the weeds in the yard. Stacks of timber were roofed, though
you would have to search and size for yourself. The sheds
were open on the south and east, with all the goods on high
racks one above the other down the length, and in the narrow
alleys you had to push, and climb, and crawl to search. If
you found what you wanted by luck, it was always best to
put everything in the yard and sit there to block the way, and
those waiting to go in joined the game by hammering all the
pieces of metal, till Moishe came running to add what you
owed, and so end the noise, that he hated, because music was
his life.

Merlin Afon was in the shed at the back, and playing the
harp for as long as anybody wanted, because in all his years
he had done nothing else, and his eyes saw the day as one
with night, and playing or not was all the same to him because
the tunes were sound in his head.

There I was, when I had finished writing the bill, listening
to the harp, and Mari Ann Gwythir came through the racks,
dressed, I believe, almost as I had seen her in Port Madryn,
and still shy, and the same look about her, though her hands
222

were whiter and she wore shoes with buckles.

'My sister said you would be here, and I have been looking to have a word with you, Mr Morgan,' she said. 'I was
there when you came from the ship, remember? Yes. Well, I
was with your family all the time coming over. Nice girls,
they are. Very nice. Well, about that I have come to see you.
Very surprised they were to hear about Morwen and you.
Perhaps for that they will stay in B.A.'

In her shyness and quietness, there was more danger than
all the shouting and bullying.

'For them to decide,' I said.

'I am well entitled to ask,' she said. 'I am the eldest in our
family, and no mean, so I have got to protect all of us. What
was your reason for such behaviour towards Morwen?'

'No behaviour to speak to anybody about,' I said. 'Less,
since.'

'Easy for a man, and no responsibility,' she said. 'Morwen
has got children, grown. Besides us, they will suffer. There is
a big debt everywhere.'

'I was a lodger and paying rent,' I said. 'I owe nothing.'

'What if there will be another child?' she said. 'What
would be your intention?'

'To have a good cup of tea, now, and nothing else,' I said.
'Is this what you told my sisters?'

'Only what Morwen wrote to me,' she said, and taking a
bundle of envelopes from the net bag. 'Would you like to see
them?'

In harp music, and nobody near, the noise farther away
from people looking for things in the racks.

'No,' I said.

'See what she says about you,' she said, holding them out.
'Everything very nice with you. No fault to find. Nobody
better, look.'

'Thank you,' I said. 'You, it was, taught me that means
Enough. No more.'

The bright look, with a lot of the freeze, came to her eyes
just like Mrs Roper Hughes that other time.

'If we find there is need, we will have an advocate,' she
said. 'Everything you have got will be attached. Leave the
country, and I will follow you. Anywhere.'

'Make good use of your time,' I said. 'I only wish Mistress
Glyn was here instead of you.'

'Remember,' she said, and off, quietly as she had come,

and she might have been a dream, on a breath, unseen, going into the light, because I went after her to ask if she knew Angharad's address in Buenos Aires, but she was neither inside nor out on the road. With such prospect to blight, there was no use to think of finding Lal, so when I got Moishe, at last, I told him I would start back in the first hours.

'They going to hold it up there?' he asked me, and pulling the little beard, and looking at the only crack of light in the clouds. 'That dam was dry from summer. Water goes through easy. They should build in concrete. They sacrifice. Always they sacrifice. Me, I like to see the sacrifice in concrete. It lasts.'

'But if it is no use?' I asked him.

'Never say no use,' he said, and turned his back, and went into the shed where Merlin plucked the deep, tri-string chords that flew a Dragon in the mind and lifted a quick, clear sense that even in the least of thinking, the Faith was there, always strong, and male, and resolute.

On the way to the Widow Glyn's I thought I would be strong, too, and showing a face of brass, and I had thought what to ask, and how to say it. But when I sat in front of her, I was like water, there. A look at her, and behind my eyes was a dream.

Nothing was changed, except that she had a lot of Mari Ann about her, and airs of patience, and looks upward slow, and down at the floor, slow, and modest with the skirts and little fingers, and speaking almost in a singing whisper.

'Mistress Mari Ann tells me you might be having another child,' I said. 'Accounting for time, I shall make up my mind.'

'No trouble for you,' she said.

'If the child is mine, none for you,' I said.

'Perhaps you have got a doubt,' she said.

'You be the judge,' I said.

'Nobody but you,' she said. 'Not before, and not after, or now.'

Never mind how badly you might have thought about somebody you met in the Garden, but if you meet again there is still a taste of the Apple and a want to strip the Tree. That little apron of leaves will hide nothing of what is known, and in a moment you are naked and the Serpent is in wreaths with him. Air comes warm, and memory is in pulse, and lungs are full, eyes heat, hands tremble, and without surprise you are ready to do what you have cursed yourself for doing before, and even while you know you will curse yourself again, yet no move is in you for those moments, and you are easy, and in sweet pain of hunger for the feel of the known and impatient to anger of any thought against.

But an Indio girl came quick from the kitchen to say something, and the Widow Glyn looked at her in the doorway, and the look stopped her like a poleaxe.

But in the look was all the ice of truth, and the Apple fell in shrivel of frost, and the Serpent slacked from a dead Tree.

An apron of leaves is not so pretty as what it hides, so everything came in its proper place, except fright in the eyes of the Indio girl.

'I tell them, and keep on telling them, to knock,' the Widow Glyn said, and for each word a fist on the arm of the chair. 'No use to speak. A stick is the only language.'

'Good-bye, now then,' I said, and a move to the door.

'Stay for tea, Huw,' she said, still sitting, and looking through to the other room. 'Nobody is in the house.'

'Thank you,' I said, and out through the front, and grateful for rain that soaked me in moments. Nothing else was in my head except to go back close to Lal, and I ran for Dalar Roberts' stable, and Kankel went to saddle Mil.

A man came to stand, and rock, heel and toe, taking snuff from a silver box in two pinches, and a red paisley from the front of his waistcoat to stop a sneeze, and back with the box and handkerchief, and hands behind a brown swallow-tail coat, and a brown bowler hat tipped over his eyes, and rocking back and fore, looking at me.

'Somebody Morgan, there is no doubt, and not long with us and covering expenses to carpenter, I presume,' he said, in English, in a voice to make your skin creep away from you. 'A hope to choosing divers of the female stamp for matrimonial. To date, no issue, is it?'

'Who are you?' I asked him, looking at a high collar and black satin folded in a diamond ring.

'To all excepts and pretences, anybody,' he said. 'If you listen to business, will you say an affirmative?'

'Where did you learn English?' I asked him. 'In chapel?'

'In the counting house,' he said, and holding up a long,

thin cigar like a pointer. 'One hundred thousand pesos, the offer. Half before, half after.'

'After what?' I asked him.

'A ceremony with Mistress Doli Corwen,' he said. 'One hundred thousand.'

'Are you mad?' I said, because I was sure I was.

'One hundred thousand,' he said, and took a case from his pocket with one hand and showed the tight pack of notes, and balancing case and cigar in both hands. 'Mistress Solva will marry Iowerth Probert. Prudent, and wide property. Business match. Mistress Doli, one hundred thousand, with property. No subtraction.'

'Why should I marry her?' I asked him, and trying not to laugh.

'She will be pleasure for espousing,' he said. 'Plenty without a coin.'

'Marry her yourself,' I said.

'I am chosen,' he said. 'We are ready now for a nuptial.'

'So am I,' I said. 'But without your help, or Mistress Doli's. Did she send you?'

'More authority,' he said. 'Her parent.'

Straight, without turning when he called I went to Dalar Roberts and asked him about the man.

'From the way he is dressed, Elias, Snuff,' he said, and looking at me one-eyed over the high desk. 'Sunday clothes every day, him.'

'Has he got a few in the belfry, there?' I asked him.

'Nobody fewer,' he said. 'Cereals, textiles and fancy goods. Machinery and general merchandise. Shipping and property. Wool buyer and sheep breeder. Living in Buenos Aires, and here on the ship just in. Step you like a dove. He has got peons very careless if he says so.'

'To the devil with him,' I said.

'A relation, no doubt,' he said. 'I will have a special bottle of reserve Mendoza to hear he has gone back to the family. But step you with ginger, aye.'

All the way up to the dam I was trying to hear what Mari Ann Gwythir might have said in front of Bronwen, and what Angharad would say to Mr Gruffydd, and how to persuade Lal to marry without telling her about the Widow Glyn, though I knew I would have to say it out loud in front of her, and the sooner the better.

But none of the girls were up there, and neither was

Vrann. Solva was ill, they said, and Doli was looking after her at the farm, and Lal had gone with others to repair the ditches feeding the top of the valley.

But the rain began again, and within a couple of hours the families were coming back and unloading pack troops, and putting their stores in caves dug from the rock, and hitching on the shovels, and down to the dam, then.

Rain settled in a weight to make the shoulders sore with the rub of wet clothing, and there was fog of water, and the only way to tell that people were still at work was in the calling of the ox drivers and the coaxing of horsemen using the shovels. Lines of them passed the hut, each dragging a couple of hundred pounds of stone, and I wondered which spirit helped through the days when the burden had been on the men and women, and in their hands, and of their muscle.

Idwyn Thomas came in with a pack troop from the Andes on his way to the City. On a white horse gone grey with rain, and a black poncho covering him back and front, and a wide-brimmed hat shedding water, I never saw anybody looking more like the soul of rain. But there was not the usual smile, and he stayed only long enough for a can of tea, and he said that the river was over its banks everywhere, and he had gone far out of his way with loss of days, and having to go back quickly or there was chance that the animals would never cross the depth of water.

Early in the morning, Lal rode down in front of the mightiest oxen teams I ever saw, and a long pack troop. I knew something was wrong when we kissed, washed for moments in rain, cooling the mouth, softer than blossom, but wondrous of another warmth and a world of beauty spun on the tip of a tongue.

'Solva?' I said, and helping her with the saddle and harness.

'Better,' she said. 'In any event, I was never one for that Slavo. One look was enough. Attraction of the skin, they call it here. I was sorry for him, of course. She was always afraid of marrying and having doubtful children. Too much inter-marriage there has been. But now Iorwerth is in the running. A good boy he is, and no relation, ever. His land, and her third of Maes Corwen and Mama's property will all be one. Very good marriage, that.'

'Then what is worrying you?' I asked her.

She put an arm on my shoulder and rested, and all other

feeling was out of me except to be a leaning post, a rock, a trust.

'Vrann,' she said. 'He lost a lot of money in bets. Nobody knows how much.'

'Is the man sure of what he is doing?' I asked her.

'Women have a serious turn when they are older,' she said. 'What about men?'

'Perhaps,' I said. 'Somebody called Elias, Snuff, offered me a hundred thousand pesos to marry Doli. Showed me the money.'

Lal laughed at the roof.

'A cow market,' she said. 'Ask my father what Matti Mumpo has offered for me. Millions, boy. Look, if Solva marries Iorwerth, that leaves Doli and me. If Doli goes, who is left? Me. Who would I marry?'

'Would you marry Matti Mumpo?' I asked her.

'You, I will marry,' she said, and pulling my ears. 'If not you, why not Matti Mumpo? He is only a man, the same as the rest. But not while Doli is alone. Who would be working? Vrann and a couple of us have always kept the canal, to begin with.'

'But you are slaves to a new Pharaoh,' I told her. 'You answer like a lot of oxen to the canal.'

'The three of us want to marry, and have our own houses, and no more running up here,' she said. 'We want to be settled. What other way is there? Without the dam, and the canal, and the water, what?'

I had the feeling of being in another case of the Widow Glyn, and everything being done for the sake of bank accounts and property, and nothing truly for the heart. With Lal, I could never keep the thought for two moments, but I made a vow to speak to her father, and when I saw Clais and some of the Maes Corwen peons coming down with a string of horses, off I went to their camp, and sure enough, Vrann was there, fitting new handles on shovels.

'Well, Mr Morgan,' he said, and using a knife to scrape, and no move to shake hands. 'Long since we met. A cup of tea?'

'Thank you,' I said, and stood at the fire. 'Let us speak without cutting patterns. Somebody called Elias offered me a hundred thousand pesos to marry Mistress Doli. He said he had your permission to try.'

'He did,' Vrann said, scraping away. 'They want the field

clear for Lal and Matti Mumpo. To me, one slice of bacon tastes the same as another.'

'I want to marry Lal,' I said. 'Everything is ready, but she wants to see her sisters married first, and living in peace, and Maes Corwen looked after.'

'I will look after Maes Corwen, girls or not,' he said, and the knife scraping slow and careful. 'True it is they have never had much peace. My fault, I suppose. Their mother said so, many a time, there.'

'But Lal is being penalised because she is the eldest,' I said. 'Why has she got to wait?'

'No got to about it,' he said, and passing the knife on an oilstone. 'You are not thinking of the Widow Glyn, are you? No father to ask there, either.'

'But you had told me never to come near,' I said. 'Lal's property is nothing to do with me. I have got quite enough for both, and in years to come, much more. I will say the rest, short. Since I have seen the work up here, I have got far more respect for all of you than will ever come in words. I would do anything to help. Anything.'

Waiting, in the fine rain, and the wind blowing against the other side of the rock face and making a sound like hidden screams, and the hollow breathing of the river beyond, and the scrape, scrape of Vrann's knife, that had never stopped moving.

'They will make their own lives by the use of sense, and I will say the yes or no,' he said, in the little voice. 'What help could you give to any of them? You know nothing of a farm, or cattle, or sheep. What do you know of a horse? What use would you be? Any peon would be better. Go now, because there is nothing more to be said.'

'Lal said to me, once, that she would be happy to have sons like you, but thinking differently,' I said. 'So I feel, too.'

He was up, and the pale eyes were all pupil in glitter of white.

'No stranger shall tell me what my daughter thinks,' he said, in a voice small even for Solva. 'Go, before I am sorry.'

'I was sorry for your horse,' I said. 'I am sorry for nothing else.'

And I went.

No Lal that evening, and when I finished work, I went down to the dam, and asked Webber Thomas if he had seen her.

'Vrann and Clais have gone to bring posts,' he said. 'She might have gone with them. Just when we could do with everybody. Be ready to move from the hut. The dam is trembling under us, now. A few more hours of this rain, and we are finished, again.'

'Finished,' I said.

He passed a hand in the air.

'Like that,' he said.

Anything I would have given to join them in the line, but I had long found out that I was useless. Working on the top might look easy, and how to catch a grip barefoot, but I had a towny's feet, and without boots I was like a winkle from its shell. One minute of the cold, and never mind the sharpness of the rocks, I was helpless, and my feet blue where they were not in blood, and days in patches and bandage. But the more shame I felt for myself, the more reverence was in me for those royal ones at the dam, man, woman and child, for they were made of another flesh, a further spirit, and one I knew well, that took me in the throat when they sang 'Jesu, Lover of My Soul'.

He was never from them, and with Him they always were.

Night came, and the roof was in thunders, and where there were holes I had cascades making rills across the floor, though thinking of families up in the caves, and those still at work, I felt like a child on the knee and off to sleep in a lullaby.

Sleeping I was, too, and a knocking woke me, I suppose, because it was not in time with the noise from the roof, and for moments I lay there. But the knocks reminded me of a song that Rhinberry's Indios had sung many a night by the fire, so I got up and the moment I opened the door, an Indio hand touched my shoulder, and I hid the lantern.

Ithel came in, part of the dark, in a leather poncho and hood, and pointed outside.

'Maes Corwen,' he said, and though I had never heard him speak, yet I knew the voice, but no time to think how or where.

A horse he had ready for me up beyond the rocks, and a leather poncho like his, so off we went, in rain to destroy your senses, and so black that although he led on a halter, I never once saw him all the way. If you had asked me before how long it would take from the dam to Maes Corwen, I might have said a good four hours or more, and many a time since I have looked at that ground, but the only way we could have come has always made me shut my eyes, with paths for goats, and cliffs for somebody not me, and clefts in rock that might pass a sheep but never horse and rider, though to an Indio, any sort of land is only something to go across. When he stopped, I could hardly believe him, and all I had to do was walk through the orchard and beyond to the house.

A rough ride, and the rain, and gladness to be seeing Lal all made me careless, I suppose, because I walked round to the front, whistling to her.

Clear to this day I remember the silly face of Clais Corwen in light from the window, and from his fist the silver spin of boleadoras, and a cruel choking round the neck, and falling flat as any ostrich. My skull was between stones, and pieces splitting, and I opened my eyes in the big kitchen, and hanging like a side of bacon, with my hands tied together behind and the thong twisted down the legs to the ankles, and a loop under my arms going up to a hook.

Lal was tied to a post, and Doli to one opposite, and Solva to a pot peg in the fireplace. Vrann was looking at me under the lantern just clearing his head. A whip he had in one hand, and a bottle in the other, and he drank. Glass was smashed and shining on the floor, and blood was over his face and clothes.

The girl's clothes were in rags about the place in colours, and they were trying to turn from me, not to be seen, and bending their heads to be covered by their hair.

'Huw, can you hear me?' Lal whispered.

'Yes,' I said.

'Thank God you are living,' she said, and tears, and the other girls were crying, soft, as if hopeless. 'We tried to fight, but he was too strong. Poor Doli is bleeding from the whip.'

'Wait, now,' Vrann said, in the little voice, and snapping the lash to sing in the ears. 'I am the father in this family. Nobody will say anything, only except me. I told you what would happen, yes? Will I be denied for ever, then? Shall I have nothing for living?'

'You have got Indios with the Justice,' Solva said, in the voice so much like his. 'Them you had. Leave us for ourselves.'

'Dada,' Lal said. 'Loose poor Doli. She is bleeding.'

'You will bleed more,' Vrann said. 'The whip never hurt anybody, look.'

Overarm he slashed and the cut brought the scalp white through her hair, and she fell sideways, and Solva screamed, and the whip turned on her and cut the long fair fall apart, and he slashed at Doli and she was cut about the middle, and he slashed at me, one side, and the other, and it felt as if Vyrnwy had laid hot iron strips there, and I was thankful for heavy clothes.

'I will say,' he said. 'Not anybody else. Nobody, only me. Years I have lived, and nothing. Three going off to others, yes. Me, nothing. One pig, more or less, what is that, if you have got plenty?'

'Pigs he calls us,' Solva said, and trying to kneel but she was tied, firm. 'Put a knife in our throats before we will put one in yours.'

'I will give you the knife,' he said, and threw the whip in the corner, and lifted the bottle. 'Wait, you. I will hit Clais from here. That one will have nothing, either. More children than me. And wives to sell. I will hit him from my place. Wait, you.'

He went out, three steps straight and one to the side, and falling against the door, and shouting for Clais out in the yard.

I was hanging, and my arms felt they would pull soft out of me.

'Why did you send the peons away?' Doli said, in whisper. 'If they were here we would go loose.'

'Would you let a peon see you?' Lal whispered. 'When he comes back, try to make him quiet. Say nothing to make him angry. Nothing more with the whip.'

'I will pay to have him in the river and no sign,' Solva said. 'Doli, are you hurting, then?'

'My breath is paining with me,' she said. 'I have got nothing to cover me. I am ashamed from my life.'

Lal cried out, and tried to move, but she was held.

'Doli,' she said. 'The last time. Brave, now then. Stand anything. The last time. The very last.'

'The morning is soon,' Solva said. 'No more. For my life. I will go.'

Vrann came in, dripping water from hair and beard, and looking as he always was, and coming close to me.

'You are the cause, here,' he said, and hit me in the face.

'If I will get rid of you, I will have peace, here.'

'Dada,' Lal screamed. 'Leave him, now. He has done nothing.'

He ran to her, and pulled up her face by the long hair.

'Say that to Tynant Lewis,' he said, in the little voice. 'Ask him who you are. Then tell that one hanging over there.'

'Cut us loose,' Solva shouted at him, and struggling. 'Doli is fainting, look.'

'Everything I want, you will do,' Vrann said, and picking up the whip, and slapping the lash on the tiles. 'See this, now.'

Dishes from the dresser he took one by one with a snap of the lash to smash on the floor.

'I could make cuts in your faces,' he said. 'I could slice pieces from you. Others will have everything, and me nothing, is it? Will you do what I want, or will you be whipped? Never mind the Justice. I am the one to say yes or no, here.'

Lal moved, and he lifted the whip to slash, and past my face flew a shadow, and his arm was pinned to the planks of the wall, and blue feathers struck from an arrow, and another went through the cloth of his shirt at the shoulder, and a third through the sleeve of the other arm, and he tried to pull his arms away, and the girls were screaming, and the whip dropped and a fourth arrow was in his trews above the knee, and a fifth was in the slack of his shirt above the waist, and a sixth went through the top of his boot.

Through the window came Michaye, and she cut the thongs about Lal, and ran to Solva, and a sawing for the arms, and over to Doli, and cutting again, and the girls helped each other, and Michaye came to me and cut the ties at the ankles. But another knife cut the loop from behind, and I was lifted to the floor.

Ithel, it was, and he cut the bindings and put a rolled rug under my head, and went over to Vrann and levered the arrows out of the wall.

Vrann was smiling at him, and quiet.

But Ithel gave him no look, and when he had all the arrows, he went out, and Michaye went with him.

Not a word.

The girls were in the other part of the house, and while I tried to have the blood moving, I could hear them talking, but Lal's voice spoke through the window, and I heard Ithel, and then I knew it was his voice that had called to me that night in Gaiman.

As if fifty years had come upon him, Vrann went to sit in the big chair, and put elbows on knees, and chin in hands, and looking up at the light.

If to be sorry for him, or not, but the girls came dressed, and lifted me to stand, and Solva went to Vrann, and hit him full strength in the face, one hand and the other, and he sat there.

'Never say my name,' she said, in his voice. 'I will never say yours. Stay from my house. Nothing I have is for you. Nothing of yours will I have.'

She went out, and Lal helped me to lean against the dresser, and gave Doli an arm to the door, and Michaye took her.

To him in the chair Lal went, and looked down.

'We have been treated like this for the last time,' she said. 'We will be at the dam or Miss Kathi's till Solva is married. Huw will give notice for our marriage as well. We will ask the Justice for our shares of Mama's property. A whip near any of us again, and this will be your answer.'

She touched the revolver holster.

But he was looking at her, mouth turned down, like a little boy ready for tears over something broken.

Slow, she went on her knees, and put her arms round him and held his head.

'Poor Dada,' she whispered.

'Lal,' Solva was shouting from outside. 'Where are you, girl? We will lose the moon, and there is water to cross, and rising fast, here, look.'

Lal kissed his cheek, and stood.

'Good-bye, Dada,' she said. 'If there was something else to say, I would say it. But there is nothing. For Doli, or Solva, or me.'

'Lal,' Doli shouted. 'Quick. The flood is coming. It is over the north corral.'

Vrann was out of the chair and running, and Lal came for me.

'I will tie you,' she said. 'You can sit a saddle. Are you hurting, boy?'

'Not now,' I said.

Water came across the kitchen with a little sound like a hisht! as if it was surprising itself.

234

'O, God,' Lal said, and looking down, and hands to her face. 'The valley must be filling.'

'Ride for the top,' Vrann was shouting. 'Never mind the animals. Ride for the rocks. Lal, can you hear? Out, girl. The dam has gone.'

18

In the first morning we saw the water coming through the cliffs, black, and smooth with force, like a street of marble, and spreading wide in foam where the dam had been, and so high that the hut was under.

Not the clouds, but all the sky was grey, and the hills dark beyond, and the air quiet as if for shame, and no sound except the long breath of the passing river.

Men and women stood looking, some in groups with arms about, and some only standing, and children by themselves, and little ones with their mothers, and they might every one have been carved from misery.

Time there was, then, to look at them in their rags, and the women with skirts tied up about their waists, and the fine strong legs under, and blouses torn and showing breasts, and most of the men bare to the trews, and beards and hair whisking in a sudden gust, and the women's hair blowing like the flame of torches. Brown, all of them, planted solid on bare feet, and if they were Welsh it was only because the seed had come from Wales, but they were a new sowing, born to Patagonia, and sprung in the heat of El Pampero, of heart and spirit fit for the work to be done.

Soul and spine, yes, but of a new country, and a new people risen up to be water carriers in the desert, and shepherds, and keepers of cattle, and reapers of all abundance.

But standing there, hopeless, and in every face, loss.

'Another good bit of work gone again, see,' Webber Thomas said, coming down with tea can and sandwiches. 'No use to swear. When the river is at the old level we will start again, but higher up. If there was enough cement and railway lines we could build stronger. But the cost is too much.'

'If everybody gave, we would have enough,' Lal said.

'Would it suit a few down there?' Webber Thomas asked

her. 'After a flood there is always somebody ready to sell. How much land went for nothing last time? How much will go after this? Put a real dam up here, and the land in the valley is worth a thousand times more. When enough of the big ones have got land enough, a dam there will be.'

'We will wait for them to pay, then,' Solva said.

'In that day, you will have nothing,' Webber Thomas said.

'Think for yourself,' Solva said. 'In that day, my children will have a lot more than I have got now.'

Strange it is, but never mind how bad the quarrel in a family or what words have been said, hate or not, all will come quiet and at peace if there is enough trouble outside. So it was with Vrann and the girls. There was no question that he would lead and they would follow, or that he would take charge of the ox carts, and they would go after with the pack troop carrying food and spares. The way to the city was under water and so was all the valley, so the only place to live was high on the edge of the pampas, where everybody else had gone. Little towns of toldos and huts were dotted over the slopes, but the best shelter was in the big wagons. We had about twenty, so everybody had good cover.

The Field of Fair-haired Little Girls was where we had our village of wagons and carts, and well named because when El Pampero was quiet, and the sun was in the west, all the clumps of grass looked like fair hair pulled up and shiny in a mother's handful ready for the comb and curlers. The girls, and more from other families, had their wagons on the other side of a ridge, but the asado pits were on our side, and they came over to eat with us, and in that way Lal and I were together except when we were at work. There was plenty to be done, too.

If I made one, I must have made twenty boats to save furniture and winter feed, and Lal and I went in the first to bring out poultry belonging to the families with us. Some of the houses were only half under water, and the family was living on the roof, but the washing was done just the same, and a couple of girls pegging out a line up there still had a hand free to wave when we rowed past.

But the river spread from our side all the way over to the hills on the south, and showing only the tips of poplars that I knew were far above any farmhouse chimney, and nothing moving except the current. We took poultry from the branches of trees, and from anything floating, and they were quiet, without a cluck or a flap, as if they knew we had come only to put them in shelter and give them to eat.

'Our thoughts are very kind indeed until they look fat enough to make a nice roast,' Lal said. 'Poor little hens, they are like us. Knowing nothing, and only eating to die.'

'Have faith, girl,' I said. 'Created things, they are. They will go back with us, with the roast potatoes, and salad, and the flowers in the window, and the wood in the fireplace. Dust we all are, and to dust we will return. Learn your lessons.'

'One good lesson I have learnt,' she said. 'To be comfortable down here.'

'One step forward, and you are with Nelya Peninnah,' I said.

'Many a time I could have been,' she said. 'It is easy enough.'

'Not with anybody,' I said.

'Anybody, you mean any man, and I will say yes,' she said. 'No need to look like that, boy. A man is the same, whether he is somebody or anybody. Nelya Peninnah is careless enough. It is not the man, or any of them. The feeling, it is, she wants. And when it is feeling, any man will serve. Why not? Take a cow, or a sow, or a ewe. Do they care? They will have their fathers, or brothers, or cousins, or anything put to them in the field. No difference in the calf or the suckling or the lamb. They will be born just the same.'

'But the human being is not like that,' I said. 'Men and women are not animals. There is law. Religion. Even a bitch will be faithful to one dog.'

I got that look, with the water shining gold in her eyes.

'Sometimes, if there is choice,' she said. 'And we are like that, too. We only pretend not. There are plenty of authorities. I have listened. But they talk for the sake.'

'Then what stopped you?' I asked her.

'Dirt, and smells, and roughness,' she said. 'And nothing settled. And babies to come. I have seen enough. I will have a home and furniture, and a girl to help. Then babies.'

'Those you have got,' I said. 'I will find a preacher the moment we get back.'

'No,' she said. 'Proper marriage in chapel, proper meeting of friends, proper honeymoon, proper house to come back to, proper life, proper everything. Forgive one, forgive the rest. Forget one now, forget everything else later. No. It will be proper, and in order, or nothing. What is an old wagon to go back to?'

'So the trappings are more important than love,' I said.

'The trappings are nothing but love, boy,' she said. 'What else is love? To give the best in us, and even more, that we have no idea we have got, even to surprise ourselves. The best, not the worst. Not something ordinary.'

'But no real giving,' I said. 'It must come as you want it. Like the money-changers. Show the coin, first.'

'Yes,' she said. 'Love is like that, with me. The better the coin, the better the love. So be patient, and a coin you shall have for that, too. You earned one for saying no to Nelya Peninnah. Not many have.'

'You know about it,' I said.

'Of course,' she said. 'Everybody does. She was standing there showing herself, and you were holding a gun. Well, we were sore for days. Doli was on the floor, there.'

'One thing this Colony will never need is a telegraph,' I said. 'Do you know about the Widow Glyn, too?'

'Well, certainly,' she said, and surprised. 'Mari Ann Gwythir saw my father. Nothing to do with me. And perhaps nothing to do with you, either. Mari Ann will do anything to have her out of that house.'

'But the house belongs to the Widow,' I said.

'To Mari Ann, the eldest, and all the land,' Lal said. 'The farm is Morwen's, and Rupert's property, of course. Mari Ann fainted when she saw the shop and sheds you were using. Everything has got to come down and Morwen will pay for that, too.'

'Not fair,' I said. 'She did it for me.'

'To keep you there,' Lal said, and no smile. 'If you pay one centavo, yes, I will be angry. For the baby, wait you. Let her have it, first.'

She put back her head and laughed, and the sound floated flat, beautiful as lilies over the water, and then it was I knew how silent everywhere, and so lonely the land.

'Poor Mr South,' she said. 'Innocent, yes, indeed. A fox in the run.'

'I am surprised you are not angry,' I said.

'I would be the same if I was a man,' she said. 'If the woman is there, why not?'

'But you are contradicting yourself, girl,' I said.

'If I was a man,' she said. 'I am not. And I am not the woman, either. So behave yourself, and have a coin instead. And listen to me. We have always bred our own livestock. That means choosing male and female, and setting them together to produce the champion. About breeding and birth we know as much as anybody. It is the same with men and women, and no use to speak as if it was something rude. Wonderful it is. Who but a fool mates wrong?'

'Well, we can get a pleasant idea or two, sometimes,' I said. 'No trouble to a few.'

'Well,' she said, and laughing. 'I can, too, I suppose. But I am not the few. And I never spoke to anybody like this before. You see? Love, it is, so be patient.'

'For how long?' I asked her.

'When the flood is down, and the chapel is dry, and our shares are in the bank, and a house is ready for us,' she said. 'That moment, we will marry. These days are for work.'

In that she was right, and I had time to feel more respect for the farmers, too. My workshop was a couple of big canvas tops over two carts, and half a tree planed smooth for a bench. Rain came down day and night, and the families without shelter slept in there. All day they worked in the rain, soaked beyond soaking, and a canvas roof at night was luxury, especially with a fire outside to dry themselves. Rock they were, and not a cough, and I never heard of anybody sick. Boys of eight and nine were tending herds and flocks out on the pampas and coming in once a week for bread and salt, and a handful of tea if their families had any. Not many had anything, so it was the Maes Corwen larder that kept everybody, and the girls opened the store cart in the morning, and it was like a shop there, except that nobody paid any money. Everybody knew that Maes Corwen could afford everything, but I never heard it said, and neither did I hear anybody saying Thank You, as if they were getting a lot for nothing. It seemed to be held unsaid that for the moment some of them were not able to feed themselves or have a roof, and others of better fortune did the sharing. In any case, whatever I had heard before, I found them more than generous and even careless. I often had thousands of pesos left in the shop waiting for somebody to collect it, without a signature, and only me for witness. Nobody bothered. Time and again I saw cattle sold with a handshake, and when Webber Thomas wanted a flock of sheep, he had them with the tip of a hat, and pay later. But it was known that he had the money. Poor men would get very little anywhere, because generally the man without money or property was also lazy, or a drinker. The earth and the animals produced more year by year for the hard-working and sober, though wealthy or not, their ways of living were as they had been in the time of their fathers. Besides, most of them in the upper part of the Valley still lived by the Bible, and worldly show was sinful, and anything over bare necessity was extravagance, and Satan was crooking a finger in all of it.

The Maes Corwen girls were thought to be very nearly queening it in Egypt because they were always buying new hats and making new clothes. But the dresses came in very useful during those weeks, and in the end it seemed that every girl and woman was wearing a bit of Lal, or Doli or Solva. We had to make several trips to Maes Corwen and I built rafts to reach the house. All the livestock was off so there was no big loss, and the house was half stone and not a crack anywhere. The water was nearly up to the roof, and we had to dive to tie ropes about boxes the girls wanted and the first out was the coffer of Vrann's grandmother, but even then he would not have it taken from the house. Up on the roof it went, and I put up a little shed, and there it stayed, with a basket for the cat, and I can see her now, sitting up there, and Solva's tears shining, and Vrann told us that the first cat of that breed had come with his grandmother, and not one of them had been known to leave the house at flood.

'Why not build the house higher up?' I asked him.

'Show me where to put a tree,' he said. 'Desert, scrub, rocks. It will be worth a bit of mud now and again to have some green outside the window, yes?'

Right, too. El Pampero blew as he pleased up there, and not a clump of grass would grow, never mind a garden.

'Even if they got water up there, nothing much could be done with the land,' I said.

'Found out a little before the arrival of Mr South,' Lal said. 'It will feed sheep. That is its use.'

'Millions of acres outside there,' Vrann said, and pointing to the west. 'Give all the water you want. Useless. The earth has lost its body. Under the sea it was at some time. We found all sorts of shells there when we were boys. On the other side, the land is not even good for sheep. Your friend Rhinberry did well. After the flood, the salt will come up.

That farm will be fallow for years. He got a good price, too.'

'Matti Mumpo will pay much more to show Huw and the Colony he is not forgetting,' Lal said.

'Nelya Peninnah, too,' Vrann said. 'And that Slavo. He was put from there quick enough.'

'Indios, I was told,' I said.

'He went,' Vrann said. 'Others can go, as well. And nobody to ask questions. Why was he there? Selling wine out in the Territory, he was.'

'Who gave him the money?' I asked him. 'He never asked me for a penny?'

Vrann laughed, and looked at Lal, but she scraped mud from her boots, busy.

'Nelya Peninnah paid for the wine, and he got her the land,' he said. 'She has got title to leagues out there. Never mind her father, she has bought plenty of her own without anybody knowing.'

'Our peons are Indios,' Lal said, without looking up. 'Nothing moves except they tell us. Even where the grass seed blows.'

'Have they told you the latest about me?' Vrann asked her.

'Yes,' she said, and sharp, and eyes up at him, wide, almost black. 'But remember what we have told you. We will never pay any loss. We have worked too hard to see it go for little games with cards. Any paper you have to put your mark on, we will deny.'

'Keep your mouth in your business,' Vrann said, and red to the neck making his eyes bluer. 'My mark has always been good enough for anybody. I will do what is to be done with my own property.'

'Ours,' Lal said, same voice, same look as a cat's waiting to jump.'

'Mine,' Vrann said, and pointed to me. 'We will speak more in private, if you please.'

'Speak,' Lal said. 'Huw is in the family.'

'Not while I live,' Vrann said, in the little voice. 'Never. Remember it, too.'

He chained the boat, and I watched him go towards the horses. Lal was looking at me, and I felt a strangeness coming cold in her, as if she might have seen somebody else instead.

'From tonight, you will have my peons near you,' she said. 'Say nothing to them. They will say nothing to you. My orders.'

But almost as soon, her arms were strong, and she was close.

'Oh Huw,' she was whispering, with all the softness. 'You are like a little baby in this country. You have got to be looked after. You know nothing, my little one, nothing, who, or where or what.'

It is silly, but I was angry that she could look on me as one to be treated as a baby, though I said nothing because I thought it was not the time, but I was wrong. Back to camp we rode at a gallop, and when the horses were quiet, we heard the harp chords and a group singing, and hand in hand we ran to join them.

Moishe Levy and Merlin Afon were there, and while we were eating, Moishe told Lal that we should bow the head and pray thanks that the dam had gone when it did.

'This much more water, all that current, nothing stands up,' he said. 'So I got a business under ten feet. Wet. But under there. Some paint I lose, and a lot of rats. Could be worse, no?'

'What of the poor ones without a house and nothing to go back to?' Lal asked him. 'You have got money.'

'Anybody comes to my place, take the pick, credit is good,' Moishe said. 'I have money, so you blame me? You got money. Build a real dam. Concrete. Sticking stones with sacrifice, does it last? For two years you have been here. Next year?'

'Find out how much it will cost,' Lal said.

'Let me sleep good,' Moishe said, and cutting more meat for Merlin. 'Get an engineer.'

'One was up here,' Webber Thomas said. 'From the railway, he was. Millions he said it would cost.'

'A company you want,' Moishe said, through beef. 'Shares. Big money, that's not for the grocers. Why not ask the bank, you people? Who has the power?'

'Between the bank and the advocates, they would have everything,' Simeon John said. 'We would wake one morning, beggars in the pampas.'

'So this minute, what are you?' Moishe asked him. 'Anybody loses his socks. Do it with brains, you lose nothing. Only the sacrifice. The sacrifice you should lose. Who talks first?'

'The Co-operative has got money,' Lal said. 'Speak to Mr Rhos Phillips.'

Moishe laughed over a rib bone.

'Who listens?' he asked her. 'Millions in the river? So they lending themselves their own money, eight per cent? Cash? Pass here the salt, please.'

Lal spoke often enough about a dam after that, but once was enough to hear about the millions needed, and everybody was quick to speak of something else to warm themselves. They were willing to give their work for all those months because there was no real cost except their time, food and fodder. Bad luck, they thought it was, that snow had fallen too heavily in the Andes, and rain on top to swell the river. Other years they were all sure it would be better, and Tynant Lewis said so when he came up.

'What will we have for the millions?' he asked Moishe, in the shop. 'Each of us is asked to spend hundreds of thousands. For what return?'

'Dry feet,' Moishe said.

'But knowing the money is safe, my feet are dry enough,' Tynant Lewis said. 'More value to the land? Who wants it? For a fraction, he will have a hundred times more land and a flock of sheep in the Territory. Fifty years of crops would never pay for it. Who will pay for repairs?'

'For me a can of coffee,' Moishe said, and holding up hands with a thick callus in each palm. 'But let me say something, eh? Fifty years a solid dam, that gives a solid people fifty years' solid work, solid savings. Fifty years, no dam, who knows you lived?'

'For one, I shall not be here,' Tynant Lewis said. 'Those coming after must do what they are able. The last two or three years we have had freak weather. Let us see what will come, and save all we can. Like that, we shall be solvent.'

He went in the back where Merlin was picking out a tune for some children and peons, and sat to hum and have his tea, and without a word, Moishe raised a shoulder.

Many a time since I have remembered that shrug, and always with the same cold feeling that I watched a prophet stamp his stone with the great seal of verity.

People knew there was food and warm shelter to be had with us, and we filled the paths with stone to keep our feet from mud, and the toldos and wagons were put in rows, always noisy with children, and crowded in the early mornings and at night. My workshop was like a hub, with a good

244

fire of sawdust, and always a crowd in there to keep warm and listen to Merlin in the back, and sing sometimes, and give themselves the pleasure of watching me work.

Late one night when Moishe had taken Merlin off, and the crowd had gone, and I had a few minutes' blessed peace to read, I heard a pack troop come down, and a little while after, Doli came in, and sat by the fire, sopping wet and weary enough to fall.

'My father has gone beyond the devil's last prayers,' she said, and putting hands almost in the flame. 'What is to happen, God knows. We were buying grain, and Mog, Moke, told us he was drunk in the city and gambling again. We looked everywhere, but nobody had seen him. So Lal and Solva stayed and I brought the troop. I will have to go back again. How would I sleep?'

'I will come with you,' I said.

She smiled and put a hand on my shoulder, another Doli, and nearly the girl I knew.

'You are like a brother,' she said. 'Everything we have had to do ourselves. It is lovely to talk and know you will be with us to help. Where else can we look? Everybody wants to take everything from us. But we will see them frizzle to a twist in the pots, first. I will have to eat, and we will go, yes?'

She had bread and a piece of meat from Mrs Davies, Tom Tiddler's, but nothing would make her change dry, and she was in a gallop all the way back, and I had nothing to do except sit there, hearing only the wind past my ears, and her voice now and again, asking if I was still in the land.

The city was pitch when we got there, and Doli went down to Miss Kathi's and I went to Vyrnwy Beris', and the forge was still going.

'Everybody is off to the Andes,' he said, black as the night, and whispering with tiredness. 'Will anybody be left here? Two troops I have got in the corral and more coming in tomorrow. What are you looking so serious about?'

'Have you seen Vrann?' I asked him. 'Lal and the girls are looking for him.'

'I should think so,' he said. 'Nobody knows what he has lost. And putting it to paper, mind. Crying drunk, and playing, and nobody can stop him. With strangers, too.'

'Strangers?' I said.

'Never seen here before,' he said, and his eyes white in the soot of his face. 'And will you wonder why the girls are having to look for him? They are out in the back at Morwen's. Where you had your shop.'

'I would never think the Widow Glyn had anything to do with gamblers,' I said.

'Lodging there,' he said, working the bellows. 'Friendly little game, see. No money on the table. No loudness or language out of place, and one got a lovely little wife, yes. And the wife ill in bed, and Mari Ann looking after her. And in the back, Vrann, losing Maes Corwen. One of the Indio girls was telling Alwen, now just.'

'I will go round there,' I said.

'I will come with you,' he said. 'Wait you, while I wash.'

A good job I waited, because Doli and Solva came in before he was ready, and their faces would have put a surprise of fear in anybody.'

'Help us, Huw,' Solva said, both hands out to me. 'My father has lost our land. Lal has gone in there. She will kill them all, and trouble with the police. Will you help us?'

Vyrnwy came shiny from a wash, and buttoning a shirt, and we ran through the back to the stable behind the Widow Glyn's, and through the yard, and I kicked open the door.

Lal was sitting in a chair and a bearded man I had never seen before had a hand on her shoulder to keep her there, and him I hit, though I forgot I had the lantern so he got that, too. Byrnwy back-handed one of the strangers against the wall to shake the house, and the girls had Vrann on the floor, and Evans, Down, kicked his chair back and stood with Mari Ann and Mrs Roper Hughes.

'Thank you,' Evans, Down, said, as if he would be sick. 'Hours I have tried to go. But they kept me. I am not sure what game we have played, here. I have lost a lot. Vrann more.'

'The signed papers are in his pocket,' Mrs Roper Hughes said, and pointing to the oldest man. 'Be careful, because they have got pistols.'

'Morwen has gone for the police,' Mari Ann Gwythir said. 'Can you believe what they would do in my house? Their portmanteaux are all strapped here, ready, look.'

'Put everything in your pockets on the table,' Lal told the men. 'The signed papers, first.'

'Listen, we could do business,' the oldest stranger said, in an English foreign to me. 'We signed as witnesses to debt.

The game was fair enough. Don't play if you don't want to pay.'

'Shut your crack,' Vyrnwy said. 'Cut the straps, Mari Ann. Where is the wife?'

'Take everything you want but leave her alone,' the man I had punched said from the floor. 'She's sick.'

'Minute we get out, we get a lawyer,' the oldest man said. 'This is robbery.'

Behind him, Solva flashed the long knife from her belt and slapped the blade flat to his face.

'One more word, and I will turn it among your teeth,' she said. 'I can throw it straight as any bullet, the rest of you. No more noise.'

'Everything is here,' Lal said, with papers in her hand, and looking at the girls. 'We would have had nothing. What can we do with this fool?'

Mrs Roper Hughes came in with long fat fingers of soft leather tied in bows at the top, and put them heavy on the table.

'Only once I have seen these before,' she said. 'My husband had them from the Andes. Gold dust, it is.'

'Give them to the police,' Lal said. 'Nobody shall say we stole. What else is there?'

'Clothes,' Mrs Roper Hughes said. 'A lot of letters. The wife has got a box of jewellery.'

'Nothing else is ours,' Lal said, and burning the papers over the lamp. 'When the police come, Mr Evans, will you put a charge? Give them these packs of cards. And Vyrnwy, will you be witness? Huw, are you with me?'

We went back to the stable, and down the street we saw the gallop of police and the Widow Glyn with the lamp in front.

'Think,' Lal shouted over the high breeze. 'This moment we would have nothing. Not a single sheep. Not a chair, not even a cup of our own.'

She was off before I could say anything, and riding as if to leave herself. But we were going up to the pampas, and not along the Field of Fair-haired Little Girls, and my poor Mil was tired, so I walked her, and she went in Lal's track, and we turned down to a small lake in a shine of dull silver under stars, and a toldo with a fire bright outside, and I knew it was Michaye going away in a gallop because of the pony with a white mane and tail.

Lal was raking embers under the grill, and she patted a place on the log.

'I wanted to jump a world away from them,' she said. 'This moment, if you can think so, we would have been three in rags. Lives lived and work done and nothing at the end. Because of a fool with cards and wine.'

'Why are we here?' I asked her.

She looked at me, and at the fire, and up at the sky and across, at the dark miles.

'If I am nervous I can never stay inside,' she said. 'Mama was the same. Out, in the pampas, and stay till the quiet has rested you.'

'Sad that you have got a house and plenty, and you must come to the desert for peace,' I said.

'Mama used to come out and sleep a few nights for a cure, and go home new inside,' she said. 'Her father was the same, and he had it from the New Testament. He was killed by the Indios before I was born. Vrann could never understand her. Will you stay with me here?'

'Of course,' I said. 'Have you thought what will be said?'

'Michaye will be back now with her sisters,' she said. 'My peons followed you. They are over there. You were a night alone with Michaye. Was anything wrong about it? Am I different?'

The look, golden by firelight and tender with sorrow, is with me now.

'Supposing you were the Widow Glyn,' I said. 'How would you expect me to answer?'

'But why, because a man and woman are together?' Lal asked me. 'Our minds go that way because we are not very far from the corral. But why should we think so?'

'Those who are innocent very often place burdens on others a little short,' I said. 'It could be called thoughtless, perhaps. Or selfish. Enjoying a testing of the weak. Like dangling toffee, and taking it away.'

'Well, think how often I have slept with my peons and a dozen other men round a fire,' Lal said, and laughing. 'What toffee was I dangling?'

'Work is another matter,' I said, but it sounded out of place, too. 'Who told you about Michaye?'

'She did,' Lal said. 'She is yours for life, a gift. Take her where you want.'

'One mistake is enough,' I said. 'I will go back to the

248

shop, if you will lend me a guide.'

'Stay,' she said, and taking my hand. 'Why is it you will stay with an Indio and not with me? I have slept in a hut with you and nobody was there. What is the difference here?'

'There, you were tired,' I said. 'Here, you are walking on glass and hoping it will hold. You are not Michaye. You are white of skin, not dark. Your eyes are the rose and gold of the wallflower, not black. Your hair is bronze and bay and in gloss of chestnut, not with ink. You are tall as the night and slender as jasmine, not little as a child. Your legs are long and straight, not shaped to the horse. You are not Michaye. You are Lal. Temptation is in her. In you is the Fall. That is the difference.'

'Wait now, till these horses are quiet and I will say something nice to you,' Lal said, and looking across the lake. 'Three, there are. Michaye is not one of them. Who could this be, then?'

Up to that moment I had heard nothing through the night breeze but for Lal it was easy to count how many horses from the sound, and sure enough, three shapes moved quick by the lakeside.

'Solva, it is,' Lal said, and surprised. 'Is that police with her?'

She ran to the other side of the toldo to whistle for her peons, and the riders came at stretch gallop and pulled in to send dust over the fire.

Solva came slow off her horse, and walked to meet Lal, no look for me, and hitting the silver crop against the riding skirt, and turning to see the police, and a deep breath, then.

'Mari Ann Gwythir's mare was cut,' she said, in the little voice. 'The police have got Doli and Kankel in the prison. She is crying for you. Nobody else knew where you were. So I left her only to come here. O, God, is there trouble on earth we have never had, then? Is there? Lal, is there?'

19

The mend in this coat always laughed at Doli's needle, and to this day it shows the rip that Kankel made when he jumped to reach it because going in a hurry, we had forgotten a rope.

Round the back of the prison, we were, and under the cell window, Vyrnwy and Eynon Caerog Evans made a back for Box, Quiff, to stand on, and Ithel climbed on his shoulders to reach the ledge, and I threw up the coat. Good job it was made of corduroy because Kankel was well over six foot and heavy. But he might have been made of pastry because Ithel had him up to the ledge in one good drag, and pull one, push the other, three-inch irons came out like milk teeth. Two stronger than them I have never seen, and even Vyrnwy shook his head to look at the bars, bedded in concrete, and torn out clean.

Kankel was in the prison hut beyond the barracks, but the police had Doli somewhere inside with an Indio girl to look after her, and because Indio girls are alike, Michaye had already changed clothes and gone in. But to have them out was not easy. A lot of money was in the rewards, and most of the police were from the Gaucho Cavalry, and not men to joke.

Box, Quiff, said that Mr Justice had told him that Mari Ann's peon had tried to hold a woman he had found with a knife beside the mare in blood, and he had torn a piece from her dress, and somebody big as Kankel had pulled him off, but he had run shouting to the house where the police were talking to the gamblers, and Doli was found near the forge, and Kankel they took from his bed at Dalar Roberts' stable.

But with nobody to watch them, the three gamblers and the woman had gone, north, south, east or west, nobody cared.

Jones, Price Special, knew the barracks well from trading,

and came with us to show the way in, and Vyrnwy brought blacksmith's tools, and Parry Jones had his keys, and Gyntaf Glyn came to help Morris, Carpenter, and of course, Tom, Tot, was small enough to push in anywhere. Over the side wall and through the stables we went, and giving the halters a good double knot on the way so that if the police wanted their mounts in a hurry they would have a quiet minute or two for prayers, there, and down to the main block, among the weeds, and kneeling to catch breath and see the best way in. A low shed it was, and mud walls and a plastered roof, and sentries standing at fires behind a door of barred logs, and a light in the cell window at the end.

The hand on my shoulder I knew was Lal's before she whispered. Like an Indio she had come, and a shadow she went, and we watched her till she stood in the light from the lantern. Not a word was clear, but if the police were angry with her for being where she was forbidden, only smiles showed on their faces, and she put her hand between the logs and pulled their moustaches and scratched their whiskers, and in a moment the gate was open and she was inside. The gate slammed, and we ran to the wall, and along, and Parry had a master in the lock, and seven of us were in before the door at the end of the passage was shut. Up we went, looking through all the peep-holes, but the cells were empty, and Tom, Tot, had his ear to the end door, and it swung open while he turned, and he nearly fell in. A sergeant we knew looked at us very sorry indeed, and pointed inside with the sheath of his sword.

Silly we looked then, and we were sillier when we were all in a line.

Tynant Lewis sat with Justice, Dab and Blow, and the Colonel of Police at a table, with Lal, Doli and Michaye on one side, and Silas Ieuan Pendar and a couple of the Senate on the other, and Matti Mumpo and a few others, and the Gwythir sisters, and old Tibbald sitting in front, and policemen everywhere.

'Good evening,' Tynant Lewis said. 'Did you know that to enter this building without a permit is a serious offence?'

'Well, sir, and begging pardon, but we were hoping to have Mistress Doli out,' Tom, Tot, said. 'Barracks is not the place for a girl of ours, see.'

'She will stay with my family, and my word is given,'

Tynant Lewis said. 'Remain where you are. Mr Tibbald, please.'

'At your service, Mr Lewis,' old Tibbald said. 'As I was saying, I am prepared to swear that the piece was torn from a dress length and a white silk lining bought from me at the same time by the girls' mother. I should say about fifteen years ago. Mistress Sabel Corwen took the largest size French corset I stocked. I should have thought that the girls might have remembered giving that dress to somebody. Italian silk, you know.'

'What did it matter who we gave the dresses to?' Lal said. 'Nobody had dry clothes. We never wore anything of hers. Never.'

Tynant Lewis talked quietly to the Justice and the Colonel in Castellano, and a clerk was writing, and Matti Mumpo was laughing himself breathless, there.

'Might have been an Indio,' Mrs Roper Hughes said, above a whisper. 'Tehuelches are big, see.'

'Italian silk to an Indio?' the Widow Glyn said. 'Go on with you. White silk lining is unusual enough, never mind throwing it away.'

'I have always been lined white,' Mrs Roper Hughes whispered to her, in a big surprise. 'What, unusual?'

'Poor Roper,' the Widow said, and looking away. 'Him in his grave, and lined white, look.'

'A comfort to me, yes, always,' Mrs Roper Hughes said, louder, and a bit of temper. 'He liked me in white because it was shining, see. With him, shining I always was, and a dozen candles in the bedroom every night, now then, for you.'

'Well, hisht, girl, Dearly Beloved, and everybody listening here?' Mari Ann Gwythir said. 'What is next, I wonder?'

'With your permission, Mistress, the Senate of Twelve will meet again at eight o'clock in the morning,' Tynant Lewis said. 'That dress I expect is in the fire by now. The area of the Gwythir stables is roped off to examine for tracks. Kankel is exonerated because witnesses testify he never left the harness room all night. We are looking, then, for two culprits. Man and wife, or even two women. It requires strength to hold a horse. Only a good horsewoman would be capable. I never thought of a woman. But Mistress Gwythir's peon is certain because he held her until he was struck on the head. The inquiry must be sent through the valley. Which peon is living with an Indio woman? Or an Indio and his woman? The police will question everybody. I impress upon you, it is our duty to help in every way. The Colonel will now tell us his wishes.'

Between the moustache and the beard, and without a move of the mouth, it seemed that the Colonel respected all national sentiments, but nobody could do as they liked, and those concerned in the attempted rescue would go to the cells for the night and have the sentence marked on their papers, and if we were in trouble again, prison it would be for a long time.

'You are the first of our people to go behind bars,' Tynant Lewis told us, and very quiet, and angry. 'The night is before you to think well about it. Has anybody anything further to say?'

'Yes,' Mari Ann Gwythir said. 'I will stand before God in the Light, and swear it was not Doli.'

'Not in the girl,' Mrs Roper Hughes said. 'I have known her since a baby.'

'The mare was only lent to Mari Ann,' the Widow Glyn said. 'Mine, she was. For me, there is no charge to make, and I will never open my mouth.'

'We shall decide in the morning,' Tynant Lewis said. 'Good night, now.'

But then we found out what a good friend we had in Mr Justice, Dab and Blow, because when everybody had gone, he told Tom, Tot, he would trust him to make certain we all went home in peace, and he would like to see the day when we would be as loyal to Argentina as we had been to one of our own.

Tom, Tot, took off his hat, and looked at us, and at Jones, Price Special.

'Tell Mr Justice the doubt is not in me that the day will come,' he said. 'Have our thanks this moment, and that day, please to remember what I have said.'

Well we were out of there in a scramble, and I have never had fresh air coming tidier to the nose. The others went off home to stop their families worrying, but I found a good place in the forge, quieter than Dalar Roberts', and happy to settle in a pile of hides, and an open door blue with the sky in front instead of a little square and iron bars.

Coming from sleep, you have always got a bit of glue in the eye, and especially in the darkness of a strange place.

Pressing on my shoulder woke me, and Orkiki whispering that Rhinberry Winn was over at Mrs Beti Bont, Cross Keys, and waiting for me. Before I could ask questions he had gone, so up I got, but I made more noise finding my other boot than he had coming or going. Over to the stable, then, and Kankel sitting at the fire with other Indios. Nothing was said, and he gave me a maté while Mil was saddled, and told me how to reach Cross Keys.

Good job it was near light, because Mil had to swim from island to island, and at last I saw the morning fires like broom in flower along the slopes and up there I found everybody in wagons. The farms were under flood, but the livestock was out, and most of the ricks and all the grain they had managed to save, so everybody was happy enough. Rhinberry shouted from a toldo near a corral full of stray cattle and horses, and happy that I was there just in time for the morning asado.

'My little one is only a throw of the hat up the mountain,' he said. 'So for a couple of days I have been making a special crate to take her with me.'

'But why take a coffin?' I asked him.

'Not a coffin, for me,' he said. 'Up in the Andes, I will find a high waterfall, and there she will stay, at the top. When it is my time to go, I will be with her. Could I leave her?'

He asked me about the night before, and laughing out loud.

'Indios,' he said. 'Which one would dare? Crossbreeds, perhaps. Peons, I am not sure. How many can ride up and down wherever they like? How many have got a horse of their own, to begin with?'

'A woman was one of them, anyway,' I said. 'But Doli never had time. Over to Miss Kathi's she went for smelling salts, and coming back when the police took her. Poor old Kankel was the only big one they knew near the place. Never out of Dalar Roberts' all night.'

'Well, eat now, and off,' he said. 'Gwenonwy sent to say that Mrs Beti Bont was very anxious to speak to you. The dressmaker, she is.'

'What would a dressmaker want with me?' I asked him.

'Not sure,' he said, and looking up the slope, so I knew he would say nothing more, and I saved breath.

Mrs Beti Bont had a rush-roofed shelter higher up the hill, and raised on a floor of stone and walled with laced branches and reeds. Eight girls were sewing, and stands of women's shapes with paper covering dresses on some of them lined the walls, and bales of cloth to the roof on shelves, with charcoal fires in open plates to keep out the damp.

'Sabel Corwen, the girls' mama, yes, a good size indeed,' Mrs Beti Bont said, and sewing almost quicker than I could move my eyes, and never stopping except to break a thread. 'Everybody is wearing thick clothes under, so a dress of hers would fit plenty.'

A little fat one in a lace cap, and cherries at the side, she was, and very comfortable, sitting there and looking to the side of small, black-rimmed spectacles, and hands in a plump of dimples.

'Lal is offering a big reward to find it,' I said, and having a maté from the Indio girl at the fire.

'There is a shame, such a lot of trouble she is having, yes,' Mrs Beti Bont said. 'Gwenonwy James will marry Donato Urrisbiscaya soon, did you know? That is her dress, the third one, there.'

'Pretty,' I said. 'Neither could choose better.'

'We were all hoping you were going to marry Lal,' Mrs Beti Bont said.

'I am,' I said.

'That dress by there is for her,' she said, and pointing the needle at a white dress with embroidery on the shape. 'Last fitting done, and ready.'

'Good,' I said, and feeling as if I had walked into chapel with my hat on. 'I shall say nothing. Her surprise. When the water is down and the chapel is dry, then we will marry.'

Mrs Beti Bont moved to turn a sleeve, and her needle clicked and clicked on the thimble, and the cherries at the side of her cap swung forward and back only a little to keep time.

But I was held by the eyes looking at me under the lace fringe, and over the spectacles, and wrinkled to see better.

'I have been very busy lately with the wedding of Miss Nelya Peninnah Morse and Mr Ambrose Elias, and all satin, and patterns sent specially from B.A., coming from Paris,' she said. 'The one for Lal was spare no expense, too. Ordered by Matithiah Morse.'

Rhinberry talked to somebody outside, and a few hens were telling everybody about eggs, and the two girls at the end were laughing about something, but Mrs Beti Bont turned her head, and they stopped as if she had used a thong.

'Strange for him to order a dress for her,' I said, and the quiet voice surprised me, anyway.

'Impatient, he was,' she said. 'And rich enough, of course. Could I be a help in any other way, Mr Morgan?'

'Yes,' I said, and putting my wallet on the table. 'Take what it is worth from that, if you please.'

Over to the dress I went and tore from hem to top, and ripped the pieces, and nobody said a word, and Mrs Beti Bont opened the wallet and took what she wanted, and went on sewing while I was pushing the rags in a page of newspaper.

'Did you say Lal had fitted this dress?' I asked her.

'No, Mr Morgan,' she said. 'Measured, and put against one of her own dresses, exact.'

'Did she know?' I asked her.

In the palm of the needle hand, Mrs Beti Bont lifted a question, and turned down her mouth.

'Mr Matithiah Morse came with Nelya Peninnah, and they brought it with them,' she said. 'All hers went in before the river was too high for me. I would have taken Lal's in days ago.'

'It will be delivered today,' I said.

'Pity I am not younger to come with you,' she said. 'Goodbye, now, and have your brains cool, and no old temper with you, is it?'

Rhinberry had his back to me when I came out.

'Well,' he said.

'First, find Lal,' I said. 'Matithiah after. Thank you for sending the message.'

'Tegwyn, Toldo, you should thank,' he said. 'She told me. From Gwenonwy she had it. Washing clothes for the families, she is. Built herself a toldo near the bridge.'

'A good wife, there,' I said.

'Yes,' he said, and pulling the sash tighter round the waist. 'Well, I will look for you in the City tonight.'

Back, quicker than I came, and Sarah, Buckets, told me Lal had taken her father in Tynant Lewis' coach to Rawson to put him on a ship for Buenos Aires.

'Here later this afternoon,' she said. 'Plenty to do, too, poor girl.'

'Any more than usual?' I asked her.

'Everything on Maes Corwen under water and no good

256

for six months, the least, and a father gone weak as old Clais, and a sister held, and nothing in the bank to pay Dalar the feed for a horse,' she said. 'Miss Kathi had to lend her some money, if you please.'

Friendly she was, but talking too much, and not to speak sharply to her I had to pretend I was taking Mil across to Vyrnwy's and I found him in the kitchen, finishing dinner.

'Matti Mumpo you will find in Damaglou's,' he said. 'It is in smells of paint for the wedding of Nelya Penninah. I am not sure who will be there, but one of them will not be me. From tomorrow, no more farriery. I have sold up. First time I have heard Alwen sing in the house for years. Off to the Andes, we are, and she can marry Mostyn Williams. Always something to stop him coming here, or her going there. Will you be long with Matti Mumpo?'

'It all depends,' I said.

'Remember what is on your papers, and be careful of the police,' he said. 'If you are put from the country, Queen Victoria will be the last to send a battleship to have you back in.'

Few people were on the streets, but a lot more Indios than usual had made a camp outside on the hill and the smoke of their fires hung in long blue streamers between the hide tents, making them look as if nothing was solid but only floating up there. Damaglou's had changed, too. The outside was all painted white with flags in a hang, and green branches over the windows and doors, and about twenty peons were in the asado pit at the back all flaying, or spitting carcasses on iron stakes.

Rhoda, Damaglou's cook, came to the door, and said the place was closed for three days and given over to Mr Elias for the wedding, and nobody was allowed in.

'Please to give Mr Morse this parcel,' I said.

'Having a siesta,' she said. 'Up till all hours, he was.'

'A surprise for him, and my compliments,' I said.

But I had the surprise, because Rhoda came back and opened the door.

'Please to take a cup of tea with Mr Morse,' she said, all smiles.

In I went, and he was sitting up in bed, with a poncho round his neck and a nightcap to his ears, and laughing fat cheeks as a baby.

'Sit down, Morgan,' he said. 'We have not been friendly,

no, but time to start, yes? Yes. That business last night did some good, no? Sixes and sevens here too long, all of us. Work together for a change. What if I put you up in a good business?'

'I have got one good enough,' I said.

'For what, then?' he said. 'That screen you made for Lal is better than the best in B.A. Have a manufactory here.'

'Where did you see the screen?' I asked him.

'Where she put it out of Vrann's way,' he said, and laughing. 'Miss Kathi's, of course. He would have broken it for the fire. A sawmill I have got, and plenty of timber. Every kind. No need to look further.'

'I hope you undid that parcel,' I said.

'Well, yes,' he said, and doubling his knees to laugh. 'Rhoda will have something to clean the windows, no?'

'Did Lal know about it?' I asked him.

'Promised, I have, only this morning, I would never say a word unless she was there, in front,' he said, hand up and the Book in his voice. 'So let us talk in friendly business. When she is here, we will say as we like, yes?'

'If you promised, very well,' I said.

The door was pushed, and Elias, Snuff, came in, tired and no shave, and sucking rain from the coppery moustache, and wet about the shoulders and knees, with a nod sideways for me, and looking at Matti Mumpo.

'Confound my soul to hell,' he said, and coughing. 'No sign of her anywhere. I will have a fever from this.'

'Have hot brandy and a lump of camphor in it,' Matti Mumpo said, and in a new fit, there. 'Gone to visit friends on the slopes, she has, somewhere. Back in time, same as ever, look now, I told you.'

'If she will do this after, there will be trouble,' Elias, Snuff, said, and dabbing a finger on the bed rail. 'Everything I tell her, she will do. Soft, for a father, you are.'

'Well, no harm in her, and good peons to keep an eye,' Matti Mumpo said. 'Once married, you will see the difference. A father is not like a husband, see.'

'It will be learnt by the heart soon enough,' Elias, Snuff, said. 'Morgan, have you been asked to my wedding?'

'No,' I said, and Matti Mumpo was wiping his eyes, with him.

'Well, come,' he said. 'Not sure when, but whenever it is,

come. Bring anybody with you. Help yourselves, and have plenty.'

He went out, and shouting down the passage for his peon.

'Brains, there,' Matti Mumpo said. 'Some more capital, see, and we will be where we like, yes. Perhaps your sister might have an interest?'

'I know nothing of her interest,' I said.

'Everybody knows about Iestyn Evans Limited, of Cardiff and The Cape,' he said, and putting hands together at the planks of the ceiling. 'Millions in sovereigns, not pesos, there. A widow, too. Good friends, yes?'

'Very good,' I said, and I was up, and going.

'Well, nothing unfriendly with us anywhere, is it, Morgan?' he said, and laughing stitches with him. 'When Lal is back, we will speak again, yes? Not a penny to her name, poor girl, or her poor sisters, either.'

'Maes Corwen under water is still worth many a good penny,' I said. 'All the livestock is off.'

'Gone to the proper owners,' he said, flat, and laughing. 'Nobody can gamble thousands of sheep here and a thousand head of cattle there, and go on years. Solva kept all the journals, but he never told her anything, see. Books and figures, mysteries to him. Everything is with the Justice these weeks. Tickling it fancy for years, yes, very well. But one day, there is the settlement, see.'

'I will speak to Lal,' I said.

'Yes,' he said, without the laugh. 'I can tell you what she will say, too.'

His cup of tea I had drunk, so there was no sense in making trouble, though I would have had him out of bed and through the window in the mud for using that tone of voice about Lal, as if he knew enough to control her in a way he had never been able to do with one of his own.

Then, it was, when I stood outside Damaglou's, looking at a sky weary of water, and the roofs of the city redder in rain, and the puddles shining in ragged lakes across the streets and water going far to the mists, and mud to the ankle everywhere, not until then had I ever felt like the homeless, or somebody without anywhere to rest.

No better than a peon.

There was nowhere.

Dalar Roberts' stable was the only place, and in that waste, a refuge to be grateful for. A fire there was, day and night, and food of the simplest, and clean straw or hay, and plenty of blankets. Perhaps that is why the Son of God was born in a stable, to give comfort of mind to the homeless coming after, and strength to their spirits only to think of that Light among cattle in a sweet crush of clover.

Dalar was still in his shed at the high desk, but what he did there except drink maté and smoke, I have never known to this day, because not being able to read or write, he never opened a book or used a pen. Everywhere was in sheaves of letters stuck on hooks, or threaded on string, or pushed on spikes or put in covers, and when more papers came in with the mail, he bolted the door, and without reading one of them, he stuck, or threaded or pushed or put, and unbolted the door, and back to sit in the desk again. If he was owed money, he wrote marks on the blackboard that nobody else could read, and it stayed there till it was paid, and after six months the debt had a coat of varnish, so when it was said you were In Varnish at Dalar's, you knew it was high time to put your hand in your pocket.

'Wait you a minute, Huw,' he said. 'Notice I have had from Mr Gruffydd. The chief mate of the ship was in old Tibbald's this morning. He said Mr Gruffydd will go direct to Vuriloche instead to come back here, and give his wagons and the troop to Idwyn to take for him.'

'Where is this place?' I asked him.

'North and west of us, and over in the Andes,' he said, and waving a hand at the paper on the back wall, 'I thought he was settled in the Territory, there. But if he will marry money, go where he likes, no?'

'Yes,' I said, and off I went to old Tibbald's, and a nice cup of tea in the side room, and toast and beef dripping with the blood in a jelly, and small pancakes with honey and rum after.

'The ladies in the party suffered from the voyage,' old Tibbald said. 'A coaster, and limited accommodations, and the worst weather for some years, I was told. They all got off at Bahía Blanca, and took coach to the west. Pity. I was so looking forward to meeting your famous sister.'

'Famous?' I said. 'Because she has got some money?'

'It does bring fame of a sort, you know,' he said. 'She seems to have brought quite a number of people with her. Servants, possibly?'

'Not if I know Angharad,' I said. 'Money will make a

difference only to others. She grew up to serve herself.'

'Then she has a right to be famous,' he said. 'If you want presents, by the way, you may take first choice. The chests are open, next door.'

'I will bring Lal,' I said.

'Ah,' he said. 'When may I expect you?'

'I am going now to see if she is back,' I said.

'Ah,' he said, again, as if there was more he could say. 'Well, I shall be ready for you both.'

Lights were in the chapel when I went out, and traps and wagonettes lined up, and more coming. Indios on the slope were making a noise with drums and singing in their own way, and a crowd of them dancing behind the wineshop farther along by the engine shed.

Sarah, Buckets, came with a candle to the side window when I knocked, and shook her head as if to say Lal was not back, but I had seen the tracks of the coach fresh from the rain of the afternoon. Another knock, and she came again, more impatient to shake her head, and let down the curtain, and darkness, then.

There was a feeling somewhere inside me that I ought to smash a window or kick a door down, or do something more than wait. But my name was on papers at the barracks, and I was in no hurry to be back there. Nowhere else to go, and the rain was in a pelt, and not anxious to talk to anybody, so back I went to Dalar's, and had a couple of quiet matés around the fire with Kankel away from the others in front and like a fool, I slept.

Silent, the place was, when I woke. Not a peon, or an Indio, and not even Kankel was there, and the fires were red ash. Out, I ran, and trying to think what time it might be. But all the lights were on in the chapel, and more lines to traps and gigs, and a few people going in, and Indios in a crowd all round. Through them I pushed, down to the school.

'Yes, Mr Morgan, we have been looking for you, too,' Sarah, Buckets, said, and opening the door wide. 'Through the classroom, if you please, and the little withdrawing room at the back.'

One lamp with a white shade, and in a white dress and silver belt, Lal stood by the fireplace looking at the china dogs and the candles, and the dark hair in loose braids had been piled without neatness, and only her eyes were turned, no smile, and deep lines new to me, and in the shoulders and the clasp of hands a tiredness I had never seen before.

But she put out her arms to stop me.

'Wait,' she said. 'Thank God nothing came to you from last night. Huw, I have got to tell you. I wish to God I could go, and not a word. But there is nothing spared for us.'

'I could have shivered to hear the mourn dry in her voice.

'If it is any trouble I can settle it,' I said. 'If it is money, I have got plenty. Go where, without me?'

She looked at the dogs on the mantel one by one.

'I am going to marry Matithiah Morse tonight,' she said. 'We will coach to Port Madryn after. Take ship in the morning for Beunos Aires. Doli and Solva, too.'

Sometimes you will think of saying something, but even before you say it, the meaning runs through your mind like a rasp tearing and bleeding but sounding such nonsense that you stop yourself and think of something else to say, but nothing will come, and you are a fool of time and despair, and ready to murder because what you want to say is so childish, and yet so true.

'Lal,' I said. 'Tell me how the words do pass your mouth. Say to me, then, flower of my heart, how?'

Through tears bright as the diamond she put on the mantelpiece she looked at the smallest dog.

'Well, I am not sure,' she said, in whispers. 'My father lost Maes Corwen. Not only in cards. Everything he gambled. Matti has bought every debt for years. He found all the Indios and bought their shares. The papers are with the Justice. What could we do? Put it to advocates, yes. We would lose the same. I have got to marry. How else will I save it? How could I think of the girls and say no?'

And, O, clearly, then, I saw that stretching of bright water, and coming wider every moment, with the bits of straw, and the tin with its hat in a lift, and everything, everything going from me and no hope to bring it back.

'Is Maes Corwen so much?' I asked her.

'Yes,' she said, and stronger. 'My great-grandfather and mother, and my grandfather and mother, and poor Mama, too, all their lives. And Doli and Solva left with nothing? Without Maes Corwen, who are we? If I marry, it will be mine, to share with the two girls. Everything is sworn and signed, and that shall be the end.'

262

Knocks on the door, and she opened it sharp.

Mr Armon Tudor is waiting,' Miss Kathi said, in whispers. 'Your cloak is here.'

'I wish I had never seen you,' Lal said. 'But I will thank God we met. Never curse me, boy. Please.'

The door was shut, and she ran, and I waited there, and I will know a china dog again, too.

Through the school I went, feeling nothing, and out to the front, and two coaches passing the gate, and I watched till they stopped in front of the chapel. But it was too dark to see more, and across the road Vyrnwy waited, with Parry Jones and Donato.

'Old Matti Mumpo is going mad,' Vyrnwy said. 'Miss Nelya Peninnah is not to be found. Elias, Snuff, has offered a thousand, cool, only for information. Nothing can start down there.'

A glass of wine he held to me.

'Luck is not always with us,' he said. 'A good one, she was. The best. But duty there is, too.'

'You knew, then,' I said.

'Well, everybody, of course,' he said. 'A place like Maes Corwen? And lose it, for what?'

'Something to bring the space in me, and I could murder,' I said.

'Think again,' he said. 'If love you have got, it is not with murder.'

Drums, there were, up the road, and chanting like a psalm.

'Indios,' Parry Jones said. 'They have had wine enough. A lot of women in chapel, too.'

'Nothing worse than Indios in drink,' Vrynwy said. 'Any mischief. And the police are busy keeping the barrels in order. A stroll, then.'

In the forge I could have sat by myself, but it would have looked like a sulk, so I walked behind, seeing only Lal, and hearing her, but nothing except a stare of china dogs in my brain, and my feet and hands were far away.

Indios crowded, shouting and stamping, about the chapel corner, and more were on their ponies riding up and down in the mud and everybody standing clear of the splashes. Vyrnwy and the others were lost in the press, and I came to a stop with leather blankets all round me, and the Indios too tall to see over and too thick to look between. But they were friendly enough, and making way for me to go nearer the chapel. A big shout all in the same voice made a move in the crowd, and in a moment I was pressed tight between them and carried like a sack to the side, and forward when those behind pushed, and swaying when the front put their heels in.

Tegwyn, Toldo, I saw on the grey pony, and holding another, with Nelya Peninnah tied back to front and mouth open and laughing in the lamplight. Police were beating at the crowds with the sheaths of their swords, but very few moved, and mounted police turned the corner, and riding sideways to ease out those in front. Rhinberry walked behind them, leading a pack horse with Nelya Peninnah's peon tied over the saddle, head down one side and feet the other.

Tynant Lewis came from the chapel with Mr Armon Tudor, but hidden by rain like silver strokes in the lamplight, and the noise was too much even to hear the Indios next to me shouting.

A sergeant cut Nelya Peninnah loose, and lifted her down, and her father ran out of the chapel door. She let him hold her straight, but without the laugh he was trying to see her face, and Elias, Snuff, put an arm about her, and for once without laughing Matti Mumpo looked round in turns of the head, quick, as a bird looks, and saw Rhinberry talking to Mr Armon Tudor.

He ran, but while his hands were out to have Rhinberry by the throat, the crowd went forward on that side, and I was thrown on my feet and having all I could do to stand in the mud, and pressed nearly flat by the bulk of big men shoving hard. Everybody was shouting and running, and I was knocked to my knees and alone in the street. Indio riders were galloping in from the crossroads, and pulling up to join the circle in the middle, turning their horses round and round, all one way, knee to knee, and the police flashing swords to break them. Vyrnwy was standing farther in front of me, and only us two left of the crowd, and a lot of our people watching under the chapel lamp.

Rhinberry ran in the middle of the ring, and shouting at the Indios, though they took no notice of him or the police, and he was pulling ponies out of the close rounds, and one by one, choosing their time, the riders broke away and turned, riding off at a gallop, and the circle got smaller and smaller, and the street was full of galloping Indios all going away, and nothing was left in the middle of the road except a heap in the mud, that first I thought had been kicked up by hooves.

But the policemen dug, and carried a man, and by the ring on the first finger I knew it was Matti Mumpo.

Rhinberry came, wiping sweat and rain together.

'If a Tehuelche is your friend, be sure to be helped,' he said, and breathless. 'Lal is safe, and so is Maes Corwen, and somebody is from us, for a riddance. I told you so, yes?'

'No interest to me,' I said.

'But look, Ithel has given it to you,' he said, and stopping to wipe. 'Everybody is ready, there. Lal, Maes Corwen, everything you could want.'

'I want nothing,' I said. 'I am off to the Andes. I have finished here.'

20

This poor little house is creaking and shuddering in the same way as Gilead Gwain's bridge when we came back with the wagons after loading my stores. The water frothed in grey spins splashing over the footway, and the crosstrees were filled with branches and furniture and coops and drowned animals, and every moment more came to pile and heave, and the footway was tilting, and all the timbers held each other and cried their pain almost in a living voice.

Idwyn sent the mules and horses swimming in a school, all heads and ears, and no trouble, and laughing while they shook drops to be safe on the other bank. A couple of hours' work we had to take the wagons to pieces and make rafts and lash the stores, and good lessons for me in the science of tying and binding. By then the water was higher, and the squeal of timber in a bend against force would make you shut your eyes for the break. Talfan Evans and Gilbert Rowlands ran across the footway, and lucky, because it shook under them, and Idwyn shouted if they were ready to play, to be off home till they were grown up and quick about it. We went over on the rafts, and if I never move from by here, they will do well without me if there is a next time.

Even with the bridge to stop it, the river ran with the strength of an engine coming from a tunnel, and though we had ropes and thongs tied to the teams on the other bank, we were slanted up by the current, so instead of being able to help we could only hang on and pray that the mules would gallop to bring us across sooner. But all we got was a good soak, and we had the wheels over and the wagons together, and nothing lost, and while the teams were being harnessed, Vyrnwy dug me in the ribs and I looked up.

Lal was driving the trap down the slope on the other side, and Mari Ann Gwythir holding a child sitting next, and Tegwyn, Toldo, holding another stood behind them in the open boot.

Idwyn ran down to the water shouting to them to stay there, and pointing to the bridge, but if Lal heard him she only waved the whip and touched the mare, and coming in a gallop along the flat, and the trap in a bounce, and straight for the footway, and standing, bent to play the reins as if she was racing, and the other two in a stare, and Mari Ann putting her feet against the buckboard and holding the baby tighter.

Timber cracked like cannons when the mare was on the planking, and Lal cut her one side and the other, and she seemed to rise and beat the rain with her fores, but her hinds were through a gap in the planks, and she stumbled cut and the trap tipped and came on. The bridge was moving, and bending in the middle, and the footway heeled, and planks flew in splinters.

'Mules,' Idwyn was shouting. 'Mules, quick.'

Everybody ran to have teams from the wagons, but Vyrnwy pulled off his poncho and trotted down to the bridge, and across the footway, but slow, not to frighten, and a hand out, and above the noise we could hear the chirrup for the mare. Lal was trying to stop the kicking and bucking to keep the trap from being smashed. but Vyrnwy reached the bridle, and led, and all the planks were going in the river like somebody throwing armfuls, and he backed out, a pace at a time and then faster, and in a run. But the timbers were breaking, and rising up, and falling in the water, and the handrail split both sides and a length fell across and jammed, and Vyrnwy had to pull it loose one hand, and on, dragging the frightened mare by the ear. Idwyn threw a lasso and Lal caught it and tied the loop to the seat, and Tegwyn knotted another from Gilbert on the other side, and all of were pulling, and the bridge seemed to rise at the back all the way up as if it might fall on top of them, but it swerved in cracks to smack the ears, and broke away and the river took it.

Then, it was, that I thanked God for Vyrnwy's strength.

The trap was off the land and going down with the last of the timber, and the lassos had no purchase. Idwyn slit the harness one side and Box, Quiff, slashed the other, and the mare ran, and Vyrnwy was left holding the shafts with the full weight of the women and the trap in his hands. Idwyn had a thong through the wheel and Talfan put one through the other, and we pulled all our strength, and the trap came inch by inch up the bank, and then on the flat, and everybody safe, and Vyrnwy looking at his hands, like claws, and no skin.

'Five of us you have saved, and nothing we can give you, only a kiss,' Lal said to him. 'But both the children have got measles, so careful how you come near.'

'Somebody will have to give me a lift,' Tegwyn, Toldo, said. 'My legs are in cramps here. Not a move is in me.'

Box, Quiff, had her down and holding her to kick and move her arms, and Morlan helped Mari Ann Gwythir, and Gilbert Rowlands took the child.

Lal came to me slow in the pace, folding her arms, and a springtime of tenderness in her eyes and a shyness in her that had never been before. But not a move was in me, not even enough to bring a smile, and if the thought was live to take her hair by the handful to kiss, my hands were still, without an order, as if I was in halves, and one was dead.

'Well,' she said. 'Did you curse me, boy?'

'Too empty,' I said.

'You shall be filled beyond the measure, and to spare,' she said. 'Were you off without saying good-bye to me?'

'It was well said last night,' I told her. 'And we were out early this morning.'

'We were out at three,' she said. 'Both the children were sick yesterday, but Tegwyn went to help Rhinberry with Nelya Peninnah. We have got plenty to thank both of them for. That fat thing was found by her tracks, and Rhinberry used his own methods on the peon.'

'I saw him ask Clais a few questions,' I said. 'No surprise to me. But what devil was in her to slaughter poor horses like that?'

'The same as a sheep or a cow to some,' she said. 'Sport for the peon, and money in his pocket. But every horse cut was owned by somebody not in her little book. Did you think of that? You, then. You said no to her. She had no liking for any of us. Davies, Tom Tiddler's, put a whip about her. Mari Ann ordered her from the house only a week ago.'

'Poor girl,' I said. 'Nowhere to turn.'

'One like that will never be at loss,' she said. 'Mrs Elias, Snuff, will go to Buenos Aires. The animals will be paid for by the estate, and the rewards will go equal between the police and Rhinberry's Indios. I am not sure how much to ask for Tanfi. Fees for stud, and the prizes he could have won, and all his winnings, anyway.'

'Would you make a claim in those terms?' I asked her.

'To the last penny, and sorry to have no excuse to ask for more,' she said, and fists on folded arms. 'That one that went in the mud, thank God, would have taken me for debt. Hell is too small for him. Fire is too kind. Make a claim? Indeed to God I will, and Doli and Solva, too.'

A feeling was growing between us, something cold, like mist, but in the head, and I was listening without patience. She stood with folded arms looking at the river, and speaking as she always had to me, as if she was telling me what she would never tell anybody else, even her sisters. But I stood and looked at her, and nothing to be felt except that coldness, like a lining in the skull. Love, yes, and I would have given anything to put my arms about her and say she was wife to me. But far stronger than that, I was empty in the brain and without a move. She was like a dream, but dreamed and gone.

She seemed to know it, because she was telling me about Doli, and she stopped, and put a hand to her throat, slowly, and tears were near, and she looked at me.

'Harm I have done to you, Huw,' she said. 'The smile is from your eyes. Gone. If you had cursed me, it would have emptied you. If I could cry, if I could scream, I would. But a heap of sacks has got more to feel. Why did you leave me last night, after? I was praying you would come.'

'You chose property,' I said. 'Now you have got plenty.'

'A third each with Doli and Solva,' she said. 'You knew why. It was my duty.'

'Whatever it was, you turned from me,' I said. 'Only a dog comes back from a kicking.'

'Well,' she said, and put up her hands. 'Nothing more to say. I have done what I swore I would do. I have got what I swore I would get. With that I will rest for now.'

'Any man will do,' I said.

She turned to me, full in the face, and a frown through tears.

'Yes,' she said. 'I meant it. There are plenty of good men. Plenty. With any one of them I could have a family. And quietness in my life. But the best quietness is to know that my sisters are safe in their lives, marry or not. If I stay single for the rest of my years, I will be happy to know it. But if I have done harm to you, I would cut my heart. Good-bye.'

She ran back to the trap, and took the mare from Box, Quiff, and walked her, talking to bring her calm enough to harness.

'If it is measles these children have got, Mistress, you must please to put warning in the City,' Idwyn said to Mari Ann Gwythir. 'Nobody coming with me will go near anybody else from this moment. Grill your own asado over your own fire. Lend nothing, not even a match. Touch nobody else's harness. Those handling the mules will stay with them. Wash everything. Carbolic I have got for the wagons and leather. I will not take sickness to the Andes. We have not got a doctor over there, and none of the women has got anything to cure. Measles is a murderer.'

'Right you, Idwyn,' Mari Ann said. 'At the first sign, burn everything near. Burn, wagon or house, everything. Burn.'

Box, Quiff, had put the harness together, and off they went in cheers, and Lal blew a kiss, though if for me or all of us I will never be sure, but I noticed that Mari Ann Gwythir never once looked where I was standing.

'What is measles?' Talfan asked, young, he was.

'White man's dirt,' Idwyn said. 'Idleness and shame brings its own plague.'

'The last anybody will say about Tegwyn,' Box, Quiff, said. 'The girl was christened and plunged with soap.'

'She has been doing the washing for half the city,' Idwyn said. 'Children will always catch what is going. A breath near them is enough. But grown men and women can die in a couple of days. I have seen it before.'

We went round the city and up, under the crest of the hills, and seeing the river far towards the dam, and back almost to the sea, and all between was a lake, with small patches of high land and tree tops, and a few red roofs with their shadows streaming like cuts, as if the poor valley lay dead like a new Christ and water bright from a body beyond life and only pale blood under wounds.

That night I was surprised to find I could enjoy the asado I had cooked myself, even if it was raw one side and burnt the other, and I slept like a Magus after the Vision. Vyrnwy threw me a cut from his beef the next morning and said he would rather have old measles than suffer to see me chewing char, and I found that if there is not an art in grilling, at least you have got to know a bit more about it than I did, and after that, even Idwyn shared bread and meat with me. But thrown, not handed.

Every morning we looked for spots on ourselves. Nobody shared a bottle or a maté or even a tin to boil water, and none of us were in yards of each other through the days, and we began to know the feeling of Lazarus. But we could sing, and we did, and even the old mules joined in, and Idwyn said it was a fact that they would pull better and farther with a song, and Vyrnwy said they would stand quieter to be shod if you sang well, but if you were only in a tra-la under the breath they would look round as if to ask where did you have the pain with you.

About then I was beginning to know only a little of a drover's life by watching Idwyn Thomas on his big black, or the bay, or the white mare, Cariad, that he loved almost as a woman, and she was beauty enough, too, and every hour he came taller in my mind. A gentle man in ways and voice, and well over six foot, big in the bone, with legs that would break ribs, and in the wide-brimmed hat, and leather trews, and top boots, and a coat of hide or a black poncho, a man to remember. A whistle from him, and the teams turned together, and the dog sat, not a sound or a move till the train was on its new rhumb, and away we would all go. Captains of ships had no more responsibility, because a little way off the path, and without water, we could all die, and losing the way was so easy, it would bring a shiver to think. Once I went out of rhumb to wring a blanket, and though I could swear I was only a step off the track, and the train not more than three or four minutes ahead, by the time I was in the saddle, they were not to be seen across the bush and thorn, and neither could I hear with the breeze against me, and for an hour or more I was pretending to track and seeing nothing and Vyrnwy came back for me, a blessing from heaven, indeed.

'Next time, give Mil the reins,' he said. 'She will find us.'

'More sense,' I said.

'No,' he said. 'Instinct, man. Purer, from God, and more of worth.'

From that moment, the dried bones out there came to have a real meaning for me, and if ever I was a yard away from the path, there was no comfort till I was back. Rain never stopped, and we were wet to the skin day and night, but used to it, and when the fires were lit, none more grateful than us to stand in our steam and feel warm again.

Coming up to The Feathers, we were, and Morlan pointed across the pampas, and I saw the two-horse wagonette and three riders behind with a pack troop, and a point of sheep, all small as toys.

'Gwenonwy Jones, it is,' he said. 'Husband and peons behind. She came across Hirdraeth Idwyn.'

Hirdraeth, in the Welsh, is a word for a grand avenue, but all I could see was the grey and green of pampas to the horizon and not a break, and I told him so and he laughed.

'Desert it is, and a lot have died there,' he said. 'But cutting across here instead of following the river gains almost a week. The river makes a big turn all round. Camwy, we call it, because it is always turning and twisting. Wait till you go over at night, and ten hours to watch the stars. You will know why it is Hirdraeth Idwyn.'

Donato turned to come up to us, and I went to meet him, and Vyrnwy and Talfan rode off to Gwenonwy. If their shouts, or a fox breaking cover, or anything else was the cause, but we heard a different shout from Idwyn, and we saw the wagonette bumping between stones and bushes and Gwenonwy standing and pulling back a runaway pair with all her strength, and the others stretch gallop after her.

She tied the reins to the seat, and crawled over to the back, and then I thought of her baby. She was wrapping him in blankets, never mind the movement of the wagonette, and when she had him tied she leaned over the tailboard and swung him like a pendulum and let him go when he was near the ground, and he rolled only a bit, soft, and we could hear him in a good bellow, too. Back she went to untie the reins, but the peon swerved and caught the near bridle, and turned in hard, and too soon, and over, wheels spinning, everything went and never mind wet ground, digging deep enough to blow a cloud of dust.

Gwenonwy came out smiling, calm, hat a bit on the side, and hair in a hang, and walking steady back for the baby, nobody the worse, and we had the wagonette upright with only a few scratches, and packed, ready, and Donato was still kneeling with his arms about her and she was rocking the baby to sleep.

'Stand clear, everybody,' Idwyn said. 'Wash everything at the river, Mistress Gwenonwy. Boil all water, and the baby's clothes. Wash out the wagonette, Donato. Three times, at least, boiling water. Come to me for strong carbolic. You shall not blame me if that baby is with sickness.'

'I will boil the old baby and us, too,' Gwenonwy said, gentle, and smiling. 'Donato, will you turn us to stone, then?'

'Let the boy have his prayer,' Idwyn said. 'If it was my girl, I would be a week on my knees, there. A miracle, it was, and nobody with a mark.'

'With Faith are miracles,' Gwenonwy said. 'A peon will drive. My hands have gone useless with me.'

Donato picked her and the baby up, clean, and set them in the back of the wagon, and got up himself, and winked at me, and off we went again.

The Feathers had always been an Indio camp with pasture for the animals and shelter from El Pampero in the rise and fall of the land, and the name it got from the ostrich feathers always blowing about that the Indios left after the asado instead of burning everything as we did. A lot of people waited there, but Idwyn shouted to them to keep away, and to put distance between each wagon, and wash everything.

Well, everybody was going mad there, washing. Long lines of hot ashes were put under drying clothes, and for hours the river was in froth with soap. The women all went one way to put up canvas and have a bath, and we went down the other, and froze, too, but willingly. One regret we all had not to have a good service or a session of hymns, and singing wide apart is not much, indeed, though it was rest to hear the children in a tune before they went to bed. Taking the animals out, and bringing them in to water, or out through the hours looking for strays will make the time pass quickly enough, but at the end of a week, nobody was less than healthy, and Idwyn said we would go on, but still at distance.

Watching him on Cariad up in front, black hat and poncho on a white horse and black rawhide and silver harness, you might think of him as one of them in the olden days, and driving six in a chariot over flaming clouds and into the morning sun. About fifteen miles a day, I suppose we were doing, to begin, and each day a little farther, until Saturday, and we stopped to rest the animals, and do small repairs, and the women baked bread and mended clothes in peace. Sunday nobody did anything, but we had a service in the morning and at night, but still far apart, because some of the children were unwell from the jolt of the wagons, but it might have been anything, and Idwyn wanted to be sure. Off again, before light on Monday, and day after day till Friday, and you could almost hear the sigh from everybody when Idwyn whistled, and stopped the leading wagon and pointed where he wanted the camp.

Once a week the pony mail passed us, one down and one up, between the City of Lewis on the Atlantic coast and the City of the Mill in the Andes, and if they had anything for us they threw the pouch down, and waved and galloped on, and everybody cheering them, and splendid to see, if it was only a man's hat and beard and four hooves, and dust. Perhaps it was the third week, and we were in the Painted Mountains, and the mailman going up to the Andes shouted to Gilbert on the way and rode on, and Gilbert came to find me.

'Message from Maes Corwen,' he said, all smiles. 'Love is following you across. Love will wait for you. From your sisters, Doli and Solva, and a good kiss.'

Out there on the pampas, and looking up at the first white light of sun we had seen for days, I saw them both and I could have ridden back there only to put an arm about them, and kiss them as sisters with the same place in my mind as Angharad and Ceridwen and Olwen. A couple like that will build a country, and I saw it done, too, and not long after.

That was the day we dreamed into the deep Indio Territory, not as if we were going in but as though land and clouds were coming out to us. Even the mountains all round us were like dreams, every one a different colour, and you could think yourself fast asleep or gone in the head to see a pure yellow mountain next to one blue, and purple the next, and apricot, and then a red, and green, and orange and scarlet and darker green and paler blue, but in a sunset of crimson clouds it was easy to believe you were finished with the Earth and waiting below the Throne for your turn to hear The Voice.

One morning I woke to see first light on the peaks, among all those tips of colour only a little breath of lilac, no more, and a tent of burning green above for a sky, with a gold coin for a moon, and a brilliance of stars, and families were singing prayers along the train, and I remembered my mother and father living in a Light even more beautiful through the

274

years, and as though told by Abraham, I knew then, that if a little part of the Earth can have such peace and wonder, Beyond must have much more, so there was no odds in being dead, and never again could thought of it come with fear, and cold.

Higher up than Indio Crossing we crossed the Camwy because the current was running strong and wagons might have worn the way too deep for those coming after.

Gwenonwy's land was on both sides of the river, and she was home, but how the girl could have thought of going to live there by herself I could never tell you. If you can think of flat, it was flat, and nothing in the sky all round. There was no track that I could see and only the pampas bush and clumps of grass, and clouds. But when Idwyn called her from the train, courage came from her as a light, in the straight back and the grey calm of her eyes and the hands steady on the reins, and in the wide hat and veil, and the whip in a guiding flick, she led us over the pebbles to show the way, and all of us gave her a good shout on the other side, and Donato, of course, the proudest man anywhere. She chose well, because when the last herd was across, the bed was still firm, and I watched Idwyn and a few more putting everything behind their eyes, and I was sure they would never again cross anywhere else.

Right, too, and Gwenonwy's Bridge it was from that day.

All the land to the south was in flood and we went more to the north to find hard ground. We were missing waterholes, and many of those we passed were filled with salt, strange to see in the middle of a continent. Idwyn said that Peak Thomas had found gold and silver and a lot of other minerals along the way, and with water to work, and good roads to carry, we were in the richest country in the world.

Happily, thinking now, Donato came on with us. Gwenonwy would have stayed, but when I looked at the little hut under winter grey, and the pampas all round, and nothing except low hills far over, and the wind in torment, I wondered how they could live a minute, never mind months, in such a place. But sense was in it, because the sheep were happy enough, and the dogs had plenty of hares to get fat on, and the horses could roam at will, and the hut was dry, with water near, and fuel outside the door, and plenty to eat always, and nothing much to do except to sell the wool as it grew. That, yes, but Donato wanted to work, and he had to have his own land, not his wife's, so without much argument they left their sheep with peons and came on with us, and I was thankful, too, because we worked well together, and two to a business is always more than twice the strength of one.

The day after, we all knew that Idwyn was silent because the pony mail had not come through, and that night we kept the fires going high, and a couple of us watched the way till morning. He had a talk with the senior men before we started, and a dozen of them saddled a mount to scout a few miles ahead, and the train turned on a new rhumb to the south-west for the City of the Mill. Before midday, two of the scouts rode back to say that a troop of Gaucho Cavalry was joining us because there was fighting with the Manzaneros.

'That explains no pony mail,' Idwyn said. 'We will close in, and travel faster to come up with them. If there is trouble, I would rather have the Gauchos near us.'

They were in camp when we saw them, and Idwyn stopped us half a mile off and rode to meet the officer, and when they moved, so did we, and when they camped for the night, we did, too, and everybody felt safer.

That night two children in the family of Rhys Owen came with spots, and Idwyn ordered the wagon burnt with everything in it and every stitch they had, and turned out a stores wagon and all the family men rode past dropping clean clothes and blankets for them. Distance, again, between the wagons and nobody going near anybody else.

And rain coming in a way you would never believe unless your face was in it, and a wide-mouthed wind to hit you from the saddle.

Scouts were out day and night, but I was no good as a tracker and not much better on a horse, so I had to stay with the wagons. Vyrnwy and Mog, Moke, rode in, split, one afternoon, without a shout or a wave, and Idwyn went with them to the Cavalry and when they came back, he called all the senior men in a ring.

'Indios have burnt houses and slaughtered herds and flocks,' he said. 'Steady revenge they are taking because their chief was killed. Our wagons will travel four in line. If there is trouble, make a circle. We will cook enough for a week, here, and travel day and night to reach the river. There, we are only a couple of days from the City of the Mill on the other side of the mountain. Women and boys drive by day. Remember that the Manzaneros have always been good friends of ours. But they have lost a good chief and now they are put from their hunting grounds and winter grazing. They are men. They will look for revenge if it takes years.'

'Who has taken their grounds?' Mistress Patti Bryn Gilfa asked him. 'I would turn now and go back if I thought I would be taking anything from anybody.'

'Nothing to do with us, rest in surety, Mistress,' Idwyn said. 'It is the new law, these days, of the Government. All the Indios everywhere must take land and settle, or leave the settled areas. The soldiers are down here to see it is done. There are hard feelings, but the last I want is any towards us. I am sure we will come to no harm. Remember your Bibles, now. Everything you could want is in there. Pray to do the best.'

And the hymn following down the train.

Snow, before, always meant Christmas to me, and doing a bit shovelling in the front and back, and snowballs on the hill and a chilblain or two, and sliding down the mountain after school and the smell of goose grease and mint my mother rubbed on our chests, and hot black-currant wine to go to bed, and sweet steam on the nose and send you to sleep.

But snow in the Andes would be very good not to think about, never mind to see.

White tips were on the line of peaks north to south and we knew we had to go over or through them to be in the City of the Mill. Snow was in the wind to freeze us in the saddle at night, and flakes came one morning, that sat all day, and more the next, until we were going through the deep slush of those in front. Fog came about us on the plain, and a fine white dew on the way up, and nobody able to see five yards. Travel, then, was a moving through white cloud, with the sound of the train somewhere beyond, and hour after hour of silence would make you want to ride closer to see a face or hear a word. If I thought I would never be glad to see the pampas, I was wrong, because when we went down to the low ground before the foothills, fog thinned and light came, and the pampas stretched the greyish green miles with the river among willows, and I could have sung for happiness, and everybody felt the same, so sing we did.

But the Andes stood in a wall of dark blue teeth all the

277

way along, and forests only to the half, and snow from there to the sky. Some of the men said they could see the smoke of signal fires, but though I looked, I saw the blue of silent mountains and tops that glared white as the point in an eyeful of hate.

During those days I had taken my turn to herd, and I was riding with Morlan Gwynn some miles from the front wagons, and plenty to do because the animals were tired, and the grass was uncut, and they were ready to stay. My arms had stopped aching from using the crop and they were like branches on my shoulders, but the dogs and horses did the work, and it was them, not me, that kept the herd on the move.

Up the rise to the mountains the mist came thick, and nothing in front except the wet brown hides and the horns of cattle, and the grey breath of ice. My name I heard shouted for a long time, but I thought it was part of the stamp of hooves, and lowing, and the winds, or perhaps some animals far off, just as in the night, I had awakened to hear a fox, and thinking he was calling Huw, Huw, and sleeping again.

But the white horse could only be Cariad, and the rider I knew by his voice.

'Rhinberry,' I was shouting, but in that noise, nothing. 'Over here, look.'

He waved in the fog, a shape, and turned off, and another rider came easy and quick through the cattle, giving me a new lesson in the use of knee and rein.

Lal.

As if I was fast asleep I looked at her.

'Are you angry I am here?' she asked me, and a smile as though we had met for the first time, the little smile of politeness that disarms a stranger.

All that time I had kept my mind from her. All those days I had turned from my thoughts. Work, movement, herding, shouting, any way of filling moments was enough, and nights were easy from tiredness. But she was always there, every second, and I knew it well, just as I knew the blood was in my veins, unfelt, unseen, until an eye caught a move of that little pump in the wrist.

The smile was enough, even without the message of Doli and Solva. We were not strangers and I was not angry and no use to pretend one or the other. My toes had been trodden,

278

and I was hit in the pride, but if she could travel that distance after me and come in a smile ready to be shouted at, it was enough, and I was off the horse, and cattle by the thousand or not I went to her, and she sat, and the tears ran though not a move was in her face.

'If you tell me to go back, I will kill myself,' she said. 'Only an hour after, and I knew I must come. I was wrong. If I had married that other one, what would I have done? What, then?'

'We will speak of ourselves,' I said. 'Who came with you?'

'Michaye and a sister, and my peons,' she said. 'Doli and Solva will come with the next train out. A misery they were making for my life. Go, girl, go on. Go, they were saying day and night. Are you pleased I am here?'

I looked at her.

'O, Huw, smile,' she said. 'I will know you if you smile. I saw you in sleep and no smile. I had to come. We were fourteen days after you but I am here. Is it you?'

Never would I have believed that she could be limp on a horse, but she fell from the saddle on my shoulders, and together we stood in the snow, and the cattle gave us ground and carefully in their courtesy turned their horns away, and their eyes seemed to smile from the side in passing, and she whispered, another Lal, a new Lal I had never known, in tears and shaking and holding fast, and whispering. Half she said I never noticed because I was doing my share, and we heard ourselves, and I suppose we saw ourselves, at the same time, and stopped together, and held away and laughed ourselves helpless. I had to push her up in the saddle, for what use my hands were, but I was too weak to climb into my own and she had to get down to help me, and up she went in a leap so I knew she was herself again, and we walked after the herd hand in hand.

Davies, Tom Tiddler's, and Blethyn Kylsant came to change places, and I was glad enough to go up front to a good fire. We were standing together, waiting for the asado, and because I was long used to the noise of the herd I noticed how quiet everybody was and no sound from the wagons.

Lal looked about at the mist, thick and grey, and ready for snow.

'Listen,' she said. 'Manzaneros are calling out there.'

In the back of the throat, a long pierce of sound in many tones, high in the head, and holding for moments to make you draw breath for them, a screech, too near the human voice to be animal, but near enough to set talons of fear in your spine. Poor Rhagwen Rowlands, with fingers pulling her hair, and eyes white with the tears of terror, had her mouth open to scream and the sound was almost out, and Mistress Eirene Vaughan slapped her hard enough to knock her flat across the fire.

'Teeth together,' she said, and settling the little spectacles in place. 'One sound, and I will have your head in a flour sack. Put the children in the wagons. Serve the asado inside. Remember, mouths shut.'

Idwyn came down the train from wagon to wagon, and whispering to everybody to close in, and no noise.

'We are going up, not along the track, and the cattle will go loose down here,' he said. 'We want to keep away from the Indios. If too many of them can come too near, they might start a fight. Take no notice of any of them. Be friendly with them. They are friendly people. The way will be steep so be careful. Call if you need help. We have got a spare mule or two.'

'Is it the Cavalry leading, then, Mr Thomas?' Mistress Eirene asked him. 'Do they know the way as well as you do?'

'No, Mistress,' he said, and smiling. 'Mog, Moke, and Idris Roberts are up there to pick a way, and when I have finished here, I will be there, too.'

'Good,' she said, and giving her bonnet a push to have it straight. 'Always I have come here without old soldiers. I never saw one to be useful before, and none have I seen this time, either.'

'But they have been both sides of us day and night for the past four days, Mistress,' Idwyn said. 'None are up front. When the mist is gone, we will pray to find the eight men they are missing.'

Mistress Eirene took off her spectacles, and put a hand to her cheek, and the little finger moved to her chin to hold the tremble.

'Forgive me,' she said. 'I will ask on the knees, now.'

'Others will join you,' Idwyn said. 'Go with God, my little one.'

Well, we had been warned of steepness, but there is steep and steep, and the way we went, you would think that steep

280

was flat. For the first time I was glad of the fog. There was nothing to see going up except the ground underfoot, and the boulders we were passing at the sides with just room to clear. How those men in front knew where to go in all those miles was a wonder to me, or what told them to turn, seeing no more than three or four yards ahead. But it made me know what little use I was, and how much I owed a couple of rough ones, though they would have laughed because they were only using the gifts alive in them, and homing with a pigeon's sureness that had never been in me.

'All the Indios want is a gifting of cattle and sheep and a few horses,' Lal said. 'If the soldiers were not in front, we might drive a bargain. My grandfather was brother-in-blood to their chief.'

'They have had plenty of time to start fighting,' I said.

'They have got more sense,' she said. 'Every time they have killed, the soldiers have gone after them. They have lost most of their young men in fights. Spears are no good against bullets. But they know we will have to go over the mountain. The flat is too deep in mud for the wagons. In the right place there is no need for them to pull a bow at us. The cold will kill us all. Look there, for a start.'

Like somebody shaking crumbs from a tablecloth, the cloud went in a rumple, and I almost fell off Mil to see a troop of Indios watching us only a stone's throw off, twenty or more, bare to the waist, and with blue feathers stuck in their headbands.

Clouds came back quick enough, but I had seen the way going up and from the side of my eye, the way we had come, and the cloud down there, and I am almost sure that my heart never went back to the place it was in before. Steep, Idwyn said. We had come up the side of a mountain and the top was overhead and stuck in the sky.

But perhaps he was right, too, because from the moment we saw what we were climbing, and the way we could fall down, nobody had much room in their heads to think about Indios, and a few of us had a bit of trouble to think of anything.

'I am going up,' Lal said. 'Perhaps Idwyn could get one of them to talk to me. We will never do it at this rate. If I am not back tonight, have no worry, yes?'

Indios were screeching on both sides out there, and a couple more times we saw parties when the mist blew, though not so near, but red paint was on their faces and striped on cheeks and backs, and the feathers were a clear blue, the colour of clouds on water.

Evening was coming, and still we went up and no word from Lal. Every few minutes we stopped to breathe the teams, and put rocks under the wheels, and give a taste of water, and in the longer stops, a few mouthfuls of hay and a piece of sugar. Boys were driving, or the mothers of families, so they knew their animals and there was no forcing, because they could feel when to go, and when to whisper to them, or when to get down and lead. Spare teams of pullers there might have been, but they would never have reached us by the way we had come, and everybody knew it without being told, so the driving was of the best and nothing left to chance. Word was passed along the line to be ready to unharness the wagons and leave them and each take a mount and the spares, and farther up we found out why.

Snow came with the darkness, and we passed from the rocks to the small, loose stones, where a slip of the wheels could tip a wagon to roll over and over, and nothing to save it. Slower we went, and then we stopped, and the whisper passed down to wrap warm, and dig deep holes for fires without flame to show in the mist.

A few matés took the worst of the cold, with a measure in each from the jar Mistress Eirene took from her wagon boot, and though it has Sal Volatile in big black letters on the label, it tasted exactly like rum to me, and her wink broke the snow crystals on her eyebrows. Many a journey that jar made during the night, but in the hole we dug, and sitting on hot stones round a little fire, we managed well, and because every wagon seemed to have its own Sal Volatile, we all slept, and only a bit stiff when light was coming, but sneezes in plenty, and ice heavy on hats and shoulders, and crusted round the lips and cheeks.

Late that afternoon, Mog, Moke, came down the wagon line and whispering for Mistress Eirene, and she put her face out of the canvas, and he showed her the swollen fingers of both hands gone black.

'Frost has put teeth in you, boy,' she said. 'Too long you have waited. Up here, now.'

Six eggs she broke for the yolks, and poured out a pot of honey, and beat them, and gave the bowl to me and I beat till I was tired. Four pairs of wool socks she put one in the

282

other, left and right, and poured the treacle in the feet, and thick over his hands, and pulled the socks over with a tie at the wrists, and a good swig of Sal Volatile, then, and he slept louder than any moke, too.

Night was pitch and we were still going up, and we stopped in a narrow place with room only for a wagon to pass and the horses were given the last bit of hay and they were looking about for more. It will pull very hard inside when a horse noses at you because he is hungry and cold, and you can only pat his neck. But there was nothing anywhere, and only stones underfoot, and without saying it, we knew there was not far for any of us to go, because with that work, and in that cold, no animal would live long, and we had no firewood. So the jar passed, and perhaps we slept drunk, but we woke and went on, with a chew of bread and raw meat, and very good, but no more bread, and the eggs were for Mog, Moke. In the afternoon we were in snow to the knee and one of the horses fell. Mistress Eirene's face was like Rhagwen's before she screamed, but her lips were too stiff, and she took out the jar and poured a couple of spoonfuls in his mouth, and he kicked, and got up, and on we went.

But she shook her head at me, and I knew she meant that none of them would stand for long.

But the people were getting weak, too, for we were up high and nobody could pull enough breath, and besides that, a hard cold needs plenty of good food and a fire. Mistress Eirene broke a cask of butter and we ate a handful at a time, and pushed it in the horses' mouths for them to lick. But there was no warmth outside, only the ice, and when we left the rock and the winds used an axe on us there was nothing to do except pray.

But the Indios were there all the time, above and below, and far at the back. We heard them, but we were used to the sound, and the shots up in front now and again were warning enough.

Mog, Moke, saddled as soon as he could stand, and when he was bound fresh, he took off his hat with both socked hands in front of Mistress Eirene, and bowed to kiss her cheek, and I helped him on his horse.

'Please to tell Lal I am waiting very patient,' I said. 'I would come up with you, but I would be a nuisance.'

Off he went, with a nod, but no word.

'The poor boy is dumb with pain,' Mistress Eirene said.

'But his hands will be whole again, see. And you stay where you are, or I will have another one to doctor.'

We stopped in the afternoon, and when it was our time to move, we found the men pulling the wagons up a short slope that anyone in his senses would look at and turn away. Teams of horses walked at the top, but no strength was in them, and in the mist you could fall over carcasses. But we were up, and the wagons were lined next to each other on a flat place that felt empty.

No wonder.

Thongs were tied across the way in front, and a step farther the rock ended, and if you threw a stone down there, no sound came after.

And the mist grey, thick and ready to snow, all the way round.

A wide shelf we were on, curving, and coming to flat rock both sides, and the way we had come was the only way out, except for a path going up to the left, and a couple of our horses lay there with arrows in them.

But no sound.

Idwyn came through the wagons, and tapping the wheels, telling us all to follow him. The crowd stretched into the mist, and he could see only a few nearer, but we could hear him plainly enough.

'The time for silence is ended,' he said. 'We hoped to find the way quicker but the Indios were strong where we wanted to go, so we had to turn. I hoped to find a safe way without fighting. If we can get into the valley without quarrelling or killing, we will have less trouble in the future. But we have gone as far as we can. The path going up will have to be dug and widened. If it leads down, good. There is no way to tell. Horses will be slaughtered for asado. The oldest wagons will burn for fuel. Bring picks and shovels to widen the path. Let us give thanks for blessing so far, and if we are to be gathered, we will go singing and in good cheer of praise.'

With pick and shovel we cleared rock on both sides wide enough for the wagons to pass, and we were out in space again. Idwyn and a few more went on, joined by lassos to find a way in the mist and everybody knotted thongs to stretch the distance down, and we started pulling the wagons to the top to save the horses.

The line of men with the Gaucho officer and Idwyn came back in slow steps and plenty to tell from their faces. In that time we laid a stone floor at the foot of the slope to lessen the incline, and when we stopped to rest, the way was almost ready.

'A word with you again,' Idwyn called, behind the shift of fog. 'There is path, but I am not sure where it will lead. The Captain thinks we should take only the horses and ride down the way we have come. It will take us two days, the least, to get back to the pampas. Same cold and no fires. Let us have a vote. Go back, and try to ride through the valley. Or go forward, not knowing where we are going. There is nothing else.'

Nobody wanted to lose wagons and stores and all the little things they had brought to make their houses prettier. More than that, for the mothers and fathers, a wagon meant shelter for the children. My stores were least in mind, because any notion of going down whether on horse or foot, and I turned sick from myself. But we knew we were getting weaker with cold, and breathing hurt in the chest and a lot of us were not sure of our knees.

'I am against any killing of Indios,' Alban Jenkin said. 'I will die and my family with me before I will take a life. From a boy I never had a moment of trouble with them.'

A murmur was with him.

'I would sooner kill thousands than let them lay a finger on my Missus and kids,' Eynon Rhys said.

Perhaps the murmur was louder with him.

'No need to speak of killing,' Idwyn said. 'Let us be gratefull none of them has got a gun. They are frightened of the sound. What else do you think has kept them off? But they can tip rock on us. What if the children are hurt?'

'Wait you a little, now,' a voice in contralto called from the mist, and everybody turned, but I stood, and loved.

'We have all been going to Chapel these years, and some before I was born,' Lal said, as if she spoke to her class beneath the trees at Gaiman. 'Most of us can count the times we have missed our mornings and evenings and Sunday school. Why were we there? The children with us are learning as we did. What are we teaching them, and what did we learn?'

'Tell us, now then, Mistress Lal,' Idwyn said, a voice and an echo. 'Silence, the rest.'

'Hear me now, because if our Sundays and our teaching and our hymns are worthless, we are put here to know it,'

Lal said. 'If there is faith, let us use it. We should lift up our eyes to the hills whence cometh our help.'

'Amen,' we said.

'We teach, as we were taught, that if we seek we shall find,' Lal said. 'That was a promise. Knock, and it shall be opened unto you. Another promise. Where two or three are gathered together, do you remember that promise, too? And you have faith the size of a grain of mustard seed, you will move mountains. One promise after another. And listen. Though I go down into the Valley of the Shadow of Death, I will fear no evil. Does it make you uncomfortable to listen? Do you believe? Do you mock? Do you mouth? Or do you slip an existence through the face of the clock? Shall we vote to go on with promise of Rod and Staff? Or make fools of ourselves, and our teaching, and all our Sundays, and go back without?'

Mist was rising and clouds with the sun in brightness rolled and rolled and no sound anywhere. Green came in patches below, and the river ran blue through willows in clumps along the banks, with a quilt of greens in the gardens and a few black roofs. Mist flew and pasture was in mile on ten miles, and tens of miles more to far mountains and wide beyond each side of the river, with paler fields where the hay was cut and patches in gold where the corn had grown. Behind us the rock was red and sheer, with cloud below the peaks. But the path went in a rise, and then down, all the way in a long curve to the meadows.

No sound, not an Indio to be seen, and no move in any of us.

'In the highest, glory, and a miracle beyond all miracles,' Idwyn said, and the whisper went up loud. 'Look, then. The City of Mill. We are home.'

'Halleluyah,' a voice called.

'Halleluyah,' one answered.

'Halleluyah,' we sang, as one, the rare, royal roar that in this small span comes only a few times to the throat from a heart gone big with the happy blood.

Idwyn was off the wagon, and waving us to harness the teams before the mist came down, and we ran, singing, and harnessed, singing, and drove, singing. Down came the mist, and the ice was in it, and close to the rock we went, and above the chorus we could hear the Indios screeching. The rise was too much for the teams, and we went in groups singing, some turning the wheels, and others at the top pulling, and the wagons went up in Halleluyahs, and the first pullers rested, lying where they fell, and singing.

Mistress Eirene took her mittens off to handle the reins, and her spectacles were at the end of her nose and she sang head up to keep them on, and behind, Enid Freeman Mathias drove with the baby in her lap, and then Beth Williams with her three little girls holding her round the neck, and old Mrs Patti Bryn Gilfa, out of her wheelchair and tied ankles and waist on the box, driving like a demon and singing for two. Lal brought the horses and we harnessed them, singing, and the wagons were passing, and thongs spoke from weight, and the whips were busy, and wheels turned in hands with blood, but the King of Kings was with us, and we passed, because He Shall Reign Forever and Ever, on, and up, into the singing mountain.